A
DARKER
SKY

A
DARKER
SKY

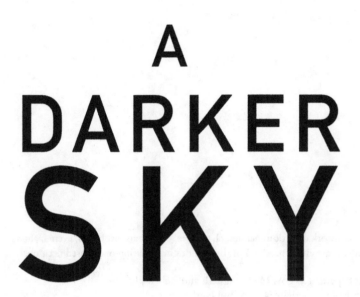

MARI JUNGSTEDT
RUBEN ELIASSEN

Translated by Paul Norlen

Text copyright © 2015 Mari Jungstedt and Ruben Eliassen
Translation copyright © 2016 Paul Norlen
All rights reserved.

Previously published as *En mörkare himmel* by Albert Bonniers Förlag in 2015 in Sweden. Translated from Swedish by Paul Norlen. First published in English by AmazonCrossing in 2016.

Published by AmazonCrossing, Seattle

www.apub.com

Amazon, the Amazon logo, and AmazonCrossing are trademarks of Amazon.com, Inc., or its affiliates.

ISBN-13: 9781503936089
ISBN-10: 1503936082

Cover design by David Drummond

Printed in the United States of America

PROLOGUE

The lighting in the small room was subdued, and there was a faint herbal scent. Soft Asian music came through a speaker in the ceiling. The walls were stained dark, and there was a green plant in one corner.

He asked her to undress and lie down on the table. She pulled on the hem of her dress, feeling naked already and unprotected. Part of her wanted to turn around and leave, but something kept her there. Curiosity, expectation about what was to come. She felt a warm tickle along her skin. Her mouth was dry. She moistened her lips. He gave her a quick glance, and it occurred to her how that might have been perceived, when she let her tongue glide across her lips. She smiled uncertainly, felt herself blush.

She fingered one shoulder strap. He was polite and turned away as she slipped out of the dress. Her hand trembled as she hung her clothes on a hook on the wall. She hesitated, uncertain whether she should keep her panties on. She'd never done this before, didn't know how it worked or what was expected of her.

She climbed up on the leather-covered massage table and lay down on her stomach. Tried to relax. Closed her eyes while she drew air in through her nose, breathed out slowly through her mouth.

The young man turned around and placed a towel over her legs and rear, adjusting it so that it stopped right below her panties. His movements were deliberate. When he grazed her with his fingertips she shuddered, although it was warm in the room. She looked up. He'd taken off the white cotton coat. She could see a suntanned, young, and firm body with swelling arm muscles. A flat, hard stomach. Narrow hips. Almost no hair on the chest and small, brown nipples. There was a butterfly-light tickling between her legs. He had white cotton pants on. The soft fabric stretched over his hips and his protruding rear end. She could not help wondering what he looked like underneath.

She turned her head down again, feeling a little guilty. She had to concentrate and just relax. Just like the man who encouraged her to go had said. Feel. Experience what's happening. Focus on the moment.

She noticed that the young man turned around again, heard him pump oil out of one of the bottles on the table and the liquid seeping through his fingers as he rubbed his hands together. She took a deep breath. The masseur placed himself next to her. Quite close. Started rubbing her bare back with long, firm strokes. Involuntarily she let out a faint moan of pleasure. His hands were strong, determined. She closed her eyes. Tried to follow the rhythm in the movements with her breathing. As the hands glided across her back, he massaged the back of her neck, her shoulders; he pulled with his hands down toward her lower back, took hold of her hips, worked with small movements in circles, his thumbs pressed against her bare skin.

He paused, pulled down her panties, and moved the towel aside so that her rear end was bare. He kneaded the buttocks, which became smooth and slippery. Again she let out a moan. He took hold of the pulled-down panties and with a slow movement drew them down along her thighs and removed them. Now she was lying completely exposed in front of him. He continued to knead her thighs with firm strokes. He carefully lifted and separated her legs so that he could more easily get at the inside of her thighs. He was a fraction of an inch from her sex. She was wet between her legs, breathing with her mouth open and pressing her face against the round opening in the table. He continued to massage her, as close as he could get without touching her sex. She was slippery and shiny all over.

He held up the towel, which had landed down by her calves, and asked her to turn over. Mechanically she did as he said and lay on her back, her breasts right next to him. He placed the towel over her so that the nipples were concealed and placed himself behind her, by her head. She closed her eyes. Tried not to concentrate on anything other than simply being in the moment.

He stood right above her. Her whole body was soft, loose limbed. She was willing now, prepared to surrender herself completely to him. He started kneading the back of her neck, let his hands glide out toward the shoulders with small pressing movements, and continued to massage down the collarbone. He stroked lightly along the edge of the towel, teasingly, close to her breasts. She was breathing heavily, and it sounded as if he was, too. She didn't know if it was from exertion or excitement. She was completely focused on his hands and where they were going to go next. How they wandered over her body. Strong caresses that made sparks fly in her belly. She felt dizzy, bewildered. His hands, warm and hard, against her soft skin.

Then, finally, he pulled aside the towel completely. Let his hands glide down over her breasts. And she was lost.

1

Erika Bergman stood in front of the mirror in the sparsely furnished room, carefully brushing her long hair. She pulled with firm, rhythmic strokes to get it smooth and shiny. Not that it really mattered; he would muss it up as soon as he had the chance. She looked at her well-proportioned body with satisfaction. Years of regular yoga training had paid off. She picked out a bra and panties with care. A wave went through her belly as she thought about what would happen later that evening. Erika smiled to herself—this wasn't exactly the kind of training she'd had in mind when she'd signed up for the yoga retreat on Gran Canaria.

She looked out the window at the mountains, which towered all around, thousands of feet high. The slopes were covered with fruit orchards, and beyond that was the glistening water of the Atlantic. Her surroundings were uncommonly green for the southern part of Gran Canaria. Plantings of bananas, papayas, squash, tomatoes, oranges, and lemons extended down toward the rocky beach. Here, out of the way, removed from the tourist complexes with their discos, bars, and nightclubs, was the Samsara Soul yoga center. The center was almost completely hidden by an old wall that provided both seclusion and protection from unwelcome guests.

Erika would be here for two months, far from everything and everyone. She planned to devote herself solely to training, massage, walks, sunbathing, and swimming. Get into balance so she could go on with her life. She already felt that she was heading in the right direction. When she'd arrived here a few weeks before, she'd been a wreck.

She hadn't counted on a romance. That was an unexpected bonus. She set down the brush and applied a little red lipstick. Took out one of the few dresses she had packed and slipped into it. Put on the high heels. Checked the clock; it was almost time.

There was a sudden movement at the window—a quick, soundless shadow gliding past. Right outside, so close that it almost grazed the glass. She stiffened. Saw her face in the mirror and recognized the harried gaze. She thought she had flown away from it, left it behind in Sweden. But it had followed her—a paralyzing feeling that someone had their eyes on her. That she had to look around before she went out. That she needed to lock the door behind her.

It didn't take much. She stood quietly while she listened for sounds, but it was silent. Almost unpleasantly so. It was rare that anyone walked past her room, which was at the far end of the building, with a window facing toward a narrow space where there were only some bushes.

She sensed another movement from the corner of her eye. It was almost like a feeling, but there was something there. She hadn't been imagining things. She felt a shiver from the nape of her neck down along her back.

Carefully, she slipped up to the window and peeked out in both directions. A lizard scampered on the ground and disappeared under the bushes.

She stood there awhile, peering out the window. Something was hiding among the trees farther off toward the wall that surrounded the center. Her heart beat faster.

Then she saw it. Coming out from the bushes, eagerly nosing along the ground. It was big and shabby-looking, with a dusty brown coat. Erika heaved a sigh of relief.

It was only a dog.

2

The scallops rattled lightly against the sides of the aluminum bucket. He'd dived for them that same morning by the rocks outside El Pajar. They weren't exactly the kind he needed, but there were no pilgrim scallops on Gran Canaria. It was the symbolism that was most important anyway. The bucket was half-full; that should be enough. The roses had been more troublesome than expected. He'd had to search around quite a while before he found the right color, in a garden by a house that seemed deserted, high up in the mountains. He'd cut as many white ones as he could take with him. He didn't want to buy roses, didn't want anything that could be traced to him.

He'd followed them the entire way from the yoga center. They got into the car about three thirty in the afternoon and drove straight to the old fishing village Arguineguín. It took an hour, and they'd arrived just as siesta was over and the shops opened again. They parked outside the Ancora shopping center and did their errands. He'd pushed his cap far down on his forehead to avoid being recognized as he walked behind them. After a couple of hours they'd had coffee at Piporro, the bar on the beach promenade, and then the man disappeared into the Norwegian Seamen's Church, which was on the cliffs right by the sea. She'd walked around alone in shops, and he'd watched her. She was so beautiful with her long, slender figure, her clean Scandinavian features and ash-blonde hair. She wore a simple blue cotton dress and sandals with high heels. He felt like going up to her and introducing himself, treating her to a drink. Sit with her and look at the sunset. She'd gone into Apollo, a restaurant down by the sea, and ordered a glass of wine. It didn't take long before the man appeared again. He was wearing sunglasses and a hat, as if he didn't want to be recognized. They ordered food and talked and laughed in an intimate way. It was apparent from a distance that they were more than friends. They'd eaten their dinner and drunk more wine, and when they left they walked close together over to some apartments above the Seamen's Church. They disappeared through a doorway, and he guessed it would be some time before they came out again. He didn't mind waiting. In fact, the later in the evening it was, the better.

He'd sat in a bar where he could keep an eye on who was going in and out of the building. Ordered a beer, lit a cigarette, and tried to calm his nerves. Dusk set in and wrapped the little coastal village in a gentle darkness. The light from the street lamps along the beach promenade was warm and welcoming, and so was the rest of Arguineguín. It was a pleasant, sleepy community on the south coast of Gran Canaria, far from the hectic nightlife that characterized the tourist towns of Puerto Rico and Playa del Inglés a few miles away. Here, most of the bars and restaurants closed by eleven o'clock.

He'd paid his bill and moved to a park bench on the street when the door through which they'd entered opened. It was already past midnight, the bar was closed, and the street was empty. He saw that the woman was alone.

She walked resolutely over to the Supermercado León, which was the only store still open. No one else was inside, and the lights shone brightly out onto the dark street. She stepped into the store, and he had a good view of her through the open doors. She picked out beer and cigarettes. His heart was pounding hard in his chest and his mouth got dry. When she came out she was stopped by one of the drunks who were usually sitting on a bench nearby. He saw that they exchanged a few words and she gave away a couple of cigarettes. She continued up the road, back toward the building she had come out of. It was now or never.

3

As she stepped out onto the dark street she heard the door close behind her with a muffled click. She realized that she had neither a key nor a code and that there was no entry phone. Nervously she fumbled for the cell phone in her handbag and breathed out when she felt it. She could just call when she got back. She had no desire to stand there yelling among the sleeping buildings, attracting attention. No one needed to know they were here. It was their secret. He'd been extremely clear about that.

He'd asked her to go buy cigarettes and beer. At first she protested. Was he really going to send her out in the middle of the night? But he insisted, and she didn't actually mind. It would be nice to get a little air.

It was almost one o'clock when she walked down the street toward the all-night supermercado. It wasn't hard to find; you could see the neon sign from the apartment. She was alone. There was not a single person to be seen, apart from a gang sitting on the benches by the beach promenade and drinking. They seemed unpleasant, and she went past without looking at them.

The store was empty. She picked out the items and paid the yawning checkout clerk, who entertained himself by watching TV as he helped her. Maybe it was the only way for him to stay awake.

When she came out a woman stepped out of the dark shadows. At first Erika was startled—it was a reminder of something she wanted to forget. But the woman clearly belonged to the little group of drunks. She was begging cigarettes. Erika gave her a few and quickly walked on.

The promenade was in darkness. The moon had glided out from behind the night clouds and cast a pale light over the sea, just barely visible in the dark. She listened to her own steps echoing against the dry asphalt. The streets were deserted. She stopped at the wall above the shore and looked out over the lava-black beach, the harbor farther off, and the residential area on the cape, which was lit up by the warm yellow glow of street lamps. It seemed to be a tranquil town with no nightlife. In the darkness she heard the light rippling of waves, a car being started far away, but nothing else—besides occasional bellowing from the drunks on the bench.

The warm night air caressed her skin. She liked standing there, all alone. A few minutes to herself to hear her own thoughts. The two of them would snuggle a while longer before heading back to Tasarte, where he would drop her off at the yoga center and she would crawl into her narrow bed as if nothing had happened. Erika smiled at the thought. If the other participants at the yoga camp only knew what she'd been up to. She felt more lighthearted than she had in a long time, as if she were very far away from all that. It was as if nothing concerned her. She could not recall when she had last felt so relaxed.

She continued along the empty beach promenade and came to the bend, where it was darkest. To get back to the apartment, she had to pass through a tunnel between a dark building and a high rock wall. Not until she was in the tunnel did she notice that she was not alone.

Someone was walking behind her. She turned around abruptly to see if it was one of the winos following her in the hope of a few coins or more cigarettes. She could see a figure dressed in black clothing and a cap, but it wasn't one of the drunks. She got an uncomfortable feeling that gave her goose pimples and she quickened her pace. Cursed herself that she enjoyed the view over the water so much that she took this route. She should have walked on the street above, where there were buildings and cars. She heard the stranger getting closer. Fear took over and made her cold in the mild night.

Then suddenly there was a low voice right behind her, a voice that said something she could not make out. It sounded as if someone was whispering to her, but she did not want to stop to hear what it was. She realized how vulnerable she was; there was no one else at the dark corner with the high rock wall, in the dark, narrow passage behind the building. She was trapped, with someone right behind her.

She panted, her body feeling dreamlike and heavy. Her movements became sluggish. There was a shadow across the light of the street lamp on the wall. She held her breath. Wanted to drop the bag of beer and cigarettes she was carrying. Wanted to run, but her legs did not obey; wanted to scream, but could not get out a sound.

Then someone grabbed her. A voice against her ear, her bare throat. And she fell.

4

Helena Eriksson was sitting in the lotus position in deep concentration. She breathed calmly with her eyes closed and felt the warmth of the sun on her face. She was drenched in sweat after almost an hour and a half of yoga. She felt the presence of the others, even though everyone was sitting stock-still. Carefully, she opened her eyes, peeked at the leader, Samsara, who was sitting with palms on the ground and both legs crossed behind his neck, muscles tensed hard, his lithe body in total balance. He seemed completely unperturbed by the complicated position. His intense gaze was aimed straight ahead, over their heads, fixed on a point somewhere else, far from there. His face was expressionless.

He looked good, she thought. Even though he must be almost sixty he was still attractive. His skin was dark brown after years in the sun, his body sinewy and muscular without an ounce of superfluous fat. His features were clean, with high cheekbones and a strong jaw that underscored his masculine appearance. That he was well-endowed could not be ignored. For days on end he went around dressed only in a thin strip of cloth around his narrow hips. It was almost irritating that he insisted on displaying himself like that, Helena thought. As if he wanted them all to be aware of what he was packing, what capacity he possessed.

Helena looked carefully at the others in the group. They were all women, most around forty. All were similarly dressed, in soft, knee-length tights and white sleeveless shirts. They got the clothes when they arrived; no one should stand out. It was part of the experience here, part of the atmosphere. They were all striving for the same goal: to find peace both in themselves and in communion with others. They had learned that physical affinity among the participants made it easier to achieve the spiritual goals.

Samsara gave a sign that they should lie down for the final relaxation. Helena got the idea that he was giving her a particularly long look and wondered why. Either he was flirting with her or she had done a pose wrong. There was always someone he took aside after class for a reprimand or extra instruction. Sometimes it was for a compliment because she'd done especially well, but that was less common. He was strict and demanding, the best yoga teacher she'd ever had.

She lay down on her side on her thin mat. Folded up her legs, bent at a ninety-degree angle. Stretched out her arms. She had plenty of room. The place beside her was empty. It belonged to her roommate, Erika, but she wasn't there. Helena hadn't seen her since lunch the day before. Erika had left at about three in the afternoon without saying where she was going and hadn't come back. Not to the evening class, not to dinner, and not back to their room during the night. She was starting to get worried. True, her roommate had disappeared before, but not for this long. And never overnight.

She didn't actually know that much about Erika. They had shared a room for almost two weeks, and they got along well, but the few times Helena tried to bring up any deeper topics of conversation,

Erika closed up like a clam. There was something melancholy about her. She was beautiful, with her big eyes and long blonde hair. She had a certain elegance, as if she was a little finer than all the others. She wasn't trying to emphasize that or act superior; it was just the way she was. She possessed a luminous quality that was almost enchanting, but she also harbored a sadness she obviously didn't want to talk about. But the darkness in her eyes disappeared completely when she talked about yoga. Erika loved the life at the center, and she was most radiant when it was time for yet another class. Helena thought about how her new friend looked when Samsara, the owner of the yoga center, welcomed them. The seriousness that marked her face seemed to be swept away. Erika was exhilarated and seemed fascinated and curious about what the center could offer her. She hadn't missed a single activity since arrival. Every morning she woke up at six o'clock to have time in the peace and quiet before the first morning yoga. Helena, on the contrary, couldn't make herself get out of bed until the last moment. Oddly enough, she found it stressful getting to class in time to relax.

But this morning Erika didn't show up for class. She hadn't slept in their room during the night either. Helena had woken up several times, only to see that Erika's bed was empty.

The class was over, and everyone got up slowly, one by one. Samsara thanked them for the time by pressing his palms together and bowing deeply toward the group. Helena left the terrace, went down the whitewashed steps that ran along the side of the building and then over to the other building where she and Erika were staying. If she hadn't spent the night in their room, where had she been? The participants at the center were mainly middle-aged women longing for peace and quiet and better balance in their bodies. There were also a few men and a few younger women. Like her and Erika. The participants mostly stayed in the area around the center. The schedule was pretty full; there wasn't much time for anything else. The days were strictly laid out with several yoga classes, body treatments, and also some work: cleaning, food preparation, and picking fruit in the nearby orchards. Helena's stay would be for two weeks. Most people did not stay longer than that. Unlike Erika, who was going to be there the whole summer. Helena did not envy her. She was already starting to get tired of the fully scheduled days and the bland food. The tasteless vegetable stews, the green tea. The first thing she would do when she got home to Stockholm would be to go to McDonald's.

She wondered where Erika could have gone. There was nowhere to go out here. There was one bar in Tasarte, but it rarely seemed to be open, and down by the sea was a family restaurant. Maybe she should go there and ask if anyone had seen Erika. Helena had already asked around the center, but no one had seen her or known where she was. Erika hadn't told her about having any friends on the island whom she might have visited.

Helena had reached their door, but stopped a moment. Suddenly everything felt foreign. She was seized by a sudden discomfort, as if something dangerous was waiting in there. She shook her head lightly at her own fantasies and tried to shake off the feeling. She opened the door and went in. The furnishings were simple. The room was painted white, and the plastered walls were bare, with no pictures or other decorations. There were two narrow single beds in separate corners. A small sink on one wall and a mirror, a thin towel hanging on a hook. Everything was spare, stripped down. In order to reach inner harmony, you must surround yourself with simplicity, Samsara had explained. He himself lived in a large stone villa some distance from the center with his wife and two children. Helena hadn't been inside, but the exterior of the villa gave a lavish impression.

The room looked just like it had when she left it that morning. She sat down on her bed. It was hard, which was supposed to be good for the circulation. Erika's backpack was half-open on the floor, and on her nightstand were a book and some magazines.

Helena wondered what kind of secret Erika was harboring. One evening they'd talked about why they'd come here. Erika had been rather evasive but said something about needing to get away. That it was unbearable at home. Helena got the impression that she was fleeing from something, or someone. A lot of people came here to recover from their stressful lives, to get closer to themselves, in solitude but at the same time together with others. Helena had a feeling that Erika was someone who truly needed a break.

Helena felt a growing, physical sense of worry. Erika didn't answer her cell phone and hadn't left any messages for her. Something must be wrong. Seriously wrong.

5

The lone fishing boat came puttering in toward Arguineguín's harbor at daybreak. A hesitant morning light spread across the sky. Manuel was tired after a night of fishing. His legs ached, and his back was stiff. He wasn't a young man anymore, and the work took a toll on his body. The catch had been good, however. They got several hundred pounds of fish, mostly tuna and sardines. It would provide a welcome boost to his finances. Times were hard; the deep economic crisis in Spain had left its mark on everyone.

He went out on deck, stretched and yawned, and then took a can of Tropical beer out of the cooler and lit a cigarette. The sea was calm and smooth.

He longed to get home and kiss his grandchildren before they went to school. His wife would serve him a warm breakfast at the kitchen table. A tortilla with potatoes and *gofio*, roasted corn that was ground into meal and mixed with olive oil, water, sugar, and salt and made into a dough that she cut into slices like bread. Gofio is high in carbohydrates and the perfect food after an exhausting night at sea. He felt hunger gnawing at his belly. He was cold and tired and wanted to get home to some food and his warm bed.

As the boat approached the harbor and the beach, he could see the black rocks below the Norwegian Seamen's Church. First he could only sense them in the light of dawn; they glistened above the seawater, which was now receding. The waves washed quietly toward land. Manuel took another puff and a swig of beer. Suddenly, he caught sight of a person on the rocks. He stiffened and instinctively took a step forward on deck, as if that might help him see better. There was a woman there—and she was naked. She was lying completely still, as if she were sleeping.

The sun was just coming up, and the morning air was damp and cool. He hurried up into the cabin to get the binoculars. His companion, Jaime, was at the wheel and wondered what was going on, but Manuel only waved his hand dismissively and hurried out. He brought the binoculars to his eyes and pointed them toward the rocks. He shuddered when he realized he'd seen right. On a flat rock below the church a woman was lying on her back, lifeless, her face turned up toward the sky. Her blonde hair fell down along her sides. Manuel shouted at Jaime in the pilothouse and gestured for him to change course.

"There's a dead woman on the rocks," he called.

As they approached the shore, the scene emerged clearly. Manuel would never forget it. The sound as the boat scraped against the black rock, a gull cawing out at sea, the distant droning of a radio from one of the beachside cafés that was about to open for the day, the clattering of tables being set out on the sidewalk for passersby hungry for breakfast. A street cleaner in green overalls was sweeping the street above the beach; another was emptying trash cans. Two joggers ran past. Someone stood down on the still-empty beach while his dog ran around in the sand. The morning light was spreading and painted the beach promenade in new colors. Facade after facade became a warmer shade as the sun climbed higher up in the sky.

Manuel made his way up to the woman on the rocks. She was lying well protected along the high wall, likely not visible from the walking path above. He recoiled and was barely able to look at her as he nervously dug for his phone in his jacket pocket.

She had a beautiful face with high cheekbones and thin lips. The skin was white, almost transparent. The eyes that stared glassily toward the sky were deep blue. There was a gash right across her neck. White roses were strewn around the body.

Manuel heard Jaime behind him.

"Por dios," he panted. "What happened? Is she really dead?"

Manuel nodded slowly.

His hands were shaking as he entered the number for the police.

6

Earlier

A cold draft woke Adriana. In her dream the Virgin Mary sat by her side, stroking her forehead, just like when she was a child. But suddenly the Virgin's face had been contorted, her forehead wrinkled and her eyes blackened. She opened her mouth and screamed, and then her teeth turned black and fell out, one by one.

Maybe it was Adriana's own anxious scream that woke her. She pulled the covers closer around her and looked out into the darkness. The shutters were slightly open, allowing the cold light of the moon in through the glass and down onto the floor. It crossed the bed like a strip of silver and crept up the wall, forming a halo around the head of Christ on the crucifix above the headboard. She had a feeling of discomfort that lingered even after she woke up, a worry in her gut, though where it came from she didn't know. It was as if the walls were closing in around her.

Then she heard him, the familiar steps across the floor. He was trying to move carefully. The door opened slowly, a faint squeak. The bed creaked under his weight as he sat down on the edge and leaned over her. He kissed her on the forehead, gently. He was unshaven, and the rough skin rubbed against her cheek.

"*Mi amor,*" she whispered tenderly.

He stroked her hair, lightly touched her bare shoulders. She took hold of his hand and pulled it to her, set it against her lips.

"Stay with me," she said.

"My darling," he said, wrapping his hands around hers. "I can't. They're waiting for me. We're taking several boats out, and I'm going with José. I can't let him down."

"Can't someone else do it? They'll manage without you for once. Call and say you're sick. Get under the blanket here instead."

The feeling was getting stronger. She felt a streak of cold inside and wanted him to warm her. The Virgin Mary had cast her cold shadow across the room.

"Stay with me, please. I don't want you to go out to sea at night." She turned her head toward the window and looked out worriedly. "A storm is brewing."

As if to confirm her fears the shutters started to rattle, and the wind sighed ever stronger in the trees outside. It was a sign from the Virgin Mary.

He took hold of her head with his calloused hands and pressed her to his chest. She took in his aroma of fish, sea, and salt. The smell never really went away. It was as if all the backbreaking years out at sea had settled in his skin.

"You know I can't," he said quietly. "Only God and the sea can put food on our table and keep us warm. Pray for me instead when I'm out there tonight," he said, releasing her. "Pray that God lets me fish gold up from the sea."

"You always laugh off questions about life and death."

"Yes," he said, stroking her cheek. "What else can you do? He who fears death does not enjoy life."

"You and your proverbs," she said with a snort, pretending to be irritated at him for making a joke about her anxiety.

"A troublesome wife makes a man a philosopher," he said, smiling at her.

His dark eyes shone at her in the moonlight from the window.

Adriana sat up in bed, took hold of his jacket, and pulled him to her.

"Kiss me," she said.

And he kissed her, long and ardently.

She'd fallen in love with him before she even turned eighteen. He'd been so different from the other boys who tried to impress her when she was young. He never made any attempts to approach her. His reserve and his cautious interest made him attractive. He didn't stand on the street corners whistling at girls like the other boys in the village. He just observed her and smiled shyly when their eyes met. One day, after she was shopping at the market, he asked whether he could keep her company, and she said yes.

He carried her box of fruit and told her stories. Tall tales about the countryside, about his grandfather, who'd come down from the mountains with goats. His father, who fished, his mother, who worked out in the fields. He had a particular warmth in his voice when he talked about his mama, her hard work and kindness.

Adriana sank back in the bed. Heard the wind sighing outside the window.

"Go then," she said, "and good luck tonight. I'll wait for you."

He nodded and blew her a kiss, closed the door behind him. As soon as he left the sense of disaster came back.

Adriana clasped her hands in prayer. Closed her eyes and whispered out into the darkness.

"Dios mio . . ."

She was startled when the wind tore open the shutters. Jesus on the cross came down from the wall and broke into pieces against the bedside table. The Son of God lay there with arms outstretched, the brown wooden cross cracked and fallen to the floor. She reached for the broken figure and pressed it hard against her chest.

"Dios mio," she whispered again. "Dear God, don't let anything happen."

7

The police radio crackled in the silent room. At first the sound seemed to come from far away, then it got stronger and stronger. The radio was always on the bedside table. As editor of the Scandinavian weekly *Day & Night* she had to keep track of what was happening. It was part of the job.

Sara Moberg was sleeping alone in the big double bed. Her husband, Lasse, was with their son in Las Palmas. They'd gone to a late soccer match and were spending the night at a hotel. Her husband was good at that, occasionally taking one of the kids on an outing, just the two of them. She sometimes felt guilty that she didn't do the same.

In her drowsy state she'd made out only fragments of the message on the police radio. A woman had been found dead below the Norwegian Seamen's Church in Arguineguín. The police suspected homicide. Sara cast a glance at the alarm clock; it said seven thirty. Suddenly wide awake, she reached for her iPhone and entered the number for Chief Inspector Diego Quintana at the Guardia Civil in Las Palmas. She groped for her reading glasses and the pen and paper that she always kept beside her when she slept, in case of an emergency. Or if she got a sudden idea for an article or something useful right when she was falling asleep or when she lay awake in the middle of the night—which happened far too often nowadays. Perhaps it was her age, approaching menopause, or just general worry.

She had to call several times before the inspector finally answered.

"*Hola*, it's Sara. Sorry to call so early, but I assume you're at work."

"On my way at least," Quintana said, practically snarling.

"I just heard something about a murder in Arguineguín. A woman was found dead by the Norwegian Seamen's Church—"

"Suspected homicide," Quintana said, correcting her. "We don't know anything yet. Damn it, the alarm just went out."

"Okay. Do you know who the victim is?"

"No."

"Has anyone been arrested?"

"No."

"Can you say anything else? Is it true that she was found outside?"

"Time to give up, Sara. I have to focus on my job. *Adiós.*"

Sara Moberg got out of bed and hurried into the bathroom. She had to get to Arguineguín as quickly as possible. A woman murdered—it was so unlikely for something like that to happen in that peaceful little resort town. Many of her readers were there. Norwegians made up a large part of the population.

She didn't bother with breakfast, but she grabbed a banana, a bottle of water, and a piece of the bread she'd baked the day before. She stuck her head into her daughter's room to tell her that she was leaving.

"Okay, okay," Olivia said from under the covers. "Have a good day, Mom."

"Just make sure you get up later," Sara called out before throwing on a sweater and sticking her feet in a pair of sturdy walking shoes. If she was going to stomp around in the rocks and sand out by the sea, it was best to be prepared.

As soon as she was outside the door of the villa she felt overdressed. The air was warm, even though the sun had just come up. She took off the sweater and tossed it in the backseat and then put in a Ted Gärdestad CD before she drove out of the garage. The iron gates opened automatically. The car was immediately filled with "The Sky's an Innocent Blue," and Sara sang along. Loud and off-key. She'd been a big Ted Gärdestad fan ever since her teens, and she never got tired of his music. He was still her idol, although he'd been dead for many years now. She still had all his vinyl LPs at home and even had an old poster up in her study.

The villa was high up on a hill with a magnificent view of the sea. All of San Agustín spread out below her. She'd lived here with her family for twenty years, almost as long as she'd been on Gran Canaria. They decided to leave the cold of Sweden when they found out Lasse was suffering from Parkinson's disease. They were newlyweds with their first child, Viktor, on the way. They'd settled in San Agustín on south Gran Canaria, where quite a few Swedes were already living. Lasse took over a dilapidated hotel right by the ocean, renovating it and marketing it primarily to Scandinavian guests. The hotel quickly became popular, and the heat, in combination with the right medications, put the Parkinson's into remission. Sara started the weekly, and after a few toilsome years it broke even. Circulation increased and advertisers flowed in. She and Lasse quickly learned Spanish, and they had many friends, both Canarian and Scandinavian. Now they'd lived here most of their adult lives, their children were more Canarian than Swedish, and their homeland felt distant. They were content to visit Sweden a few weeks every year. That was more than enough.

Arguineguín was only fifteen minutes away, and Sara drove straight to the Norwegian Seamen's Church. It was located in the middle of the town, high and beautiful on a promontory with a view of the harbor, the beach promenade, and the sea where the cliffs over by Puerto Rico and Mogán descend sharply into the depths. Even from far off it was apparent something had happened. A dozen police cars were parked by the church, uniformed officers were everywhere, and police tape was fluttering lightly in the morning breeze. Sara collected her camera bag and notebook before getting out of the car. A group of people stood outside the tape, and she could hear agitated voices. Someone asked what was going on while another shook her head. Several people were taking pictures with their cell phones. Curiosity seekers were approaching from both directions along the beach promenade.

Arguineguín was squeezed in along the south coast of the island, between the major tourist towns of Playa del Inglés and Puerto Rico. It was extremely unusual that something as sensational as a murder happened.

As Sara approached she saw Chief Inspector Quintana, who was crouching by the victim along with a person she assumed was the medical examiner. The body was barely concealed behind a provisional curtain. She made her way to the police tape and called to the inspector, completely ignoring a policeman's attempt to get her to back up. Her camera naturally indicated that she was a journalist. Diego looked up and their eyes met. He waved to her. He tossed off a comment to the medical examiner and walked over to her. He smiled weakly when they greeted each other—he was clearly bothered by what had happened. Diego Quintana was a well-built and unusually tall man for a Canarian, well over six feet. He had dark hair that was combed back, a thick mustache, and well-groomed sideburns.

"I thought I'd see you here," he said.

"What happened?" Sara asked.

"Some fishermen found a dead woman here on the rocks just this morning. There's no doubt it's a homicide."

"Still no arrests?"

"No."

"Can I get closer?" she asked.

"This is a crime scene, the technicians are gathering evidence, and the medical examiner is here. You'll have to stay outside for now."

"Please—if I stay in the background? I won't disturb anything."

"You know I'll do anything for you, but there are limits."

Quintana winked at her and went back to the curtain, where the medical examiner was making an initial examination. It sounded like a joke, but she knew he was serious. Diego Quintana had been in love with her since they'd met ten years earlier. But both were married to other people and she didn't feel the same way, so she tried to pretend not to notice.

"Can you at least say how she died?" Sara called after him.

Quintana stopped for a moment, and then turned around and stroked his index finger across his neck in a rapid movement.

Sara shuddered. She climbed up onto a section of wall outside the tape, where she had a better view of the rocks below the beach promenade. When the medical examiner moved she suddenly caught sight of the body.

The woman was perhaps in her thirties. She was naked, stretched out on a flat rock. One hand was placed over her chest while the other covered her lower abdomen. Right across her neck she had an ugly knife gash, but it was strangely clean. Her light skin glowed against the shiny black rocks around her. Sara's gaze fixed on something lying around the body. She put the telephoto lens on the camera. Then she saw. White roses had been strewn on the ground. The dead woman's pose looked arranged, as if the murderer had wanted to illustrate something.

Around the crime scene more people started to gather. Curious villagers and tourists streamed in from all directions, forming a small crowd outside the tape. Sara noted several other journalists and photographers.

She looked at the dead woman. *Who are you?* she wondered. *And what in the name of God happened to you?*

8

The morning sky was just getting light and the air was already warm when Kristian Wede staggered out of his apartment, still not entirely awake. He had a hangover and was tired and would have given anything to be able to stay in bed after the phone rang. It was his boss at the Swedish-Norwegian consulate, Grete Jensen. She sounded stressed.

"Something serious has happened in Arguineguín. A woman who is probably Scandinavian was just found dead below the Norwegian Seamen's Church. Everything indicates that it's a murder. You'll have to go there and try to find out who she is. The Foreign Ministry is already breathing down our necks. Speak with a Chief Inspector Diego Quintana. He knows you're coming."

On his way to his car, which was parked on a narrow back street, he took the snuff box out of the inside pocket of his jacket and put a pinch between his upper lip and gums. The snuff didn't make him feel any better, but he needed the stimulation to wake up.

He pulled his hand through his dark curly hair, which had a tendency to stick out in different directions, and settled himself in the car. Opened a can of Coke he'd taken from the fridge on the way out. Took a few deep gulps, put in a CD. His little bright-yellow Morris was so boxed in that he barely managed to get it out. He'd bought the car new as soon as he landed on the island three months earlier. The Swedish-Norwegian consulate had found lodging for him in a duplex apartment in San Cristóbal, a suburb of Las Palmas. It was right by the sea, with a view of the beach promenade and the skyline of the big city in the background.

The engine roared as he pressed the gas pedal to the floor and turned onto the *autopista* heading south. He stifled a yawn and turned up the music. Considering how late he'd been out the night before and how many beers he'd consumed, it was early, much too early. A glance at the clock showed eight thirty.

He accelerated, the car eating up the highway ahead of him, mile after mile. He passed the airport, the Vecindario area, San Agustín—the favorite of many Swedes—and the enormous tourist complexes in Playa del Inglés and Maspalomas.

The night before he'd gone to the local bar, situated on a corner by the beach promenade just a stone's throw from his apartment and only a few yards from the wall by the sea. Sometimes the waves came so close that the bar owner had to move the outdoor tables higher up on the street so the customers wouldn't get drenched. Mar Cantábrico had quickly become a favorite and Kristian often ended his workday there with a beer, or several, while he sat and stared out toward the horizon and thought over the events of the past year and how drastically his life had changed. But yesterday evening he'd had the company of a new friend, the artist Jorge, and had knocked back way too many Tropicals while they discussed the major issues of life. He stumbled home at two o'clock in the morning and fell asleep fully clothed on the couch in front of the TV.

Kristian Wede passed the sign that said "Welcome to Arguineguín." He drove straight ahead after the first roundabout, continued past the Spar grocery store, and then turned left at the next roundabout and parked outside the Danish hair salon, which was on a street above the beach.

He got out and took off his jacket and left it in the car. It was considerably warmer here than in Las Palmas. Because the island had four climate zones, the weather could vary greatly. It was not unusual for it to be ten degrees warmer on the south part of the island than on the north side. Many freezing tourists were disappointed when they landed in Las Palmas and were met by clouds and temperatures in the 60s. But the farther south the charter buses drove, the more the sky opened up. The very best weather, with the least wind, was on the coastal strip between Maspalomas and Puerto de Mogán. A few miles away in Playa del Inglés there might be gale-force winds while it was dead calm in Arguineguín. The strange name of the town, which came from the language of the native inhabitants, simply meant "still water."

Kristian rolled up his shirtsleeves as he walked to the Seamen's Church. As he passed the diving center, he saw the police tape and a gathering of people. The police had blocked off the stairs to the rocks and the promenade along the beach. Among the onlookers was an elderly couple trying to get a glimpse.

"Do you know what happened?" the man asked when Kristian reached the plastic tape. He and his wife were dressed in matching workout clothes in a screaming shade of green.

"I'm sure it will be on the news later today," Kristian answered, looking for someone who could let him through. When no one reacted to his discreet signs, he raised the tape and ducked under it.

"I don't think that's allowed," the woman protested.

"You're right about that," Kristian answered and continued down the stairs to the rocks.

A police officer came hurrying toward him.

"Stay there," he called, making lively signs with both hands.

"I'm sorry," said Kristian. "But I'm supposed to meet—"

He took out his notepad; he couldn't remember the name he got from the consulate.

"Sorry," the policeman said, taking hold of his arm.

"Diego Quintana," Kristian read. "Can I speak with him?"

"You can't come in here. This is a crime scene, and it's closed to the public."

"I'm from the Swedish-Norwegian consulate in Las Palmas, and I've been sent here at the request of the consul. I'm responsible for contacting the victim's family."

The policeman guided him firmly back outside the tape.

"Do you need help?"

Kristian turned around, surprised by the friendly voice. The woman who was standing right outside the plastic tape spoke Swedish, was quite a bit shorter than him, and had dark, shoulder-length hair. She seemed self-confident and calm and had a direct gaze. He guessed that she was in her mid-forties.

"You look like a policeman," she said frankly.

"That's an old habit I have, looking like a policeman," he said, extending his hand. "Kristian Wede. I'm from the consulate in Las Palmas, and I'm supposed to speak with a Chief Inspector Diego Quintana."

"My name's Sara Moberg. I'm the editor of the Scandinavian weekly *Day & Night*." A frown brought out the lines on her forehead. "I don't remember seeing you before. Are you new?"

"Yes, I guess you could say that. I've been here for three months. But I know your paper."

"Come with me," said Sara, going to the wall where she was standing earlier.

A flock of seagulls sailed peacefully over their heads. A few fishing boats were on their way in to land and on the beach people were starting to put out towels and parasols. As if nothing had happened.

Under the canvas tent inside the police tape he could glimpse the dead woman. He sensed the contours of the body; she was lying on her back, and her face was turned upward. Kristian raised one hand toward the sun to see better. Had she been alive lying there? Did she know she was going to die? A shiver passed through him.

Sara asked him to wait while she went to get Quintana. He measured Kristian with his gaze as they introduced themselves.

"Have you identified the dead woman?" Kristian asked.

"No," the chief inspector answered. "She had no ID on her. She was found naked, without a bag or any clothing. But we're guessing she's from Scandinavia."

"Why do you think that?"

"The pale skin, the height, and the blonde hair. The eye color. She's sunburned, too, in a way that shows she wasn't used to the sun. And ninety-five percent of the tourists here in Arguineguín are from Norway or Sweden. What is it you Norwegians call Arguineguín? Isn't it 'Little Norway' or something like that?"

"Yes, I've heard that," Kristian said. "Although I'm new here, so I'm not that well informed."

He had already taken a liking to the burly policeman. There was something sympathetic about his slightly boorish appearance.

"What makes you suspect homicide?" Kristian continued.

Quintana cast a quick glance at Sara.

"You don't have permission to print anything. It's much too soon."

Sara raised one hand in the air.

"Scout's honor, I promise."

"Her throat was cut."

"Have you found the murder weapon?"

"Not yet."

"How long has she been dead?"

"That we don't know exactly, but the murder happened during the night."

"Can I see her?"

Quintana shook his head.

"We can't let you in. This is a crime scene. Excuse me, we'll have to talk later."

Quintana nodded curtly and returned behind the tape.

Kristian asked to borrow Sara's camera and raised it to his eyes.

"Do you see her? Awful, isn't it?" said Sara.

"Truly," Kristian mumbled while he observed the dead woman sadly. It was frightening to see the woman lying there lifeless—and also bewildering. He looked searchingly at Sara.

"Doesn't this seem staged?"

"Yes, absolutely," said Sara. "The perpetrator was careful. The way she's lying. And the roses around her. You see how clean she is, although the blood must have sprayed when he cut her throat. The murder site is farther away, by the wall. There's a lot of blood there."

Kristian was taken aback. The journalist seemed rather thick skinned. She stood there and observed the body as if she were studying dirt under her nails. She seemed completely unmoved. She took back the camera and zoomed in. Suddenly Kristian heard her take a deep breath.

"Look at this," she exclaimed, handing the camera over to him. "Do you see the bracelet around her wrist? It's a Swedish brand, Sahara. I'm quite sure."

Kristian focused the lens further. The bracelet was silver with double chains and two large interconnected rings.

"I love their jewelry. I have several pieces at home," Sara continued. "It's a very special style. You recognize them immediately, and I'm almost certain they can only be bought in Sweden. Quintana! Come here!" Her powerful voice echoed over the barricaded area.

The chief inspector, who was conversing with a group of policeman a little farther away, looked up with surprise. He seemed to realize it was important because he hurried out past the tape and over to the wall where they were standing.

"What's going on?"

"The woman's bracelet comes from a Swedish designer," said Sara. "I have that kind of jewelry myself. If you want to check, look for the name, Sahara."

Quintana raised his eyebrows.

"Well, that may mean that she's Swedish, but that's not certain. She may have gotten the jewelry as a present from someone from Sweden."

He disappeared over to the victim along with a crime scene technician. Sara saw through the camera how the technician put on a pair of plastic gloves and carefully removed the jewelry.

Quintana pulled his glasses out of the breast pocket of his jacket. He studied the bracelet carefully. Raised his head and nodded over toward Sara. She'd been right.

Sara turned toward Kristian.

"I have to go. Nice to meet you, even if it could have been under more pleasant circumstances."

She extended her hand and he took it.

"If you need help, you know where to find me."

Kristian wondered how they would be able to identify the woman. Hopefully someone would miss her and be in touch with the police. There was nothing more to do here at the moment—the police were fully occupied with their work. He would have to await the identification and talk with Quintana later.

Just as he was going to jump down from the wall he discovered something lying on the ground. A brown, fan-shaped scallop shell. How did it end up here?

Without really knowing why, he leaned over, picked it up, and put it in his pocket.

9

It wasn't until he turned onto his own street that he felt his breathing calm, felt his heart no longer beating as violently. The whole way home he'd been on edge. He'd chosen to take the new, faster freeway, but just as he drove out of Arguineguín and turned off toward Puerto Rico, it occurred to him what a risk he was taking. He was much more likely to be stopped by a police car there than if he'd taken the old road along the coast. He wanted to get home as fast as possible, crawl into bed, and know that he'd escaped. Wanted to close the door behind him and be alone. But he'd forgotten that the police were much more active on the freeway.

Every time a car showed up behind him on the road, he peeked nervously in the rearview mirror. Was careful not to drive too fast or too slow. He didn't want to arouse suspicions. He'd stared straight ahead, concentrated on the road, held on hard to the steering wheel. The cars passed him, the taillights like evil, red eyes in the darkness. At any moment he expected a police car to drive up alongside him and see that something was wrong. They would wave him off the road and make him stop. He would roll down the window and they would know that he was the one who had killed the beautiful Swedish woman who was on the rocks. Naked, abandoned, her life taken away. It would show in his face that he was the one who'd done it.

But that didn't happen. The cars simply drove on in the dark of night.

His body felt stiff, and his mouth was dry. He looked down at his legs; his pants were stained with blood. Her blood.

Ever since he'd first caught sight of her he couldn't stop thinking about her. He could see in her eyes that she was a woman you could love. The way she smiled, the way she pulled back a strand of hair from her face when she was complimented.

She was so innocent, so pure. He'd loved the brief moment right when she stopped breathing, the moment of death. The sense of power, of taking God's place. Nothing could be loved for eternity; it was only those few seconds, and then it was over.

There was a lot more blood than he'd expected. He must have struck the carotid artery, because it sprayed all over him and on the ground all around. He recoiled so violently that he almost fell backward. He was soaked with blood and he'd been forced to take off his sweater and jeans and wash himself in the sea. It was not only his clothes that were stained, but his face, his hair, his shoes. He'd rinsed off the worst of it, hurrying in case some nocturnal wanderer happened to walk along the beach promenade and catch sight of him. She'd lain soiled in her own blood, and it had gathered around her body and made her ugly, repulsive. That wasn't what he'd intended, and he had to do something about it. First he moved the body a little, and then he undressed her. He'd devoted a good amount of time to cleaning her throat, breasts, stomach, arms. Fortunately he'd had the foresight to bring a sponge, and he went down to the sea and filled the bucket. He wanted her to be clean when they found her.

It had gone well. He didn't think anyone had seen him, even though it had taken at least an hour.

Before he left her, he stood quietly and observed her for a few minutes. Her nakedness and the white roses around the body against the black rocks. He took out his phone and snapped a few pictures before he hurried to his car, which was parked above the church.

As he approached home it was after three o'clock in the morning. The streets near his house were deserted, not a person was out, and his car was the only one on the road. The apartment was on the top floor of a small building on one of the pedestrian streets downtown. He opened the door and slipped in, hoping that no one noticed him. He had only one neighbor, an elderly lady who lived with her cats.

He undressed and put his clothes and shoes in a garbage bag; he would have to get rid of them later, burn them. If he'd known there would be so much blood, he wouldn't have worn his new shoes, he thought, feeling irritated as he got into the shower. He washed his hair and scrubbed himself, rinsed off carefully, scrubbed his body again. His irritation changed to a sense of sorrow. He got out of the shower, and the water ran down his body and gathered like a pond on the floor, just like her blood had gathered around her body. He observed his face in the mirror, took his razor and followed the contours of his face. With every stroke of the razor he got rid of something of himself. He discovered that he even had blood in his ears. He dabbed at his ear with a cotton swab and met his own eyes in the mirror when he saw the cotton stained dark by her blood.

Suddenly he felt how tired he was. Exhausted, he staggered over to the bed. Before he slid into sleep he thought about her. He was filled with calm.

Now, since he'd started, there was no going back.

10

The newspaper offices were on a back street in San Agustín, only a stone's throw from her husband's hotel. The proximity was practical; Sara was able to help out at the hotel when needed, and she and Lasse could meet for lunch on occasion. She stepped out of the car, unlocked the office, and stepped inside. The offices consisted of two rooms: one larger room with a couch for visitors and a round table with a few chairs and two work stations and an inside room, where the graphic designer worked and all the pages for the next issue were taped up. Along the walls hung a selection of framed front pages from the weekly since its start in February 1999, along with a map of the island and various notes. Hugo Pérez, the weekly's other writer, was on vacation in Sweden with his Swedish wife and family, so Sara had to manage all the coverage herself. Normally this was the low season, and the majority of Scandinavians had returned to their homelands for the summer.

When Sara came in, the offices were empty and silent. Javi hadn't shown up yet. He pasted up all the ads, edited the weekly, and made sure it reached the printer every week. Per, who was responsible for advertising, wasn't there either. The weekly was distributed to a couple hundred places frequented by Scandinavians: the big hotels, shopping centers, churches, various meeting places, restaurants, and cafés.

Sara set down her bag, took out the camera, and started uploading the images. She was happy that so many were good. She not only had her own paper to think about, she also had a contract with one of the largest tabloids in Sweden. Sara had been a freelancer for *Aftonbladet* for several years, and it worked out great. She saved all the money she earned from her second job in a separate bank account, which she called "Sara's Hoard." She never touched that money, so the account grew steadily. She would use the money for herself, but on what, she hadn't decided yet. But it wasn't just about the money. The news editors at *Aftonbladet* pressured her a bit when things heated up, but Sara thought it was stimulating and fun to work for them. And she felt a certain pride when she saw a major spread with her own picture and byline published in the major newspaper.

Where *Day & Night* was concerned, there was time to get the murder into the next issue. Handling news for a weekly was problematic. Because there was a whole week between issues, many events no longer seemed current by the time the article was published. While she had no ambition to put out a daily newspaper, *Day & Night* had to include issues that affected the readers. Like the murder in Arguineguín.

The last time Sara had heard of anything like it was a few years earlier. A thirty-one-year-old mother of two from Tauro, on the south coast, not far from Arguineguín, had been knifed to death by a Swedish tourist in Las Palmas. The woman had met him on the Internet only a few weeks before. It was a frightful, meaningless murder, and Sara felt sad when she thought about the victim's two sons and her extended family.

Sara devoted a good amount of time to the story of the woman left at the church, wrote articles about the murder for both *Aftonbladet* and

Day & Night with various angles, and managed to drink a number of cups of green tea in the meantime. She closed out the articles with reactions from the community and a description of the agitated atmosphere in Arguineguín. She had interviewed several people at the scene, and all displayed the same shock and concern.

Every single person she'd interviewed had wanted to talk. It was often that way, she thought. People had a need to vent after harrowing events. She was glad that her Spanish was fluent; it created trust when she was out among people. And after twenty years on the island she'd developed a Canarian accent, which made things even easier.

By the time she was finished, she'd put together several articles for the tabloid and two double spreads for her own paper. She quickly emailed the text and images to the waiting editors in Stockholm and then focused on *Day & Night*.

We'll have to leave out the article on the new café that serves Swedish pastries, she thought. The enthusiastic couple who owned it—recent arrivals to the island—would be disappointed, but there was nothing to be done about it. It would have to wait until the next issue, as would the article on the plans for a new water park in San Agustín.

Sara leaned back in her leather chair and sighed. Her eyes fell on the drawer where she'd stored a pack of cigarettes. Even though she was in her mid-forties, she still smoked in secret behind the backs of Lasse and the kids. It was absurd, as if she wasn't adult enough to do as she pleased. But she couldn't bear the nagging and the laments. She'd stopped smoking ten years earlier and didn't want to hear the whining she'd been forced to endure then. Lasse had never smoked and didn't understand how you could do something as idiotic as consciously shortening your life just to have a cigarette. Besides, he loathed the smell and would constantly say how unattractive it was when a woman reeked of smoke. At last she gave in and quit, even though she wouldn't have done it for her own sake. Recently she'd been at a women's dinner and yielded to temptation on the terrace along with the smokers. Since then she'd started smoking a little when she was alone.

Sara removed the pack from the drawer and fished out a cigarette. She got up and opened the door to the street wide. Sat down in front of the computer again, lit the cigarette, and clicked open the few pictures she'd quickly taken of the victim. *Who are you?* she thought. Considering the bracelet, the unknown woman was probably Swedish. Sara went onto the jewelry brand's website and confirmed that all store locations were in Sweden.

Then she clicked open a close-up of the dead woman's face. Her intense blue eyes were staring up toward the sky, her mouth half-open. She almost looked surprised, as if she'd been caught off guard the moment before she died. Why did something so awful happen to her?

Sara browsed through the full-length shots she'd taken of the body and studied them carefully. The victim appeared to have been arranged, as if the perpetrator wanted to leave a message. The question was, what was it?

A few minutes before four her watch beeped a reminder—the police would be holding a press conference at the station in Las Palmas. She was content to follow it on TV and turned on one of the local channels, which was broadcasting it live. The room was filled to bursting with journalists and photographers. Sara could see Quintana take his place behind the podium along with the press spokesman. The information they gave was meager, but they did say that the victim came from Sweden and gave her age. Otherwise, they were tight-lipped, mentioning neither a murder weapon nor suspects. They also didn't say anything about the victim's peculiar arrangement or how she'd been killed.

Sara waited an hour after the end of the press conference, and then she called Quintana.

"Hola, it's me, Sara."

"I hear that."

"I understand that you've identified the victim. Can you say who she is?"

"Why should I do that?"

"What if I promise not to publish it until I get the green light from you? You know you can trust me. Who is she?"

She could tell that Quintana was hesitant, but they had a long relationship, and she was well aware of the inspector's weakness for her. Besides, he owed her a debt of gratitude after she'd done him a big favor a few years earlier.

Quintana sighed dejectedly.

"Okay, but keep the information to yourself for the time being. The woman is, as you thought, from Sweden. Erika Bergman, born in 1982. Thirty-three years old. From Stockholm, single with no children. She was studying social anthropology at the university. Parents and a brother live in Stockholm."

"Has the family been informed?"

"I don't know. We've contacted the consulate of course, but we don't know how quickly that will happen."

"Was she on vacation?"

"You might say so. She was participating in a yoga retreat on the west side, by the village of Tasarte. I've only had time to speak briefly with the director, a Frank Hagen. He's Norwegian, by the way."

"What kind of yoga center is it?" Sara frowned. "I don't think I've heard of it."

"It has the exotic name of Samsara Soul," Quintana said drily. "It sounds very New Agey."

"Strange," said Sara thoughtfully, still surprised that she didn't know about the place. "And it's run by a Norwegian, you say?"

Generally all Scandinavians who ran any kind of business on the island were in contact with her and had tried to get her to do a feature on them. An article in the weekly meant coveted free advertising because many tourists read *Day & Night* and often visited the places they learned about in the paper. Sara had often heard stories from pleased business owners about tourists coming through their door with the paper in hand.

"Yes, although he's probably lived on the island a long time. He speaks fluent Spanish, admittedly with that singsong Norwegian accent, but it's fairly faint."

"Was Erika Bergman traveling alone?"

"As far as I know, although she shared a room with a Helena Eriksson, also Swedish. It was thanks to her that we identified the body so quickly. She called and reported Erika missing."

"Does anyone know what she was doing in Arguineguín? I mean, that's a fairly long way from Tasarte."

"No idea. We haven't gotten that far yet. Frank Hagen is on his way in for questioning."

"Okay, thanks very much. Truly," Sara said with emphasis.

After getting off the phone she found the Samsara Soul website. There was a picture of a sinewy, suntanned middle-aged man with a ponytail, dressed only in a colorful, ankle-length piece of cloth that reminded her of some kind of Indian tunic. He was barefoot and standing on a hilltop, looking out over the landscape. Along with the picture was text about how life could be changed with yoga at Samsara Soul. Evidently yoga was combined with various forms of therapies: conversation, massage, creative work, and meditation. There was a gallery of pictures of people in various yoga poses, mostly women. Other galleries showed images of massage and people dyeing clothing. Interspersed with these were beautiful nature photographs of the beach, the sea, and the area around idyllic Tasarte. Judging by the price list it must have cost a small fortune to stay there for several months as Erika Bergman planned to do. Sara frowned. Quintana said that she was studying at the University of Stockholm. How did a student have the means to spend so much money on yoga? Why did she want to stay so long? Did she have some other connection there?

Sara leaned back in the chair, rocking lightly while she looked at the pictures on the computer. According to the website the business had been in operation for ten years. Although it was on the undeveloped west side, and apparently the owners had neither the need nor desire to make use of column space in *Day & Night,* she could not let go of the thought that it was strange she'd never heard of the place.

If a story about the yoga center had not been done before, perhaps this was the time.

11

The Swedish-Norwegian consulate was on Calle Luis Morote and had a view of Catalina Park in central Las Palmas. Because of reduced appropriations, the two consulates had merged a few years earlier and Kristian worked equally for both.

After visiting the crime scene in Arguineguín he'd gone home briefly and had time to wolf down a sandwich, lie down on the couch, and take a nap for an hour before showering and driving to the consulate. Without the break, he simply couldn't have handled it. The morning's hangover had been replaced by growing fatigue.

Now he drove his yellow Morris up in front of the building. It was three o'clock in the afternoon. Before leaving Arguineguín he'd found out the victim's identity. The Foreign Ministry was informed about the case and had contacted the parents, who expressed a desire to travel to Gran Canaria as soon as possible. They wanted to be in contact with the consulate, and he'd called them repeatedly, without success. He left messages on their answering machine and asked them to get back to him as soon as possible.

In Las Palmas the sun was broiling hot, and the asphalt quivered in the heat. He parked and got out of the car. It was hot, damned hot, and he was already sweaty.

As he stepped through the glass door into the building, he ran into Diana. Just as cool as always, she was dressed in patterned harem pants and a black tank top. She had on flat sandals, and her short black hair was glossy and well coifed around her face. She had no makeup on except her blue-violet lipstick. She worked at a law office one floor up. They'd met a month or so earlier and gone out and had a beer. The evening ended at her place and since then they'd met at regular intervals for uncomplicated sex. Neither of them was interested in having a serious relationship. Right now the arrangement suited him fine. Kristian's life was sufficiently complicated without him making it even more difficult.

"*Hola, guapa, buenas tardes,*" he said in greeting, kissing her soft cheeks.

She smelled fresh, as if she'd just stepped out of the shower.

"*Hola, guapo,*" she said in return, responding to the customary cheek kisses.

"Mmm." He sniffed the back of her neck. "You smell good," he whispered in her ear.

"Thanks, I just came from a boxing workout," she said, pulling away from the fleeting embrace. "The air conditioning in the gym broke down so I must have sweated buckets."

To underscore her words she greedily drank from a bottle of water. In the other hand she was holding a gym bag.

"I must be crazy, spending my time boxing in this heat instead of having lunch at some cool restaurant indoors with functioning air conditioning like a normal person."

"Absolutely." Kristian looked furtively in both directions. "By the way, do you have any interest in getting a little crazy with me tonight?" he whispered.

They were careful to be discreet; neither of them wanted their colleagues at work to guess what was going on.

"You dog," she said, poking him in the side. "Okay, ten o'clock at my place? I probably won't make it home before then."

"Agreed," he said contentedly. He winked at her and continued on his way, whistling under his breath. Suddenly his fatigue had disappeared, and for a moment he forgot the unpleasant task he had ahead of him: talking to people who had just lost their daughter.

As soon as he stepped into the office, the consul approached him. Grete Jensen was a stylish woman in her fifties, always immaculately outfitted in a dress or skirt and blouse, her long hair done up in an impressive bun on her head. A little too much makeup, with a thick layer of black mascara, eyeliner, and red lipstick, but she was a strikingly beautiful woman, the kind who never passed by unnoticed. It was not only her exterior that attracted attention. Her deep, dark voice and thunderous laugh could make her colleagues jump in pure terror.

"So nice that you're here," said Grete, waving him into her office.

The window was open, yet it was hot as an oven in the ample corner office with its high ceiling and magnificent view of the park. She plopped down on the chair behind her elegant mahogany desk and looked inquisitively at him.

"Have you spoken with Erika Bergman's parents?"

"I haven't got hold of them yet, but I've left several messages."

"That's just as well. I just spoke with the dad. He called here directly for some reason."

Kristian frowned. He picked up his cell phone and discovered that he had several missed calls from Sweden. When he was driving with the music loud it was impossible to hear the phone. A little awkward, he had to admit. He was new at the job and contact with relatives was one of his duties. He wanted to perform well, make a good impression.

He'd been sensitive after the incident in Oslo, lost some of his former self-confidence. Sometimes he felt like a wounded bird and wondered if he would ever get back to being the person he was before everything happened.

"I'm sorry, I didn't hear the phone in the car."

The consul waved her hand dismissively.

"No problem. That sort of thing happens. They're coming here tomorrow in any event. Can you pick them up at the airport?"

"Of course." Kristian paused. "How are they doing?"

"As I said I only talked with the dad. He was extremely taciturn, but that was probably the shock. What did the police say?"

"Not much. They don't seem to have any idea who murdered her."

The consul looked at the clock.

"The Guardia Civil has announced a press conference at four o'clock that will be broadcast live on TV. We should watch it."

"Sure. Is there any point in my trying to get hold of anyone there before that?"

"Yes, we have to know where the body goes. Presumably she'll be taken to forensic medicine as soon as possible."

"Okay."

Kristian got up and went to his own office at the other end of corridor, which was considerably more modest. The consulate was empty and silent; only he and Grete were there. It was vacation time for the employees, and the operation was at its quietest this time of year. Normally. But things were no longer normal.

He spent the next half hour trying to get as much information as possible from the police. No perpetrator had yet been arrested, and they could not reveal anything about the motive behind the crime, but simply referred him to the promised press conference. It turned out that the body was at the forensic medicine department in Las Palmas and would undergo a preliminary examination that evening. The autopsy would wait until tomorrow.

He hung up with the police, got a glass of water, which he downed in one gulp, and took a pinch of snuff. Sank down in the armchair behind the desk and leaned back. A child's drawing was hanging on the wall. It depicted a giraffe that was smiling broadly and had flowers on its body instead of spots. It was a florafa, Valeria had explained. So a florafa was a flowery giraffe, from the Spanish *flor* and *jirafa*.

How would I react if something like that happened to Valeria? he thought. Even though he'd only had contact with his daughter the past three months, his feelings for her had already grown strong, and now he could not imagine life without her. His daughter was ten years old, but he'd missed her entire childhood until now.

He'd met her mother, Pilar, when she'd come from Las Palmas to study in Oslo for a year. They started a relationship. After Pilar went home, she called and said she was pregnant. She wanted to keep the child, but Kristian wasn't at all prepared to become a father. The girl was born with Down syndrome, and Pilar moved home to her parents and broke off contact with Kristian. But when he was offered the job at the consulate in Las Palmas he saw it as a sign; moving there was simply meant to be.

When he'd called, Pilar had been discouraging on the phone at first. They'd had no contact for almost ten years, so why was he calling her now? She was married to a Canarian and had a son together with him. She was living her life with Valeria and her family, and he was living his. He was the one who had chosen this, she said. He hadn't even wanted to keep the child. That he was moving to Gran Canaria made little difference. Valeria had grown up so far without a biological father who cared about her, so why should she suddenly be available to him after all these years, just because he now had the desire to see her?

Kristian could understand her feelings. Yet he didn't give up, but stubbornly continued his attempts. At last Pilar gave in. They had a tense meeting at a café in a park. When Kristian saw the short, dark-haired girl with the round face and the slanted eyes smile broadly and openly at him, he started to cry.

He and Pilar talked while Valeria hummed to herself. He hadn't thought about the fact that she had Down syndrome, only felt the warmth from her soft hand in his. They sat down on a bench. *This is going to happen my way,* Pilar had said, and he answered that that was completely okay; he was simply happy to get to be with Valeria, to get a chance to be her dad.

Since then they had met several times, and he hoped to be able to see Valeria more regularly.

But he had to take one step at a time.

12

Earlier

The seagulls sailed across the sky on their outstretched wings, high above the spot on the stony beach where the woman with the long, curly dark hair stood looking out over the sea. It was relatively calm now. The waves struck rhythmically against the shore. The stones on the bottom rolled along with the movement of the sea; back and forth they were dragged against the seabed. The dull sound usually calmed her, but now it only made her more worried. She looked up at the cloud-free sky, which seemed bluer than usual. *Why don't I hear any birds?* she thought, fingering her skirt nervously. *Why don't they shriek and yell like they always do? Make a racket.* She squeezed her son's hand, which was holding firmly on to hers. The seabirds glided soundlessly past, high above their heads. *Like clouds,* she thought, feeling at the same moment that she herself was like a cloud. Empty, weightless, gliding around without purpose or meaning, separated from everything. She felt loosed from her moorings, from solid security. She had never felt so alone.

"Papa's coming back," she said consolingly to her son, who looked up at her suspiciously. He had his father's dark-brown eyes and thick eyelashes. He was a slight boy with thick, black, slightly curly hair like hers. His face was beautiful and childlike. He looked younger than his twelve years. She could not allow herself to believe that her little David would already be fatherless. The thought was frightening, awful, unreal.

"He's coming back," she repeated with certainty, as if to convince both herself and her son.

The other fishermen's wives in the village had already started dressing in black. They had started the grieving process. But Adriana could not make herself—she still imagined that her beloved would return home from the sea and come toward her with outstretched arms and his crooked smile. She imagined that she could dress in white the rest of her life. Not in black. That she would never have any reason to grieve.

She was well aware that the others felt sorry for her because she could not accept that the men were not coming back. Because she stubbornly refused to believe that they had gone to the bottom of the sea, along with the fishing boat that had not yet been found. Adriana felt sorry for the others, that they had let go. José's wife dressed in black and wore a dogged expression. She had started planning for life as a widow. But Adriana could not imagine what life would be like without her beloved. She simply could not accept it and continued going to the same place by the sea every day with a desperate hope that the little fishing boat would show up on the horizon.

"Are you sure Papa's coming home again?" David asked.

"Yes," she answered, and somewhere inside her she still had faith in that, faith that he would come back to them, to her, and love her as he'd always loved her. His strong hands would lift her up, whirl her around, and he would laugh his loud laugh. So loud that everyone would hear it.

She sighed, and then they went home, hand in hand, exactly as they had come.

• • •

The day approached evening, and she stood out on the walkway looking toward the sea for her husband, in case he should come walking. She ran over to the door and opened it when she heard sounds, hoping it was him. She missed him when she went to bed alone at night, when she woke up in the morning. With bare feet against the cold floor she went to open a window, leaned out, and looked for him.

But the days passed and weeks turned to months. Slowly she lost hope, stopped waiting. She stopped looking for him, but it didn't stop hurting. She could still recall his smell, his voice, but the memories became weaker with every day.

At last she realized the awful truth. The realization happened suddenly, even though deep inside she'd known for a long time. She was sitting alone on yet another evening with her arms crossed, staring vacantly at the wall. Then she understood deep down for the first time that she would never see her husband again. The insight was devastating, and she rocked back and forth without being able to cry.

She didn't know how much time had passed when she finally came to her senses and stood up. She looked in on her son, who was asleep in his bed. She sat on the edge of the bed and watched him, stroked his cheek carefully while she whispered that she loved him. Then she went into the lonely bedroom, undressed, and lay down in bed. The place beside her would remain empty.

13

The house on the hill was large, much bigger than they needed. It was reminiscent of a South American hacienda with its grand style and its arches, the warm-colored facade and the enormous terrace with its glistening black-speckled marble patio. The villa had nine rooms and a large outdoor dining area with a grill and fully equipped kitchen. A balcony ran along the whole front side of the house and had a view of San Agustín, the surrounding mountains, and the sea. The stone house had beautiful Canarian carpentry, using the dark pinewood typical of the islands. The rooms were amply proportioned and furnished with heavy, dark furniture that underscored the feeling of grandeur and luxury.

After all these years in the house, Sara still sometimes thought it was unreal that she could live in such a beautiful home, that she actually had permission to wander through room after room and know that it was hers. Unreal that she had it so good. She came from a simple home and was unaccustomed to luxury. Now she lived in a house that appeared to belong to someone beautiful, rich, and famous. Not someone like her. Sara and Lasse were anything but glamorous. She was a hardworking journalist who was passionate about her paper, and Lasse toiled every day at the modest little hotel, where he did everything from managing bookings to cleaning rooms, making sandwiches, and carrying luggage. Sometimes she worried that they didn't live up to the grandness of the house. But she loved it, enjoyed living there, and thought every day about how fortunate she was.

She had just watched the TV news and was sitting in the roomy, rustic kitchen checking the day's newspapers on the Internet and listening to local radio while she had coffee with the obligatory crispbread sandwich. Despite spending over twenty years on Gran Canaria, she hadn't abandoned the habit of Swedish crispbread for breakfast. Thanks to all the Swedes in San Agustín, crispbread was on the shelves at the local supermercado, and she enjoyed a couple of slices with pesto, cheese, and tomato with her morning coffee. She went through the news every morning, primarily because she was interested and it was an old habit, but also for work. She had to keep herself updated on what was happening in the world. The big news in the local media was naturally the murder of the Swedish woman in Arguineguín. Everyone basically reported the same things: the victim was staying at a yoga center in Tasarte, she had traveled there alone, and both perpetrator and motive were unknown to the police. The police had chosen to reveal that she'd been killed with a knife, but nothing about how she appeared when she was found, that she was naked, or that the murder scene seemed to be staged. Her identity was not revealed. Sara had no intention to reveal it either. It was far too soon, and it was unlikely that all the relatives had been informed.

She sipped her coffee, heard Lasse puttering around in the living room. He'd worked late the night before due to a busload of late-arriving guests, and was giving himself the morning off. The children's summer vacation had started, and they were still snoozing in their beds.

She sat there, thinking about what had happened to Erika Bergman. A young woman who'd come to Gran Canaria to practice yoga, one of the quietest, most peaceful things you could devote yourself to. And then she encountered a brutal murderer. What was she doing in Arguineguín, so far away from Tasarte? Was she there to visit someone? Did she know her murderer?

Sara picked up a pencil and chewed on the end as she looked out the window to where the cat was jumping after small birds on the terrace. It seemed undeniably planned, but that didn't have to mean that they knew each other. Perhaps the perpetrator had chosen Erika Bergman simply for her appearance, because she fit into some scheme. He'd cut her throat, yet there was hardly a trace of blood on the body, meaning he must have washed her off. And thoroughly. How did he manage to do all that without being seen? The perpetrator had had luck on his side. If, in addition, he'd specifically planned to kill Erika Bergman, then he'd been more than just lucky. How did he know that she'd be in Arguineguín? And that an opportunity would arise to strike?

She took out her notebook and searched for the notes from the crime scene. Erika Bergman was murdered some time during the night of Wednesday. Even during low season, a number of people passed the Norwegian Seamen's Church in the evening. There was a walking path right above the rocks. She thought about the restaurants that were nearby. She knew of an Italian one, and a Canarian tapas restaurant. Farther away there was a supermercado. *I'll have to go there,* thought Sara. *I'll go and ask around. Perhaps someone saw or heard something suspicious. But first the yoga center.*

She realized she had a full day ahead of her and was just about to get up from the table when Lasse called to her.

"Sara, come and look at this!"

She went into the living room, where he was sitting at the dining table browsing through old photo albums. A feeling of tenderness passed through her when he looked up and peered at her from behind his reading glasses, his hair disheveled. He looked happy. She stood behind him and stroked his back lightly.

"What is it?"

"Look here," he said happily. "Do you remember how much fun we had?"

He pointed to a picture of the two of them with their arms around each other, each with a glass of champagne, on a gondola on the canals of Venice.

"We look so young," she noted, without a trace of melancholy in her voice.

The picture was taken when they celebrated their tenth anniversary with a weeklong trip to Italy. They'd visited Rome, Venice, and Florence, and it had been marvelous. Florence in particular had made an impression on her.

"I have to go," she said but remained standing a little longer.

It had been a long time since she'd looked at those pictures.

"Maybe we ought to go there again," Lasse said enthusiastically, continuing to look through the photographs. The cathedral in Florence, the amazing Ponte Vecchio bridge, and the Uffizi Gallery. She remembered that Lasse had taken pictures inside, even though it was prohibited, and that she'd been a little irritated with him. Several well-known paintings showed up in the photo album, and suddenly she stiffened. There was the most famous: *The Birth of Venus* by Sandro Botticelli from the late fifteenth century. Both she and Lasse had seen the image on posters and in many other contexts, but it was a completely different experience to see the painting in reality. Sara stared at the photograph. Why hadn't she thought of it before? Lasse kept talking and tried to turn the page, but she placed her hand over his to stop him.

"Wait," she said in a breathy voice. "Wait a little."

She stared at the picture of the well-known painting. It showed Venus, the goddess of love, tall and slender, standing naked in a shell by the sea with one hand over her breast and the other placed over her lower abdomen, holding onto a strand of hair. On one side was Zephyr, the god of wind, and his wife, Chloris. On the other side she was received by the goddess of spring, Flora. White roses fell from the sky.

Sara's mind went blank. For a long time she stood with her gaze fixed on the picture.

"What's wrong?" Lasse asked with surprise.

"Wait, I have to . . ."

Sara fumbled for her phone while thoughts whirled around in her head. In her mind she saw the police standing at the crime scene, the medical examiner. She wondered whether any of them had realized the same thing.

With trembling fingers she entered the number of Diego Quintana. He answered immediately.

"¡Hola! Excuse me for bothering you. I understand that you have lots to do, but there's something—"

"Sure, out with it, but make it brief." The inspector sounded out of breath. Apparently he was in a hurry.

"Absolutely. I'm sitting here looking at pictures from the crime scene, and it appears as if the murdered woman has been arranged—"

"Yes, that's nothing new. We see that, too."

Sara ignored the comment.

"Do you know the painting *The Birth of Venus*, by Botticelli?" she continued eagerly. "From the fifteenth century. The victim isn't standing in a seashell like in the painting, but otherwise it all matches: the nudity, the hair, one hand in front of the breast, the other below the abdomen, the roses around the body—"

Sara heard the inspector draw a breath.

"Do you know what I just found out the technicians picked up at the scene?"

"No."

"Scallop shells below the body."

14

His shoulders ached. Sweat was running down his forehead. He wanted to wipe his face, but the box of papayas he was carrying made that impossible. He set it down on the edge of the back of the truck and pulled his sleeve across his forehead. The dust from the dry ground along with the burning sun made the work almost unbearable. Although it was past six o'clock in the evening it was still broiling hot. If it were not for the cooling breeze from the sea it would have been completely impossible to work outdoors.

The fine-grained dust worked its way under your clothes, sticking to your damp skin, settled on your tongue, and stung your eyes. There were twelve laborers picking papayas from the trees and placing them in wooden boxes that they then carried to the truck, which was parked on the dirt tractor path that ran into the orchard. He recognized a couple of the other fruit pickers—they were actually fishermen but supplemented their meager income by helping out with the harvest.

He went over to the bucket of water, filled a container, and greedily drank before rinsing his face with the rest. He looked over toward the yoga center, where four women had gathered in the shade under the trees. From this vantage point he could see through an opening in the surrounding wall that faced toward the papaya field. The women were standing barefoot on blue mats that they had set out on the ground, each with her left foot placed by her right knee and her hands held with the palms against each other. He wondered how long the women would endure in the same position. The trees protected them from the sun, but not from the heat.

"The idea is that we should work."

A hand on his shoulder made him turn with a jerk. It was Alvaro, the foreman, a burly man who hadn't bothered to shave for a while. The skin under the beard and on his body was dark after years of hard work under the Canarian sun.

"Sorry," he said. "I've been working hard all day and needed a break."

"We don't get paid to take breaks. Do you see anyone else here who's not doing something?"

He looked at the other men, their worried eyes; some shook their heads and signaled to him to brush off the rebuke. Alvaro was known for his lack of patience.

"I'm a person, not an animal," he mumbled.

"Excuse me," the foreman growled. "I don't think I heard what you said."

He tried to pull loose, but the powerful man's grip hardened, and his dirty nails cut through the cloth of his thin T-shirt.

He was about to respond when he saw her come running across the road, past the yoga center. She was dressed in tight pants, a bright pink tank top, and flashy running shoes. She turned around and caught sight of him, flashing a self-confident smile before she continued on her evening run down toward the sea. He followed her with his eyes. She had lipstick on and her hair in a ponytail with a visor over her forehead, reminiscent of the chic big-city girls on the Las Canteras beach in Las Palmas. A feeling of contempt welled inside him. She looked as if she had not a worry in the world. As if she were a completely privileged person, totally cut off from all the shit he had to stomp around in. She radiated a superior air and wore a slightly condescending expression. As if she felt sorry for him, pitied him because he was one of the less fortunate. One of those who could never get what she had. Or even come close. He was a person in squalor, at the bottom of society. And there he would stay. She belonged to those who enjoyed the fruits that he and other wretches picked by the sweat of their brows. She was the kind who took without being ashamed, as if it were the most natural thing in the world. The fury welled up inside him when he saw her disappear with light, carefree steps behind the banana plants in the adjacent orchard. They did hard physical labor in the heat while she enjoyed a jog to make herself sweat. It was an insult.

"I'm talking to you."

The irritated voice made him react. Before he had time to think, the blow was already on its way. His fist against the jawbone, the pain in his hand, the skin that cracked. He was shocked at himself; that wasn't what he'd intended. He had only reacted instinctively. The foreman lay on the ground, spitting blood. He leaned down, took him by the arm, tried to help him up.

"Keep away from me, damn it," Alvaro hissed, pushing him away.

Someone came to the foreman's rescue and helped him to his feet. Alvaro took out his wallet and tore a few bills out, which he crumpled up in his hand and threw on the ground.

"There's your pay for today. I don't want to see you here anymore. Get out of here! And stay away, otherwise . . ."

Alvaro did not complete the sentence, just turned on his heel and walked decisively away toward the truck. Someone picked the money up from the ground and gave it to him before everyone returned to work without further comment.

He remained standing a moment with the crumpled bills in his hand before he turned his back on the papaya field and walked away toward the sea. Perhaps it was just as well. Maybe he shouldn't waste any more time here.

15

The sun was high in the sky. Some children were swimming and splashing in the pool. The grown-ups had placed themselves in rows on lounge chairs, each under a parasol. Right now she would have done anything to enjoy a cooling dip and then lie down and do nothing, like the tourists. Her back ached, her head was pounding, and to top it off she had her period and kept having to run to the restroom so as not to bleed through. Ana wiped the sweat off her forehead; it was almost insufferably hot. The bucket holding cleaning solution seemed heavier with every minute that plodded along. With all the stairs it was impossible to pull a cart, so she was forced to carry what she needed.

She was behind on her schedule and felt stressed because she was in a hurry to get home to the children. Their summer vacation had started, and her old mother could only manage the two wild ones for so long. Her husband wouldn't get home from work until eight o'clock.

A younger couple had had a party in their unit last evening, and then checked out and left the hotel without telling anyone. Considering what the room looked like, it was strange she hadn't heard any complaints from other guests. She'd had a shock when she opened the door to clean. Empty liquor bottles strewn everywhere, overflowing ashtrays, burn marks from cigarettes on the table, a picture torn down, and the floor full of beer cans and food scraps, chips crushed underfoot. Not to mention the bathroom where someone had thrown up, not in the toilet, but on the floor beside it. It was incomprehensible how people could be such pigs. Ana knew very well who the couple were. Fresh-looking youngsters in their mid-twenties, nicely dressed in summer clothes, him with sunglasses and hair combed back, her with a ponytail. They looked sporty and neat and were always friendly when she met them in the corridor. She would have never imagined them leaving the room in such a condition. They must have some conscience anyway because they left a twenty-euro tip.

It had taken her two hours to get the unit clean. She couldn't do anything about the burn marks, and she had told Lasse that the table ought to be replaced, along with the picture that was ruined. He hadn't been happy when he heard about it, but luckily such incidents happened very seldom. Sun Suites Carolina was primarily a hotel for retirees and families with children, who had the sense to behave themselves.

It was after three o'clock, and her stomach was screaming with hunger. She needed to grab a *bocadillo* or something, but her lunchtime had been eaten up by the trashed apartment. Ana tried to push the irritation aside and forget how sweaty and hot she was. Only one unit remained, and then she would be done.

The scent of poinciana spread as she walked outside toward the access balcony. The big tree bent its branches over the path below, red flowers covering the ground around it. She stopped for a moment and massaged the small of her back where she could reach. She took a deep breath and enjoyed the scent and the quiet. They'd made it nice here: a lemon tree, a papaya, and a banana palm that Lasse tied firmly to the fence so that it wouldn't give way under the weight of the bunches when it was full of fruit. *I'll be home soon,* she thought, trying to console herself. *Then I can eat some leftovers, take a cold shower, and go down to the sea with the kids. At least there will be a little breeze there.*

Unit number 201 was at the far end of the row on the third floor. Ana knocked lightly on the door. There was no sign hanging on the handle to signal that the guest did not want to be disturbed, so after knocking once more without an answer she unlocked it and went in. A faint stream of light from the gap in the door filtered in across the floor to the far wall. The room was dark and smelled stuffy. She called out, but no one answered.

Some clothes were strewn on the floor inside the door. She leaned over and picked up the garments, folded them, and set them on a chair before she went past the little kitchen and pulled open the curtains that concealed the view to the pool area and the sea. Sunlight flooded into the room and blinded her for a moment.

She opened the balcony door to air out the room. The sweat was running under her shirt while she wiped off the table and chairs. A reddish-brown layer of desert sand was stuck on the rag. The sky was hazy. The *calima* came early this summer, she thought, wringing the rag out in a bucket of water. The railing and floor on the balcony were covered by the North African sand that blew in with warm winds from the Sahara at regular intervals and raised the otherwise very pleasant temperature considerably. Sometimes it got up to 100 degrees in the summer.

Ana coughed, then put her hand to her mouth to stifle the next coughing attack, but it didn't help. The air was dry, and the fine grains of sand made their way everywhere: into your hair, inside your clothes, into your throat.

She let the balcony door stand open and returned to the combined kitchen and living room. Here it was tidy, and to her relief the cleaning went quickly.

She opened the bathroom door and was startled when the front door shut behind her from the draft from the balcony. She remained standing a moment in the darkness before she reached for the switch on the wall. Then there was a crunching under her shoe; the ceiling lamp was broken and lay broken on the floor. *What is it with everything today?* she thought. Was there no end to the misery?

"Good Lord," she mumbled when she caught sight of a dark reflection of herself in the bathroom mirror. As if someone else was staring at her.

The only sounds she could hear were her own breathing and happy shouts and laughter from the children playing in the pool outside. *I have to pull myself together,* she thought. *And be done with this seemingly never-ending workday.* She went out of the bathroom and let the door stand open so that light came in from outside and she could clean. The bathroom was just as neat as the rest of the apartment. A black toiletry case and a bottle of aftershave were by the side of the sink, along with an electric toothbrush and an electric shaver.

The bedroom door was ajar, the bed was made, and it did not appear as if anyone had slept there during the night.

Then her gaze fell on the wall across from the bed, and she froze. The wall was covered with photographs, all of the same subject: a young, beautiful woman with long blonde hair. In one picture the woman was sitting on a pier with her feet in the water, smiling at the camera. In another she was standing on a balcony with a wineglass in her hand as she made a toast toward the photographer. In several others she was sitting on a couch with a cat on her lap, bicycling on a gravel road, practicing yoga on a beach in evening light.

On all the pictures someone had drawn tears in red ink that ran from the woman's eyes. It looked like she was crying blood.

Ana's hands flew to her mouth, and she shook her head in terror.

"Madre mía," she whispered.

16

The Norwegian Seamen's Church was actually a rather modest building, but its location, with its brilliant view of the sea, was without a doubt the best in all of Arguineguín. The church served an important function, and not just for religious activities. It was also a social institution, a gathering point for all the Norwegians who lived not only in Arguineguín but all over south Gran Canaria. And that was particularly noticeable now, after the horrifying murder that had been committed right outside its doors. The minister, Finn Nydal, had worked there for five years and was very popular among his church members and other visitors, as well as the local authorities. The church contributed collections to the poor, made home visits to needy souls, and provided musical events for people in the area.

As Sara stepped in the door of the church she joined a stream of people. There seemed to be a great need to talk. The church was full; some were there purely out of curiosity because they hoped to find out more, others had come to talk about their growing worry and fear. There was a perpetrator loose out there, a perpetrator who could strike again. It was still unknown who the murdered woman was; all the police had released was that she was Swedish. What if it was someone they knew?

Sara made her way through the throng and caught sight of the man from the consulate she'd met at the crime scene the day before. What was his name? Kristian? He seemed nice, she thought. There was something interesting about him. Maybe she could make use of him in some way. She saw that he was talking with the minister. They stood with their heads close together and seemed unaware of their surroundings. The man was actually very attractive, she thought. Tall, in good shape, handsome. He was casually dressed in a shirt, a jacket, and narrow blue trousers. He had dark, curly hair, which was a little unruly, and a lovely face. She guessed that he was in his mid-thirties. His position at the consulate was newly created, and she wondered where the need came from. Had the number of Scandinavians getting into trouble increased?

She went over to the two men. They turned as she approached.

"Hi," she said. "Am I interrupting?"

"Oh, no," Finn Nydal answered. "No problem. You're very welcome here."

"What happened is terrible," Sara said sympathetically.

"Yes, truly," the minister agreed. "I still can't believe it's true."

He shook his head and looked at her with a worried expression.

"I was thinking about talking with the people here in Arguineguín, get their reactions and such. I assume the murder has stirred up some emotions," Sara said.

"Of course everyone is very shaken up. We don't know who she is yet, only that she's from Sweden. The police don't want to say more about her identity. I assume that all the family members haven't been informed yet. There may actually be relatives and friends here in the congregation."

He concluded by nodding at the people who had gathered. Everyone was standing in small groups, talking, with coffee cups and paper plates with *mazarin* cakes in their hands. It looked like any coffee hour.

Sara and Kristian exchanged glances. Both understood that the other knew the victim's identity, but neither said anything. Sara had promised Inspector Quintana not to reveal the identity or to say a word about the art theory. She took her notebook out of her bag.

"Can we go outside and talk?"

"Of course," said the minister.

The three went out on the terrace, which had a magnificent view of Arguineguín's shoreline, the harbor, and the big, glistening Atlantic. Below were the rocks where the dead woman had been found the day before. The caution tape and the police cars were gone, and it was hard to imagine that a brutal murder had happened here only a little more than twenty-four hours before. They sat down at a table in the shade. Sara turned to the minister.

"How did you find out what happened?"

"The police called me in the morning, and I came here right away." He shook his head. "I was questioned by the police, who wondered if I'd seen anything, but of course I hadn't. I was at home asleep and didn't know a thing."

"And you haven't noticed anything peculiar around the church lately? Anyone behaving strangely, wandering around here or anything?"

"The police asked the same thing, but no, I haven't."

"How are the members of your congregation reacting?"

"People are extremely upset, and of course they wonder what kind of lunatic is running loose. Information has leaked out that evidently he cut her throat." The minister shook his head. "This naturally makes people worry. Everyone is wondering who she was and why this happened in our little paradise, our idyll. Many Norwegian citizens come here because of the quiet, and now everything is turned upside down. No one feels secure."

"I understand," said Sara. "And what are you doing here at the church?"

"We've set up a kind of crisis center. A room where people can go and light a candle and leave a final thought. Then there is a need simply to meet, as you see." He pointed toward the church. "We're also adding an extra service this evening because many have requested it." Half to himself, he mumbled, "I hope we'll find out more before then."

They were interrupted by a plump younger woman with a long blonde braid down her back.

"Finn, can you come in? There's someone over here who wants to talk with you."

The minister placed his hand on her arm.

"Of course, Reidunn, I'm coming." He turned toward Sara and Kristian. "Excuse me, I think I'm needed by my congregation."

They shook hands with him before he went back into the church. Sara fixed her gaze on Kristian.

"I assume you know the victim's identity, too?"

"Erika Bergman, from Stockholm," Kristian said quietly, looking around to assure himself that no one could hear.

"Perhaps you can help me make contact with the parents?" said Sara.

"Take it easy. I haven't even met them yet. Keep in mind that they just found out that their only daughter was murdered. I hardly think they'll be inclined to talk with journalists."

Sara took a pack of cigarettes out of her bag, shook one out, lit it, and took a puff before she answered.

"Obviously it wouldn't be for the next few days, but once the initial shock has subsided. I assume that the parents are going to stay awhile. They'll presumably be here until they can bring home the body, and that will probably take at least a week. There will be an autopsy and as long as the murder isn't solved the police won't want the body taken away from here. It could take a long time for the perpetrator to be arrested."

She took another puff and squinted at him.

"Well, I don't know," he said. "We'll have to see."

"Here, take my card." She extended her hand. "Do you have one?"

He pulled a business card out of his inside pocket and handed it over to her.

"Do you know anything about how the murder happened? Do the police have any leads?" he asked.

"All I know is that she was murdered right here and that he used a knife. But there are other circumstances that are strange."

Kristian leaned forward.

"Like what?" he asked eagerly.

Sara got up from her chair.

"You'll find out when you've arranged a meeting between me and the parents," she said teasingly. She put the cigarette out in the ashtray, turned on her heel, and left.

Kristian had no time to say anything before she disappeared. He just sat there, looking foolishly after her.

17

Sara passed the exit to Puerto de Mogán, the last in the chain of tourist towns along the south coast, at the far south end of the autopista. Then she turned off up into the mountains.

She drove past one small village after another before continuing due west on a narrow road that wound its way upward. There was not a house here as far as the eye could see, only high mountains rising up around her.

Tasarte was a remote village people rarely visited by chance. Sara looked up at the precipices on either side of it. The landscape was reminiscent of the American West, with the bare hills and dramatic ravines, the dusty, reddish earth, and the slender, thorny cactuses growing by the side of the road. She seldom had business on the west side of the island. In some ways it was the forgotten part of Gran Canaria. Here the beaches were stony and inaccessible, and large areas were uninhabited.

The road cut straight through the enormous massif down toward the little village. White-plastered houses were crowded along the curving roadway. Beyond, the sea could be seen, big and blue, glistening in the sun. Along the barren rock faces goats climbed, their bleating echoing between the hilltops.

She drove through Tasarte and continued down into the valley, toward the ocean. The yoga center was out of the way, secluded, and several times she had to stop and ask people along the road for directions.

She parked outside the tall, worn stone wall that enclosed the center and was met by a locked iron gate. She pressed on a buzzer, and the door opened automatically. *Samsara Soul,* she thought. *It sounds a bit New Agey.* She'd looked up the name and found out that the word *samsara* came from the ancient Indian language Sanskrit and meant "to flow together or pass through various stages, to wander." *Is that what happens when you practice yoga?* thought Sara, who had never tried it herself. The word could also mean "cycle or reincarnation." The Norwegian, Frank Hagen, who ran the center, called himself Samsara. *I guess that sounds more exotic than Frank,* she thought.

When she'd called and asked for an interview he'd been reluctant at first, but when she explained that she was going to write about the center regardless, he let himself be convinced. Sara was looking forward to meeting him and hoped to find out a little more about Erika Bergman.

Inside the gate was a large paved terrace with two white-plastered buildings, one on each side. The two wings were connected by a trellis with climbing grapevines, forming a lush lane between the buildings. The stone-paved path was in shadow, providing protection from the burning sun. In the middle of the terrace a fountain rippled restfully next to a pond with goldfish, and wind chimes hanging on the branches of the lemon trees tinkled softly in the faint breeze. Lounge chairs were set out here and there, where she assumed the guests could recover and relax in the shade, read a book, or simply rest.

A sinewy, tan middle-aged man came toward her. She recognized him from the pictures on the website. His grizzled hair was pulled back in a ponytail, and he was dressed in an ankle-length tunic and had sandals on his feet. He did not extend his hand in greeting or kiss her cheek in the customary Canarian manner; instead he pressed his palms together and bowed slightly. He showed her into a room that was furnished with a low couch on either side of a table. The room had an impressively high ceiling and picture windows offering a ravishing view of the surrounding mountains. The ceiling fans kept the room comfortably cool despite the heat outdoors.

"I thought we could sit here and talk. We won't be disturbed here," he said. In the corner was a refrigerator, and she gratefully accepted when he offered her a glass of water.

"Thanks for meeting with me," Sara began. "I understand it must be a shock for one of your guests to be found murdered."

Frank Hagen filled the water glass while he answered.

"Yes, it's completely incomprehensible. We're all deeply shaken, and I cancelled the yoga classes when we got the news." He raised his eyes. "That's why it seems so empty here right now. We're almost completely booked, but no one seems to want to go outdoors. The police have been here, closed off Erika's room, and interviewed staff and guests. Most of them are very upset. To be honest, I don't really know how we can go on."

He spoke in a soft yet penetrating voice. His accent was melodious, and he rolled his *r*'s. Sara listened attentively. She recognized this way of talking after all the years of speaking with Norwegians through her work.

"You're from Bergen?"

Frank looked at her, slightly amused.

"Is it still that obvious? You're right, but it feels strange to talk about where I came from. It's been so long since I left Norway. I moved away thirty years ago. I lived in India for ten years, then I came here."

"So that's where the interest in yoga is from?"

"Yes, I was saved in Kerala," he said. "That was long before yoga became so popular in the West."

"How well did you know Erika?"

Frank frowned. His gaze wandered. He changed position.

"Not very well, actually. Here we meet mostly when we have yoga classes and then we're busy with other things besides conversation. It's more about body language, so to speak. Breathing and movements."

"What do you know about her?"

"She came here alone and had plans to stay a long time, at least for the summer. It's unusual that we have guests who stay more than a week or two."

"Why was she going to be here so long? Did she say anything about that?"

"No, she gave no explanation, and I didn't ask her. I don't think anyone else did either."

"Do you know whether she was in any kind of relationship? At home or here?"

"We didn't talk about her personal life in that way."

The answer came a bit too quickly. He obviously knew more than he wanted to disclose. Perhaps it was the police who had put a muzzle on him. They, of course, would not want him or anyone else to reveal details to her that might jeopardize the investigation. Sara chose to change tack.

"What was Erika like?"

"She was an experienced yoga practitioner; that was apparent at once. Muscular, balanced, with a flexible body. Good body control, strength in the movements, and she actually had proper breathing. Unfortunately, that's much too rare."

He sighed lightly.

Sara could not help but be puzzled by how unmoved he seemed by the fact that the woman they were talking about, one of his guests, had just been murdered.

"Do you know whether Erika knew anyone in Arguineguín or if she had business there?"

"No, but maybe she didn't go there on her own initiative. The murderer could have picked her up somewhere and driven her there, right?"

"Sure, that's a possibility of course. Did she know anyone in Tasarte, besides the people at the center?"

"No, not that I know of. We deliberately chose an inaccessible location, far from the major tourist areas. The idea is that you should come here and relax and take care of yourself and your body, settle into the yoga. That's impossible if it's too noisy. If the guests want a change they usually go down and swim or have a glass of wine at the beach restaurant. Up in the village there's a grocery store and a bar that's open sometimes, otherwise there's nothing right here." He paused and appeared to be thinking. "But of course a number of tourists come here and rent rooms down by the sea. It's possible she met someone there."

"Did you notice anything about her? Did she seem worried or anything?"

"Now you sound like the police," Frank said with a hint of irritation in his voice. "No, I didn't notice anything. Listen, I have forty yoga students. I can't keep track of them all. Besides, these are adults we're talking about."

"How have the other guests reacted to the murder?"

"As soon as I found out it was Erika, I gathered everyone for a meeting, and naturally there were a lot of emotions. Erika was popular among the employees and the guests. She was a pleasant person. Then the police arrived and were here all day yesterday and that didn't exactly calm things down. Several have said they want to go home . . ."

His voice trailed off, and he sighed deeply. Suddenly he looked tired under the deep suntan. Sara realized that she would not get much further. Frank Hagen didn't seem to have much to contribute. She hoped she could talk with some of the guests.

"Can you show me around?" she suggested.

"Of course," Frank said, getting up quickly.

He seemed relieved that the conversation was coming to an end.

They went back through the empty yoga hall and out onto the terrace. A woman was sitting on one of the benches under the lemon trees. Her thin shoulders were shaking; she appeared to be crying.

"That's Erika's roommate, Helena," said Frank. "She was probably the closest to Erika."

He stopped hesitantly and looked perplexed. Sara took the opportunity to go up to the crying woman.

"Are you okay? Can I help you in any way?"

Helena looked up, her eyes red from crying.

"Who are you?"

Sara introduced herself and extended her business card.

"May I sit down?"

Helena nodded and dried her tears with the handkerchief she was holding. Sara turned toward Frank.

"Thanks for your time. I've probably found out everything I need. Here's my business card in case you think of anything else."

She extended her hand in farewell, but Frank did not take it. He simply bowed lightly as he had when they met and disappeared along the path under the grapevines.

"I'm here to find out more about Erika, who she was," Sara explained. "Do you think you can help me?"

"I don't know," Helena whispered. "I . . . The whole thing is so awful. The police have been here, but I didn't think about it then."

"What? What was it you didn't think about?"

"That Erika was running away from something. I'm sure that she was."

"What sort of thing?"

"She never said flat out. I asked once, but she was evasive. It was clear she didn't want to talk about it. The police asked me if anything in particular had happened, but I said no. I was in such shock that I couldn't think. Today, though, I happened to think that actually something strange happened last Friday. Erika had been out walking down by the sea—she would go there and be gone for several hours. When she came back she went and lay down immediately and stayed in bed all evening. She didn't want to go to dinner or to the evening class either. And she never missed a yoga class. She really loved yoga."

"Did you ask what was going on?"

"Of course I did. She pretended that everything was fine. But I know there was something, something she didn't want to tell me about."

18

Earlier

Adriana was standing in the cramped kitchen preparing potato soup for lunch. She set the table with two plates and two spoons. She set out two glasses.

Not three. His chair was still in its usual place. Neither of them could make themselves sit there. Not yet. It was dark in the room, but the sun filtered in through the cracks in the shutters that faced out toward the narrow walkway. She kept them closed, as protection against both someone looking in and the strong sun.

She stood quietly a moment and observed the old, worn drop-leaf table where they'd sat—all three of them—and shared countless meals together. Their little family. It would never be that way again. The Lord and the sea had taken her husband from her. She'd stopped praying to God and the Virgin Mary; they didn't hear her. The simple wooden chair at his place was a constant reminder of how it should have been. He should be sitting there. But it didn't turn out that way. Sometimes she thought she saw him, thought he was sitting there by the window. His broad back and strong arms. The hairy chest that heaved under his shirt when he laughed or breathed heavily. How she worshipped his body, his face. Every wrinkle he got from sun and laughter, every line and change. The straight nose, the soft mouth, and the eyes that glistened like precious stones under the black, dense eyelashes. He was an unusually handsome man.

When she complained that he was away from home too much he'd say he had to go out while there were plenty of fish in the sea. Work as a fisherman provided no certain livelihood, and he was forced to take every opportunity to earn money. As the years passed he made her feel so loved that her worry disappeared. He made her strong and secure, and she relied on him. And now he was gone forever. Vanished on a nighttime fishing trip, and his body had still not been found. Maybe it would float up on land one day. Maybe not. Maybe it was just as well that she didn't have to see him. This way she could remember him as he was.

Suddenly Adriana realized that she was standing in the middle of the kitchen, still with a kitchen towel in her hands. The soup had thickened in the pan. She stirred it and took it off the stove. Sliced bread and placed it on the table along with the olive oil and the saltshaker.

She called to David, but he didn't answer. He was probably sitting on the steps outside, as he often did, perhaps still waiting for his father. She'd stopped waiting, even if she didn't want to admit it to anyone other than herself.

She dried her hands on her apron and went out to look for the boy. The facade of the building was bathed in light, the sun high in the sky. Adriana peered in both directions but didn't see him. She called his name several times, with no answer. There was no one to be seen; there was no one to ask. The heat meant that everyone either had gone down to the sea or was staying indoors.

She was seized by a sudden worry, without knowing where it came from. There was no reason for it. Her son could be anywhere. It was completely normal that a twelve-year-old was out with his friends somewhere. Bicycling around the village like they did, playing soccer on the field behind the school, or swimming at the shore.

She ought to eat by herself, and then he would come when he wanted. But she couldn't. She had a creeping sensation of discomfort and she could not get rid of it. She knew that she had a tendency to worry unnecessarily. But she was unable to escape the feeling. She had to go out and look for him.

She took off the apron, placed it over a chair, and went out, closing the door carefully behind her. The sun burned on her back as she hurried away, past the neighboring houses that crowded along the narrow ledge toward the sea, where you had to tightrope your way along. The worn shacks were close to each other, pressed together as if they could give each other protection from the hard winds and waves that struck them. They were painted different colors and were in varied conditions. They had small square windows with closed shutters, sheet-metal doors with images of the Madonna. Farther up, where there were real streets, there were stone steps and balconies by the entries with potted plants, cages with canaries hanging on the buildings, and decorations in the form of fishing boats, nets, and fish. Here and there was a Canarian flag, a Spanish *bandera*, or a pennant for a soccer team. An occasional plastic chair sat outside a door, where the older ladies would sit and talk toward evening, when the sun was low on the horizon and it was cooler out. Every house had its own color, its own cracks and expressions. They reflected who lived there. Doors that stood ajar to let in air. The sounds from TVs. Children playing on the floor while a grandmother watched. Women preparing dinner in the kitchen, men watching the news or standing in groups on the street corners smoking. The men went to work, and when they came home they played with the children. After dinner they kissed their wives and took them to a bar on the corner, ordered beers and asked what they wanted, cheered when the soccer team made a goal, kissed their wives again, and twirled them around in a joyous dance at the successes of their team. Or at life itself.

How I miss him, she thought, feeling a tightness in her chest.

Old Fernando was sitting outside his door. Bent-backed, he leaned toward the radio with the broken antenna that he had taped together. A crackling sound came out of the speaker. He had a pocketknife in one hand and an apple in the other. He got up when she came walking by.

"Poor you," he said, lightly kissing both her cheeks and looking sympathetically at her.

"Don't feel sorry for me. He's coming home soon." She smiled, making an attempt to keep going. "Soon."

She said that, although deep down she knew it wasn't true. She couldn't handle all the sympathy that was forced on her.

"Of course," said Fernando, letting her go. "Maybe your boy is going to find him. Now that he's going out to fish."

She stopped and stared at her neighbor.

"What did you say?"

"David borrowed Pablo's boat. He's going out to sea to fish. The boy wants to earn his keep, and I guess that's good." The older man turned his eyes up to the sky. "Who knows? Maybe God will show him what the sea is hiding."

The sun disappeared behind a cloud, and all the shadows pulled back. Adriana turned cold inside.

"Is David down at the shore?"

"That's where Pablo has the boat."

She ran to the sea and the shore where the boat was. Her legs felt weak and she had a hard time getting air, her heart pounding in her chest. When she got to the water she saw David putting all his weight against a small fishing boat, forcing it toward the water. A few older men were helping out. Adriana ran, screaming and waving at them.

"What are you doing? Are you out of your minds?"

The men looked at each other, stopped pushing, straightened up, and shrugged in incomprehension. David had politely asked for help, his dad had been a fisherman, and now it was the boy's turn. At his age they'd been out to sea themselves, fishing to help support the family.

They shook their heads at the upset woman, trudged a short distance away, and sat down on some wooden crates, each of them lighting a cigarette and observing how Adriana threw out her arms toward her son. David stood on the stony shore, his legs apart, his mouth a narrow slit in his face, his eyes staring hard at hers.

"What are you thinking?" she screamed at him. Not because the boy couldn't hear her, but because she was afraid, scared to death of losing him.

"I wanted to go out and fish," he said sullenly. "We'll be out of food soon."

"That's nothing for you to worry about, you're just a child."

"I can be useful, too. Someone has to provide for our family, and you're not."

"What is that you're saying?" his mother burst out in despair.

"Papa's not coming home. It doesn't help that you're waiting for him. He's not coming back, he's dead."

At his words everything turned black in front of her eyes and before she could stop herself she struck him—a sharp, open-handed slap right across the cheek. His expression did not show what he was thinking, he just kept staring at her. Defiantly he stood there, as if anchored to the ground, and looked at her while his cheek turned red. She placed her hand over her mouth.

"Never say that again," she said calmly. "Never, do you hear?"

"I won't," he answered. "Sorry, Mama."

She got down on her knees and threw her arms around him. She never wanted to let go.

19

Kristian had fallen asleep on the couch after work and woke up with a start when the doorbell rang one flight down. For a few seconds he lay there trying to collect his thoughts. He was sweating, and his mouth was dry.

"Damn," he mumbled, realizing to his dismay that the apartment looked as if someone had turned it upside down and shaken it hard and long.

He had only been going to close his eyes awhile before getting to work on the chaos. Kristian hadn't been able to keep his promise, which was apparent from the state of the apartment, and he cursed himself. He never had control over all the things that needed to be taken care of. Garbage to be thrown out; clothes to be washed, folded, and put in the closet; the dust that gathered under the furniture; the sand that blew in through the door and windows; the papers in piles.

The Vespa that took up the better part of the space in the hall. He'd just brought home a new carburetor that he'd ordered over the Internet, firmly determined to get the Vespa in mint condition, replace everything with original parts. But that took time.

Kristian forced himself to clear his head. He'd only meant to rest a few minutes when he got home from work. The meeting with Erika Bergman's parents had been strange and not at all what he'd expected. He picked them up at the airport, drove them to the medical examiner's office, where they identified their daughter, and then drove them to the hotel. They'd been cool and distant, and they barely uttered a word. Both were in their sixties, elegantly dressed, and remarkably controlled. He'd perceived them as unusually cold, and that in itself had bothered him. Much more than if they'd wept hysterically and been hopelessly heartbroken. Mentally, it had taken a toll.

Laboriously he got up from the couch when the doorbell rang again. Kristian opened the door right as Pilar and Valeria were about to leave.

"Sorry," he said. "I fell asleep on the couch."

"Perhaps this isn't a good time?" Pilar said sarcastically, observing him with her scrutinizing gaze.

Kristian knew that he wasn't showing his best side. He pulled a hand through his hair and tucked in his shirt.

"It's just fine," he said.

"What's that smell?" Pilar asked, casting a glance up at the stairs behind him.

At first he thought she meant the garbage bags lying all over the hall, but then he noticed the cooking odor and realized where it was coming from.

"Damn," he said, hurrying up to the kitchen.

He tore open the oven door, and black smoke rolled out. He'd put in a pizza when he came home, and now it had been forgotten for almost an hour. Kristian turned around and discovered Pilar in the kitchen door, holding Valeria by the hand. She shook her head skeptically.

"This wasn't what I imagined when we agreed on you taking care of Valeria sometimes," she said, putting her arms protectively around her daughter.

"It's just a pizza. It's not exactly the end of the world," he said.

"Maybe not," Pilar replied. "But I'm not just talking about you forgetting a pizza in the oven. Look at the rest of the apartment. I thought you were serious when you said you finally wanted to take some responsibility for Valeria."

"I'm doing that," said Kristian, setting the charred pizza on the kitchen counter while he opened the window. The smoke stung his eyes, and he started coughing.

"How will you manage to take care of a little girl when you can't even take care of yourself?" She sighed, took Valeria by the hand, and started walking toward the door.

"Please," Kristian said quietly. "Don't go—"

Pilar turned toward him and said in a hard voice, "You weren't the one who bathed her before the heart operation. Knowing it could be the last time you would see her. Who was ready to cry her insides out when the surgical nurse came and got her. Who sat up for nights on end because you didn't dare fall asleep when she was sick. You weren't the one who turned your life upside down while you did everything not to lose her. Who was forced to give up everything to take care of her."

Pilar's mouth was small and tense, and her eyes filled with tears while she talked. The pain in her face was merciless. She paused briefly and caught her breath. Kristian wanted to say that it meant a lot to him to be able to take care of Valeria now, but he realized that Pilar was right. He hadn't been there when she needed him, when Valeria needed him.

"We should probably wait with this," Pilar said at last with a sigh. "Call me when you've got things in order, Kristian. Don't think you can just come along and play Dad. Valeria has special needs. And if you're unable to take that into consideration, maybe it's best that you don't take care of her."

Valeria looked back at him as her mama pulled her away from him. His daughter held a stuffed animal, a giraffe, tightly under her arm as if she were afraid of losing it. And then they went out the door and disappeared.

Kristian sank down on the kitchen floor and leaned against the wall; all the air had gone out of him. He'd been excited about having Valeria with him. He'd really looked forward to it.

He rested his head against the wall. Pilar had explained that Valeria needed stability and routine; otherwise she felt insecure. He'd meant to get everything in order before she arrived. He just happened to fall asleep.

After a while he got up. He had to pull himself together, deal with the chaos. He started cleaning and airing out the apartment. He changed the sheets on the bed, the towels in the bathroom. Took out the garbage. While he was cleaning he thought about Valeria and how she'd looked at him as she'd left, as if she understood that it was his fault that she couldn't stay with him.

As soon as he was done cleaning he sat down on the couch and called Pilar, but she didn't answer. He listened to Pilar's happy, slightly breathless voice on the voice mail asking the caller to leave a message after the beep. Heard Valeria's laughter in the background, then her voice, and then a cry of joy as if her mama were tickling her. Then there was silence and the beep.

He hung up and sank back on the couch, setting the phone aside on the coffee table. Sat and rested his face in his hands. He thought about his own voice mail neutrally saying his name and making a dry request to leave a name, a number, and what the call was about.

Formal and sad. There was no one laughing in the background, no cries of joy.

When he'd gotten the job offer in Las Palmas he'd felt like he was getting a new chance.

He couldn't sit and watch his life slip through his hands once again. He had to do something. For Valeria's sake, and for his own.

He leaned over and reached for the phone again. He entered Pilar's number, listened to her voice, Valeria's laugh. Then the silence and the beep.

20

Sara was waved past the guards at the entrance to the Guardia Civil headquarters in Las Palmas. Chief Inspector Quintana had evidently notified them of her arrival. She parked her car and checked in at the front desk. It didn't take long before Quintana came down the polished corridor. He was dressed in jeans, a white shirt, and a jacket. Despite his size he moved lithely and always looked fresh, as if fresh from the shower. It was late afternoon and nearly 90 degrees. She smelled after-shave when they kissed cheeks.

"Do you want coffee?" he asked.

"Please," she said. "I really appreciate your taking the time to meet."

They went to the cafeteria, which was several flights up. It was cozy, with a dark counter and several small tables. The atmosphere was relaxed and pleasant. A loud murmur and happy laughter met them as they entered. There were policemen both in the green Guardia Civil uniforms and in plainclothes. Several had beers in hand and must have ended their shift for the day. Quintana greeted several colleagues before he and Sara sat down at an outdoor table. Sara sipped her double espresso and met his gaze.

"Anything new?"

"The autopsy is happening right now, but I've received a preliminary report from the forensic medical examination done last evening. The cause of death is established. Erika Bergman was killed with a knife and died from loss of blood when her carotid artery was severed. It's quite clear that the murder occurred at the scene. She also had semen in her and had had intercourse in the hours before death. Skin was found under her nails, which suggests that she put up a fight. We'll probably have findings on the DNA analysis within a few days. No other bruises or signs of a longer struggle. It probably went pretty fast."

"Okay," said Sara, looking at him thoughtfully. "Semen, you say. Does that indicate she knew the perpetrator, that she had a relationship with him?"

"Possibly, if it's even his semen."

"Doesn't that seem pretty likely?"

"You might think so, but it's far from certain. She may have had intercourse with someone and encountered the perpetrator afterward—maybe by chance, on her way home or whatever."

"By chance?" Sara put her cup down and looked skeptically at him. "What about how she was arranged? And the perpetrator being inspired by *The Birth of Venus*? That suggests careful planning."

"I assume you're right," Quintana said with a sigh, taking a bite of the chocolate doughnut he had in front of him. "For some reason Erika Bergman was in Arguineguín, but no one knows why. We've questioned everyone at the yoga center, knocked on doors in the area, asked around among the restaurants and shops in the area, taxi drivers, neighbors, and God knows what. No one noticed her, and we haven't found anyone who was acquainted with her."

"Surveillance cameras, then. Are there any?"

"None that work, unfortunately. Of course we've checked that, too."

"What conclusions do you draw from that?"

"None at all so far. It's too soon for conclusions."

"I was at the yoga center earlier today and met Erika's roommate, Helena Eriksson," Sara continued. "She told me that Erika seemed down. She had a feeling that Erika had left Sweden for the summer to escape something or someone. Maybe it was about a man."

Quintana frowned.

"I haven't questioned her myself, but I can't recall her saying anything in the transcripts I've read. I hope to find out more when I meet Erika Bergman's parents."

"What do you think about the art theme?" Sara said.

"It's extremely interesting. What does the murderer want to say? What message does he want to leave by arranging the body like that?"

"He really went to a lot of trouble," Sara pointed out. "He got scallops and roses, washed the body carefully . . . and I'm guessing he was extremely careful about his choice of victim."

"The question is, what kind of person does this," Quintana said. "Who plans so carefully and succeeds in executing the whole thing without being discovered."

"Probably a pretty cunning and controlled person," Sara said. "The arrangement suggests intelligence."

"Yes," said Quintana, smiling. "And you're just as engaged as you usually are."

"Thanks," Sara responded, feeling herself blush. Not because Quintana said it, but because it was true. She wasn't a police officer.

"This isn't exactly an everyday murderer," Quintana continued. "I've never seen anything like it. The approach is brutal, but everything indicates a certain level of education. Maybe he studied at the university in Las Palmas. Maybe he's from there."

Sara looked searchingly at the inspector.

"The birth of Venus," she said hesitantly. "Could it be a love story? Unrequited love? Jealousy? Erika Bergman was unusually beautiful."

"Indeed she was."

There was silence for a while. Quintana drank his orange juice, then looked up at Sara.

"How are things otherwise?" he said in a considerably softer voice.

"They're okay," she said, feeling embarrassed by his gaze, which was open and full of warmth. She tried to pretend it wasn't there, but sometimes she couldn't ignore his interest in her.

"Everything's going fine? At work and at home?"

Sara laughed.

"Yes, fine, thanks. How about yourself?"

Quintana didn't say anything, only looked at her slyly.

"Okay, if we return to what we were talking about," she said, "what's the next step?"

"Take it easy," he said. "I've told you more than enough already. Now I'm just wondering—what do I get in return?"

He leaned forward and looked expectantly at her.

"How about dinner?" Sara suggested.

The chief inspector's eyes glistened.

"That sounds almost too good to be true," he said eagerly.

He brought the glass to his mouth again.

"Saturday evening, at home with me and Lasse. You and your wife are very welcome."

Diego Quintana choked on his juice, which resulted in a long coughing fit.

21

Lasse Moberg glanced at the clock as he updated the hotel's guest list. It was already just past ten and dark outside. The hotel was quiet, most of the guests having gone to dinner at one of the nearby restaurants. A few had gone to bed for the night in preparation for the next morning's outing. The bus would depart at eight o'clock for the long trip up to Pico de las Nieves, seven thousand feet above the sea.

Lasse had promised to make dinner for the children but hadn't been able to tear himself away from work. A lot had happened. He'd called and told Olivia and Viktor to heat up pizzas from the freezer. The kids would have to manage on their own. He felt a strong physical unease. It was likely that they'd harbored a murderer as a guest at the hotel, and Sara was out playing homicide investigator. His hand trembled against the reception counter, and he placed his other hand over it to keep it still. The twitching came and went, although it had gotten worse lately; his doctor had warned him about stress.

Ever since a shocked Ana had called to him and shown him the unsettling pictures of Erika Bergman in unit 201, he'd felt shaky. He immediately notified the police, who were there in ten minutes. They stayed the whole afternoon, questioning all the staff and gathering the guests in the common room to try to ascertain whether anyone had noticed anything unusual. Most of the guests were older people who came there to relax. They'd been worried when the police cordoned off the room.

Lasse told the police everything he remembered about the guest, which wasn't much. Adam Fors hadn't stood out other than for checking in late in the evening, but it wasn't the first time that had happened. He'd only stayed a couple of days before he'd disappeared. He kept to himself and didn't speak to anyone at length.

Lasse logged off the computer and stood up. He saw his own silhouette in the dark glass of the entrance door. He'd been standing right here when Adam Fors came to the door and asked if they had a vacancy. Lasse had taken his passport and registered him in unit 201. He made a copy of the passport and gave him the key. He'd been curious about the young man having so little luggage and about the late hour, but not curious enough to ask any questions. The late-arriving guest appeared orderly. He had a sad look in his eyes, but he was neatly dressed.

Although it was late and Lasse should have gone home long before, somehow he couldn't quite leave. He felt compelled to do a final round of the hotel. The blossoming flamboya with its red flowers met him as he left the reception office. He noticed that the banana plant was hanging down toward the ground, and he tightened up the rope that tied it to the fence. Lasse was very pleased with the various plants around the hotel. The flamboya had started to bloom a week ago, and now it was releasing its red blossoms, which were starting to cover the ground. In the pool area there were also a few citrus trees and luxuriant hibiscus plants with red and yellow blossoms.

As he passed unit 201 and saw the police tape, he felt his stomach knotting up. He didn't like seeing his hotel like this. He'd been forced to move the guests staying in the unit next door. They didn't want to be neighbors to a possible murderer.

When he finished his rounds and saw that everything was quiet, Lasse went back toward the office and into the common room. He could picture Adam Fors. Several times he'd seen him reading in the corner by the bookcases. Even though he'd only stayed at the hotel a few days, the young Swede had managed to pass quite a few hours in that spot.

Lasse went over to a bookcase and let his fingers glide over the spines of the books. One of the books stuck out a little and he pushed it in. He liked the books to be in order. Not many of the guests sat there and read; most lay on lounge chairs by the pool, browsing glossy magazines or reading paperbacks they brought from home.

He was about to turn around when he saw that the book he had pushed in was upside down. He pulled it out all the way and glanced at the cover, which showed a woman in a red dress. The title was *And She Should Be Red*, but someone had taken a black marker and changed the *Red* in the title to *Dead*. He felt a shiver down his spine and the involuntary twitching in his hand again. The book was by an author named Annika Frostell. Lasse couldn't recall having seen or even heard of the book before. Presumably one of the guests had left it behind; people didn't often bother to take home the books they'd brought with them. For that reason the library was steadily growing.

He flipped through the pages, browsing randomly. On page 277 he stopped—someone had underlined the words *forgive me . . . forgive me!* And farther down on the same page: *Don't leave me!*

Lasse set down the book and felt his stomach contract.

Once again he had to call the police.

22

He'd been standing in the bushes so long his toes had gone numb. The moon was resting pale and dull on the velvet sky, making the trees cast ghostly shadows across the dry ground.

He crouched down when the door opened and Luísa came out on the steps with a wineglass in her hand. She stood looking out over the garden, which was lit up by the pale moonlight, and raised the glass to her mouth. Her lips opened carefully. She closed her eyes as she drank.

The first time he'd met her she'd been exciting, as if from another world. Like a light puff of wind from the sea, she had whirled up the dry leaves lying on the ground. Then reality caught up, and he saw who she really was. Saw that she'd taken what was his and crushed it like a cockroach under the sole of her shoe. He'd learned to despise her, her laugh, her smiles, the playful glances she gave him. Then she betrayed him.

The hand with the wineglass was lowered, and she lifted her chin, looked up toward the sky, searching for a star she could rest her eyes on. He peered up, observed the same constellation as she did. He could hear her sigh. It came from a place deep inside her, as if her carefree mood had turned into a great sorrow. A movement behind her made him freeze. A woman appeared wearing an apron, her dark hair pulled into a hard bun at the back of her neck.

"Sorry, but the children won't go to sleep until you've read to them."

The woman in the apron looked older in the glow of the outdoor lighting. It deepened the sad look on her face. The slow movements, the caution when she addressed her employer, the way her gaze wandered when the younger woman turned toward her.

"I'm coming soon," Luísa answered.

"Can I go home?"

Luísa looked despondently at the woman standing in the doorway waiting for her to answer. Then she waved her aside as if she were an irritating fly. The housekeeper hurried down the steps and continued on the narrow path toward the gate.

He stood and watched her leave, felt stiff, almost numb. The woman closed the gate, locked it, and disappeared in the darkness outside.

He curled up when Luísa peered out into the night before going back into the house.

Soon he would put his hands around her and whisper in her ear that time no longer meant anything. Just as he'd done with Erika. Time no longer means anything—when you're dead, you're free.

The light in the window turned off, and he pictured Luísa going up the stairs and into the bedroom, undressing, setting her clothes on a chair by the bed, and crawling under the sheets.

He felt a kind of warmth when he thought of her lying there with her eyes closed. He waited awhile before he stepped out of the bushes and positioned himself in front of the house.

Even in the shadows there was no room for him when she was around.

23

It was nine o'clock before Sara was finally back at the office, and her stomach was growling with hunger. The graphic designer was in his usual place, working up to the last minute to get everything ready before sending the paper to the printer.

"Hi, Javi," she said, sticking her head into the inside room. "How's it going?"

"Fine, thanks. I'm about done. You're not bringing in a lot of new material now, are you?"

"Uh, sorry," she said, smiling. "I was thinking about putting together a quick feature on the yoga center. It feels extremely current. That was where the victim was staying."

Javi tore his eyes from the screen and turned toward her with a gloomy expression.

"How many pages?" he grumbled.

"I need two, with pictures. So to make it work we'll need four new pages, then I'll also have room for an article with the latest news." Sara glanced at the clock. "Is it too late to call one of our advertisers? You can offer a real deal—half price for a full page."

Javi threw up his hands.

"You can't be serious. I promised to take my girlfriend out for dinner."

"And how can you promise that the night before we go to press?" Sara said angrily. "We have a murder to cover. This is the biggest thing that's happened since the newspaper started. And by the way, I've been working like a dog all day without eating. I've barely had time to go to the bathroom, so the last thing I need right now is to argue with you. In an hour I'll have the articles ready, then you put them in. Period. You can help me upload and select pictures in the meantime."

The young graphic designer looked subdued after his boss's outburst. Slowly he got up from the chair and walked over to her. Put his hands on her shoulders.

"Of course, you're right. Obviously we'll help each other out. Sorry. But before I get started on the pictures I'll go and get pizza. You look like you need it. Do you want a Diablo with salami and pineapple as usual? Arugula and fresh tomatoes?"

Sara nodded and felt her eyes tearing up from his kindness. He knew exactly what she wanted. She'd ordered that pizza so many times over the years that at the pizzeria around the corner they'd started calling it the *Sara especial*. She yawned, much more tired than she wanted to admit. It had been an eventful day.

She sank down at the computer and started writing the article about the yoga center, working to avoid revealing too many details. The headline was in the best tabloid spirit: "Where the Victim Lived." It was a perfect fit for *Aftonbladet*, whose evening editor was also waiting for more articles. Of course I can report where Erika had stayed on Gran Canaria without revealing her identity, she told herself while the keys clattered. Besides, it was only a matter of time before it leaked out who the murdered woman was. The police clamming up wouldn't stop that. The immediate family had been informed, and there were plenty of journalists without scruples. General interest in this case was much too big to keep the identity out of the news for long.

She chose to include the interviews with both Frank Hagen and Helena Eriksson.

She was interrupted in her writing by the door opening and the aroma of freshly baked pizza wafting in. Gratefully she accepted the box along with an ice-cold can of cola. She ate while she finished the two articles. When she was done and had turned the text over to Javi, and they'd chosen which pictures should be included, she sank back in the chair and lit a cigarette. The door to the street was open to let in air. The nights were warm this time of year, and the full moon shone in the black sky.

The phone rang; it was Lasse.

"Please come home. It's late and you've been up since six o'clock this morning. Have you had dinner?"

"I just pigged out on a pizza."

"Good, but now you have to come home. It's past midnight, and I have a lot to tell you. Some sensational things happened at the hotel today."

"What?"

"It has to do with the murder. The police were at the hotel all afternoon."

"What happened?"

"I'm not saying a word until I have my wife beside me in bed."

24

On a day just over a year earlier, the salute from the cannons fired from Akershus Fortress at the mouth of the Oslo Fjord had sounded with a hollow boom. The weather was beautiful and sunny, unusually warm for a late spring day in Norway.

Tens of thousands of people had gathered along Karl Johan Boulevard carrying trumpets and flags. Many wore folk costume. It seemed as if every single Oslo resident had turned out to celebrate Constitution Day, the seventeenth of May. Norwegian nationalism was strong and showed itself most clearly on this particular holiday.

They were standing outside the parliament building. Kristian felt the festive atmosphere in the air, the joy in the celebration mixed with expectation for the arrival of summer. He had just counted the eighth round from Akershus Fortress. There were five seconds between rounds, and a total of twenty-one shots would be fired off before it was quiet again.

Suddenly the police radio attached to his shoulder crackled. The alarm concerned all units in the vicinity of Karl Johan. There was a burglar alarm from a jewelry store at Egertorget, very close by. An armed man had broken into the closed shop and threatened the employees, who were taking advantage of the holiday to do inventory. The man had shot a female clerk in cold blood, and she was lying seriously wounded on the floor of the store. When the robber rushed out of the store, he'd shot wildly around him before running from the scene.

Kristian and another police officer elbowed their way through the crowd in the direction of the square. When they finally reached it, there was complete chaos. People had fled from the open plaza, and it was strangely deserted in the midst of the festivities. A motorcycle with its engine revving was overturned outside the jewelry store, and terrified people took shelter behind benches or hid in restaurants and in the entryways of surrounding stores. Several ran crouching toward the stairs down to the subway. A couple stood holding each other. Others stood crying openly. An older man got Kristian's and his partner's attention and told them that there'd been several shots fired and that an armed man had disappeared down a side street, Øvre Slottsgate. Kristian rushed in that direction. He immediately caught sight of the fleeing man ahead of him.

Then everything happened extremely fast. The sound of screeching brakes, rubber against asphalt. The robber running across the street holding a pistol in his hand, the car stopped in the middle of the street. The robber tore open the door and grabbed hold of the woman sitting behind the wheel, pulling her out. Kristian stopped when the woman, lying in the street, reached her hands out to him.

"My child! Rescue my child!" she screamed.

In the backseat he glimpsed a little girl. She looked scared out of her wits. Everything went black before Kristian's eyes. The sounds around him became hard to make out and he felt nauseated. His hand flew up to his head, cold sweat broke out on his forehead, and his intestines churned.

Other images played out in his mind: a boy with an ice cream in his hand standing outside a car where a child was sitting in the backseat.

Then something happened. A stranger showed up, the car drove away, and the boy was left alone.

The boy's eyes—there was something familiar about his gaze, as if everything a child can experience in the way of pain was written on his face. He stood there barefoot and stared past the surrounding landscape.

Then Kristian was back in the moment, back in Oslo. He twirled around and got hold of the robber through the open window. The car skidded. The sound of glass breaking, metal twisting. The man in the car hit the steering wheel. Kristian felt an inconceivable pain as his shoulder went out of joint. He tore the pistol from the robber's hand, struck him with it, closed his eyes, felt his face getting warm and sticky. Couldn't make himself stop hitting, as if something had taken hold of him. He struck and struck, uncontrollably. The robber whimpered and tried to protect himself, but his resistance got weaker and weaker.

As Kristian was aiming the next blow he made eye contact with the girl in the backseat. Everything stopped. She stared at him with panic in her eyes; her mouth was open, but no sound came out. In the next moment Kristian felt someone grab him and pull him backward so that he lost balance and landed on his back in the street. His partner put a knee on his chest and held him firmly.

"What the hell are you doing, Kristian? Are you trying to kill him?"

Then all the sounds came back, as if someone had held them back and then suddenly emptied them over him like a bucket of ice-cold water. The sound of the pistol butt against the man's face, the mother's desperate scream, the child in the backseat, the people on the street, the braking cars, a dog barking, his breathing, and his heart beating, wicked and hard in his body.

In a cold sweat Kristian sat wide awake in bed while all the sounds still echoed through the room. It was dark; the door to the balcony was cracked open, but it was still night. Kristian pulled back the covers and got up. The sheets were damp with sweat. He opened the balcony door and went outside. The night air was warm and barely cooled him.

Once again he saw the boy in his dream. He was leaning against the stone wall that ran along the road. He had an ice cream in his hand and was looking out over the road. His skin was pale, and his hair moved slightly in the wind.

"Go home," Kristian said quietly. "There's no one out there."

He leaned against the railing. Far away a light was visible out on the sea. Then his nose started bleeding. *Damn,* he thought, wiping under his nose. *Not again.*

25

The minister at the Norwegian Seamen's Church, Finn Nydal, sat with his hands clasped and his elbows against the desk. He had opened all the windows wide and there was a breeze from the sea. The church's air conditioning, which had been donated a few years ago, wasn't working. He'd called a repairman, but that was over a week ago, and no one had shown up yet. The minister concentrated on his breathing: in deeply through the nose, then slowly out through his mouth. It usually relieved his anxiety, but this time nothing helped. He hadn't slept a wink the night before; his thoughts had twirled around in his head, leaving him no peace.

"Dear God," he whispered. "How could you? She was so young."

He got up from the chair and went over to the window, which faced the sea and the cliffs below. He remembered the first time he'd stood here enjoying the view from the Seamen's Church and thought how beautiful it was. That was exactly what he was thinking now. The sun was shining, making the sea glisten. A few fishing boats were on their way out, and he watched them plow through the waves, as if the sea and the boats had found their own rhythm.

Finn Nydal had concluded yesterday evening's sermon with a prayer and a minute of silence for the young woman who had been found on the rocks. For a while he'd thought about cancelling the service, but changed his mind. The parishioners had a need to talk, with him and with each other.

He usually came to work early, before anyone else arrived, to enjoy the quiet. He felt closer to God at that time, as if Our Lord was more occupied when everyone else was awake.

There was a knock at the door. Before Finn had time to respond, it opened, and Reidunn's rosy face appeared in the doorway. She was one of the younger church volunteers.

"There's someone who wants to talk with you. Is this a good time?"

"Who is it?" he asked.

"A Norwegian woman, but not anyone I recognize from Sunday services. She said that she wanted to talk with you and that it's important."

"Send her in," he said.

The minister clasped his hands behind his back, a gesture that perhaps was old-fashioned but which he had nonetheless borrowed from one of the older teachers from when he studied theology. Finn Nydal was just over forty, relatively young to be minister at the Seamen's Church, so he told himself that the gesture made him look more mature and responsible. He straightened up and craned his neck.

Reidunn opened the door for the woman to come in.

She gave the minister a fleeting smile that did not reach her eyes and extended her hand.

"I'm Merete."

"Finn Nydal."

The woman was middle-aged, skinny, with sunken cheeks and missing teeth in her upper jaw. She looked scarred and haggard. Her heavily dyed yellow-blonde hair hung in thin wisps around her face.

Her gaze was glassy, and her wrinkled clothes appeared to be in urgent need of a wash.

"Sit down," he said, making a gesture toward the chair on the other side of the desk.

Merete did not seem to hear the invitation; instead she looked around. When she caught a glimpse of the green plant in the corner, which he'd inherited from his predecessor, she marched resolutely up to it.

"This needs a lot of sun," she said, rubbing the leaves between her fingertips. "It doesn't do as well in the shade."

"You had something important to tell me," said Finn, ignoring the information about plant care.

"I get so thirsty this early in the morning," Merete began, grinning at him with her toothless mouth. "But perhaps that's asking too much."

"You can have a glass of water," he said.

Now he recognized her. She was often part of the group who sat outside the Supermercado León and drank beer or smoked pot. Several times he'd sat down and talked with them. The group was made up of a motley collection of Canarians and tourists who had come to the island not to sunbathe and swim but to drink; liquor was cheap, and beer cost no more than water. Then many got stuck—on the island, in alcohol dependence. Some of them eventually managed to make their way home; others simply gave up. They slept on the beach and carried their few possessions around in plastic bags or backpacks. He'd first noticed the woman in front of him several years earlier. She'd looked different then; she'd gone downhill considerably.

They sat on either side of the desk. Merete sighed in disappointment. She'd evidently hoped for something besides water to drink, but she took the glass he served her. Swallowed it in a few gulps and then held out the glass to him again.

"I think I saw the woman who was murdered. She was shopping at León that same evening. Or I guess it was night. It was probably almost one o'clock."

Finn Nydal stared at her.

"How do you know it was her?"

"I heard that the woman they found dead had long blonde hair and that she was Swedish. And it was right in the area where I met her. I talked with her. When she came out of the store I asked her for a cigarette. And she answered in Swedish. She gave me several. She was nice."

The minister swallowed hard. His mouth was dry, and he reached for a glass of water.

"Was she alone?"

"Yes, I didn't see anyone else."

"Why are you coming to me? Why don't you go to the police?"

"I don't trust the police down here. I haven't done anything wrong, but I've heard stories about how they treat people."

Finn leaned forward, observed her attentively from behind his glasses.

"What did you see exactly?"

He twirled his chair around and took a bottle of Arehucas and a glass from the cupboard on the wall. He filled the glass and pushed it to her.

She looked happily surprised and leaned forward and eagerly took hold of the glass. She closed her eyes as she emptied it in one gulp.

"Try to remember all the details."

"At first I noticed her outside the Danish hair salon. She must have come out of one of the apartments there. Then she went to the León. I wanted to ask her for cigarettes or a couple euros. She looked nice, like someone who can't say no when you ask, so I went up to her when she came out of the store."

She brought the glass to her mouth again, but discovered at the same moment that she'd already emptied it. Finn reached for the bottle and refilled the glass.

"And what do you want me to do with this information?"

"Can't you go to the police? Everyone in the village knows you and trusts you. No one will believe me."

He took out a piece of paper and a pen.

"Write your phone number down here. Do you have one?"

Merete nodded and carefully wrote her name and a Spanish cell phone number. Then she pushed the paper over to him with a satisfied expression. She remained sitting and waiting, stealing a glance at the bottle.

"Two glasses is enough," he said firmly. "This is a church, not a bar."

She did not persist but got up and nodded in parting. He stood up and opened the door for her, assured her that he would contact the police about her observations.

He closed the door behind her and then leaned against it. Breathed out.

Took his wallet out of his inside pocket and fished out a photograph of her. She was smiling in the way that young people do, with her eyes, with her whole face. Her hair fell softly over the face and cheekbones. He let his finger sweep across the picture.

"Forgive me," he said quietly. "Forgive me because I couldn't love you as I should have."

He turned around and discovered that the laptop was open on the desk. His secret was there, a secret only he and God knew about.

26

Juanita Díaz opened the one window in the kitchen of the simple restaurant on the pier in Tasarte and let the fresh sea air stream in. Outside there was white foam on the waves; the wind had picked up. The water struck the sea wall and splashed up on the wind-whipped facade. A few boats were bobbing on the water. Down here by the deserted rocky beach there was not much other than the sea and the solitary building, far out on the pier, in which the restaurant was housed. Her family lived on the top floor above the restaurant. They also had a few extra rooms to rent out.

It was just past eight o'clock in the morning, and the restaurant would open soon.

How many guests to expect was hard to estimate. Mostly it was the individuals who rented a room or folks who worked at the fruit orchards in the area. Now and then spontaneous visitors found their way to the shore for a meal.

She peeled potatoes and beat eggs for the tortilla, peeking out the window while she worked. She saw that her supplier had left the sacks of fresh bread outside, straight from the bakery in Tasarte. She opened the door to bring them in and caught sight of a man standing on the shore, looking out over the sea. Juanita was surprised that anyone would be here so early in the morning. She stood quietly a moment and observed him. He was standing by himself under a projecting rock, throwing stones into the sea. At regular intervals he bent down to pick up more. There was something mechanical about his way of moving, as if he was not really present in what he was doing. He wasn't very old, she thought. Around thirty, tall and muscular, blond, dressed in jeans and a T-shirt. She didn't recognize him, but there was something in the way he moved that interested her. She set the sacks of bread on the kitchen counter, swept out a cockroach, got her pack of cigarettes and a cup of coffee, and sat down on the steps outside the restaurant. Managed to light the cigarette after several attempts in the wind and once again turned toward the sea.

The man had not seen her and continued with his monotonous occupation. She observed him while she smoked, couldn't decide what it was about him that caught her interest. She looked over toward the little parking lot. She recognized all the cars there. Where did the man come from? What was he doing here? He didn't look like a visitor at the yoga center, nor did he seem to belong to the group of surfers who rented out the simple stone houses a little farther up the beach. She took a sip of coffee, couldn't keep from staring at him. A thought struck her. Perhaps she should go out and ask him if he wanted to come in and have a cup of coffee? He looked like he needed to get something warm in him.

The truth was that she would have appreciated a little company. Not much happened at the deserted rocky beach surrounded by the high mountains, and there weren't many people to talk with this early in the day. Later she had more than enough to keep her busy—cooking and serving the guests.

The wind from the sea was blowing cold this morning, and she pulled her sweater tighter around her and took cautious steps as she went out to the man, who was standing with his back to her.

"¡Hola!" she called as she approached, but he showed no signs that he'd heard her.

Suddenly she stumbled on the slippery stones that the sea had washed clean.

"¡*Mierda!*" she exclaimed when her skirt was soaked.

When she looked up, the man was standing in front of her. He was bleeding from the temple but didn't seem to notice it. The blood ran down onto his thin shirt. She got to her feet and backed up a step; there was something in his eyes that frightened her. It was as if he was not fully present in reality, as though he stared right through her at something ghastly that existed only for him. Then his eyes became glassy, and his shoulders lowered.

"I'm not feeling well. Can you help me?" he asked in broken Spanish with an accent she couldn't place.

"You can have a cup of coffee, then I can wash your wound," she said, touching her own temple with her fingertips to show what she meant.

They went into the restaurant, which was still empty, and she motioned to him to sit down by the window. She took out the first-aid kit and fetched a bowl of lukewarm water. The wound was deeper than she thought. She washed it carefully and removed the dried blood around it and then dabbed with disinfectant before she put on a bandage.

"How did you get this?" she asked while she put the things back in the first-aid kit.

"I stumbled last night . . . on the stones. It was dark and I couldn't see . . ."

"What were you doing out by the rocks?"

For a moment it appeared as if the man didn't understand what she was asking. He fidgeted. Juanita stood up and got two cups of coffee. He followed her with his eyes as if he was afraid of what she would do.

When she sat down again across from him, she pushed his cup across the table.

"Careful, it's hot," she said, smiling.

"Thanks," he said. "You're very kind."

Juanita reached across the tabletop to pat him on the arm, but he started and pulled back. There was a pain in his eyes that worried her. She sank back down on the chair and let him have the distance he needed. She didn't want to worry him, but at the same time she felt foolish for trying to console him. She didn't even know who he was.

"Sorry, I'm not completely . . ."

He didn't finish the sentence; instead he just sat staring vacantly into space. It seemed as if he was about to say something else, but she wasn't sure. Did he want to tell her something, or did he prefer to be alone?

"It was silly of me to ask what you were doing out by the cliffs. That's your business. Sometimes it's nice to be by yourself."

Suddenly he looked right at her.

"Yes, but sometimes solitude is unbearable," he said, smiling faintly. But the smile never reached his eyes.

27

Erika Bergman's parents were staying at the San Agustín Beach Club hotel. It was strange that the parents chose such an elegant, charming place to stay, thought Sara as she stepped into the lobby. Decidedly luxurious vacation lodgings, first-class restaurant, exotic garden, and swimming pool with a view of the wide waters of the Atlantic.

They'd arranged to meet in the breakfast dining room, and Sara had to explain that she was meeting someone before she was let in by the stern breakfast host. He showed her to a table at the far edge of the terrace, where the two of them were sitting, each stirring a cup of coffee. Bo and Eva Bergman were a stylish couple in their sixties; he was silver haired and impeccably dressed in long pants and a button-down long-sleeved shirt despite the heat, while she was wearing a pink dress with the hair around her small head freshly blow-dried.

How can they look so perfect when by all rights they ought to be crushed? thought Sara as she shook hands with them. But perhaps that was just it: to hold up you made sure the externals worked. She sat down and ordered a double espresso.

"Let me start by expressing my sympathy," she said.

"Thank you," said Mr. Bergman.

Mrs. Bergman only nodded weakly.

"I wanted to meet you to find out a little more about Erika, to be able to tell her story. And I want to let you know that I won't publish anything you're not comfortable with."

"Good," said Mr. Bergman. "We appreciate that."

"Do you mind if I tape the conversation?" Sara asked, starting to dig in her bag.

The parents exchanged glances.

"That's fine," said Mr. Bergman.

Erika's mother squirmed. She looked uncomfortable, but not particularly heartbroken. Both seemed noticeably controlled. Sara had a hard time concentrating. If it had been her Olivia who'd been murdered she would have been in the mental ward at this point.

"Can you tell me why Erika came here?"

"She loves yoga. Or loved . . ." Mr. Bergman's voice died out. "She did yoga several times a week, and had for many years. She thought it changed her life. She became calmer, more balanced . . . She studied at the university and made great demands on herself. Yoga meant that she could concentrate more easily. It made her more harmonious."

"Why was she going to stay so long?"

Sara turned directly to the mother, who so far had not uttered a single word. She stared at Sara, but apparently could not bring herself to say anything. Once again it was the father who answered.

"She wanted to get away. She'd had a hectic spring with lots of studying and several big oral exams at the end of the semester. She was worn out and wanted to be gone all summer until school started again in early September. That's understandable. I guess it's not so strange. Of course, as a student she was short on money, and she asked if I could pay. It cost a pretty penny to stay at that yoga center so long. I agreed because I could see that she needed to get away, but if I'd known . . . I mean, if I'd had the slightest sense of what would happen, I never would have . . ."

His face darkened. Mrs. Bergman sat without saying anything. Nothing suggested that she felt a need to console her husband. Instead, she put one leg over the other.

There was silence for a while. Sara felt a sudden tension around the table. Mrs. Bergman brought the cup to her mouth and carefully sipped her coffee. Sara noticed that her hand was trembling.

"There's one more thing," the mother said almost in a whisper, as if she intended to stay silent but couldn't keep from saying something.

"Yes?" said Sara. "What is it?"

"Erika had a boyfriend, but they broke up not that long ago," Mrs. Bergman said.

"And?"

Sara leaned forward, interested.

"His name is Adam Fors. Well, it was Erika who broke up with him. They'd been together less than a year. He was jealous and controlling and she wasn't doing well because of it. Her studies suffered, too. She missed several oral exams and fell behind. She had to study twice as hard the last few months before summer. She got pretty seriously off track during that time."

"So how did he take it? Her breaking up with him?"

"Not good at all. He went to see her again and again and refused to accept that the relationship was over. He didn't want to accept it."

"What did he do? Did he threaten her?"

The parents looked at each other.

"No, not as far as we know," said Mr. Bergman, who had pulled himself together. "But Erika was bothered by the fact that he was stubborn and kept insisting they should get back together. He wouldn't leave her alone. I think that's why she wanted to stay away as long as possible. She hoped he would get tired of it."

Sara felt a shiver inside. She thought about the photographs of Erika at the hotel room that Lasse had told her about the night before.

Adam Fors was the guy who'd stayed there. The parents had evidently not been informed about that yet by the police.

"Did he?" she asked at last. "Get tired?"

Bo Bergman met her gaze while his wife Eva stared vacantly in front of her.

"To be honest I don't know," he said. "Maybe he didn't."

28

Earlier

The door opened with a creaking sound, but David didn't say anything. He looked in hesitantly from the street. His hands were at his sides and his gaze wandered, searching for a point to rest his eyes on.

Adriana smiled at him, held open the door.

"I can make a *café con leche* for you, with a lot of milk," she said.

He turned around and looked in. The chairs were stacked on the tables. Long shelves along the walls. He looked up at her.

"It's our bakery now, and there's a real espresso machine behind the counter," she said.

David understood that his mother was trying, that she was smiling to make him happy. He took a step forward and went inside. It was dark and dusty in there.

"Should we sell bread?"

Her son looked at her skeptically.

"Bread, cheese, olives. I'll make flan, *mousse de gofio, tarta de plátanos* . . . It's going to be nice when we get everything arranged. And you'll get to help me every day when you come home from school. You can serve the customers who come here to have coffee, and there in the corner we'll have a TV with a big screen that shows soccer when Barcelona or Las Palmas are playing matches. And we'll save money for a bicycle for you, a bike that's all your own."

Adriana turned on the ceiling light. She started taking the chairs down from the tables. She wiped off the tabletops with a damp rag while she observed David looking around the place.

It had been six months since the night she'd kissed his papa goodbye and he disappeared at sea. When she closed her eyes she could still feel his nearness and wished that she had held him a little longer, that she'd kissed him one more time. Wished that he had turned around in the door and looked at her one last time.

Now she was forced to go on with her life—if for no other reason than for David's sake. On the same day that she'd opened the closet and taken out the black dress, she'd decided to move to the little town of La Aldea de San Nicolás on the west side of the island. Adriana had set the dress on the bed and looked at it. She had inherited the dress from her mother. She sat down on the bed and cried and then dried the tears with the fabric of the dress. She was unable to put it on. The sorrow was too heavy. On top of it all, should she have to wear a dress that would force her down to the earth? Down on her knees before the altar in the church, with clasped hands, to pray to a God who hadn't shown her any mercy?

One bright spot in all this was that her husband had taken out a life insurance policy. She'd been against it, thought the money could be better used, but he'd insisted. Every month he paid a premium, year in and year out. She was grateful to him for that now. The insurance money gave her the opportunity to move and build up a new life together with David. She had a small pension and could buy the bakery.

Inside were eight tables so she could also run a simple café. A few of the chairs needed to be repaired, but it was nothing she couldn't manage by herself. The kitchen wasn't large, but the previous owners had recently renovated it and acquired an espresso machine and a new oven. The walls had been painted white a few years ago. In some places the paint had flaked, but she could cover that with a fresh coat. The café had a window out toward the street, and the previous owners had applied for outdoor serving. *That might be good,* she thought.

She felt a tap on her shoulder.

"It's nice," said David, smiling cautiously.

"Thanks," she answered. "I think we're going to feel at home."

Adriana went behind the counter. One of the chairs scraped against the floor as David pulled it out and sat down. She opened the refrigerator, took out milk, and set it on the counter.

His hands were dirty; there was dirt under the nails. He stuck one finger in his mouth, bit the nail, felt the taste of soil and salt. He didn't know what absence tasted like, but he missed his friends, the street they'd lived on, the shore where the old fishermen sat. The sun that sparkled like diamonds as the sea struck lightly against the rocks. Above all he missed his papa.

"Do you think I'm going to make any friends here?" he asked, tearing loose a piece of a nail; his finger started bleeding.

"You're going to make lots of friends," Adriana answered, pouring the black coffee into a big glass. "Just give it a little time. School just started."

She set the glass on the table and poured in hot milk. It turned into lines in the black beverage. *Like tentacles,* he thought.

"Say 'stop' when there's enough milk."

David looked at her.

"What happens if I forget to say 'stop'?"

"Then it will run over," she said tenderly, tousling his hair.

She placed the pitcher of milk beside the glass and sat down on the chair beside him, placed her arm around his thin shoulders.

"You miss papa a lot, don't you?" she asked gently, and his eyes got shiny.

"Don't you?"

"Every day," she answered. "Every time I see myself in the mirror, every time I see you. You are so like your father."

The boy did not answer, just stirred the coffee and watched the black mix with the white.

"Will you be happy if I'm happy?" he asked, setting the spoon down on the table.

He didn't look at her, just looked at the drink that was moving in the glass.

"Yes," she whispered. "Then I'll be happy. You know that it's not anyone's fault that Papa is dead."

"It must be someone's fault," he answered. "But it's not yours."

"What do you mean?" she asked and released him, looked into his mournful eyes and noticed that they got darker.

"I don't pray to the Virgin Mary anymore, not to God either."

"But you should," she said, pressing him to her. "You should pray every day and every night before you go to bed. Promise me that, my boy."

"I promise," he answered quietly. He wanted his mama to be happy, like before. Before his papa disappeared.

But he would never pray to God again.

29

His childhood home was at the far end of the row of houses closest to the sea. It was a narrow three-story building, painted white, with blue around the windows. It had been beautiful at one time, but was now marked by salt, wind, and water. The paint had flaked off in many places. The walkway that ran between the houses and the sea was so narrow he had to balance as he made his way. The old iron railing was rusty and looked like it might break apart at any moment. Fallen pieces of mortar that had crumbled from the facades crunched under his feet. Most of the windows were dark, but once the residential area had teemed with life. When he closed his eyes he could hear children's feet running over the paving stones. So many memories; he'd once been happy here. He barely remembered how that felt.

Now only a few scattered old people seemed to be left, and when twilight fell they went inside and locked their doors. As if they were afraid that the sea would crawl up on land and take with it the people it had still not managed to conquer.

He reached the house. He still had the rusty old key, and it fit the door, which was painted dark green. After a little shifting back and forth, the door opened with a drawn-out screech. For a moment he stood outside and looked in, as if he feared that his emotions would overpower him.

Then he gathered his courage and stepped inside. The house was very dilapidated; the dampness had made the paint on the walls come loose in large sheets and settle along the floor. It was stuffy, and a sharp odor of mold stuck in his nose. It had been a long time since anyone had made it smell cozy with the aroma of freshly baked bread, the polish Mama scrubbed the floor with, or grilled fish.

He closed the door behind him, stood awhile to get a sense of the room, the windows nailed shut, the floor with its cracked boards, the crumbling brick fireplace. On the ground floor was his parents' bedroom. The door into it had lost its hinges and fallen down; he leaned it against the wall so that he could go in. There stood the rustic old iron bed his mother and father had slept in. He felt the tears burning behind his eyelids when he thought about it. He could picture them so clearly. She with her long dark hair, the corkscrew curls that coiled along her back, the white cotton nightgown that ended at the knees. His father with his muscular, tanned arms. So many mornings he had gone in to them when he was little, crept between them.

That was why he was here, to retrieve the old bed. He'd chosen to come in the evening so as not to attract attention when he carried it out and up the steep stairs to the truck parked on the street above.

He looked at the head- and footboards and saw that he'd be able to unscrew them and drag the pieces out of the room, out of the house, and up to the small truck, which he'd borrowed from one of the fruit farmers, saying he was going to help a friend move.

His gaze fell on the large, decayed wardrobe by the wall. He opened the doors and recoiled from the strong smell of mold. There were old clothes in piles, along with cans of paint, boards, and other trash. Mice had built nests in the rags and the bottom of the wardrobe was covered with droppings. He saw a doll sticking up out of a bundle and recognized it immediately. It had belonged to his mother when she was a child. Eagerly he pulled it out, held it carefully in his hands. It was a plastic doll with chubby arms and legs. Time had darkened the plastic. It was actually a sleeping doll, but one eye was missing and the other stared at him with an ice-blue, glassy gaze. He rocked it a few times, and the one eye still closed.

He sank down on the bed and set the doll carefully next to him and took off his shoes and socks, wanting to feel the warm wooden floor against his bare feet. Once it had been soft to walk on; now it was dry and cracked. Broad gaps had formed between the wooden planks, and he could see the cockroaches running below, making rustling sounds as they moved. He lay on his back on the hard bedstead base, which swayed under his weight. He placed the doll on his chest; it felt secure somehow. He stared at the ceiling. In several places it had fallen in, and he could see the evening sky above. It was beautiful, he thought, taking a pack of cigarettes from his chest pocket and lighting one. He took a drag and felt a strange peace he had not experienced for a long time.

He looked at the doll sitting on his chest, staring at him with her one eye; where the other had been there was only an empty, dark hole.

"Can you keep a secret?" he asked in a low voice.

The doll looked back at him but didn't say anything.

30

Luísa Hagen sat on the stone stairs and looked at the children, who were playing in the last rays of daylight that fell between the trees.

She had set the table on the veranda. Frank liked Adalia and Jonatan to be done eating and in bed before he came home. He said he gave so much of himself to the yoga center's guests all day that he needed to relax when evening came. Now, after everything that had happened, this was particularly important. All of his waking time was spent calming guests, talking with the police, keeping the media as far away as possible, and at the same time continuing to run the operation. As well as possible. For now, all yoga classes were cancelled.

After dinner she would bathe the little ones and read a story until they fell asleep. She never knew when he would come home, and she'd learned not to ask where he'd been or what he'd been doing. It was best that way, to pretend not to notice, to breathe calmly and simply be.

Luísa watched the children as they ate. Five-year-old Jonatan was only a year younger than Adalia, but the age difference seemed much greater. He'd always been sickly and was the one who was most tired after a long day. He was skinny and slight and ate carefully, as if he were afraid of not being able to pick up the fork. Adalia was tall and sturdy for her age, borderline chubby. She had her father's blue eyes and long black hair that curled down her back.

Suddenly Luísa heard a rustling sound from the bushes next to the wall that surrounded the property. The sound made her turn around. She thought she sensed a movement, had the idea that someone was there, that someone was looking at her. Suddenly she felt uncomfortable. She waited a moment, but nothing happened. She must have been imagining things. Perhaps it was just a bird hopping around among the dry leaves; snakes were uncommon in this part of Gran Canaria, and rats didn't stray this high up. Luísa was well aware of her fear of the dark. That the house was secluded, out of close contact with neighbors, didn't make it any better. She would probably never get used to the desolation out in the country.

She tried to concentrate on the children and chatted with them about their day, stroked their hair tenderly.

Now and then she peered out into the garden where the lights along the gravel path to the gate had just turned on automatically. But there was no one there, only the tall papaya trees by the wall.

Her gaze fell once again on Jonatan and Adalia. That was the best thing about Frank, that through him she'd had her beautiful children.

She didn't really understand how she'd ended up in this isolated spot. Everything had gone so fast. She met Frank at a yoga center in Le Vegueta, the old district in Las Palmas where she'd lived. He was filling in for her regular yoga teacher. He was intense and demanding, with a body so perfect it was as if created by God himself, and she fell in love at once. After the class they took a walk in the warm evening and sat at a bar and drank wine until sunup. When the morning dawned and ordinary people rushed past them on their way to work, wearing their freshly ironed office clothes, she'd gone with him to his hotel room, and they made love the whole day. During those hours in the cramped, dark room she'd been intoxicated in a way she never wanted to recover from. Her previous sexual experiences meant nothing in comparison.

She'd never been anywhere close to the heights Frank, or Samsara as she called him then, could take her to. He was like a storm wind that occupied her, and he did not let her out of his firm grip until she lay naked and exhausted beside him in the bed, shiny with sweat and limp with satisfaction.

After that, everything seemed so obvious. Only a few weeks later she quit her job and gave up her apartment and moved in with him at the yoga center in wild, desolate Tasarte, as far from her hectic big-city existence as you could get. She had accommodated herself to the new life, tried to forget the old one, all her friends, and everything the big city had to offer. The children had come in rapid succession, and she was suddenly very busy. The first few years she hadn't had much time to think, but it was different now. Both kids were in school in the village, and she had most of the day to herself. She'd seen more and more clearly how her husband controlled her life and how monotonous and isolated her existence had become. Her home had begun to feel like a prison. The one time she felt free was during her runs. For that reason, she ran more and more often and for longer distances.

I have to get out of here, she thought. In secret she'd started planning how she could get away and start a new life with the children, as far from Frank and Samsara Soul as she could get.

Her thoughts were interrupted by a branch snapping over in the bushes. Luísa quickly stood up, which startled Adalia and made her knock over her glass of milk. The white milk ran over the table and formed a little pond around the fruit bowl.

"It's okay, honey," she said, picking up the glass, which fortunately hadn't rolled over the edge and broken against the stone terrace. "Mama will get a paper towel and wipe it up."

Adalia looked frightened. Her papa was not equally merciful when she happened to spill something. She was much too used to being scolded if she did something wrong. His eyes would turn completely black.

While the children finished eating, she straightened up the kitchen. Her head was full of contradictory thoughts. Earlier in the day she'd talked with her one remaining girlfriend with whom she kept in touch after moving so far away to such an isolated place. Elena had been there to visit a few times, and she liked neither Frank nor the area in which they lived. She'd shown this clearly, and now she was no longer welcome, according to Frank.

That really makes no sense, Luísa thought. I have nothing left of my old life. Barely even my best friend.

The phone call that morning had been about her marriage with Frank. The conversation had taken an unpleasant turn. Elena started questioning her about him and made insinuations that Luísa wasn't sure how to interpret. Then Jonatan suddenly started screaming at the top of his lungs because he'd fallen down and hurt himself, and she'd been forced to hang up, without really understanding what Elena meant.

When she came back out to the terrace Jonatan was no longer at the table.

"Where's your little brother?" she asked Adalia, looking around.

"He said he found something over by the wall," her daughter answered, continuing to eat.

"I don't see him," said Luísa, setting the rag down on the table. "Jonatan!"

She went down the steps and out into the dark garden.

"Here I am, Mama."

"Don't hide like that when it's dark out, do you hear?"

"But I was just here," the boy said sullenly.

She heard from his voice that he didn't think he'd done anything wrong. And he hadn't. She was the one in the wrong.

"You have to sit at the table and finish your food," she said. "Not go out in the garden when it's dark so that Mama has to hunt for you."

"But there was someone there," said Jonatan. "I just wanted to see who it was."

Luísa stopped and looked at him.

"What are you talking about? There's no one there," she said uncertainly.

"Adalia said it was just a dog, but it wasn't. I went and looked, and it wasn't a dog."

Luísa looked nervously around, but she couldn't see anything. The branches of the trees hung over the ground as if they were trying to hide something from her.

"What did you see?" she asked.

"Come on," said the boy, taking his mama by the hand and dragging her with him between the trees. "Do you see? She's still there."

Luísa leaned under some bushes that were growing wild between the trees, but she couldn't see anything.

"Don't you see her?" said Jonatan, pointing eagerly. "Why is she sitting there, do you think?"

And then Luísa saw the doll that sat leaning against the wall, staring at them with its one eye.

"Come," she said, taking hold of the boy's arm. "Let's go inside."

31

Sara hadn't noticed that it was getting dark outside the windows of the newspaper office. It was Friday evening, Lasse was waiting at home with dinner, and it was time to leave. But she couldn't quite tear herself away. She thought about the scallops found next to Erika Bergman's body. The question kept spinning over and over again in her mind. Where would you find scallops on Gran Canaria? She'd had them at restaurants a number of times. As far as she knew they lived at depths of at least sixty feet, and you had to dive down to gather them by hand or with a net. Perhaps the perpetrator harvested them somewhere. But where? If she could find a place where there were scallops it might provide a lead.

Her thoughts went to Tasarte, where the yoga center was and where Erika Bergman had been staying. The beaches there were rocky, the bottom gravelly, and the water deep, so it was probably a good place to dive for scallops. When Sara visited the yoga center she'd driven down to the rocky shore and seen a restaurant. The people there ought to know if you could find scallops there. She looked up the number and called. Even though the restaurant was small and isolated, hopefully they were still open on a Friday night. A woman answered immediately, with clatter and talking in the background.

"Tasarte Restaurant, *buenas noches*."

"Hi," Sara said and introduced herself. "I was wondering, do you serve scallops there?"

"No, sorry," the woman answered. "But we have other seafood dishes. I can tell you what's on the menu if you want to reserve a table."

"That's not necessary," Sara hurried to say. "But can you harvest scallops in Tasarte?"

"No, I've never heard of anyone doing that."

"Do you know where you can find scallops on Gran Canaria?"

"They're not that common. I know they're found farther north, but here on the south side, there's only one place I know of."

"Where's that?"

"In El Pajar, in front of the rocks beyond the beach. Why are you asking? I recognize your name. Don't you work for that Swedish newspaper? Or is it Norwegian?"

Now the woman sounded curious.

"Yes," said Sara. "Sorry, I probably should have said that. I'm the editor of the Scandinavian paper *Day & Night*."

"Right, that's what it's called. You did a story about my sister and her Swedish friend's tapas bar not too long ago. They serve Swedish-Canarian tapas at a bar in Las Palmas."

"Yes, I remember that very well," Sara exclaimed. "Great food. It seems like it's a very popular place."

"The article in your paper didn't hurt. They've been packed since then. If you go there I'm sure they'll treat you to dinner."

"I'll keep that in mind," said Sara, who couldn't help smiling.

"My name's Juanita Díaz, and I'm the cook here," the woman said. "My family runs the restaurant. Perhaps you ought to write about us? Now that Tasarte is getting so much attention?"

"You're right about that, but a restaurant review will probably have to wait. Right now I'm mostly concerned with the murder of the

Swedish woman who was staying at the yoga center. By the way, did you know her? Perhaps she ate at your place sometime?"

"No, I've never seen her." A brief pause at the other end. Sara could hear the cook's hesitation. "But there was something else . . . that happened this morning."

"Yes?"

"A man whose head was bleeding came into the restaurant, and he wasn't from here. I got the impression he was from Sweden or Norway."

"Why do you think that?"

"He wasn't German or English, I could tell by his accent. It seemed like he was living in one of the caves here along the rocks."

"What did he look like?"

"Tall and fairly athletic, blond. In his thirties. But he looked shabby."

Sara stiffened. The description fit Adam Fors.

"What happened?"

"I cleaned the wound and gave him breakfast. Then he just disappeared. There was something unpleasant about him. And then I thought about the murdered woman in Arguineguín. I don't know if there's a connection. But I realized I recognized him. I was up at the yoga center the other day to see my girlfriend who works as a housekeeper for Frank Hagen. I saw him right outside. But maybe he's just one of the surfers who hang out along the beach, even if he didn't look like a typical surfer guy."

Sara thought feverishly. So far the police had only circulated a facial description of Adam Fors internally. The general public didn't know what he looked like.

"I'd like to send a picture to you," she said. "Do you have access to the Internet?"

"There's poor coverage at the restaurant."

"Can I send you a text and call you in a few minutes?"

"That's fine."

Sara ended the call and searched for Adam Fors's Facebook page. Suddenly it struck her that she didn't know how to download images from the computer into the phone. The opposite was not as complicated.

It irritated her that Hugo wasn't there when she needed him. Finally she held the phone up to the computer screen and took a picture. Then she checked the picture; it was a little blurry and there was reflection from the screen, but you could still see his face fairly clearly. It would have to do. She sent the picture, waited a few minutes, and then called Juanita again. Sara was well aware that she was out of her depth and that Quintana would be furious if he knew what she was up to. But she couldn't help it.

"Was he the one you saw?" Sara asked before Juanita had time to say anything. There was silence for a moment. Then she heard the woman on the other end.

"I—I'm not sure," she stammered. "It may be him, I mean . . . it's not impossible, but . . . He was thinner and looked harried. He just seemed different somehow, if you know what I mean. Besides, the picture is blurry. I just don't know if it's him."

Sara sighed; that wasn't the answer she was hoping for.

32

Kristian woke up early, with Diana trying to shake some life into him. The phone was ringing and apparently it had been for some time.

There were four missed calls: one from his boss at the consulate, who apologized for calling so early, the others from some hysterical parents shouting at the same time so that he couldn't actually hear what they wanted.

At his boss's request he called the Policía Nacional in Playa del Inglés. They had arrested a seventeen-year-old Norwegian boy during the night; he was suspected of assaulting a Spanish police officer. The parents demanded that their son be released immediately. Kristian had to go to the station to help out, although he didn't really understand what he could contribute. The police seemed unwilling to release him, and he could understand that. Although the boy was under eighteen, he'd attacked a policeman when he was being arrested for disorderly conduct outside a disco. It was an idiotic thing to do when you were on a two-week vacation with your parents. Actually, it was an idiotic thing to do at any time.

Kristian parked on the street outside the police station, got out of the car, and locked it. The street was quiet; not even the birds had managed to open their beaks this early.

The uniformed man behind the counter looked stern. He cast a quick glance at Kristian. He evidently understood immediately who Kristian was, because he pulled out some papers and handed them to him. Kristian didn't know if he should say good night because it was still dark out or good morning because it was past five a.m. Even if he spoke Spanish relatively well, sometimes he was unsure about greetings. He chose the latter.

"*Buenos días.* Are those papers about the boy?"

Before he could get a response, the chief inspector, Javier Herrera, came out of his office. He greeted Kristian with a handshake and showed him into an adjacent room. They sat down on either side of the desk. Herrera looked at Kristian.

"Don't the young people in your country have any respect whatsoever for the police?"

"That's a question I've had occasion to ask myself many times."

Kristian started skimming through the thin report.

"How long have you had this job at the consulate, helping tourists who are unable to behave themselves?"

"Three months, but it already feels too long," Kristian said with a sigh, looking up. "You don't have a job opening here?"

Herrera smiled crookedly.

"*Hombre,* hardly for a foreigner like you. And why did you quit the force in Norway, by the way? I heard a rumor you got fired. May I ask why?"

"I didn't get fired, I resigned," Kristian said curtly. "What kind of report is this?" He read through the papers once again before looking up at the chief inspector. "It's impossible to understand the course of events."

Herrera shook his head. He looked tired and pale and had dark circles under his eyes.

"You're here two hours after the kid is brought in—in the middle of the night—and expect to have a written account of the case. Don't complain. If it wasn't for me you would've had to wait until tomorrow to get a report."

"Sorry, I'm just tired. Yesterday was a bit much. I should've stayed in bed."

"You're not alone if you'd rather spend your night somewhere else. My little six-month-old *señorita* has kept me awake nights for a week and now my wife wants to have a little *señorito*, too."

"You're a fortunate man," said Kristian.

"I don't know if I agree. Not today anyway," Herrera mumbled drily.

Kristian browsed through the papers.

"The police were in plain clothes when they arrested the boy?"

"They showed identification."

"No chance to get him released?"

"No," Herrera answered, shaking his head. "You work for the consulate, and I'm sure you can pull some strings, but believe me, he deserves to sit in jail. And yes, I know he's only seventeen. But that doesn't excuse everything."

Kristian sighed.

"I'm sure you're right."

"Of course I am."

"But I have to go try in any event. The family is going home to Norway in a couple of days."

"Do what you have to. I know you're just doing your job, but I'd really like to have a few words with the idiots responsible for bringing up that punk."

They stood up and were about to go meet the youth in question when Kristian's phone rang. He saw that it was Sara and excused himself.

"Hi, sorry about calling so early, but we have to go to Tasarte," she said eagerly. "Now. I've got wind of something big."

Sara quickly recounted the cook's story.

"I think Adam Fors is there; we have to go."

"Have you notified the police?"

"No, not yet, because she's not sure. But it's really worth checking."

"You'll have to wait until I'm through here."

A few hours later Kristian was standing on the pier outside the little restaurant in Tasarte with Sara and the cook. He scanned the steep cliffs. He was tired and irritated. First the consul wakes him at an ungodly hour as he was lying in bed, Diana beside him. And now it's Sara and her ideas. Instead of spending a lovely Saturday morning with Diana, here he was in the wind and the damp.

"Are you sure it was here you saw him?" he asked Juanita.

She nodded seriously.

"It's not even certain that it was Adam Fors," he said, turning to Sara. "It could have been anyone."

"Well, I think a lot suggests that it was him," Sara objected. "A man who's probably Swedish wandering around here outside the yoga center. A man who seems completely out of it, which would make sense if his girlfriend has just been found murdered and he knew he was being chased by the police. Just think, he left his hotel in a hurry, and he's probably still in the country. No man with his passport has left Gran Canaria, as far as I know. And think of the pictures on the wall, the book with the underlined passages. He's sick. Maybe we ought to call the police? He may be dangerous."

"Since you've dragged me here anyway, we might as well keep going."

"What are you going to do if we find him?" Sara asked worriedly.

"I intend to talk with him," said Kristian. "Although I must admit I don't like getting wet."

"You're the only one who has shoes suitable for wading in the water. If I'd known the water would be this high I would've brought rubber boots."

"Do you even own rubber boots?"

"No," Sara admitted.

He sighed and cast a final glance toward the mountain that extended like a dark wall toward the cloudless sky. He walked past the restaurant, past the boats pulled up on land, and continued over toward the smooth rocks. He could not see anything or anyone, but Juanita had said that there were several caves in the rocks where someone could hide. Apparently it wasn't unheard of for tourists to try to spend the night in the hollowed-out nooks, only to be surprised when the sea rose and forced them to wade back with their soaked belongings and book a room in the middle of the night.

Kristian was careful where he set his feet; the water had made the rocks slippery, and it would be easy to slip. He stopped on a ledge and watched the waves heave in from the sea and crash against the stones. He shook his head.

"This is madness," he said, preparing to jump to the next slippery rock.

At the same moment he registered movement along the rock wall. In a moment of distraction he landed wrong, slid over the smooth stone, and ended up standing with water up to his knees.

"Damn it," he mumbled, looking around, and it was then he saw him.

A man about his own age was standing behind a protruding rock, staring at him guardedly. Kristian rooted in his pocket and took out the copy of Adam Fors's passport. It could be him. He looked haggard, as if he hadn't slept in a long time. His shirt was dirty and his pants torn.

"Hello! Are you Adam Fors?" Kristian called over the thundering sea. He raised one hand in greeting and started walking toward him.

"Stay where you are!" the man yelled in Swedish and picked up a stone, big as a fist. "I mean it," he added, raising the stone as if to underscore the seriousness of the warning.

There was no doubt that Kristian had met Erika Bergman's ex-boyfriend. He sighed and stayed where he was with the water rushing around him. He held his hands in the air to show that he meant no harm.

"I just want to talk."

"I didn't do it!"

"What didn't you do?"

"I loved her."

"Do you mean Erika?" said Kristian, slowly approaching.

"I loved her." He let his hands fall, dropping the rock, and stared down into the water that roared around him. "But she couldn't love me . . ."

Kristian was so close now that he could almost take hold of Adam, if it weren't for the slippery stones. The Swede looked up in surprise and recoiled when he realized how close Kristian had approached. He picked up the stone he'd dropped and stood up. Then he took a step backward, as though to turn around and run away.

"Wait," Kristian pleaded. "I don't mean you any harm. I just want to talk with you. Tell me about Erika."

"Are you a policeman? You look like one."

"I hear that a lot, but no, I'm not a policeman. I work for the Swedish-Norwegian consulate in Las Palmas."

Adam nodded.

"She said she didn't love me anymore . . . That she couldn't love me anymore, that everything inside her was dead. As if someone had killed that part of her." His eyes narrowed. "She said she'd met someone else."

Adam slid down on the stones, the rock wall against his back.

"What do you think happened to her?" Kristian asked.

"I don't know. She's dead, but I didn't do it. I know that some people think I did. But I loved her! I could never hurt her!"

"I understand," Kristian said soothingly. "Who was she involved with?"

"She didn't want to tell me. She just said that he did things with her that made her feel like a woman, that he knew how to satisfy her. I yelled at her and slapped her, but I didn't mean to. I never would have hit her."

Kristian could see that he was glassy eyed.

"Did you hurt her?"

"I'm so tired," said Adam, turning his head to look out over the sea. "All I want is to sleep and not dream." He leaned his body slowly to the side. "I loved her. I would never do anything to hurt her, ever."

"The pictures," said Kristian. "Why did you draw red tears on the pictures of Erika? Were they her tears?"

"No," Adam answered. "They were my tears. I wanted her to see them, but she never did."

33

The hands that glided over his thigh muscles were hard and strong. He had hardly dared look up from the table when the young man took off his white tank top and set it aside on a chair. The young man was slender, golden brown, resembling the young men on the beach in Playa del Inglés, where he sometimes went. Or the teenagers he saw on the beach in Arguineguín. He would sit down at Piporro at a table along the street. Drink a glass of red wine and peek furtively at the young Canarian men splashing in the water, chasing each other, wrestling in the sand, and playing soccer. He smiled when they yelled names at each other after someone missed the ball and had to throw himself into the water to retrieve it. Today's young people had a particular way of being vulgar that he thought was titillating, even if deep down he was ashamed of his thoughts.

The masseur asked him to spread his legs and he obeyed, but clearly did not spread them wide enough because the young man moved one leg to the side before he continued kneading. Before he lay down on the cot, he'd asked the young man's name. Felt that he had to do that, it was more personal, even if a name really didn't mean anything other than something he got from his parents.

Thinking of the boy's parents made him even more ashamed. For a brief moment he felt like getting up and apologetically saying that the whole thing was a misunderstanding, that he'd changed his mind. Tell the kid to keep the extra money.

"Rafi," the guy with the sinewy, golden-brown body had said. That was certainly not his real name, but it felt nice to have a name to relate to. Made him feel closer.

The hands massaged the inside of his thighs with smooth fingers, hard and sure against his skin. He realized he was shaking.

"Can you turn around?" the masseur asked.

He obeyed. The masseur had a soft, pleasant voice, not like others his age who had a hint of harshness in their voices that would follow them the rest of their adult lives. He felt ashamed of his growing member. But it didn't seem as if Rafi noticed it; he simply continued massaging his thighs and hips.

He closed his eyes and pictured her. He tried to think of something else, but the image of her face in his mind would not let go. Her light hair like a halo around her beautiful face as she was lying there. He'd loved her but not the way she wanted him to or the way he'd hoped he could. It was God's law, He who had created everything and determined what should be natural and condemned everything else, but it had never felt quite right. He was born different, unnatural. And he'd been ashamed; he felt worthless not being able to love her as she loved him. God didn't want to bless him with the ability to be happy with a woman. It felt like it was a punishment that she was dead, like God had punished him for what dwelled inside him.

The young hands moved in circles around his member. He suddenly felt sad.

"Perdón," he said in a thick voice. "It doesn't feel quite right."

"It's fine," Rafi answered. "Just lie down and relax."

He closed his eyes and exhaled. Tried to concentrate on the hands that continued untiringly. He got harder again. Suddenly he felt the hand around his member.

He sat up on his elbows, embarrassed but at the same time aroused and expectant.

"I can't relax. May I kiss you?" he whispered in a hoarse voice.

Rafi tipped his head, observed him.

"I don't do that normally . . ."

"Normally?"

"You're a special guest, *señor*, and I like you." Rafi took a deep breath. "But it costs extra."

He felt the shame plastered on his face. It made his hands cold and his heart hammer. He swallowed and got up from the bench. Felt unsteady on his legs as he walked naked over to the clothes he'd folded and set neatly on the floor, crouched down, and took the wallet out of his pants pocket.

"How much do you want?" he asked as he turned toward him.

Rafi had taken off his pants and his member hung down along his thigh. It was bigger than he'd expected, and he felt a tingling between his legs.

"*Cincuenta euro.*"

He fished out fifty euros and handed them to him. The masseur folded up the bills and set them on the table.

He put his arms around the young body and pulled him to him, felt Rafi's hand around his sex as he closed his eyes and kissed him.

He'd kissed her the same way, twined her blonde hair around his fingers, one hand on her hip, and pulled her to him. But he hadn't felt the same thing.

"I've never kissed a minister before," Rafi murmured, caressing his member.

"We are all alike before God," he answered, and felt that he was lying.

He just wanted so much to be loved and this was the closest he dared embrace the love that had grown big and ugly inside him.

34

After the morning's outing to Tasarte, Sara was back at the office. They'd called the police to help escort Adam Fors to the station in Las Palmas. Quintana insisted that Kristian go with them. He wanted to talk with him. Sara wondered whether this meant her friend would get a reprimand or praise for his effort. She hoped for the latter. With her help, Kristian had achieved something the police had been unable to do: locate the murder victim's ex-boyfriend. Whether Adam Fors was guilty or not, it was a major success that he was now in police custody.

Sara was alone at the office. Her associate, Hugo, still had a few days left of his vacation; she was eager for him to get back and relieve her. Normally she had no problem updating the website and being in charge of everything herself, but the situation right now was anything but normal.

She sighed, absentmindedly taking a bite of her crispbread sandwich. She sipped her green tea. Did Adam Fors murder his ex-girlfriend? She thought about the book with the underlined passages that Lasse found at the hotel. At the spot where Fors usually sat. It was really awful.

There was no doubt that he was mentally fragile. There was a lot that pointed to the ex-boyfriend as the perpetrator, but it still didn't quite add up. She'd checked him on Facebook, Twitter, and other social media and found nothing to suggest he knew anything about art, or was even the least bit interested in such cultural things. He was a soccer guy who worked with computers, and seemed into sports and technology and nothing else. Would someone like him, who almost exclusively posted pictures of himself holding a beer bottle at a bar, cheering at a soccer arena, or flexing his muscles in his underwear, go to the effort of making the murder of his ex-girlfriend look like Botticelli's fifteenth-century painting? She didn't want to be prejudiced, but it seemed far-fetched.

She was feeling very restless. Adam Fors was mentally unstable, but she didn't think he'd murdered Erika Bergman.

She thought about the scallops found below Erika Bergman's body. Scallops were evidently not found in Tasarte, but Juanita had said you could find them in El Pajar. Sara glanced at the clock. She could think of nothing more sensible for her to do right now.

She got up, grabbed her bag, and left the newspaper office.

Without really having a plan, Sara got in the car and drove toward El Pajar, a pleasant little village neighboring Arguineguín. It was in the shadow of a large cement factory. There were plans for the factory to be moved north and replaced by a hotel in a few years, which would change the character of the village considerably. The town planned to build sports facilities and bungalows on the surrounding land, where there were now banana orchards and a campsite. Sara wondered how that would affect Arguineguín, which still maintained many of its Canarian features. The tourists hadn't taken over there like in other places. The one beach would be improved, and that would certainly mean a boost for the local restaurant owners, but at the same time it would be sad if Arguineguín were to meet the same fate as Puerto Rico or Playa del Inglés.

Sara drove toward El Pajar along a road bordered by enormous eucalyptus trees. The trunks were a beautiful, glossy gray because as the leaves slowly turned to follow the sun the trees lost their bark. She parked outside one of the village restaurants, right by the cement factory. As she got out she caught sight of a gang of cats prowling around an old wrecked car, where they seemed to have made themselves at home. The doors of the car were missing, and cats were lying on the seats, on the floor, and in the front window. A few kittens were toddling around outside.

Sara strolled along the beach promenade. As it was a normal weekday before the Spaniards started their vacations, the fine sand beach was almost empty of people. A woman with a child was playing by the water, and a couple of girls were sunbathing. Otherwise it was deserted. At the far end, the mountains towered. The church was also located nearby, housed in a grotto, but it seemed closed.

She took off her sandals and carried them as she walked down to the water. The water felt cool against her skin. Farther off she caught sight of a man walking out of the water. He set a harpoon against some stones and then wriggled out of his tight wetsuit, picked up a towel, and started drying himself. Sara hurried up to him.

"Hola," she said in greeting, nodding at the harpoon. "Is there any chance you're fishing for scallops?"

For a moment she worried she'd been too direct. On the island people usually introduced themselves and exchanged a few words before they started asking questions.

"My name's Sara," she added.

The man laughed curtly.

"Miguel," he said. "No, I catch octopus." He held up a mollusk that was clinging firmly to the tip of the harpoon. "There aren't many scallops here, and besides it would be pretty hard to hit them with the harpoon. There's probably a better chance of finding scallops at one of the restaurants in the area. They'll prepare them for you, too."

"You don't say." Sara smiled. "Someone told me you could harvest them here, but it doesn't matter. Maybe I'll have a bite to eat later."

"You're not properly dressed for harvesting scallops anyway," the diver said with a glint in his eye.

Very charming, thought Sara. Tall, muscular, his hair dark and wet. She guessed he was in his thirties. She sensed that he was flirting with her, and she felt flattered.

"You need a wetsuit. The scallops don't exactly come creeping up on shore when people are hungry, you know." He winked at her. "You have to go down at least sixty feet to find any."

"So then there are scallops here?"

For a moment he looked surprised at her persistence.

"Well, maybe not right here. Like I said, you have to go farther out."

"Are there many who fish for scallops?"

"No, but it's interesting that you ask. A few days ago I met a guy, and he wasn't out for octopus. It's not often someone comes here to harvest scallops, that's why I remember it."

"How do you know he wasn't fishing for octopus?"

Miguel held out the harpoon.

"You have to have one of these. Plus, he left behind some scallops and a plastic case with some papers. I tried calling after him but suddenly he seemed to be in a big hurry and rushed off. You know how people are—who knows why they do the things they do?"

"Can you describe him?"

Sara felt her pulse rising. It could have been the murderer. True, she was grasping at straws, but that was all she had at the moment.

"No, he was too far away. Besides, I only saw him from the back. But he looked pretty normal, normal height and build, wearing a cap. I turned in the plastic case at the bar up there."

The diver nodded toward the buildings above the beach. Outside one of them were a few tables and chairs.

"I threw the scallops back in the water."

"Thanks very much," said Sara, shaking his hand, which was cold and wet.

She thought he held on to her hand a little longer than necessary.

She hurried up toward the bar he'd pointed to. After a little convincing she found herself with a plastic folder and a glass of wine in her hands. She sat down at an outdoor table and carefully pulled out the papers from the folder. They were stiff from salt water. Sara carefully spread them out, only to determine that they were illegible. The text had blurred together, ruined by the water. She sighed with disappointment and took a sip of wine. Then she noticed it.

There was a folded business card in one corner of the case. She unfolded it. There was the name Samsara Soul in gold and red. It was from the yoga center. She turned the card over. In ink on the back someone had jotted down "Friday at 9:00" and a telephone number. The card was damp and some of the numbers had been smeared. There was no name or identifying information. Only a number. With trembling fingers she fished her reading glasses out of her bag. The number was a Spanish cell phone number, but the last two digits were hard to make out. Sara swallowed hard.

The business card she was holding in her hand could not have ended up there by coincidence.

35

Kristian had intended to go home after the day's exploits out in Tasarte and the arrest of Adam Fors. He'd gone with Quintana to the police station in Las Palmas, where Erika Bergman's ex-boyfriend would be questioned. But after his encounter with Fors, Kristian was convinced he wasn't the murderer. Quintana confirmed this only a few hours later. It turned out that two German surfers had been drinking with Adam on the beach in Tasarte the entire night of the murder. They had treated Adam to food and beer while he told them about his unhappy situation with Erika. The party didn't break up until after three o'clock in the morning. They remembered him very well, and several other surfers who hung out on the beach had also seen the three young men.

Kristian did have an interesting meeting with Chief Inspector Quintana, who offered him a position helping the police part-time with the case. He decided to consider this at least, even if he didn't feel mentally prepared to return to police work. Besides, he had his position at the consulate to think about. He would have to speak with Grete, although Quintana had said that he intended to call the consulate himself and tell her of the offer.

Instead of going home, Kristian turned onto the autopista heading south. Once again he was driving toward Arguineguín.

Kristian could not let go of the thought that someone must have noticed Erika the evening before she disappeared. During their conversation earlier in the day Quintana had said that the police had a dozen witnesses, but none were able to confirm that they'd seen Erika Bergman in particular or identify the person she'd been with. That was all they had, various witnesses who'd made observations, none of them certain of what they'd really seen.

He went into the Supermercado León and bought a bag of beers and a bottle of whiskey liqueur—Southern Comfort—the same kind Janis Joplin always drank before she took the stage.

He sat down on one of the benches in the corner, right across the street from the León, where the winos usually hung out. It might be fruitless, but he hoped he'd find out something if he sat there long enough. Someone in that crowd must have seen something the night Erika Bergman was murdered. Maybe they were scared of the police or wanted to avoid getting involved, so they hadn't come forward to make a statement.

Kristian opened a bottle of Tropical and knocked it back greedily. The beer was cold and refreshing in the evening heat. He needed it right now. It gave him a little break from everything happening around him, all the experiences that had washed over him that day.

He was immediately joined on the bench by several Canarians and Norwegians who'd seen better days. They sat awhile, had a few beers, and let themselves be treated to his bottle of Southern Comfort before moving on. A few disappeared to buy pot before they came back to smoke; others had several beers without saying anything.

Kristian was aware that he didn't fit in, but as long as there was something in the liquor bottle being passed around he was accepted. He asked about the night of the murder and any observations they'd made, but an hour or two passed without him finding out a thing.

Among those who kept him company was a Norwegian named Rolf, who told him he was in Arguineguín while awaiting a prison sentence. While he waited, he was living on Norwegian social assistance. He looked older than the forty-three years he claimed to be. His face was marked by years of drinking. His fingers trembled as he rolled a cigarette and lit it.

They talked about the Norwegian rock band Jokke & Valentinerne. Rolf had been at a concert in Trysil where Jokke fell backward onto his amp but continued playing guitar as if nothing had happened. Jokke was his role model and according to him no one was a greater poet, not even Dylan or Springsteen. Kristian wasn't completely convinced.

Rolf sang some of Jokke's lyrics quietly and barely in tune while he raised his beer bottle in a toast.

Kristian tapped his bottle against Rolf's.

Rolf laughed and emptied the beer in one gulp. Kristian opened another.

"You're a hell of a good man, damn it." Rolf gave Kristian a friendly pat on the shoulder. "Where'd you say you come from?"

"Oslo," Kristian answered, once again bringing the bottle to his lips.

"What're you doing here? Vacation?"

"Drinking," Kristian answered.

"We've all got a reason to drink," said Rolf. "What's yours?"

"You know the girl who was found murdered down by the Seamen's Church?"

"Yeah, what about her?"

Rolf had a serious look on his face.

"We grew up together. She was the youngest. Now there's just two siblings left," Kristian said, letting out a sigh.

"I'll be damned. Then I know why you're sitting here. Damn it, what a mess. At first I thought maybe you were a cop or something. I've got some unresolved business at home so I'm trying to keep a low profile down here, if you know what I mean. Sorry about your sister, buddy."

"Thanks, it's too awful," Kristian said. "And the police haven't found who did it. No one seems to have seen anything either. Can you believe that? Even though it happened right here in the middle of the village."

Rolf coughed and looked down into his bottle.

"There's a broad who usually hangs out here, Merete. She saw something that night. I know she went and talked with the minister about it. But she's not here. Haven't seen her for days. Maybe she found someone to take care of her, who knows."

"What did she see?"

"She didn't say much, just that she bummed cigarettes from someone who looked like the girl they found and talked with her right before she was murdered." He looked at Kristian. "She was actually pretty sure it was the girl who was murdered."

"Why didn't she go to the police?"

"Merete's here on Gran Canaria with two of her kids. Got taken off welfare in Norway 'cause she drank. There was something wrong with the dad. I think he hit her. That's why she started drinking. So she came here. Didn't have a chance against the legal system."

"I understand," Kristian mumbled.

He hadn't heard about this witness statement. Quintana had said there was not a single person who could say with certainty they'd seen Erika Bergman. Either Quintana was withholding information for some reason, or else the minister hadn't bothered to inform the police. If that was the case, the question was why.

"But I know something Merete doesn't know," Rolf continued.

"What's that?"

"The apartment your sis came out of before she went down to León is the minister's."

Kristian looked at his newfound drinking companion with surprise.

"The minister has an apartment here, and Erika was there? Are you sure?"

"Yes, I know it's true. But if you go to the police don't mix me up in it. I won't say a word."

Kristian paused to digest what he'd just found out. He finished his beer. Once again he happened to think about the Norwegian rock band.

"Here comes winter," he said, looking over toward the Norwegian Seamen's Church.

"Here comes the cold, fine time," Rolf said and started humming along. "Jokke was a cool guy. He understood people like us. And now he's gone."

"That was a long time ago," Kristian said quietly and got up. He'd found out what he needed. "Take the rest of the beer in the bag."

He took out his wallet, removed a fifty-euro bill and gave it to Rolf, who took it with surprise.

"This stays between us."

"Of course. It stays between me and you and Jokke." Rolf grinned, quickly tucking the bill into his pants pocket.

36

Kristian had left Rolf on the bench and was standing outside the Norwegian Seamen's Church a short distance away. It was dark at the church and the big windows gaped vacantly toward the sea. Everything was deserted. It was just past midnight. Why hadn't the minister told anyone about the witness? Or about the apartment that Erika was in the night of the murder? Had she been there with him?

He tried to call Quintana several times without getting an answer.

The sea breeze came in from behind him, and the images of the murdered woman lying on the rocks below made him shiver. At the entrance to the church he looked carefully around to assure himself that no one was in sight.

A few scattered cars drove past on the road above, lighting up the silent facades before they were consumed by the darkness.

It took Kristian a few minutes to pick the lock—a click in the door, and it opened. He slipped in, took the phone out of his pocket, and used it to light his way ahead in the darkness. He didn't dare turn on any lights. The scant light cast shadows into a hall with office doors. He held his breath, listened tensely, but heard no sounds.

The phone vibrated in his hand; he'd set it on silent. It was Quintana.

"You called." Quintana was curt.

"I've found out something you have to check."

"Do you know how late it is?"

"The minister at the Norwegian Seamen's Church in Arguineguín has a studio apartment on Calle Graciliano Afonso. I think you're going to find Erika Bergman's fingerprints there."

"What are you talking about?" the inspector exclaimed.

"A witness saw her coming out of there. Check it."

Kristian repeated the street name.

"It sounds like you've been drinking. Where are you?"

"I'll call you later, Diego."

The office had a view of the cliffs and the sea below. He let the light from his phone wander across the room. Kristian went over to the desk and sat down in the chair, turning on the desk lamp and lowering it so it wouldn't be seen from outside. He let his eyes glide across the bookcase. There was a row of binders labeled by year. On the shelf below were various editions of the Bible, along with Kåre Hansson's book about the Norwegian minister and poet Petter Dass—the minister who was said to have sold his shadow to the devil. There were also other biographies, a book about church architecture in Norway, and a number of history books.

Kristian turned on the computer; the screen lit up in blue and asked for a password. He sighed and leaned back in the chair. Considered a moment whether he should just take the computer with him, mess up the office, and make it look like a break-in.

Randomly he pulled out one of the drawers in the desk. It wasn't uncommon for people to have their usernames and passwords written on a scrap of paper in a drawer. He found a brown leather wallet. It was old and worn. He set it on the table and rooted through the pens and paper clips in the drawer. He browsed through a notebook, but it contained only notes with Bible references.

Kristian closed the drawer and picked up the wallet. He glanced at the clock; he didn't want to stay any longer than necessary.

The wallet contained a driver's license, a few bills and coins, and a passport photo of a young, beautiful woman. Kristian took out the photo and inspected it. She was not unlike Erika, with the same light hair, big blue eyes, and high cheekbones. The photograph was worn at the edges and the colors were faded. He put it back and concentrated on the computer. He leaned down under the desk and used the phone to light up the underside, looking for a piece of paper with passwords that might be stuck there, but he saw nothing.

He looked at the screen, which was still waiting for a password.

Most people used the name of a pet, their partner, or a child as a password, but the minister had none of those as far as he knew. He wore no wedding ring and hadn't said anything about family or children when they met.

Kristian looked around. His gaze landed on the book about Petter Dass, and he tried the number of the beast from the Book of Revelation. Three sixes in a row, the sign of the devil. The square with the minister's username and image vibrated, which indicated a wrong password. Kristian tried a few more: Dass, Yahweh—God's name in Hebrew—SonofGod, but every time the same thing.

A sudden impulse made him open the wallet and look at the picture of the woman again. On the back, written in red, was "Marita 1995." And a heart with an arrow through it. Cupid's arrow.

Kristian entered her name. Wrong password. He tried again, adding *1995* after the name. He was in. The screensaver showed a beautiful image from the harbor in Arguineguín. Kristian took out the flash drive he had on his key ring and inserted it in the computer before he searched through the folders. He immediately found one marked

"Personal." It wasn't encrypted. Kristian thought that if people knew how simple it was to retrieve information or steal profiles and identities, they wouldn't dare have a connected computer.

Then he opened a browser and started checking the search history but was suddenly interrupted by a sound out in the hall. He jumped up from the chair, pulled out the flash drive, turned off the screen, switched off the light, and hid next to the wall behind the door.

The door handle was pushed down, and someone entered the room. In the darkness he recognized the silhouette of the minister: the sharp profile, the hair that was combed back but protested by falling down on his forehead. Kristian held his breath. If Finn Nydal turned around he would see him despite the darkness and the door he was partially hidden behind.

His eyes fell on the wallet, which was still lying on the desk. *Damn,* he thought: he'd forgotten to put it back.

A ringtone cut through the room. For a moment he thought it was his own phone, and his heart almost stopped. He was sure he'd put it on silent. The next moment the minister took out his phone and answered.

"Finn Nydal," the minister said. "Yes? You need access to my apartment? Now, in the middle of the night? Are you on your way? Okay, I'm coming."

Finn Nydal clicked off the call and put the phone back in his pocket. He remained standing and looked out the window.

"Lord Jesus," he whispered out into the darkness. "It's not true."

He left the room, and Kristian stayed pressed against the wall until he heard the outside door close. Now he had a little more time. He hurried back to the computer and searched through it without finding anything remarkable. Then he went into the minister's personal pictures. The first one he opened showed Finn Nydal tightly entwined with another man in a tender pose. They were clearly in love with each other. *So that's your little secret,* thought Kristian.

37

The car headlights barely showed the way. He was alone on the narrow road that curved along the rock wall. He'd traveled the same stretch more times than he could count, but this time it was different. Everything around him was black, an impenetrable darkness. It was the middle of the summer and almost seventy degrees outside. Yet he was cold. He turned up the heat in the car and felt the sweat running down his face, over his collarbone, between his shoulder blades. No matter what he did it was as if there was something wrong with him, as if he were not properly assembled. Something had gone haywire inside.

The headlights caught a sudden movement on the road ahead, and he reacted instinctively by pressing the brake pedal to the floor. The tires screeched against the asphalt, and the car stopped abruptly. In a daze he sat petrified, gasping for air while the headlights played across the roadway and disappeared in the pitch-black night. A minute or two passed while he tried to regain his composure. He stayed sitting there a little longer before he heard the whining sounds, like a child crying. He looked in the rearview mirror but couldn't see anything, only the red brake lights reflected on the rock wall.

Then he opened the door, got out, and discovered a bundle lying on the road behind the car. Had he run over a child?

It felt as if a hand was squeezing his chest. Things just couldn't be that bad. He walked hesitantly toward the body that was lying there shaking, and the twitches made cold shivers run down his back. When he got closer he saw that it was a dog. It let out a weak yelp as if it was asking for help. He'd run over the animal, and its hip and back leg were crushed. The most humane thing would be to kill it. He had the knife, but he didn't want to use it for that purpose, and he couldn't risk the dog biting him. Not now.

"Quiet now," he shushed, holding his finger over his mouth.

As if it understood him, it set its head back against the ground and sighed heavily. He took a step backward toward the car, felt his eyes tearing up. He couldn't do anything for it; it would die anyway. The next car would put an end to the dog's suffering. But how long would it take? He turned around, climbed over the railing and searched for a stone to strike it on the head. But he couldn't find one big enough. Frustrated, he looked at the animal lying there panting in the road. There was nothing he could do. He had to move on. He couldn't lose focus, couldn't lose control. Soon day would break; hopefully it would not be long before another driver came. He opened the car door and got in behind the wheel. Glanced in the rearview mirror, but it was too dark for him to see anything. With trembling fingers he turned the ignition and drove away.

The high mountains towered on either side, and he knew how steep the drop below him was, even if he couldn't see it right now. He held steady in the middle of the road, the white streaks disappearing at an even tempo under the tires of the car. Everything he needed was in a black garbage bag in the trunk. He hung on firmly. He couldn't forget the dog's look as it laid its head against the ground and sighed. He should have helped it, put it down, driven it to a vet, but he couldn't. He was incapable right now.

"Damn it," he screamed, striking his hand against the steering wheel. "Damn it."

Then the exit finally showed up; the sign flared up in the headlights. He slowed down and signaled, even though there was no one to see it. When he got onto the smaller road, he froze. There was a van with its lights off by the edge of the ditch. He managed to make out a bald man sitting at the wheel, smoking. The cigarette glowed in the darkness. For a moment he thought it was a Guardia Civil officer. He dismissed the thought; he couldn't let himself panic. It was probably just someone waiting to pick up a coworker on their way to an early job.

He glanced at the clock: five thirty. The road sloped down steeply and seemed much longer than in daylight; he concentrated on the curves. Nothing could happen now. Along the way he passed the deserted stone building right by the road. It had once served as a warehouse but had stood unused for many years. All the windows were gone, and the dark openings gaped at him as the car's lights played over the facade. He continued on, leaving the building behind him. The road turned into a tractor path, and the asphalt changed to dirt, becoming stony and bumpy. He passed lush banana plantations and densely growing papaya fields. Out here there were only fields, no houses. It would be another few hours before any workers showed up. The darkness was dense around him. He had chosen the place well and knew exactly where he should go.

At one spot the road widened a little, and he parked and turned off the ignition and the lights. It was pitch dark. He rolled down the window, heard the cicadas singing intently in the warm predawn. A solitary rooster crowed far away. There was a strong odor of manure.

He fished out an already-rolled joint and lit it. Took a deep puff and closed his eyes; his heart was beating so hard in his chest that it hurt. He couldn't let go now, had to keep a cool head. He visualized everything like in a slow-motion film. Felt the knife he had inside his shirt. He had to calm his nerves, get into the right mood. This was even more important than the last time. He couldn't lose his concentration; he just had to get sufficiently relaxed.

He waited until it started to get light.

Waited for daybreak.

38

Sunday, June 29

Kristian looked around the café. It was the first time he'd been here, and he'd chosen it because it was close to the consulate. He had to stop by work even though it was Sunday, and then he intended to spend the rest of the day with Diana. He was worn out after the drama of the night before, but he dismissed his tiredness.

The sign outside advertised Dorada beer; the image was in red and white with Spain's highest mountain, Teide, on the neighboring island of Tenerife, in the background. Like many other cafés in the city, it was barely more than a hole in the wall. A narrow bar ran along one side; the lighting was dim, and the furniture was dark wood. Faded signs hung on the walls showing the dishes that were served, mostly hamburgers and other sandwiches. The pictures were so bleached out it was hard to see what was what.

Sara was already there waiting for him at a table at the back. She had on earphones and was listening to music. She was sitting with eyes closed, rocking along and humming off-key. *Good thing she's doing it quietly,* he thought. When she noticed him she took out the earphones and handed them over so he could listen.

"Listen to this," she exclaimed enthusiastically. "A song by Ted Gärdestad. A classic that never gets old. You've heard of him, haven't you?"

Kristian shook his head and put the earphones to his ears. It sounded anything but modern. Just some Swedish crooner from the seventies he wasn't familiar with.

"This isn't exactly contemporary, is it?"

"No, it must be at least forty years old. But it's still so freaking good!"

Kristian took off his light suit coat, hung it over the chair, and sat down across from her. "I saw that you called last night. Unfortunately I couldn't answer; it was late."

Sara raised her eyebrows and turned serious. "Diego called me. He wondered if I knew where you were. Don't ask me why he was calling so late on a Saturday night asking for you. He must have the idea we're hanging out together a lot. He didn't want to say what it was about, but maybe you can?"

"Have we gotten to that point? That we're sharing information with each other?"

"Seems like it," said Sara, smiling. "That may turn out to be a smart move for both of us."

"I went to the Norwegian Seamen's Church last night and did a backup of the minister's computer."

"You did what?" Sara burst out, her eyes opening wide.

Kristian told her about meeting Rolf the evening before, the nocturnal visit in the church, and the tip about the minister's apartment, where Erika Bergman had been the night of the murder. He also told her about the picture on the minister's computer.

"So Finn Nydal is gay," said Sara. "But what significance does that have? The only thing I'm wondering about is why he hasn't told anyone about his apartment and that Erika was there. But you broke into the Seamen's Church?"

"Not at all. I happened to have a key that fit," said Kristian, firing off a sarcastic smile. "You were going to tell me something. You haven't forgotten, have you?"

Sara observed him while she sipped the strong coffee. There was something both fascinating and alarming about Kristian Wede. He was completely unpredictable. The way he acted, how he looked at her while he waited for her to tell him something. She felt herself being drawn further and further into the case. It engaged her, and however absurd it might sound, she hadn't felt this kind of job satisfaction for a very long time. She wanted to tell Kristian about the art theme and hear his view of the matter—and also about the business card she'd found at the beach in El Pajar. But she chose to wait; she wanted to provoke him a little.

"But what would you even do with the information?" she said skeptically. "You're working for the consulate, and you don't have anything to do with the murder investigation, do you?"

"Now you're just teasing. Have you read my job description?" Kristian retorted drily.

Sara shook her head. "Come on, Kristian. I'm a journalist. Do you really think I haven't checked up on you? In this case, your responsibility extends to helping the victim's parents get here, keeping them informed, and then putting them on a flight back to Sweden."

Kristian looked at her with an unfathomable expression.

"That's about to change."

"What do you mean?"

"Quintana called me in for a meeting yesterday. He wants me to help with the investigation."

"Are you serious?" Sara said in surprise. "As thanks for nabbing Adam Fors?"

"Maybe so. The police need help with the language, questioning witnesses. I'm Norwegian and have police experience. Quintana talked with my old boss in Oslo and evidently liked what he heard about me."

Sara let out a whistle.

"Impressive, but how will it fit in with your job at the consulate? And what does the consul say?"

"Grete thinks it's okay if I temporarily divide my time between the consulate and the police. But I'm not being given insight into the whole investigation. I'll be on the sidelines and only jump in as needed."

"Too bad," Sara said with a grin. "You could've been an even better source than Quintana."

"Take it easy. Don't go thinking you'll find out everything just because I'm assisting the police a little."

"So why did you quit being a policeman in Norway?"

"What does that matter?"

"Being curious is part of my job. I guess you've never worked as a detective—as far as I know you were mostly on the street?"

"'Investigator in the field' is more correct. I served on street patrol in central Oslo. Have you been rooting into my past?"

"I wouldn't say that exactly, but I do know that you were suspended after an incident, and there was an internal investigation."

Kristian leaned back in his chair while he observed Sara.

"A jewelry store in central Oslo was robbed. I followed the perp, and he would've gotten away if I hadn't stopped him. The accusations of excessive force were found to be groundless, but I was taken out of operational service. There, you have the story. Satisfied now?"

"You almost killed the perpetrator. That's what I heard anyway," said Sara.

"There was a child in the car," Kristian said calmly. "I took his pistol and then . . . I don't remember anything until I was lying on the ground."

He took out a box of snuff and put a plug inside his lip.

"Did you see anyone after the incident?" Sara asked.

"The guy was pretty messed up, but he wasn't seriously injured. The misconduct charges were dismissed. But yes, I went to a psychologist. She was mostly interested in my dreams—"

"What dreams?"

"About a little boy eating ice cream who sees a car disappear."

"And where does that dream come from?"

Kristian raised his eyebrows and shook his head.

"Thanks, but I've already talked with a psychologist and have no need to dig deeper into that. You said you knew something else about the murder?"

Sara sipped her coffee, which had started to cool down. "Can you order another espresso?"

Kristian waved to the man behind the counter, who reluctantly came over to their table.

"Otro espresso doble," Kristian said. "Now it's your turn."

"Have you heard of a painting called *The Birth of Venus*?" Sara asked.

"The painting by Botticelli?"

"You're familiar with it?"

Sara was surprised that he answered so quickly. She knew the picture was famous, but not everyone knew the artist's name right off.

"My father worked at the National Museum in Oslo before he retired," Kristian said as a cup of coffee was set on the table. "He met my mother when she was going to the music academy. I come from a—how shall I put it—cultured home. You can imagine how they reacted when their only son wanted to be a policeman. So, yes, I'm very familiar with *The Birth of Venus* by Botticelli. The original is in Florence. I haven't seen the painting myself . . ."

His voice died out, and there was a tense silence. Kristian stared at Sara.

He gasped. "You don't mean . . ."

Sara took a gulp of coffee before she gathered up her things and stood up.

"You know how to get hold of me."

She gave him a pat on the shoulder and left.

Kristian followed her with his eyes as she disappeared. He remained seated awhile and watched the door as it slowly closed. Put a hand in his pants pocket and took out the shell he had found on the rocks below the Seamen's Church. It was fan shaped and brownish-white. He'd looked it up; it was a scallop, which was not natural on the beach. They were found out on the seabed.

He'd wondered why it was there. Now he understood.

39

The sound of the front door closing woke Luísa Hagen. A glance at the alarm clock showed a quarter past five. Frank was much earlier than usual; the first yoga class didn't start until seven o'clock, and the center was only a ten-minute walk from their house. She lay there thinking awhile, looking out into the darkness. Maybe he was taking the opportunity to visit someone when he thought she was asleep. She was well aware of his affairs with women and of course he knew that she was—even if they both chose to pretend otherwise.

On the other hand this would be the first yoga class held since the murder of Erika Bergman, so maybe that was why he wanted to be at the center early. The guests were still upset, and Frank was naturally also shaken by everything that had happened and probably wanted to be there well ahead of time to prepare himself. Not that she really cared. He'd been even more distant and closed-up after the frightful incident. Luísa barely had any contact with him, and he didn't seem to want to talk about it. When she commented on it or tried to start a conversation, he only answered in monosyllables and seemed bothered and absent. She wouldn't be surprised if he'd had something going with the beautiful Erika. Even if he was approaching sixty, women still fell for him like bowling pins, and it didn't matter how young they were. Erika was a little over thirty, so at least she was a full-grown woman.

Her husband's escapades no longer affected her. There was only one occasion when Luísa put her foot down: last Christmas when a mother was staying at the center along with her daughter. At first Frank had been in close contact with the mother, who was a little older than Luísa, almost forty. Luisa didn't care about that; she was used to it. But when he started showing interest in the teenage daughter, Luísa thought it had gone too far. She'd told him off, and for once it seemed as if he listened. After that she hadn't noticed him getting involved with any younger girls.

She lay there in the darkness, staring up at the ceiling. It was impossible to go back to sleep. It was still completely dark outside. The children would sleep a few more hours, and even if, against all odds, they woke up before that, the housekeeper arrived by eight o'clock. She acted as a kind of second mother for them, and they felt safe with her. She'd even nursed Adalia and Jonatan when Luísa had plugged ducts. She must remember to put a few euros on the kitchen counter so that she understood how much Luísa appreciated what she did for her and her family.

She got out of bed. She'd always had self-discipline. Quickly she changed into jogging clothes. She gulped down a glass of water, looked in on the children, who were snoozing in their beds, and then she was out the door. She drew the morning air deep into her lungs. It was still dark and relatively cool. She made her way down the dirt tractor path outside the house and ran in the direction of the sea. Slowly at first, to wake up properly. Her body felt stiff and heavy with sleep, and it took some time before she got going. Running made her feel good. She liked getting out and clearing her thoughts. Recently it had been even more important. Her life had become more and more untenable. If she continued in this loveless life with Frank, she would go crazy. She had to get away. She just didn't know how to go about it.

The ground was uneven and she had to pay attention to where she put her feet. Around her the dark orchards spread out: papaya, squash, lemon, orange, and banana. Farther away she saw the outlines of the mountains, and as it got light the nuances in them emerged. She could make out a flock of goats climbing along the mountain crest far off. A rooster crowed in the silent dawn and was followed immediately by several in answer. Their complaining calls echoed between the mountains. The local bus working its way down here rumbled a short distance off. So far there were no people to be seen. The rustling in the bushes on either side of the little road made her heart beat faster than her measured pace would suggest. She felt tense but didn't know why. Perhaps the uneasiness from the other night was still on her mind. She'd felt like someone was spying on her. She tried to shake off the feeling. Quickened her pace and kept going.

Down by the deserted crossing to the highway she turned off onto the valley path to the extensive papaya fields, heard the roar of the sea and her own breathing. In here the vegetation was denser. She started to sweat. It was nice to run. Her steps became lighter; it was almost as if she were flying along. The longer and faster she ran, the better she felt. She managed to shake off the discomfort and let her legs go almost by themselves.

Her thoughts revolved around how she could get away from Frank without him getting his hands on the children. He was domineering and manipulative, talented at convincing people of his own excellence, and good at casting suspicion on others. His bad side had shown itself soon after she moved in. He wanted to control her, like he wanted to rule everything around him. At first her infatuation with him prevented her from seeing clearly. But in time it occurred to her what kind of person he really was. When he was with the guests, he seemed lovable and accommodating, but as soon as they turned their backs he would describe, often exhaustively, how clumsy they were when they practiced yoga. He would make disparaging comments about their appearance or the stupid things they said. Deep inside, he looked down on his guests—the very people he made a living from. She couldn't put that together. She didn't understand how he functioned. It made her insecure, uncertain. It was as if he had several faces. She didn't know what he really thought about her either, or what he said about her when she wasn't around. The longer they were together, the clearer it was to her that her husband was mentally and emotionally disturbed. He'd started to frighten her.

A car parked next to the papaya field caught her attention. What was it doing there? Maybe it was one of the fruit pickers waiting for the day to begin. She saw the silhouette of a figure in the driver's seat. As she ran past, quite close because the little road was narrow, she could only sense the driver's face. The hands rested on the steering wheel. She glanced into the car as she passed. She felt a wave of fear when she perceived what had been placed in the passenger seat next to the driver. Was it the same doll that had been in her garden staring at her and the children? And what about the shadow she thought she saw moving between the trees? She remembered the feeling of being observed.

She had no time to think further before the car's headlights switched on, and the car door opened. She turned around instinctively to see what was happening. The lights blinded her, but she saw that someone was coming after her. She ran for all she was worth, with spots of light dancing before her eyes. Her heart was hammering in her chest. Then she stumbled and hit the ground shoulder first. The pain burned in her body. She felt a hard knee between her shoulder blades pressing her down against the ground. The stranger leaned over her; she felt the warm breath against her face.

She tried to scream when a hand was pressed over her mouth and nose. She lost her breath, tried to wriggle loose. In her mind she saw the children's faces; she should be with them. Not here, in the dark, among the densely growing papaya fields, the expansive orchards. Out here she didn't have a chance. No one could see her; no one could hear her. The tears welled in her eyes while she smelled the nauseating odor from the hands. She managed to get hold of one hand in a final, desperate attempt to get loose; her nails tore up the skin, but her attacker said nothing. Only breathed heavily. The blood made her fingers sticky. Then it was as if all the energy had run out of her and down onto the dry, stony ground.

Then everything went black. Nothing could save her now.

40

Earlier

Adriana noticed him as soon as he came in. His eyes were a shining blue, and he had long blond hair fastened in a bun on his neck, and his skin was golden brown. *He's not from here,* she thought. He stopped, looked around the place. A few old men were sitting in one corner playing cards while they had coffee and freshly baked *churros*, deep-fried bread sprinkled with a lot of sugar. The bakery was off to a good start, and she'd been well received by those who lived in the little town. She and David were still living off the life insurance; the bakery wasn't breaking even yet, but it had just opened, and she hoped it would soon get better. The stranger placed his hands on the counter, waiting for her attention.

"Hola, buenos días. How can I help you?" Adriana said, setting down the rag and wiping her hands on the apron tied around her waist.

"I have a car full of ripe papaya, bananas, oranges, and lemons. I see you have a juice machine," he said.

He nodded toward her most recent investment, which admittedly had cost a pretty penny, but she hoped it would pay for itself soon.

"I heard you just opened," the newcomer continued. "Maybe I can be your personal fruit supplier."

"That would be very nice," she said happily. "But I already buy oranges from Pepe, who runs the *mercado* on the corner."

The man had a charisma that was hard to resist and a charming smile. He got a shrewd gleam in his blue eyes. He leaned over the counter and lowered his voice.

"May I tell you a secret?"

She nodded, a little unsure of how she should meet this obvious charm offensive.

"Pepe buys his oranges from me."

Adriana shook her head.

"No, is that true? Do you mean he sells them to me for more?"

"He has to add something. What's the point otherwise?"

She observed him a moment in silence. He was truly attractive, and of course he was right.

"I get them for seventy-five *céntimos* a kilo."

The man on the other side of the counter looked surprised and backed up a few steps. "What?" He threw his hands out in an overly dramatic gesture. "What kind of power do you have over poor Pepe?" he exclaimed. "That's the same amount he buys them for! But I support women who start their own businesses, so for that reason alone you can buy my oranges for seventy céntimos a kilo."

"So generous," she said coquettishly. "But I'll pay sixty céntimos."

He looked deeply into her eyes.

"I have a magic effect on women," he said quietly. "I'm used to getting what I want. I actually think that you're going to give me seventy céntimos a kilo, just to see me again."

His gaze was serious, as if he meant what he said.

"Then you're mistaken," she said with a laugh. "Sixty céntimos, not one céntimo more, and then I only want the best fruit!"

She shook her head, even as he made her uncertain with his shameless audacity.

"I take a woman with a mind of her own as a challenge. You'll get what you want, you rose of the mountains and sky. This time," he said slyly, pressing his palms together while he bowed and closed his eyes. "It's good you're striking while you can. When I've saved enough money I'm going to open a yoga center in Tasarte and then you'll have to find someone else to buy oranges from."

Adriana could not keep from bursting out in laughter. This man was truly special.

"My name's Adriana."

"And I answer to the name of Samsara. I've forgotten my original name."

"Where do you come from?" she asked.

"From Norway," he said, shaking his head. "One of the coldest and darkest countries in the world. And I'm not just talking about the weather. So, unfortunately, I would also prefer to forget my origins."

"Sometimes it can be nice to forget," she said.

At the next moment the door opened, and David came in.

"Is there anything I can help out with?" he asked, taking no notice of the man talking with his mother.

"You can clear the tables," she said, forgetting for a moment that she had just done that herself.

David looked around.

"Maybe I can take out the trash?"

She nodded. He disappeared through the door and out to the street with his boyish gait, carrying a not-very-full garbage bag. The door swung shut behind him slowly, as if it did not want to close before he came back again. The older card-playing men looked up when he ran out the door, longingly following him with their eyes. Once they, too, had been young boys, and now they were old men trying to remember what that was like.

"You have a fine son," said the man in front of her. "How often do you want me to deliver oranges? I'm in Aldea once a week, every Monday."

"That sounds fine."

She smiled at him, perhaps a little too broadly, she thought, ashamed the next moment.

"How much do you need?"

"I guess we can start with ten kilos at a time."

"Okay, then I'll get the fruit," he said, going out the door.

She leaned against the counter. There was something in his voice, how he looked at her. He seemed so self-confident. She immediately felt guilty, standing there thinking about another man with interest. It was not that long ago that she had stood looking out over the sea and was finally forced to realize that her beloved would never come back. Her mother had sniffed at her when she did not want to wear the black dress and shawl; she herself had worn mourning dress for several years when she lost her husband. But Adriana felt compelled not to give up for David's sake. He needed her, not her sorrow.

The door opened again, and the man who called himself Samsara was standing there with the orange crates in his hands. She saw that he had dirt on his face. She did not notice David when he came back. She saw only the man's face, his smile, the long hair that was pulled back, and the dirt on his face.

There was something about him.

41

The foreman, Alvaro Mendez, was in a lousy mood. Not that he was normally a cheerful guy, but now he was really irritated. The well-to-do farmer he worked for had called and complained that the watering system out by the biggest papaya field had broken down and told him to check on it immediately. It was Sunday, Alvaro's only day off. The fact that he'd gotten up in the middle of the night because his son wet the bed and couldn't go back to sleep didn't make things any better.

Alone out in the field, he brooded about what could have caused the problem. He knew it had to be remedied right away. It hadn't rained for months. The water in the system came from rainwater ponds up in the mountains and was transported through pipes down to the orchards in the Tasarte Valley. Without them, they wouldn't be able to do any farming. Here in south Gran Canaria, with an average of three hundred sunny days a year, it was crucial to make use of what little rain fell.

Up at the field he discovered that the lock on the chain that hung on the high fence by the entrance had been broken off.

He swore silently. Someone must have come in and pulled apart the water pipes at the connection point. It had happened a few times before—some idiotic surfer had decided to have a drinking party in the fields. He cursed the damned foreigners who didn't have the sense to stay in their home countries. They had no respect for ordinary people who toiled from morning to night to afford the things tourists took for granted.

He stepped over the network of black rubber hoses lying on the ground. Everything appeared to be in order. He'd expected bottles and shards of glass on the ground, but it looked just like it had the other day when they'd finished the harvest. No one seemed to have moved anything. The palmlike papaya trees grew close together and the vegetation was dense, even though the branches were now cleared of the green, pear-shaped fruits. When he pulled back a branch to get a better view, he caught sight of something that made him freeze. At first he wasn't sure what it was, and he had to take a few steps forward. An old, black, rusty iron bed was partially hidden among the trees.

"What the hell?" he exclaimed. "Is anyone there?" he called. Whoever had dragged the bed there was presumably asleep. But how in the world did they transport it here? And why go to so much trouble to sleep outside when you could just as easily lie right on the ground?

It had to be some young people who'd been fooling around and drinking and then fallen asleep drunk. Once again he called but got no answer.

At a loss he stood there for a moment, wondering whether he should go back to the car to get his tools. Wake whoever was lying in the bed and then get them—and the bed—out of the papaya field. He shook his head with irritation and approached the bed. First he had to see if he could even pull it by himself. He was unlikely to get any help from a bunch of sleepy, hungover adolescents. He went closer and saw long dark hair flowing out over the mattress. A woman was lying so quietly she must have still been sleeping.

"¡Perdón!" he called.

But the woman on the bed didn't react. He definitely did not have time for this. He came closer but stopped abruptly. The dark hair was plastered to her face. He met her lifeless gaze and saw blood running out of the corner of her mouth.

"Dear God in heaven," he whispered while he stared at the naked woman on the bed. He staggered backward, stepped on something soft that crunched under his boots. A little black cat. He wanted to scream out loud, but not a sound passed over his lips.

42

Kristian disliked the sight of blood. He always had, ever since he was little.

Now he was standing by the main road, looking out over the valley, with a nosebleed. The blood dripped down onto the guardrail, and he felt nauseated and dizzy. The sun rested on the massive mountains that beautifully framed the little village far below. The ocean wasn't visible from where he was standing, but he knew it was there, blue and glistening.

Kristian had stopped the car by the side of the road and gotten out; he wanted to have a few minutes alone before he drove down to the scene of the crime. He'd been walking on the beach promenade at Las Canteras, his arm entwined with Diana's, when Quintana called and told him it had happened again. Another woman had been murdered. She'd been found at a papaya plantation in Tasarte, not far from the yoga center.

He wiped away the blood that ran over his lips and chin with the piece of paper where he'd written down the contact information for Erika Bergman's parents when he picked them up at the airport. He wadded up the paper and let it fall down the mountain.

• • •

Kristian saw the police barricades as he drove down the narrow gravel road between the banana plantations. A policeman from the Guardia Civil met him.

He followed the uniformed man, who took him to the tape and raised it so he could pass. The police had cordoned off the whole gravel road that led to the beach.

Sara stepped out through a gate and came to meet him.

"What are you doing here?" Kristian asked, not really surprised.

"Police radio," she said, winking. "I'm just going to get the camera from the car. Quintana's there."

Kristian looked over toward the papaya field and caught sight of the tall man amid the dense foliage. The papayas had been harvested, and the leaves from the trees covered the ground. He went in, crouching under the branches, and his eyes fell on the rusty bed standing in the middle of the field.

"Watch where you put your feet!" Quintana roared, and Kristian automatically took a step to the side so as not to tread on anything important. Right next to him was an old doll leaning against a tree. It looked up at him with one eye; the other was gone.

"Sorry," he said, giving Quintana an apologetic look.

The next moment he noticed her. The woman lay on her back on the bed, staring up through the foliage and the trees that leaned toward her. The perpetrator had undressed her, so she was naked on the dirty mattress; her abdomen was torn apart, and large quantities of blood had stuck to her thighs and the mattress. She was lying a little on her side with her knees drawn up. Kristian felt his stomach churning and reflexively placed a hand over his mouth to stop the nausea welling up in his throat. He swallowed, tasting sour belches. He backed away from the bed and found a tree he could lean against, felt the pressure in his head and the nosebleed start again.

Kristian leaned his head back and fixed his eyes on the sky to stop the nosebleed, trying to subdue the pressure.

"Is it that bad?" Sara handed him a paper napkin.

"Thanks," Kristian replied, taking the napkin and holding it against his nose. "What kind of sick person are we searching for?"

Sara shook her head. She didn't need to say a thing.

They stood there under the tree while they observed the dead woman on the bed.

Several CSIs with masks and plastic gloves were walking around the scene. They worked slowly and thoroughly. Marked various places around the murder scene with plastic signs and took pictures of objects they found that didn't belong in a papaya field.

Quintana walked toward them and extended his hand to Kristian.

"I hope you can help out here," Quintana said. "It seems we'll be making use of you sooner than we thought. The police chief in Oslo said you were capable and perhaps you can contribute some new perspectives."

"Perhaps, although you know I no longer work as a policeman," Kristian said, still pressing the napkin against his nose.

"Once a cop, always a cop," Quintana said, handing him a face mask. "Do you want this instead?"

Kristian took the napkin from his nose; it was stained with blood, but the bleeding seemed to have stopped.

"Stress," he answered. "I've had nosebleeds since I was a kid."

"We all have different ways of dealing with stress," Quintana said drily. "Everything indicates that this murder was committed by the same perpetrator. The victim is Luísa Hagen, married to Frank Hagen. She has a connection to the yoga center and is arranged in a very particular way, just like the case in Arguineguín."

"Frank Hagen?" asked Sara.

"He's obviously a suspect; he's a common denominator. He's been brought in for questioning." The chief inspector abruptly fell silent and his eyes turned dark. "I assume it's not necessary for me to point out that what you see and find out is information that can't be disseminated?"

"Naturally," Sara answered, feeling the notepad resting heavily in her hand.

"How long has she been dead?" Kristian asked in a subdued voice as he pressed the piece of tissue up his nose.

"The crime scene investigators think it's about six or seven hours. The medical examiner hasn't arrived yet. Luísa usually went out for a run in the mornings, at seven. This is as far as she got," Quintana said with a sigh.

Kristian turned around to look for the villa where Frank Hagen lived with his family but couldn't see it.

"It can't have taken more than a few minutes to run here from the house," Sara said. "Even if it's not visible from here, it's close by."

Kristian looked at his watch, which showed a little past two in the afternoon. "What have you found so far?" he asked.

Quintana turned toward Luísa Hagen.

"The papaya field has just been harvested, so apart from cigarette butts and water bottles and some other garbage . . ." His voice died away. "The victim is placed on the bed, arranged, he's used a bigger knife and cut apart her abdomen and let her bleed to death. The bed is old, but it must have been transported here quite recently. The fruit pickers were done with the harvest only a few days ago, and it wasn't here then."

Kristian could not take his eyes from Luísa Hagen's face. The half-open mouth, the flies that had gathered at the corners, where the blood had flowed. The dead eyes staring up through the leaves.

"How do you manage to be so cold?" he asked Sara, who was busy taking notes.

"I try to forget that there's a person lying there," she answered without taking her eyes from the notepad. "I'm good at compartmentalizing."

"I wish I could do that."

Kristian's eyes fell on Luísa Hagen's clenched hand. Her fingers clung firmly to some threads of red yarn that ran between her fingers and down to the ground. He leaned over, following one thread, which was tied to some animal bones. A little yellow sign with a number written in ink was next to it. Quintana followed Kristian's gaze.

"We think it's from a dog," he said. "She has a number of threads in her hand that lead to various objects. The whole thing is extremely peculiar. I've never seen anything like it. Behind you is an orchid. And farther away by the headboard is an old radio."

Kristian saw the flower, which was trampled down in the leaves that had fallen from the trees; the red thread was tied around the stem. Next to it was another sign.

He turned his gaze toward the animal bones, which were close by. A cold feeling of discomfort crept along his spine. He got up and walked around the bed. On the other side there were more red threads hanging down; one was attached to the doll that he almost stepped on when he arrived at the scene. At the end of another thread was a dead cat.

Suddenly the crime scene felt like some kind of bizarre theater production, and Kristian staggered backward, his eyes still fixed on the spot. He let go of the bloodstained piece of tissue, which fell to the ground.

"Pick that up!" Quintana said sharply. "You don't want to lead the CSIs astray."

He did as the chief inspector said. A thought began to take form far back in his head as he stared at the scene before him: the naked woman with the long black hair, on the iron bed, the blood between her legs. The red strands of yarn like umbilical cords leading to the various objects. They were symbols—the flower, the cat, the doll, the radio, and the bones, which he now decided were a pelvis. He assumed the dead cat—a symbol of the vagina—was female.

He could hear himself breathing heavily and out of the corner of his eye he saw Sara and Quintana staring at him with surprise. His head was whirling while he tried to remember. Something was missing. He searched feverishly along the ground.

"There must be one more thing," he mumbled. "One more thing."

He carefully rounded the bed, caught sight of yet another red strand of yarn and there, among dry leaves and grass, he saw it. The object he was searching for. A snail with the yarn tied around the shell.

"Exactly," he panted, half to himself. "The snail represents slowness. The drawn-out pregnancy. The miscarriage."

Kristian backed away from the crime scene and sank down against a tree, sitting right on the dry, hot ground. He was sweating profusely. Quietly he observed the dead woman on the bed and the strange objects all around her.

"Frida Kahlo," he said quietly.

"What do you mean, 'Frida Kahlo'?" Sara asked indignantly.

Kristian looked up at her.

"Frida Kahlo, the Mexican artist. She was married to the artist Diego Rivera. She had a miscarriage and did the painting after that. The murder is arranged almost exactly like the painting."

Quintana gave Kristian an admiring look and for the first time in a long while he opened his mouth.

"Once a cop, always a cop."

43

Earlier

Adriana saw David walking beside Samsara on the path. Her son laughed loudly when Samsara told him one of his many stories. For the first time since his father had disappeared out at sea, David seemed really happy. The leaves on the ground crunched beneath her feet. The big stone house they would live in was farther up from the sea. She had seen it at a distance as they drove into the valley, and it looked grand. Samsara had insisted on showing them the newly opened yoga center first. Adriana tried to tell him that she was hot and sweaty and would prefer to start by seeing the house, but he didn't want to hear that. Just held her next to him. Then he put his hands around her face, rested his eyes on hers, and kissed her lightly.

Things had happened quickly between them, too quickly, some would say, but Adriana didn't care. When Samsara suggested that she and David move in with him in Tasarte, she'd been hesitant at first, but he'd pressed her. Adriana couldn't bring herself to say no. She was already his. She had been from the first time—she felt that she would belong to him, and he to her.

At first David stayed out of the way, didn't want to speak to the strange man, just gave him one of his dark looks and slipped into his room. She'd been irritated, wanted to grab him and tell him to behave himself, but Samsara stopped her and said David needed more time. She appreciated him for that. She admired his wisdom and calm. And the darkness in her son's eyes slowly got lighter.

One day the two of them showed up together in the doorway to the bakery, the man she had fallen in love with and her spindly son. When she saw that they were standing with their arms around each other, she set down the tray. A cup fell off and broke when it hit the floor. She collapsed on the nearest chair and covered her face with her hands so they wouldn't see her crying. David ran over to her and hugged her. He asked why she was sad, and she answered that she was crying because she was happy. Then she kissed his cheek through her tears.

It had been difficult to get rid of the bakery, but Samsara convinced her to turn over the sale to him so she wouldn't have to worry. He took control of her bank accounts and managed everything. He would see to it that the money left over went to David, to secure his future. He told her she didn't need an income now; she had him. And Adriana went along with it; she was glad not to have the responsibility. There had been so much on her shoulders the past year.

Now the two of them walked ahead of her on the path to the yoga center. Samsara leaned over and whispered something to David before he turned around and laughed in her direction. Her heart felt warm. Samsara had said something funny that made the boy laugh; he was good at that. It was easy for him to make them happy.

On the way to Tasarte, Samsara sang a song in a foreign language. David was sitting between them and with fascinated eyes he observed the man who was driving and tried to sing along with the refrain. Adriana didn't understand what he was singing, but that didn't matter. Samsara laughed and tousled the boy's hair, said *mi amor* to them both. The look he gave her, warm and glittering, told her that she was loved, that he was serious.

"We'll unload the car later," he said and parked. "I want to show you something first."

He'd taken them to a banana farm. The workers in the field were sweating, their torsos bare as they harvested. They wiped the sweat from their faces and greeted Samsara as a brother and friend, and he did the same with them. She liked that. They weren't just workers, he explained. They were brothers and sisters. They were all one family. And now he wanted her and David to be part of it.

His pride, the yoga center, was a little off the road inside a high stone wall. Samsara told her that everything he earned at the fruit farm he'd invested in the center, and soon he would only work as a yoga teacher. It was just a matter of time. Adriana didn't care much about that, as long as she could be near him, know that he loved her. That they were together.

He showed them the twin buildings, located opposite each other. A young woman looked out a window. She cast long looks after the three of them.

"Who is she?" asked Adriana.

Samsara stopped, took hold of her arm. "Why do you ask?"

"I don't know," Adriana said uncertainly. "I was just wondering."

The grip on her arm hardened. David was walking a fair distance ahead, playing with a stick in the grass and didn't notice anything.

"I hope you're not the jealous type."

Adriana wanted to ask him to loosen his painful grip, but she didn't say anything. There was something in his eyes.

"I can't handle that," he continued. "I've had enough of jealous women. I've been in those kinds of relationships before, and I don't want to go there again. I associate with a lot of women. Most yoga students are women. I hope that's not going to be a problem."

"No, of course not," she said quietly.

She glanced again at the young woman, who was still in the window; her long light hair played in the wind. She was beautiful, and Adriana suddenly wanted to cry.

"It's okay, my love," he said in a considerably gentler voice, letting go of her arm.

He stroked her cheek, and they continued up toward the house where they would live. It was so high up that it had a sea view, and she could see how the water glistened in the sun. She took his hand and pressed it hard, to show how much she appreciated everything.

Then they went down to the sea. Adriana stopped and watched the waves, which were born far out where no one could see them and then grew and became foaming white and raging over their surface before casting themselves against the rocks. David sat on the gray concrete pier, his legs dangling over the edge. He laughed loudly along with the roaring of the sea, and she thought that nothing could drown out his shouts of delight. It had been a long time since she'd seen him this happy. Samsara crouched, protectively holding his arms around the boy.

For a second she felt excluded. She stood there and observed them. They were in a world of their own, and as she looked at them, her distance made her itch all over. She turned her gaze back to the sea, searched for what she had lost long ago. The salt-drenched air reminded her of David's father. He had always smelled of sea, salt, ebb and flow. She closed her eyes and evoked his image in her mind, the sunburned skin, the dark eyes. How she missed him. And now she was missing the memories of him.

Adriana turned toward Samsara, and he saw her and waved her over to him. He put his arms around her, and she felt a flash in her chest, a reminder of happiness.

They sat down at an outdoor table at the only restaurant far out on the pier. The wind was brisk, and the water cast itself against the rocks, drowning the black stones in white foam.

"He loved the sea," she said, and the absence was surely reflected in her face.

"Loves," he corrected her. "Your boy loves the sea."

She nodded. He didn't like it that she thought about David's father. You have to look ahead, stop digging in the past, he said. She had to forget the man who had loved the sea.

She glanced toward David, who was sitting far out on the pier, but let him be although the water striking the blocks sprayed up and made his clothes wet.

Samsara ordered champagne, the drink with the name from a region in France she would never travel to. She said she was content with a glass of water, but he didn't listen. She was relieved that they had only cava. He could frighten her. For brief moments she got glimpses of something different in him, something threatening and dark. But she was never able to pin it down before he returned to his usual pleasant self. It was as if at certain moments he fully showed himself to her, but just as quickly the door closed again and the frightening image disappeared and she thought she'd imagined it.

They toasted, raised their glasses, looked at each other. She'd been keeping an eye on David, who had moved even farther out to the edge. The wind picked up. She didn't like that he was drawn so much to the sea.

"Sit farther back," she called in a sharper tone than she'd intended.

David turned toward her, and she could see that he didn't understand why she was upset. Samsara placed his hand on hers.

"Let the boy be, he thinks it's fun," he said soothingly.

"I'm afraid he'll slip and fall into the water."

"He's a big boy, he'll manage."

Samsara raised his glass and wanted her to do the same. At the same moment a scream was heard, and David disappeared from sight. She got up abruptly and ran to the far end of the pier where David had just been sitting. Adriana called desperately and saw her son struggle in the water. The forces of the sea were strong, and he wasn't a good swimmer. At a distance she heard calls that came closer. Several men came out of nowhere, running to the rescue.

The waves struck against the men who had thrown themselves into the water, as if it were trying to fight them off so it could keep her boy.

"He's mine," she whispered to the sea. "Don't take him." And just as she said that she knew that it was the one who smelled of sea and salt who wanted the boy. It was David's father who'd come to get him. He needed him now. Like God needs small children to be his angels, because children are more beautiful than all else he created on the earth.

"I've got him," someone shouted, and she started to cry.

They set David down beside her, and she hugged him. He was wet and shaking with cold, or perhaps with fear. She held him pressed hard against her until Samsara took hold of her and said that she shouldn't suffocate him, otherwise everything would have been in vain. He laughed and the others joined in, presumably out of relief—what he'd just said wasn't funny. She couldn't make herself laugh, but lightened her grip on the boy.

"I'll never lose you again," she said but realized that she couldn't keep that promise. Inside her something had already let go.

44

Chief Inspector Quintana was at the restaurant at the far end of the pier at Playa de Tasarte eating grilled tuna with Canarian potatoes. Hungrily he dipped the small, wrinkled, salty potatoes into the spicy red sauce and stuffed one after another into his mouth. He was exhausted and famished. Although he didn't usually drink alcohol on duty he ordered a cold Tropical, which he drank in deep gulps. After the macabre sight of the poor woman on the old iron bed out in the papaya field, the bloody abdomen, and the peculiar objects on the ground all around her, he needed something strong. He finished what was left on his plate and seriously considered ordering a Veterano with coffee. He'd gotten drunk on the cheap cognac many times. Usually in solitude when his wife was away and he was left in peace with his thoughts and could reveal what was hidden deep down. His hopeless love for Sara Moberg. It was irritating that he was never able to free himself from dreams of her.

He'd been enchanted since the very first time he'd met her ten years ago. It was at the opening of a cultural festival in San Agustín. He was there with his wife, Dolores, who was the director of the main library in Las Palmas. Sara was so beautiful with her dark pageboy and her blue eyes. He knew that she was married, but she was there alone. He'd never heard anyone from Scandinavia talk so much or laugh so loud. There was an easygoing spirit about her that charmed him at once. He'd been like a teenager in love. Even his wife, who generally wasn't jealous, had noticed his fascination. She'd made a gibe or two about it when they got home that evening.

Only a week or so later he saw her again at a cocktail party hosted by a mutual acquaintance. He'd blushed up to his ears and acted very nervous when Sara spoke to him. He stumbled over his words. He, who was usually so self-confident and cocksure. He didn't recognize himself. He and Dolores lived a pleasant life, and he liked and respected her. But Sara surprised him in a way he'd never before experienced.

Once past his fumbling introduction at the cocktail party, they'd had a real conversation. Sara Moberg was unpredictable. Perhaps it was because she was Swedish. What did he know? The only thing he knew for sure was that he'd been struck by lightning that evening ten years ago and the attraction had not gone away. And that annoyed him.

Just as he finished the last bite on his plate he caught sight of Sara approaching the restaurant. She was walking resolutely into the restaurant with her phone pressed against her ear; she hadn't seen him yet. There was an involuntary stir in his abdominal region.

As she got closer she spotted him, and her face broke into a quick smile. She raised her hand and waved. There was something girlish about her. Even though she was a mature, extremely competent middle-aged woman, she had an exuberance that she would surely never lose.

"Hola," she said, giving him a couple of kisses on the cheek and sinking down on the chair across from him. She ended the call and set down the phone. "Good Lord, what a sight. Just horrible."

"One of the strangest and most awful things I've ever seen," Quintana said. "What would you like?"

"Club soda and a glass of wine, thanks."

Quintana waved the waiter over and ordered. There would be a Veterano for him, after all.

Sara took her laptop out of her bag. "What do you think about the murder?"

"Macabre. Even more studied than the last one. And more brutal. This is a refined perpetrator we're dealing with."

"Finn Nydal, the minister at the Norwegian Seamen's Church?"

Quintana raised one eyebrow and looked at her inquisitively.

"I've heard about the minister's apartment in Arguineguín," Sara continued.

"You're always two steps ahead, aren't you?"

Sara didn't answer. She simply smiled at him as if to confirm that was exactly the case.

"Finn Nydal is out of the picture," Quintana continued. "He had dinner with a friend the night of the murder and then went home with him. The friend has attested they were together the whole night. That said, we did find Erika Bergman's fingerprints in his apartment—along with Frank Hagen's. Apparently they had a sexual relationship. That's been confirmed from several sources. And they were at the apartment the night she died. But that doesn't mean Hagen murdered her."

"Why not?"

"She was alone for a few hours that afternoon. You see, Hagen and Finn Nydal regularly play chess and drink rum together, and they did that day, too. They have a regular time when they meet. The appointment was in a diary we found on Nydal's computer. Erika could have met someone during that time."

"Someone who came back to murder her?"

"Exactly. Besides, the minister has been in the station for questioning the whole night and so he couldn't have murdered Luísa Hagen. He's still at the police station."

"But why didn't he tell the police that Hagen and Erika were at the apartment?"

"I suppose he wanted to protect Hagen. Call it misplaced loyalty. It's punishable, but I don't think we'll take it any further."

"And Hagen?"

"He's still a wild card."

"How strong are your suspicions?"

"He's in for questioning. More than that I won't say."

"Okay," said Sara, looking searchingly at him. It was obvious that Quintana did not intend to reveal more about Frank Hagen.

"I've checked on the painting it seems Luísa's arrangement was based on," she continued. "Look at this."

Quintana leaned across the table. He smelled the faint aroma of her perfume.

Sara clicked open the painting *Henry Ford Hospital*, painted in 1932 by Frida Kahlo.

In the picture a naked Frida Kahlo is shown in an old iron bed, with a bloody abdomen and six objects around her. In her hand, which she is holding against her stomach, six different red threads radiate like umbilical cords from her body. It almost looks like the bed is floating freely in the air. In the background are the factories of Detroit.

Sara pointed at the various objects.

"Kahlo was married to the famous artist Diego Rivera," she said eagerly, "and the painting depicts her despair after a miscarriage at Henry Ford Hospital in Detroit. The fetus in the picture she called Diegito, the little child who was never born. The child is symbolized by the one-eyed doll that the perpetrator placed beside the bed. Then you have the apparatus that depicts the cold, impersonal, mechanical nature of the hospital. The perpetrator used a radio instead."

"That I understand," Quintana mumbled, "but what did he mean with the dead cat? There isn't one in the picture."

"No," Sara said thoughtfully, twining a strand of hair around her index finger. "But you see the snail. That's there. Also the orchid at the crime scene. The snail symbolizes the slowness of the miscarriage, the drawn-out pain of losing a child. The flower she got from Diego as consolation when he visited her at the hospital. The part of the skeleton from the dog is a pelvis and represents Frida's ruined pelvis. She was seriously injured in a bus accident at the age of eighteen, and parts of her pelvis were destroyed."

"So what's missing is the anatomical model?"

"Yes, and the dead cat, which I assume is female, had to serve as a symbol for that. Frida Kahlo wanted to underscore the complexity inside a woman's abdomen."

Quintana leaned back in the chair and threw out his arms.

"Who in the name of God are we dealing with?"

"You have to wonder," Sara agreed. "But you can assume that the person we're searching for is interested in art. Wonder how interested in art Frank Hagen is."

"I checked on that," said Quintana. "He actually went to art school in Norway when he was in his twenties."

45

The sheet was warm against his skin. Kristian heard the traffic outside the open window. Diana had put on an album by the Spanish singer Bebe at a low volume, and her voice vibrated gently in the room. He threw the covers to the side, got out of bed, and walked naked to the window. The cool night air cleared his thoughts and made the hairs on his arms stand up. He took a deep breath and looked down at the street; a taxi had stopped at a red light, and passing cars and pedestrians went by. The screeching sound of car tires made him lean out to see better. A silver-gray sports car came around the corner at high speed. Without being aware of it Kristian's knuckles whitened as he held firmly on to the windowsill. He felt his stomach knot up. His body reacted automatically. The images flickered past in his mind.

The man who had run from him on Slottsgate in Oslo one year earlier. Kristian was close behind, one hand on his radio, breathlessly reporting that he was following the suspect. He'd been warned that the robber was armed and dangerous, but Kristian ignored the warning. He was in good shape, his boots pounded against the cobblestones, and the distance between him and the man decreased. He didn't care that he didn't have his own weapon. Something else took over.

Kristian watched how the silver-gray sports car braked and stopped behind the taxi until the light turned green, and then continued down the street, but his thoughts were elsewhere. Back to that day.

The robber stopped a car, dragging the female driver out. He could still hear her cry for her child, who was in the back-seat. Something misfired in his skull. He hit and hit until the man was unconscious. He didn't know what would have happened if he hadn't been stopped.

Kristian heard a door close behind him and turned around. Diana came out of the bathroom. She smiled when she saw him standing by the open window.

"Would you like something to drink?"

"A glass of water?"

She blew him a kiss and disappeared into the kitchen.

Kristian sat on the windowsill and looked down at his naked body. He was in good shape after all the years at the police station gym.

There was an internal investigation of the incident and he told them what he could recall. He was exonerated but taken off active duty anyway, which meant that he was given a desk job and forced to go to a psychologist. He went there a couple of times a week, sat in a chair, and talked about himself, talked about the dream he'd had since he was little. Posttraumatic stress, the psychologist said. There was something in his past that meant that he forgot parts of what had happened that day.

In the dream he was always a little boy. He never grew, just stood watching how the sky above him got darker and darker, until at last it was black and whirling like a tornado over his head. Then the car drove up, and he screamed until his voice disappeared. After that he could make no more sounds. Always the same dream. Always the same car. Always the same scream.

He'd been unhappy in the new job. He missed interacting with people out on the street, the sense that he made a difference. Being exonerated didn't make it any better. Sitting in an office pushing papers felt like a punishment. Finally he couldn't take it anymore and submitted a letter of resignation and applied for a job as a guard with Securitas. The police chief asked him to withdraw his resignation, but Kristian said he couldn't stay.

"I figured as much," the chief said, taking out a sheet of paper, which he set on the desk in front of him. "The Swedish-Norwegian consulate in Las Palmas on Gran Canaria is looking to hire a person with your background. I suggested you. I know you have a daughter there and it might be good for you. You don't need to answer right away. Think it over first."

Without waiting for a reply he stood up and left the office.

Ten years earlier, when Valeria was first born, Kristian had started to drive to the Oslo airport on several occasions but turned around or stopped by the side of the road each time. Even with his suitcase in the car and an airline ticket in his pocket, he couldn't do it. Each time he called Pilar and said he couldn't come yet, something had come up. In the dream where he was a little boy with the sun in his face, he was on Gran Canaria. It was the little boy in the dream who didn't want to go.

Later, when he got the letter from the consulate in Las Palmas, he knew he'd been given another chance. He went to the police chief and said that he was taking the job and then went home and packed.

His thoughts were interrupted by Diana's soft hand stroking him lightly across the small of his back.

"What are you thinking about?" she whispered in his ear.

She had to stand on tiptoe to give him a kiss on the earlobe.

Kristian turned around, placed one hand around her waist, and took the water glass in the other. Kissed her gently.

"Can you manage one more time?" she whispered before releasing herself from his grasp and slipping between the sheets.

He didn't say anything, simply slid down into bed and let himself be encircled by her warmth.

46

When he got out of the car in Playa del Inglés he was met by newspapers screaming headlines about the murder: "Unknown Perpetrator Strikes Again." "Woman-Killer Still on the Loose." "Tasarte in Terror." They were all about him. He swallowed hard. His heart hammered in his chest, and he had a bad taste in his mouth. It was as if he couldn't swallow everything that had happened. As if all the evil had sneaked into him and he had the taste of death on his tongue. He couldn't forget Luísa's expression when she saw the knife in his hand.

The first thing he did that morning was to buy the papers and check the news. According to the articles and news stories, the police had hardly any leads. His stomach knotted in nervousness. He looked around. Tourists strolling around in the hot sun as if they didn't have a single worry in the world. Most were dressed for vacation in sunglasses, shorts, and flip-flops as they made their way down to the cooling sea, beach towels and beach bags in their hands. The traffic was light; only the occasional car drove past. He caught himself looking for police officers. Sweat broke out on his forehead. He had to try to pull himself together, maintain control. He looked at the clock. He still had another half hour.

He crossed the street and sat down on a wall under a tree. Took out the joint he'd rolled before he left home. He didn't smoke much, but right now he wanted to dampen his pain. He lit it and took a drag, felt the smoke sting his lungs, deadening his thoughts and the pounding worry. A sound startled him, and he saw a street dog come running up on the other side of the wall, barking. He was on tenterhooks; he had to calm down. Try to keep his head cool. He took another puff and slowly exhaled the smoke.

The massage institute was on a back street, a stone's throw from the Yumbo shopping center in the middle of Playa del Inglés. A steep staircase led up to the entry. Halfway up the stairs he was forced to stop to catch his breath. He felt as if he'd been running. He dried his face with his T-shirt. Two middle-aged women stood on the landing, deep in conversation; they were having difficulty deciding whether to go in. When he passed they gave him furtive glances and discreet smiles. He tried to smile back, but it was fake. He felt his stomach churn and almost turned around on the stairs to go back.

The sign over the door was discreet, just "Lotus Massage" in gold-colored letters. The prices for the various treatments were listed on a sign in the window.

He opened the door, and a bell announced that he'd entered. The waiting room was not large: a leather couch and a couple of brown chairs around a glass table, a table with a pitcher of water and some glasses. The walls were white, with close-up photographs of shoulders, lower backs, and thighs being massaged by skilled hands. A sun-bleached calendar with the text "Dream Boys" was hanging by the counter, still open to April; no one had bothered to turn the page since then. The lighting was subdued, and Asian music streamed through the speakers in the ceiling. He felt slightly nauseated, and a headache came creeping up the back of his head.

"*Hola, hermano.*" The guy with a shaved head behind the counter greeted him as if they were old friends.

His biceps swelled under a tight T-shirt. He'd seen him here before, but couldn't remember his name.

"I'm not your brother, *cabrón*," he muttered. "Just give me a key."

"We're all in the same boat." The guy handed over the key. "Room 21. How are you doing, really? You look a little glassy-eyed."

"What the hell do you mean by that?"

"Relax. You aren't the only one who has a joint before coming."

"Don't tell me what goes on here."

He took the key, a towel, and a bottle of oil and left.

The room was at the far end of the corridor. The walls were stained dark, and the music from the ceiling drowned out the sound of a fan. At any moment the door would open.

He tried to breathe deeply, concentrate. He swallowed hard when he realized that the last time he'd touched another person it was her. Suddenly he felt it so clearly—the memories from daybreak out in the papaya field. Felt them physically. Her astonished look. How she whimpered when he held her firmly from behind and forced her down onto the ground. She'd been stronger than he expected. He'd covered her mouth so she couldn't scream. She'd fought for her life. Tried to kick, bite him. That was when he struck her on the head. She lost consciousness for a few minutes, long enough for him to drag her over to the bed and bind her firmly to the headboard. He felt dizzy and had to support himself against the massage table when he thought about what she'd looked like when he drove the knife into her. How she howled into the scarf he'd tied around her mouth.

He didn't notice when the door opened. He stood with his back turned and his eyes closed. He had disappeared into another world. A place that was his alone, where he could lie down to rest.

47

Earlier

Adriana stood in front of the mirror and looked at her growing stomach, stroked it mournfully. Her feelings were mixed. While she was happy about the child, she was more and more uncertain about Samsara. She saw him looking at other women, and he pointed out how fat she'd become, complained about the food and about what she said, commented on how she did things at home. More and more often she felt like an idiot.

After she got pregnant he spent even more time away from home. He explained his absence by the steadily increasing number of yoga students. Explained that they needed money to add onto the house so they would have more room. Recently he'd also been gone a lot during the evening, and he was tired and worn out when he came home. Couldn't bear to talk, couldn't bear to touch her as he'd done before. She didn't say anything when he went to bed right away, didn't dare make him angry. He flared up so easily these days. He didn't have time for David either, who always stayed awake and waited hopefully for him. Many times she'd sat with him on the steps up to the house and explained that Samsara had to work. As soon as the little one growing in her belly arrived, everything would get better. But it was as if David didn't believe her.

She heard the front door close and David's quick steps across the floor.

"David, I'm here," she called, straightening her hair before coming out of the bathroom.

The sound of steps disappeared up the stairs to the top floor.

"David!" she called again, and this time her voice was sterner.

Not a sound came from the top floor; it was completely still, as if the boy was holding his breath. She sighed and went after him. It was hard to walk. The doctor had said that she had to be careful and not exert herself too much, not go up stairs or carry anything heavy.

She was forced to stop and catch her breath at the top of the stairs, supporting herself against the handrail.

"David, open up!"

The door to his bedroom slowly opened and he looked out carefully. His eyes were shiny and red rimmed.

"Come, I want to look at you," she said. "How was school today?"

"I don't want to talk about it," he said quietly.

"Come out here at once!"

He came out with his head lowered and his eyes staring straight at the floor in front of him. Immediately she saw that something was wrong. His shirt was missing a button, his pants were torn across the knees, and his shoulders were shaking, as if he was crying but trying to hide it from her.

"What happened?" she asked.

He raised his eyes and looked at her. His lip was cracked, and one eye was swollen.

"They called him a womanizer, and I said it wasn't true."

"What?"

"They said that Frank's a womanizer and that he sleeps with all the women at the yoga center."

"Come here," said Adriana, trying to embrace him, but he took a step back and looked at her with narrowed eyes. "You shouldn't believe everything people say."

"I defended him," he said, his voice trembling. "But they were right. Why do you think he's never at home?"

"How can you say that?"

"Everyone knows it, everyone except you. I don't want to live here anymore. I wish Papa was here! That we'd never moved from Aldea! Why do you call him Samsara? That's not even his real name. Everything's just fake. All he cares about is fucking—"

The blow struck him under the right eye. His cheek turned red, and tears welled up in his eyes. But he simply stared back at her.

"I'm sorry," Adriana said. "I shouldn't have done that."

"Don't bother. You don't care about anyone but him anyway!" he screamed, shoving her away from him.

It was more forceful than he intended.

Adriana staggered backward, groped for the railing but couldn't reach it. For a moment she saw the fear in David's face while she desperately tried to keep her balance before she lost her footing and fell down the stairs. David's arm, which was too far away for her to take hold of. The white ceiling above her and the pain in the back of her head when she hit the wall. Instinctively she held her hands around her belly to protect the baby. Her face against the stone step, everything swimming before her eyes—she blocked out what was happening. Adriana thought she could hear the child who was growing inside her scream in terror and pain as she lay at the foot of the stairs. As if in a fog she saw David standing there frozen, shocked at what he'd done.

"Sorry, I didn't mean it!" he called desperately. "I didn't mean to."

"I know that," she said weakly. The pain inside her quieted. "It's fine, just help me up, then we'll set the table."

She took hold of the railing and stood up, felt like she was about to faint but tried to breathe normally. Everything would be fine once Samsara came home. Everything would be fine.

David helped her into the bathroom, where she got into the shower. He hurried into the kitchen and set the dinner table as she'd asked him. The warm water felt good against her skin. The water around her feet was red at first but slowly ran clear. She stepped out of the shower and dried off, changed, and went out to the kitchen, where David had set the table for three and lit candles, which he set on the table.

"Are you okay?" he asked.

"Only a few scrapes, nothing to worry about," she answered, smiling faintly.

The bleeding had stopped, and she was no longer in pain. There was probably no danger.

They sat down next to each other. She took his hand and squeezed it carefully, and David leaned his head against her shoulder.

"Everything's going to be fine," she said quietly, stroking his face. "Everything's going to be fine, just wait and see."

Night had fallen, and the moon shone palely in the dark sky when she finally heard Samsara carefully close the door behind him. She was sitting at the dinner table in the dark, waiting for him. The candles had burned out, and the food was cold. He stood and looked at her in the darkness.

"I've been working late," he said. "The last thing I need is a guilt trip."

"Is it true what everyone is saying about you? That you're not content with me . . . that you have others?"

"Who says that?"

"Just answer me, is it true?"

"You're the one I love," he said. "We can talk about it tomorrow."

She remained sitting in the dark and looked at him. She wanted so much for him to say something, something to convince her that it wasn't true.

"I'm tired. I have to sleep," he said, going upstairs.

And she knew that she could never lie beside him again in the way she had before. She would feel his breath against her hair, his warmth against her body. She always lay close beside him to have him near.

Now she was filled by an emptiness inside. She had no one she could confide in.

The pain she carried inside her was hers alone.

48

In the sun-drenched idyll a darkness spread that cast horrid, demonic shadows. Apprehension was growing in Tasarte.

"What hysteria," Sara said with a sigh, reaching over and turning off the car radio after listening to the latest news broadcast, by a host who excitedly discussed the murders' art theme with an expert. Speculation about the motive and the reasoning behind the arranging of the murder victims based on famous paintings ran high.

"It's hardly surprising. It's like something out of a Tarantino film," Kristian said, unrolling his window.

The murder of Luísa Hagen in Tasarte had not only shaken the whole area but had received major coverage in all the newspapers and on TV and radio, both locally and nationally. All of Spain was shocked by the brutal murders of the two young women. An ice-cold, calculating murderer was on the loose. The police were barraged with phone calls from worried people who wondered what they were doing to find the murderer and how close they were to an arrest.

The police had held a press conference after which no one felt any calmer. No one could understand how such a thing could happen in the peaceful little valley.

"Can I put on some music?" Sara asked after a period of silence.

"Not that Ted person again, please."

Sara sighed and appeared to concentrate on the road, although Kristian wondered what she was really thinking about while she drove.

He started to feel carsick from all the curves in the desolate mountain pass. Sara was not the smoothest driver he'd ever met—she braked often and abruptly, and she swung from one side of the road to the other seemingly without any logic whatsoever. Several times he'd tried to point out that she ought to drive slower, but she glared at him so fiercely he realized it was wisest to keep quiet. He wished he hadn't let himself be convinced to leave his car and ride with her. "We're going to the same place," she said, but she hadn't said that she drove like a drunk racecar driver.

Erika Bergman's roommate had called Sara earlier that morning and asked her to come see her at the yoga center. She wanted to talk with her, but didn't feel she could say what she wanted on the phone.

Kristian was going to meet Frank Hagen, who had just been released from the jail at the Policía Nacional in Playa del Inglés. In Kristian's work with the consulate he helped Norwegians who were in dire straits, and Hagen was still a Norwegian citizen even though he'd lived on Gran Canaria for many years. Although the police did not have enough to keep him in jail, he was considered the prime suspect in the investigation.

Kristian felt himself being drawn more and more into the investigation and reluctantly realized how much he missed police work.

"Do you know why the police didn't keep Frank Hagen in jail?" he asked. "I talked with Quintana on the phone very briefly early this morning, but he didn't want to say anything."

"It turned out he had an alibi," Sara said, rolling her eyes. "Guess where he was while his wife was being murdered?"

Kristian shook his head.

"In the bed of one of the female guests at the yoga center."

"Nice. The guy has young children," said Kristian.

At the same moment he felt the guilt that was constantly hanging over him. What had he been doing when Valeria was little?

"For what that alibi's worth," Sara said drily, interrupting his thoughts. "Maybe he got her to vouch for him. I have a feeling that man is frighteningly manipulative."

Kristian looked searchingly at Sara, whose hands were on the steering wheel, her eyes on the road.

"How is it that you find out so much from the police? What kind of hold do you have on Quintana really?"

To Sara's dismay she felt herself blushing. "We have a special relationship," she said after a brief pause. "The old goat has a soft spot for me."

"Good Lord, Sara—a soft spot? As if that is enough? I'm a cop myself, damn it. Homicide investigations are serious matters, and details that leak out to the public can harm the investigation and hamper the work of the police. Quintana can't reveal things to you about the investigation just because he has a 'soft spot.'"

"I thought you didn't call yourself a policeman anymore," she said, giving him a teasing look.

"Don't try to change the subject," Kristian protested.

"I already have," said Sara, grinning while she turned into the grounds of the yoga center.

They had arrived.

The normally peaceful place was completely transformed. The police had cordoned off the yoga center, the papaya field, and the entire road that ran between them. After Luísa Hagen's body had been found, there was intense activity, with searches by dog patrols, door-to-door inquiries, questioning of possible witnesses, and a hunt for traces of the perpetrator.

They got out of the car and rang the bell to Samsara Soul. It took only a minute or two before they were let in by Helena Eriksson. She'd been waiting for them. Sara noticed that she looked pale and exhausted. When they greeted each other her hand was shaking, and she seemed jumpy.

"How are you doing?" Sara asked, giving Helena a quick hug. It felt natural both because they'd met and talked in confidence before and because the young woman seemed to need an embrace.

"Not so good. It's so awful, everything that's happening. I don't understand it."

"I know," said Sara, patting her consolingly on the arm.

Helena walked ahead into one of the common rooms, where green tea and water were set out.

"How much time do we have?" Kristian asked Helena, glancing at the clock.

"Thirty minutes. The bus is coming to pick up the last of us in an hour and I need half an hour to pack up my things."

"So then it will be completely empty here," Kristian said, pouring a glass of cold water.

"Yes, only Samsara will be left. The children are evidently with their grandparents in Las Palmas."

"You had something you wanted to tell us?" said Sara.

Helena fingered her long tunic nervously and glanced constantly at the door, as if she feared that someone would step in at any moment.

"I would prefer to talk just with you," she said to Sara.

She gave Kristian an apologetic look.

"Sure, that's okay. I'll go look for Hagen in the meantime," said Kristian.

"Shall we sit down?" Sara suggested.

They sat down on one of the low couches by the window with its panoramic view of the mountains.

It was obvious that the woman beside her was upset. Sara thought she had something important on her mind.

"I don't know if this has anything to do with it," Helena began hesitantly. "But there's a massage institute in Playa del Inglés that I think Samsara is part owner of, and he recommends it to all his students."

"Yes?" said Sara.

That sounded logical; yoga and massage fit together. Even if Playa del Inglés was a good distance from Tasarte—it had to take at least an hour to drive there and an hour and a half by bus.

Once again Helena looked over at the closed door and leaned forward before she continued. "It's not an ordinary massage place. Their big thing is *massage erótico*, and it's young guys who perform it. That's their concept. Most of the guests at the yoga center are middle-aged women, and Samsara encourages them to go there and relax and accept what they get. Learn to live in the present, enjoy the moment. I don't think the women who go there the first time realize what it's really about. They think they'll get a massage to stimulate sexuality, but then it gets more and more intimate. Then, in the heat of the moment, so to speak, they're offered sex for payment."

"Why haven't you told this to the police?"

"I felt stupid . . . I've been there myself . . ."

"So the police don't know anything about these sex transactions?"

Helena shrugged. "I don't think so. On the other hand it's not against the law to sell or buy sex here in Spain, is it?"

"You're right," Sara said with a sigh. "There doesn't seem to be any oversight at all here where the sex trade is concerned."

"Whether the police know about it or not, they wouldn't do anything anyway," Helena continued. "I was just thinking whether the sex trade at the massage institute could have anything to do with the murder cases. I wanted you to know."

"I'm glad you told me," said Sara. "We'll keep in touch. I'll let you know what's happening."

"Thanks," said Helena. Her eyes were moist. "I liked both Erika and Luísa."

"I know you did."

Helena glanced at her watch. "I have to go."

They hugged good-bye, and Helena disappeared out the door. Sara's thoughts were whirling. This was a lot to digest. She felt a pressing need to smoke.

She went outside and sat down on one of the stone benches in the garden. As she was digging the pack of cigarettes out of her bag, she came across the crumpled business card she'd found at the beach in El Pajar. She hadn't been able to decipher the very last digit yet, but she guessed it was an eight. What if Helena was right and that massage place was connected in some way to the two murders?

Suddenly she had an impulse. She took out her cell phone and tried entering an eight as the last digit. It took a moment before anyone answered. Then a young man's voice.

"Lotus Massage, buenos días."

Sara hung up.

49

Kristian had found twenty-three euros and thirty-five cents between the sofa cushions, and he'd been living in the apartment barely two months. After a quick calculation he determined that he'd be fairly rich if he didn't vacuum the couch for a few years. He hit the cushions so that the dust whirled and then set them back and folded up a blanket he'd just bought to make the living room cozier. He stood and looked around the room. The two-level apartment hadn't looked like much when he moved in. The former tenant, an employee of a Norwegian manufacturer, had let it fall into disrepair. The calendar in the kitchen was several years out of date. After the tenant had moved, the apartment had stood empty. According to the rumors, he'd had an affair with a married woman and had had to move out in the middle of the night by lowering himself down from the balcony while the husband pried open the front door.

The door had, indeed, been scraped on the edges when Kristian moved into the apartment, but it could just as well have been from a break-in. A 1977 Vespa PX had been left behind in the hall. It didn't run, but Kristian decided to try to get it out on the road before the end of the year.

It had been hard to get hold of original parts. He'd bought some on the Internet, and it took time to get them transported to Gran Canaria. Now he was replacing the parts as they arrived, disassembling it and putting it back together again. He liked puttering with the Vespa, getting grease on his fingers, being occupied with something completely different from his ordinary life.

Although it was run down, Kristian had liked the apartment from the first moment. The paint on the exterior of the building had flaked from being by the sea. Inside there was mold and fungus in several of the rooms.

The consulate had brought in some workers to fix it up, and Kristian had stayed at a hotel the first month he was on Gran Canaria. They'd done a solid job, changing all the pipes and fixing the electrical. It had been like moving into a new apartment. He'd picked new tile for the floor, in a warm ochre color, while the walls were white. He thought the light surfaces made the atmosphere peaceful. He liked the balcony best. It faced toward the long beach promenade and the sea, and he could sit there for hours, gazing out at the horizon.

He thought about the day when he drove Pilar to the airport in Oslo, when she was going home so many years ago. He'd promised her that he would follow her, but he was never able to. Not even when she called and told him that she was pregnant, that she was carrying their child.

What do you want me to do? she'd asked him. He'd answered that he couldn't take responsibility for a child, not then. How would he do it? He had no money and several years left in his education.

He'd suggested an abortion, and she'd started crying. He hadn't been able to say anything to make it better. She'd called repeatedly, and more and more often he didn't answer. He had run away from his responsibility.

Kristian was interrupted in his thoughts when the doorbell rang. He almost tripped over the vacuum cleaner as he ran toward the stairs. Valeria and Pilar were standing outside when he opened the door.

"Hi there. Welcome. Come in!"

"I don't have much time, Kristian," said Pilar. "Nice to see that you've cleaned."

Kristian felt something hard and painful knot up in his stomach but ignored it and smiled.

"I can make coffee."

Valeria tore herself loose from her mama and ran into the hall and over to the Vespa.

"Why do you have this inside?" she asked, setting the giraffe she'd carried under her arm on the seat.

"One might ask that," Pilar said drily. "Make sure Valeria doesn't hurt herself on it or get oil stains on her clothes."

"Of course," Kristian answered. "No problem. It's just a hobby project—the former owner left it here."

"Maybe there's a reason he left it," Pilar observed.

Kristian took a deep breath.

"Listen to me, Pilar," he began. "Can't we start over? I know you have every reason to be angry and disappointed in me. I show up here after ten years and suddenly want to be part of Valeria's life. I understand that's not easy, but it's not easy for me either."

Pilar looked him straight in the eye, her mouth drawn tight.

"There are two things that make it possible for you to get to see your daughter at all. First and foremost, it's because your mother has always been there for me and Valeria. She never betrayed me. She always supported me during the ten years when I barely heard a word from you. The other reason I'm letting you see Valeria is that, despite everything, she wants to see you. To be honest, I don't care in the least whether this is easy for you or not. I only think about what's best for Valeria. By the way, she can only stay overnight."

"Pilar," Kristian pleaded, placing a hand on her shoulder.

"Don't make it harder than it already is," she said, twisting away. "You can drop her off at my place tomorrow at nine o'clock. She has a physical therapy appointment."

"I can go with her."

"I don't think so," Pilar replied.

She kissed and hugged her daughter and went out the door.

Kristian followed her with his eyes as she crossed the street and went over to her car, which was parked a short distance away.

He remembered the first time they met. He was sitting in Palace Park with some buddies and had just found out he'd been accepted at the police academy. They were out celebrating. She'd come walking along with some friends, and he'd noticed her at once. The dark hair that fell softly down over her shoulders and the way she walked, as if her movements were small dance steps. Her laugh that made everyone nearby turn around. She made him happy. He'd asked her out, and they fell in love in a flash.

"Mama doesn't like you very much, does she?" said Valeria.

"No," said Kristian, closing the door. "But maybe she will someday."

"I don't think so," Valeria answered. "She's in love with Antonio."

"How do you know that?" Kristian asked, following Valeria up the stairs.

"They have children together. That's what happens when you're in love."

He followed the chubby little girl around the apartment. Valeria investigated everything carefully, opening closets, pulling out drawers, peeking under the beds, picking things up and studying them before setting them down.

Kristian walked right behind her, at first around the top floor and then down the stairs to the ground floor. Then she went upstairs again and sat down on the couch. She leaned her head back and sighed.

"You haven't seen the balcony," said Kristian, sitting down beside her.

"Are you tired, too?" she asked.

"I just might be," he answered, peeking at her out of the corner of his eye.

Kristian wondered why the British doctor, John Langdon Down, who gave his name to Down syndrome, couldn't have had a different surname. Why couldn't his name have been something more positive, something that would have suited Valeria better? Something that made people know that she always smiled?

"I'm glad you only have one staircase," said Valeria. "At home with Mama and Antonio we have three, one for each floor. What can you see from the balcony?"

"I have a view of the sea."

"I've seen that before. Mama says you come from another country that's far away."

"Yes," Kristian answered, noticing that Valeria had placed her hand beside his. He could feel the little hand against his own. He stroked her little finger with his index finger, rather carefully.

"It's called Norway, and it's very cold in the winter. It's so cold that the bears are white there."

Valeria cocked her head and looked at him with her small peering eyes, as if she didn't really believe what he'd just said.

"Do you have jirafas there?" she asked, looking attentively at him.

"No, we don't. But in Norway we call them *giraffer*."

"If you don't have jirafas where you come from, why is there a name for them there?"

Kristian smiled. "I don't know. There are lots of things I don't know."

"If you're my papa, why weren't you here when I was little?"

"I don't know that either," Kristian answered seriously and swallowed hard.

50

Sara parked the car a few streets away and walked over to the building where Lotus Massage was. It was housed in a small, dreary shopping center that looked run down. On the ground floor was a supermercado, a café, and a knickknack store, which, judging by the sign in the window, sold everything from mattresses to souvenirs and decorative objects. On a sign was "Lotus Massage" and a Buddha figure. She took the stairs up to the entry and hesitated a few seconds before going in. A bell rang, signaling her arrival. Behind the counter stood a young guy with muscular arms and a white sleeveless shirt that fit tightly on his trim body. He gave her a dazzling smile.

"Buenas tardes, how may I be of service?"

Sara was disconcerted. Suddenly she didn't really know what she should do or why she'd come. What had she hoped to achieve with her visit? She cursed her impulsiveness. All too often she did things spontaneously without thinking about the consequences. She had a newspaper to run. It would still be a few days before Hugo was back, and she didn't have time to play private detective. Besides, it was crystal clear that this guy, who was only earning his daily bread, would never reveal anything to her that might jeopardize his job. In the wake of the financial crisis, unemployment among young people on Gran Canaria was about 60 percent. Sara suddenly felt ashamed. What had gotten into her?

"A massage, perhaps?" the young man asked.

"Well, I don't know," she said hesitantly.

He set a brochure in front of her on the counter. There was a list of what the business had to offer.

"Have you heard about us? Are you here on a recommendation?"

"Yes, I heard about it from a girlfriend. She's a student at the yoga center in Tasarte, Samsara Soul. Have you heard of it?"

"Of course, we get many customers from there."

"She was very satisfied with the masseur she had. I just don't remember what his name was . . ."

Sara looked searchingly at the man behind the counter. His expression did not show what he was thinking. She needed names, some kind of information, anything at all that might lead further. She didn't know if only customers from Samsara Soul were offered sex or if that offer applied to everyone.

"And you want him in particular? All our masseurs are capable. I think you'll be satisfied with whoever you get."

Sara hesitated. She was unsure how to continue. She didn't want to raise suspicions. She hadn't told Quintana about the information she'd found out about the massage parlor. She knew all too well how furious he would be if he knew. She was running her own private investigation in the middle of one of the most sensational homicide cases in years and doing things the police ought to be doing. She was walking into a minefield, and she knew it. Even so, she couldn't let it be.

"Yes, but I'd actually really like to have him. He was evidently . . . very special. If you say the names of your masseurs maybe I'll think of it."

For a moment the amiable man looked uncertain.

"There are quite a few who work here. Let me see: Pepe, Nacho, Toni, Rafi, Paco, Goyo, Dido, Chema, Isco . . . Those are the only ones who do massage. Some of us work in reception, but we only take care of the administrative part."

Sara raised her eyebrows. "I'm sorry, none of those names sound familiar. I guess I've just forgotten it. But those can't be their real names, can they?"

"No, those are nicknames, of course. I'm called Ossi. Here we only use nicknames."

"Why?"

"It's company policy. Don't ask me, I'm not the owner."

The receptionist shrugged and started to demonstratively shuffle some papers, as if he had just become seriously occupied.

"But you do know what their real names are? Maybe he told my girlfriend. I know she's seen him several times."

"I don't think so."

"But if I find out their real names, maybe I'll recognize it. And maybe their last names, too . . ."

The kid behind the counter got a suspicious glint in his eye. His smile stiffened, and he suddenly turned serious.

"Last names are confidential. I can't give those out. What is it you really want?"

Sara had no time to answer before she heard a voice behind her.

"What's the problem?"

A young man had shown up out of nowhere and stood right beside her. She felt his arm against hers, the smooth skin. She looked into a pair of dark eyes. He was standing a little too close, and Sara involuntarily backed up a few steps. His intense gaze disturbed her.

"Problem?" she stammered. "I don't have a problem."

The young man smiled disarmingly. He didn't look older than his early twenties.

"My name's Dido," he said, extending his hand. "And I'm not referring to your personal life. More like the muscles in your neck."

Sara shook his hand.

"Sara," she said uncertainly. "I was just a little curious, I didn't mean to snoop," she continued, turning toward the man behind the counter.

His scrutinizing expression had disappeared, and he seemed to see her now as just another middle-aged woman yearning for physical touch and sexual stimulation.

"I can't help noticing you pull up your shoulders," the young man pointed out. "You're tense."

Sara looked around. Ossi leaned forward and smiled at her again without saying anything. He only nodded in agreement.

She felt pressured. There was something intrusive about the two men, an intimacy she didn't feel comfortable with. She knew it was crucial to approach them the right way. She realized she would never find out anything if she asked flat out or said she was a journalist.

"Well, perhaps I should take advantage of the opportunity," she said with a quick smile. "How much does it cost?"

"That depends on what you want," said Dido with an unfathomable look.

Sara instinctively rubbed one shoulder. "I am pretty stiff. Perhaps I should just do the neck and back?"

"Sure, that's fine."

"Do I pay now?"

"We can wait until after the massage," he suggested. "We'll have to see how long you want me to carry on."

Sara felt her stomach burning. The best way to get information was probably to be alone with him in the massage room. Was he one of the masseurs who offered sex for payment? Maybe they all did. The receptionist hadn't listed a single female name. What if he tried to get her to buy sex—what would she do then?

A woman around her own age came out of an adjacent room. Her hair was tousled, her eyes shiny. Sara wondered what kind of treatment she'd had. She nodded curtly and disappeared down the steps.

• • •

The young man who called himself Dido showed her to a corridor with a row of closed doors. He opened one at the far end, and they went into a smaller room with a massage bench in the middle. The lighting was subdued, and she heard soft Asian music. There was a scent of herbs.

"Undress and lie down on your stomach on the bench. I'll be right back."

"Undress?" The thought of being naked frightened her. "But I just want you to do my neck and shoulders."

He smiled at her. "I just want you to feel comfortable, and if I'm going to massage then I need to touch you. You can keep your panties on."

He left the room. Sara felt her heart pounding hard in her chest. What had she gotten herself into? It was too late to stop now. She put her cell phone on silent and noticed several missed calls from both Lasse and Kristian. She would have to call them later. She slipped out of her skirt and hung it up on a hook on the wall, along with her top and bra. She lay down on her stomach on the bench and tried to relax. She didn't want the masseur to notice from her breathing that she was nervous. On the other hand, perhaps he would just assume she was inexperienced and tense about what was going to happen.

She heard him open the door and come in. To stall him she opened her mouth at once.

"Like I said, I'm only interested in having you massage my neck and back. Nothing else."

"Of course," he answered, and she thought he sounded slightly amused.

She heard him pumping out oil, and then he started by stroking across her whole back with rhythmic tugs. Sara could not help letting out a sigh of satisfaction. It was really nice. She closed her eyes, listened to the restful music, and breathed in the scent of aromatic herbs. Truth be told, this was exactly what her poor stressed-out body needed. She felt her blood circulating as her body was wakened to life. The masseur worked in silence and performed the massage firmly and professionally. It didn't feel at all like the right situation to ask questions, but she had to seize the opportunity.

"That feels really nice," she mumbled.

"That's good, I'm glad."

"What was it you said your name was? Dido?"

"Yes. You speak very good Spanish. Do you live here?"

Sara did not want to get tangled up in any lengthy lies about who she was, so she chose the simplest route.

"No, I'm Swedish, and I'm just here on vacation. I'm staying in a hotel here in Playa del Inglés. We're staying for two weeks. We got here yesterday."

"How did you learn to speak such good Spanish?"

"I studied Spanish at the university and worked as a travel guide for many years. Mostly on Mallorca," Sara fibbed.

"You're very suntanned, but perhaps the weather is nice in Sweden?"

"Sure, it's been pretty good so far this summer. But I tan very easily."

Sara was starting to feel a bit self-conscious. Now he was the one asking questions instead of her.

"How long have you worked here?" she asked.

"Not that long. A few years."

"How did you learn to do massage?"

"I took a course."

"It must have been good," she said appreciatively.

"Thanks."

There was silence for a while. Sara wondered how to continue.

"This business of massage erótico—what is that really?"

"It's a massage that stimulates sexuality. Was that the kind of massage your girlfriend got?"

"Yes," said Sara. "I felt a little stupid out there, so I didn't want to say that."

"It's nothing to be ashamed of. It's a very good massage. Everyone ought to do it."

"Do you give that kind of massage?"

"Of course. Maybe that's what you would like?"

As he asked, his hands slid down to the small of her back. Involuntarily she twitched.

"No, no," Sara assured him. "Not now anyway. But do you do what comes afterward, too?"

"What do you mean by 'afterward'?" The masseur's voice was sterner.

"Well . . . This feels a little embarrassing, but my girlfriend told me that she and her masseur . . . Well, I don't know . . . Maybe it's a secret. Maybe it's only something that happened between them."

Unperturbed, the handsome young man continued the massage. He added more oil, and Sara got the idea that his movements became more caressing, more intimate. It was some time before he spoke again.

"That's the kind of thing you don't talk about. What happens, happens."

His hands stroked along her sides, he massaged her waist and hips, and once again his hands glided down toward the small of her back. She felt how he pulled aside the towel that covered her and pulled down the edge of her panties. He was getting ready to massage her buttocks. Sara stiffened. She didn't want to go that far.

"Listen, wait a minute," she asked.

He stopped. "Yes?"

"I think that's enough now."

Sara tried to get up. She took hold of the towel and covered her body. The masseur backed up a step. He looked surprised.

"Sorry," she said, excusing herself. "But I have to go."

She grabbed her clothes and took out her wallet.

"How much do I owe you?"

"Thirty euros."

As Sara was taking out the money she noticed the business card she'd found at the beach in El Pajar. She had an impulse and pulled out the card.

"Do you recognize this handwriting?"

The masseur took the card. Sara thought she saw his hand tremble almost imperceptibly. Perhaps not so strange after he'd just been massaging her.

"Where did you find this?"

Sara did a double take. "What makes you think I found it?"

"You asked whether I recognized the handwriting. I assume you wouldn't have to ask if someone gave it to you."

Sara smiled. He was right. She was fascinated by the young man who stood before her. He didn't seem to belong here; there was something about him. His gaze was sharp and alert, and the way he carried himself puzzled her. He seemed well educated. Sara was usually good at reading people, a quality she'd made use of many times in her work as a journalist.

"But you do recognize the handwriting?"

He inspected the card carefully. "No, I don't. Why should I?"

"Do you see that the number is for here?"

Dido held the card even closer. It was dark in the room. "Yes, but the handwriting . . . I don't recognize it."

"Okay," said Sara, taking back the card. "It doesn't have to belong to anyone from here. It may be one of your customers. And you probably don't have a list of them, I assume."

"No, we don't register our customers, if that's what you mean."

He fell silent and looked at her suspiciously. "Why are you show-ing me this?"

"It doesn't matter."

Sara thanked him and quickly left the room. She felt embarrassed and unsuccessful. Why had she come here? It hadn't led her any closer to finding the murderer.

When she left she saw in the corner of her eye how the young mas-seur watched her for a long time.

51

To Kristian, it seemed almost unreal to sit across from his daughter at the kitchen table in his apartment. It was the first time they'd had dinner together on their own. He felt warm deep down in his heart. Even if it was unaccustomed, it felt completely right and natural. Valeria would spend the night at his home with him. That was a big deal. He hoped for all the world that it would go well and that she wouldn't miss her mama. He wanted this time with her. Pilar had told him that Valeria wasn't used to sleeping away from home, so to be on the safe side he rented videos and bought a book of bedtime stories, which he intended to read to her.

He put things away in the kitchen while she sat and played with her toy giraffe and hummed a song he didn't recognize. He rinsed the plates in the sink before putting them in the dishwasher. He thought he was getting better at this. When he was done he turned toward Valeria.

"What do you want to do, my little princess?"

"Can we have ice cream?" she suggested hopefully.

"That's a good idea," said Kristian. "I know a great place."

They walked hand in hand over to the little beach in San Cristóbal. The sun was just going down on the horizon. Valeria's eyes sparkled when she got to choose the kind of ice cream she wanted.

They sat down on a bench where they had a view of the sea. Some children were playing with a dog down by the edge of the water.

Kristian watched Valeria as she tore loose the paper around the ice cream before carefully biting off the nuts embedded in the chocolate coating.

Suddenly he was struck by an intense feeling of discomfort. In the recurring dream that woke him up almost every night, the boy had an ice cream just like that in his hand. And he ate it exactly the same way as Valeria. He could remember the red-and-blue logo on the ice cream wrapper, how he took off the paper and threw it in a trash can hanging on a brick wall. The trash can had "Kalise" written on it in red and blue. It was hot, and he was enjoying the sunshine and the taste of ice cream, chocolate, and nuts in his mouth. Then the sky above him turned black. The ice cream melted in his hand, and he dropped it on the ground.

Every time, he woke up, scared to death that someone was in the room, that someone was watching him while he slept. The psychologist said he ought to talk about the dream with his parents. It could have been something that happened in his childhood. Maybe they could help him fit together the puzzle pieces. He was doubtful. In his family they never talked about feelings, only about practicalities. He and his parents didn't have the kind of close relationship that allowed them to talk about everything. He often felt that he didn't know them very well. In fact, he didn't know them at all. What did he know about his parents' inner feelings and thoughts? Basically nothing. And what did they know about his?

He pushed aside the thoughts and tried to concentrate on Valeria. He was sitting on a bench by the sea with his daughter, and that was a wonderful thing.

"Is it good?" he asked.

"It's really good," she said, smiling at him so that her eyes became narrow streaks. She wore braids and a pink dress. It was her favorite color, she'd proudly announced when he said it was pretty. Kristian was struck by the fact that he knew so little about his daughter. What foods she liked, her favorite subjects in school, what she liked to do, who her friends were. The only thing he was sure of was that Valeria loved everything to do with giraffes. He wondered where she got that interest from. He guessed it wasn't just part of her syndrome. Most children her age probably had something they loved more than anything else. Kristian didn't know. There was a lot he didn't know.

It was a sad fact that he'd missed out on a large part of her childhood. He wondered what she felt deep down and what she thought about. He wondered how much she actually understood. He was well aware that he had to proceed carefully.

"Can I go on the swings?" Valeria asked, pointing toward the play area in front of them.

"Of course," said Kristian. "I'll sit here and watch you."

"Thanks for the ice cream," she called with delight, licking her fingers as she ran off on her chubby legs. She wore pink sandals.

Kristian watched his daughter while she swung. He let his thoughts wander.

He had taken the psychologist's advice and gone home to his parents and sat down on their soft couch. His mother set coffee out, white cups against the dark living room table that was so low he had to lean over. As soon as he started telling them about the dream, his father looked embarrassed, and it wasn't long before he got up and stomped out of the room.

"Why haven't you ever said anything before about this dream?" his mother asked.

"Why does Dad always have to close up inside himself?" he'd shot back.

His mother leaned over the low table and took Kristian's hands. "Dad doesn't want to talk about it," she said.

Then she told him about the boy with the ice cream who'd been standing outside the store. His father was afraid that he would make a mess in the car they'd rented to drive around the island, so he had to stand outside and eat his ice cream while his parents were inside the store paying. She told him about the man who came running down the road, who tore open the car door and started the car in which they'd carelessly left the keys in the ignition. She described how Kristian couldn't stop screaming at night, how he'd stopped talking. He hadn't uttered a word for a long time afterward. And she told him about the car that was found the next day, empty.

"What do you mean, it was empty?" Kristian had said. "And why wouldn't I talk?"

His mother covered her face with her hands before she answered. "You were so little, Kristian, you were so little," she said, crying. "You didn't talk for months, and we couldn't do anything to help you. You thought it was your fault . . ."

"My fault?" he had asked. "I don't understand."

"You had a sister. She was two years younger than you. She was in the backseat."

Kristian felt himself turn cold inside. "When they found the car it was empty, Kristian," his mother continued. "Your sister was never found."

"Do you need a tissue?" Valeria asked suddenly, taking hold of his arm, pulling him back into the present.

Kristian looked down at his daughter, who was sitting beside him on the bench.

"What would I do with a tissue?"

"Dry your tears," she said. "You're crying, Papa."

52

Earlier

The gurney felt cold and foreign. The sheets seemed freshly laundered, but Adriana could not detect any scent of detergent, only her own sweat. A nurse walked alongside her and dried her forehead. The rubber soles of the clogs tapped softly against the stone floor. From below her the rhythmic screeching from the wheels of the gurney was heard. Adriana caught herself counting them, the steps. The fluorescent light in the ceiling was bright and vibrated slightly. The doors they went through opened without a sound.

"Are you doing all right?"

She turned toward the nurse who had dried her forehead; she was the one who'd asked the question. Her hair was in a tight bun behind her neck; she wore no lipstick, only a faint hint of mascara. In her breast pocket she had a pen, which had run onto the white dress. Adriana could not read the black name tag. She felt tears coming to her eyes but was unable to wipe them away. The nurse saw that and pressed a napkin against her cheek.

"Is it going to be okay?"

Her voice was weak, so thin that it almost drowned in the sounds from the corridor. The squeaking of the wheels, the footsteps, the low voices from patients and visitors who sat lined up along the walls.

"We'll do the best we can," the nurse answered, stroking her cheek.

She thought, What happens if the best we can isn't good enough?

Samsara had wakened her early in the morning in the chair at the kitchen table, where she'd fallen asleep. He was forced to help her up, and she started to bleed heavily. He escorted her out to the car, where he placed her in the backseat. David had awakened and was standing in the front door, the black doorcase like a frame around him. Samsara asked him to get a sheet to put under her. The boy ran in and came out with a blanket. David said he wanted to go along, but his stepfather said no. She didn't have enough energy to argue but took hold of Samsara and held on tight until he gave in and said that David could sit beside her in the backseat.

She had drifted off on her son's shoulder while Samsara drove to the hospital. Fell asleep to the scent of her firstborn.

The double doors opened, and she was rolled into a sterile room. A man came in, dressed in green. He was wearing a mask; she could see his eyes. He seemed to see right through her. The wrinkle between his eyes was deep and serious. She wanted to say something but before she could, a mask was put over her mouth and nose. It smelled bitter, her fingers started to tingle, and she had a hard time keeping her eyes open. The room got blurry, and then there were only shadows around her. After that everything turned black, and she found herself in nothingness.

The first thing she noticed when she woke up was her hands resting on the white sheet. She tried to move her fingers, but they were stiff. She felt the presence of someone in the room, right beside her. She looked up but was unable to raise her head. She had no energy. She felt heavy and drowsy, listless, barely conscious.

Samsara stood bent over her—a familiar figure in a strange body against the whitewashed wall and the window that someone had opened. She could see that the sky was blue, not a cloud visible. Inside her the clouds were dark and heavy with rain. She caught sight of David, standing over by the wall. He cast cautious glances at her, as if he wanted to say that it was all his fault, his guilt to bear. She knew that it was too heavy for him, and she wanted to raise her hand to him, stroke his cheek, wipe away his tears and the pain he felt. But she was unable to move her face enough to force a smile.

"Are you thirsty, my love? Do you want water?" Samsara held out a glass.

Adriana felt the cold water run between her lips and down over her cheek. It was as if she had lost all feeling in her face. He took a paper napkin and wiped her mouth. Set the glass on the table beside the bed and sat down on a chair. Neither of them said anything. She could hardly hear them breathing. The child was out of her body, she felt that. There was a vacuum where it had been and nothing filled the space now. She felt paralyzed. Why didn't anyone say anything?

Someone had put flowers in a vase on the nightstand, a bouquet of roses. The red flowers moved slightly in the light breeze from the window.

She swallowed, licked her lips. Her mouth was like sandpaper. Her fingers prickled; she bent them slightly, tried to shake off the anesthetic. Slowly the pain grew in her; it was like an insect coming to life. Impatiently it moved, traveled around in her body. She moaned weakly when the pains struck her in the abdomen and spread up over the pelvis and along her spine.

Samsara stood up again with the water glass, which he set against her mouth. She twisted her face away, and he set the glass back.

"Where's my child?" she whispered and saw that David trembled, as if he understood that he wasn't the one she was asking about.

The door opened, and she heard Samsara breathe out as though relieved not to have to answer.

The doctor who had been in the operating room stood by the bed. She recognized the serious gaze. His eyes and the deep fold between them. He sat down on the edge of the bed.

As he placed his hand over hers, he knocked over the vase of flowers. Adriana heard the metallic sound when the aluminum vase hit the floor. Felt the doctor's hand on hers. David quickly crouched down and picked up the flowers. She could see that his eyes were red rimmed, that he'd been crying. He handed her the bouquet.

She could not make herself take it.

53

He was outside the Casa de Cultura building in the little village of Aguïmes, up in the mountains. Aguïmes was a lovely, peaceful village, with its narrow streets, light-colored houses, town square, beautiful church, and sleepy atmosphere. There was something both beautiful and overwhelming in its stillness. It was a village you could fall in love with.

He visited the cultural center often; admission was free, and usually there were few visitors so he could enjoy the exhibit in peace and quiet. Right now it felt especially liberating to be here. Leave all the excitement, escape to rest for a while. A new art exhibit had opened a few days earlier.

He'd learned to appreciate art as a teenager, and it had acquired a very special significance in his life. He'd realized that it was about life. And about death.

The door creaked lightly as he went in and climbed the stairs. It was the middle of the day, and he was all alone. In the large hall there were pale portraits of people who seemed almost to float out of the dark wooden frames. One of the paintings was so unclear he had to stand very close to see the expressions and gestures. He reached out a hand and carefully touched the lips of a woman who was on her knees, leaning over her child, her mouth open as if she were calling desperately. The child was staring at a bird sitting on a stone, with its head under its wing, sleeping. It was a peculiar painting, ominous somehow, and he felt unpleasantly affected.

Suddenly his concentration was broken when someone entered the hall. He turned around and saw an older woman walk slowly up to the first piece of art, which hung on the short wall beside the entry. He hadn't noticed it before.

The woman looked right at him. Her hair was white and gathered in a small bun at her neck. She had dark sunglasses on, checkered suit pants, and a bleached shirt she'd stuffed down inside the waistline. There was a narrow leather belt around her waist.

"Así es la vida," she said in an ominous voice. "Such is life."

He stopped before the painting, which depicted a wrinkled old woman with a hunched back. She was similar to the woman beside him. The figure in the painting was dressed in a coat and wore a hat that was pulled down over her forehead, covering her eyes. In her hands she held a jug of blood, which she was emptying on the ground. A little child lay shrieking, its arms raised toward the woman holding the jug.

"It doesn't look like life," he answered. "More like death."

The strange woman smiled faintly. "The old person is pouring out her life onto Mother Earth, and the little child lying on the ground who is being rinsed off was once her. It's life and death. Can anyone really say what the difference is?"

He looked at her with curiosity; she had expressed exactly what he'd been thinking.

"Are you an artist?" she asked. "I notice you have that special aura."

"No, unfortunately," he said. "I only like looking at art."

She observed him without saying anything and then lifted the sunglasses. Her gaze was glassy, milky white.

"Most people are shocked when I take off my sunglasses. I don't use them to protect myself from the sun but to protect myself from curious looks. They call me *la artista ciega*, the blind artist. That's a little exaggerated because I can see shadows . . . and things people with normal vision can't see. I painted these pictures. Do you like them?"

"I just got here," he answered. "I haven't had time to see them all, but they're a bit frightening."

She put the sunglasses back on.

"They're supposed to be frightening," she said. "Like life. And death. I like your voice. Can I look at you?" she asked, raising a hand toward his face.

He did not answer, simply leaned over and let her stroke his face. She lightly felt his forehead, let her fingers glide down over the eyes, the bridge of the nose, along his mouth, and down over his chin.

"You're a handsome man," she said with a smile. "Too handsome for an old woman like me."

She took his hand and placed it in hers, stroked it across the palm, lifted her face as if she could see him.

"You have blood on your hands," she said seriously.

He pulled back his hand and looked at her in dismay.

"All artists have," she said, smiling at him. "Will you follow me around the exhibit? It's so long since I've had company that I've almost started to miss it."

He took her arm, and then they walked slowly through the rooms.

54

Frank Hagen stood before the window in the bedroom and looked at his reflection. Absentmindedly he gathered his hair in a ponytail behind his head. The bus with the last guests had left, Luísa's parents had picked up the children while he was being held by the police, and now he was alone.

He'd been questioned for hours and interrogated about his relationship with both Erika and Luísa. He'd admitted that he'd had a brief relationship with Erika. They conducted a search in the villa and took the computers and a number of other things, including several of his paintings. It was evident that people had been there, rummaging around. He clenched his fists, felt fury inside him. Luísa was dead, and everything was in chaos. He was on the verge of losing control. The yoga center had been fully booked for several months ahead, and now it was empty. He put his fists against the window and rested his forehead on it. It would be a while before he could open the center again. And where the massage institute in Playa del Inglés was concerned, the other partners wanted him out. Ever since Erika's murder they'd made insinuations that he should stay away until the investigation was completed.

Now he represented a problem for the business, and there was a major risk that the police would realize what was going on there.

Frank observed his face in the window. He looked old, tired, and worn out. Like a loser, a man going downhill. Just days ago he'd been an esteemed yoga teacher, a desirable business partner, a successful entrepreneur, an attractive lover, a husband, and a father. Now he was about to lose everything.

Suddenly he noticed a figure by the gate. He sharpened his gaze. Was it one of the guests who hadn't made it to the bus on time or changed their mind and came back? Or a journalist? If there was even anyone there. He could have seen wrong. Maybe the darkness was playing tricks on him.

The thought of someone standing outside the gate worried him, and he knew he wouldn't be able to relax until he'd gone over to the center and double-checked that everyone had left. He closed the door behind him and locked it. He didn't usually do that. There was always someone in the house, but now it was just him, and with that came a kind of insecurity. The gate creaked on its rusty hinges; he needed to oil it.

The road over to the yoga center was deserted, and although he couldn't see far ahead in the dark, he'd walked it so often he could do it blindfolded. Someone had left the light on in the common kitchen. He continued up the path; the door was wide open.

"Hello, is anyone here?" he called. No answer. He called again to be certain, before closing the door behind him. In the kitchen he found a bag on the dining table. When he picked it up he saw that it was empty. It felt as if something besides the people had moved out, as if they'd taken the soul of the building with them and left behind a devastating vacuum.

Frank continued through a common area, leaning over and picking up a magazine that was on the floor and then tossing it in the magazine bin, before continuing upstairs. There were guest rooms on either side of the corridor, where the landline phone he'd had installed a few years before was.

When he looked into the first room he heard a chair scrape against the floor on the ground level. He stopped, not quite sure he'd heard right. He ran down the stairs to the kitchen but was uncertain whether any of the chairs had been moved. He hadn't noticed how they were placed. Out in the hall the front door was ajar. He was sure he'd closed it. He opened it all the way and looked out. It had gotten darker. The branches of the trees spread out against the deep-blue sky. Then he went in again, but couldn't shake off the worry that had started to grow inside him: there was definitely someone nearby.

"Is anyone here?" he called again, but got no answer.

He returned to the top floor. Checked room after room, opened the cupboards, pulled out the drawers in the nightstands, peeked under the beds. In one of the rooms he found a pink T-shirt that one of the young women had left behind. He recognized the motif, Jesus in the lotus position, smoking a water pipe. He sniffed it and closed his eyes. He remembered her well; it hadn't taken long for him to get her into bed. He wouldn't have objected to a little female company right now.

His gaze fell on the little house next to the yoga center. Now it was just the two of them.

The silence was broken by the jangling ring of the telephone. He stiffened, held his breath, and listened. He came to his senses, hurried into the corridor, and picked up the receiver.

"Samsara Soul," he said, hearing how his voice was shaking.

Someone was breathing at the other end, but otherwise it was silent. He repeated the name of the yoga center and felt himself turning cold; his fingers were tingling. Still the person on the other end didn't say anything. Then the line went dead, and he stood alone in the big, empty building, the hollow tone echoing in his ear. He put the receiver back in the cradle and felt a physical discomfort, as if someone were watching him. He turned toward the empty rooms but couldn't see anything. Everything was quiet. He would have to look through the rest of the building tomorrow, he thought. The sound of his steps against the stone floor was loud now with everyone gone.

It was just a wrong number, he tried to convince himself. The railing felt cold against his palm. Halfway downstairs he saw movement and stopped. When he looked down he saw that the front door was wide open again, swinging slowly in the breeze.

The wind had picked up.

55

Tuesday, July 1

Sara was waiting on the low stone step outside Kristian's building in San Cristóbal when he came hurrying around the corner. She was sitting with her back against the facade, her eyes closed to the morning sun. He had two rolled-up posters under one arm and carried the linen jacket he'd been forced to take off in the heat. He looked stressed, his forehead was damp, and the light shirt had patches of sweat under the arms.

Sara raised her eyes when Kristian approached, demonstratively shook her head, and stood up.

"Sorry," he said guiltily, digging for the keys in his pocket. "I left Valeria with her mom and had to do a few errands. It took longer than I thought."

"Don't worry about me," she answered, throwing out her arms. "My time is certainly not as valuable as yours. What does forty-five minutes here or there matter?"

"I said I was sorry," Kristian replied with an edge of irritation in his voice.

He opened the door so she could go in.

Sara stopped in the hall and looked at the Vespa leaning against the wall. Kristian had gotten some new parts and disassembled the motor, which was spread out on a sheet along with tools and a can of oil. She turned toward him and raised her eyebrows.

"I thought you worked for the consulate, not a garage. Don't misunderstand me, for God's sake. It's admirable to bring work home."

"It's a Vespa PX 77," Kristian answered, making his way past her and up the stairs. "If you're having a bad day you don't need to take it out on me."

"I was having a completely fine day until I had to wait almost an hour for you in the heat," Sara countered.

She hesitated before she continued into the apartment, considering whether she should take off her shoes. She chose to keep them on. Slowly she went up the steps. Kristian had already jumped up on a stool with a roll of tape in one hand and a poster of *The Birth of Venus* in the other. He taped it on the wall and turned toward her.

"Will you hand me the Frida Kahlo picture? It's on the table."

Sara took the other poster, which was lying amid a couple of empty beer bottles, a plate with a half-eaten pizza, and old snuff packets. On the kitchen counter were unwashed dishes, bowls that had contained various kinds of batter, and dirty whisks and spoons. An open package of flour and cocoa and sugar. A shirt was carelessly slung over a chair. A basket filled with laundry was on the couch beside a pile of newspapers.

"This place is a mess," Sara muttered.

"I cleaned yesterday," Kristian protested. "Although Valeria was here and we baked. I haven't had time to put things away."

It was dusty and smelled stuffy. Sara wrinkled her nose as she handed him the poster.

"Is it okay if I open a window?" she asked, going over to the nearest one and, without waiting for a response, opening it wide.

Kristian took no notice of that, simply unrolling the Frida Kahlo painting, *Henry Ford Hospital*, and taping it alongside the other.

He got down from the stool, took a few steps backward, and observed the two pictures.

"It looks like these were printed out from the Internet," Sara commented.

"They were," Kristian answered. "I downloaded some high-resolution images and went to a printer in Las Palmas, close to work. That's why I was late—I didn't count on it taking such a long time."

Sara moved beside him and inspected the pictures: he'd printed them out poster-size. It was strange to view them now after seeing the two murdered women arranged almost exactly like the figures in the paintings.

"What the two motifs have in common is that they tell about births," Kristian said thoughtfully. "The birth of Venus and then Frida Kahlo's miscarriage. The subjects are women, and they've inspired someone to commit murder."

"That's nothing new."

"The murderer wants to tell us something. He's done this with something in mind, a meaning. The question is simply what."

Kristian paused and drew his hand across his beard stubble. He looked at Sara.

"Would you like something to drink? You must be thirsty. There's a little pizza left over from yesterday, too."

Sara cast a glance at the coffee table and the plate with the leftover slices of pizza. They looked dry, to say the least.

"A little club soda, please," she answered. "How can you live like this?"

Kristian looked around, bewildered.

"It's not so bad, is it? Like I said, I cleaned yesterday before Valeria came, but with kids it gets messy quickly."

Sara pushed aside the things on the couch to make room and sat down. Kristian came in with two glasses, which he set on the table.

"Adam Fors was put on a flight home yesterday, but you've probably heard that. Maybe that's why you didn't want to meet?"

"No," said Sara, leaning back on the soft couch. She let out a light sigh. "I got a massage."

"Yes?"

"Massage erótico."

"Erótico? Are you trying to tell me you paid for sex?"

"No, dear, you know perfectly well I didn't. I followed a lead. Did you know that Frank Hagen is a partner, or at least has some financial interest, in a massage institute in Playa del Inglés called Lotus Massage?"

"No, I didn't know that."

"The customers are offered sex. And it's young men who are selling it. I think it's primarily aimed at women, but I imagine there may be male sex buyers, too."

"And you?"

"It didn't go that far, and of course I would have declined. Good Lord."

"That's good."

Kristian stretched and took a long look out the window, as if his thoughts found the surroundings too cramped and needed to be let free into the fresh air.

"Do you remember what I said about the business card I found in that folder left at the beach?" Sara continued.

"In El Pajar?"

"The number that was written on the back was for Lotus Massage."

"I'll be damned." Kristian raised his eyebrows. "Did you find out any more when you were there?"

"Not much, other than getting the nicknames of the masseurs. They refuse to give out their real names."

"Well, that's something, anyway. Have you told Quintana this?"

"Not yet." Sara sighed guiltily. "What do we really know?"

"Not much when it comes down to it. It's only a jumble of circumstantial evidence and speculation. Nothing that leads us to the perp. Adam Fors was the strongest bet, but he's presumably sitting in a pub in Stockholm getting drunk right now. Anyway, that's what I'd do if I were him."

"We know that Frank Hagen has something to do with the murders."

"We don't know that," Kristian corrected her. "We have circumstantial evidence."

"Erika Bergman was at the yoga center and had a relationship with Hagen, Luísa was married to him, Hagen studied art when he was young, and I found a business card with the number of the massage place Hagen is involved in at the same place where the murderer gathered the scallops found by Erika's body. Isn't that a lot of evidence?"

"We don't know for sure that was where the murderer dived for scallops—or if he was the one who lost the business card."

"Frank Hagen's interest in art, then? I heard from Quintana that Hagen studied at the art school in Oslo for three years. When he was in India he helped support himself by painting portraits. He was evidently involved in an art project, and that was how he ended up in Kerala to start with. Then I guess yoga took over." She frowned. "Hagen said nothing about that when I met him. I wonder why. Maybe he has something to hide."

"These are still only speculations," Kristian objected.

Sara got up from the couch and went over to the posters Kristian had put on the wall.

"So all we actually have are the ways in which Erika and Luísa were arranged. Why did he go to the trouble to do that? What is in these pictures that can tell us something about the murderer? He must have left some traces that make it possible for us to find him. He's an art connoisseur, if nothing else. And as I said, Frank Hagen at least fits in there."

"The first is a birth," Kristian said slowly. "*The Birth of Venus* by Botticelli depicts how Venus, the goddess of love, is brought to land by Zephyr. The goddess of spring, Flora, is standing on the island of Kythera to receive Venus. Venus means love and desire, although I don't know if that has any relevance."

"Where are you going with this?" Sara asked.

"I'm not sure yet . . . Frida Kahlo's painting is also about birth, in a way. A failed birth, a miscarriage. The artist painted the ground in earth tones to symbolize her solitude, and her bed seems to float freely in the air, which could symbolize helplessness and the feeling of being disconnected from everything. In the background are the car factories where her husband, the artist Diego Rivera, was making sketches for the murals. Kahlo said herself that when she painted the picture she had an idea about something sexual mixed with the sentimental . . ." Kristian stared glassy-eyed at the pictures.

"And your conclusion is that the similarity between the two murders is birth, love, and desire?"

He turned toward Sara and looked at her without saying anything. Sara suddenly felt a cold shiver up to her neck.

"You mean that the perpetrator could be . . . a woman?"

Kristian nodded.

56

The medical examiner's office in Las Palmas was located just behind the police station. Sara had been there a few times before, but that was long ago. It was only after strong persuasion that Quintana agreed to let her be there when he met the medical examiner, Santiago Suarez. The two men had been good friends for many years.

Quintana greeted her at the entry with a warm smile and an appreciative look. Sara felt a sting of guilty conscience. She still hadn't told him about Lotus Massage and its connection to Samsara Soul. But the fact was they hadn't had time to talk the past twenty-four hours. Quintana was fully occupied with the investigation and couldn't always make time for her.

The autopsy on the latest victim had just been completed when they knocked on the glass door to the autopsy room. The medical examiner stood with his back to them. As soon as he caught sight of the two visitors he pulled off the plastic gloves, threw them in the trash, and washed his hands.

He kissed Sara quickly on both cheeks and gave Quintana a handshake and a pat on the shoulder. Poor Luísa Hagen was lying naked on the wheeled steel table.

"What can you say about the cause of death?" Sara asked.

Santiago Suarez frowned. "She received a powerful blow to the head with a blunt object, but that wasn't what she died from. She had extensive injuries to the abdomen, probably caused by multiple stabs with a large knife. No trace of semen. He mauled her, and evidently the death was drawn out. It took time before she expired."

"You mean she was conscious while he was at it?" Sara looked searchingly at him. Although she'd asked the question, she really didn't want to know.

"Unfortunately I think it took several minutes. She was tied to the bed and the marks on her wrists show that she pulled and tore and tried to twist herself loose."

He went over to the body on the table and carefully lifted up one forearm.

"See for yourselves. The wounds are rather deep. That indicates that she struggled. Under her nails she had both skin and foam from the mattress she was on. It took time."

"Does that mean you have the perpetrator's DNA?"

"Yes, although it will take a day or two before it's processed," said Quintana. "But if he doesn't have a record, it doesn't help us that much, other than letting us compare it with the DNA on the other body."

"Both victims were naked," Sara said while she let her gaze travel across the body on the steel table. "Erika Bergman had sex with Frank Hagen earlier in the evening, but not with anyone else—at least there are no traces of that, are there?"

The medical examiner nodded in confirmation.

"The perpetrator stabbed Luísa Hagen in the abdomen," Sara continued. "What does that mean? Do the murders have a sexual motive?"

"Hard to say," said Quintana, rubbing his chin. "At the same time you have to remember that both victims were arranged according to artworks in which the women are naked, so that could be reason enough. There doesn't need to be any sexual motive behind it."

Silence settled over the room. Daylight made its way in from behind the thin cotton curtains; the stainless steel counters and the instruments on their white cloth shone in the light. With the polished stone floor, the chill and sterility around them, a peculiar stillness set in as the three stood around the table and observed the dead body. As if they were hoping for an answer. Sara thought about her conversation with Kristian earlier that morning.

"If you think about the art motif," she said, "the first one is about birth, the second about a miscarriage. What does that tell us?"

Quintana met her gaze.

"Yes, what the hell does that tell us?" he said with a sigh. "There are several connection points between the women. They were about the same age. Both had a connection to the Samsara Soul yoga center. Both were murdered with a knife, and everything indicates that it's the same murder weapon, right?"

He turned toward Suarez, who nodded slightly in response.

"All things considered, it's the same perpetrator we're dealing with. But what is the motive? If the perp is not Frank Hagen, who is it?"

Sara looked at him seriously. "What if it's a woman?"

Quintana looked at Sara with surprise.

"A woman?" he repeated. "What makes you think that?"

"I don't think anything, I'm just asking. In purely practical terms, it wouldn't be impossible for a woman to commit the murders. Erika Bergman's throat was cut, which is completely possible for a strong woman, and Luísa Hagen was first struck on the head, then tied to a bed and stabbed multiple times in the abdomen. A woman could also manage that."

"The murders do both seem to be about birth," Suarez added. "The arrangements are studied and refined. We're dealing with an extremely uncommon murderer. There is a carefully thought-out plan, and the theme feels female in a way."

"I don't think we should get locked in to a male perpetrator is all I'm saying," Sara said.

"Take it easy now. You're not leading this investigation. But maybe you're right," Quintana said at last. "Maybe it is a woman we're looking for."

Sara ignored Quintana's comment. "What women are in both Luísa Hagen's circle and Erika Bergman's?"

"Just so you know, you're not writing a word about this—so far these are only speculations," Quintana said sternly. "Keep in mind that you are neither a police officer nor part of the investigation team. If you don't keep quiet about this you won't find out a thing more from me, and I don't care about the consequences. We're hunting a dangerous double murderer and you could expose yourself to danger if you're not careful."

"Take it easy. I'm not writing anything about this," Sara assured him. "Not yet, at least. But if you're trying to find connections between the victims, there is another possibility."

"What's that?" Suarez asked.

"There's a massage institute in Playa del Inglés called Lotus Massage," Sara said. "Have you investigated it?"

Quintana shook his head. "Not that I know of."

"Frank Hagen is evidently involved with it in some way, but not on paper; there's nothing registered anywhere. He has a financial interest in the massage institute and apparently many of the guests at the yoga center go there to buy sex during a massage treatment."

Quintana stared at her in astonishment. "Where did you hear this?"

"As a journalist I protect my sources."

"Fine. So how can I take this seriously if you don't give me more?"

Sara told him briefly about going to El Pajar to search for scallops and finding the business card from Samsara Soul with the number of the massage center jotted down on the back.

Quintana turned toward Luísa Hagen's dead body. "Maybe we were too quick to release your husband. Maybe we were."

57

Earlier

The small truck braked and turned a short distance onto the dry ground before backing up toward the house. The driver put on the parking brake, opened the door, and got out. He opened the tailgate, leaned in, and picked up a box, which he handed over to David, who was standing waiting. The sun was high in the sky, and the temperature had climbed to over a hundred degrees. David's clothes stuck to his body, and sweat was running down his face, making his eyes sting. He dried his face with his sleeve and carried the box up to the house where Adriana was unlocking the front door. Inside it was dark. There was thick dust along the windowsills and floor as though no one had been there for years. She went in and opened the shutters to air it out.

"It's nice here," she said when David came in with yet another box, which he set down on the floor near the wall.

David looked questioningly at her. He didn't understand why she felt she had to lie. She didn't even try to sound convincing, said it only as if they were words without meaning, as if the words would take care of themselves after she'd said them. They didn't; they died as soon as he heard them.

"Why do we have to move?"

"David, we've talked about it. Samsara—"

"His name's Frank, Mama."

"He needs a little time alone. It hasn't been easy for him, what happened with the baby."

"Why don't you ever talk about yourself? Or me? It's always him you're worried about. It's as if you and I don't feel anything. It hasn't been easy for us either," said David.

"I know it hasn't been easy for you . . ."

He looked at her, and his young face became more serious than usual. "What you're saying is that we have to move out of the house because Frank is sad that the baby died."

"Something like that," she said, stroking his hair. "Samsara was just going to finish a yoga class, and then he'll come and help out. We have to paint, but first I'm going to clean."

David stood and looked at her as she walked around the room like a ghost. He'd never seen her like this before; she was present but also . . . not. Her fingers wiped the dust from the molding, and the dust particles danced like stars in the living room when they were caught by the sun coming in through the window.

David went outside and walked to the truck, where the driver had taken out the rest of the boxes, now standing stacked on the little gravel patch in front of the cottage.

"I have another move. I can help with the couch, but the rest you'll have to manage yourself. It's not that much."

David nodded without saying anything, just took hold and lifted.

Adriana stood in the door and watched David push the couch against the wall. They'd gotten it from someone who didn't want it anymore.

It was shabby, and the fabric was faded and worn. David gave the piece of furniture a final shove before he stood up and turned toward her. Outside, the sky was burning in beautiful colors, as the setting sun painted the clouds red and orange.

"Will you help me with the last box?"

"Shouldn't Frank help out?" David asked.

"I'm sure he's busy over at the center," she answered vacantly. The words sounded false and hollow.

David looked around. The living room wasn't large. They'd acquired an old TV, which they set on a table in the corner. Along with the couch, it took up almost the whole room. There was also a small kitchen, and a bedroom they would share.

He got two bottles of water from the refrigerator and went out and sat on the steps. Adriana sat down next to him, and he gave her one.

"What's in the last box?"

"Things, your books."

He turned toward her.

"We don't have room," he said, and she could see in his eyes that he really wished they did have room for the books he loved to read and browse through. She didn't have the heart to discard them even though he'd said he didn't want to keep them. He'd packed the things in his room, the souvenirs, the pictures he'd had on the wall, his favorite shirt—everything he didn't need but still depended on. The things that had made him the person he was. He would sit on the bed and look at a book, even one he'd read many times before. Just to experience the paper, the aroma, the memories that he himself had written down between the lines.

"I couldn't throw the box away," she said, putting an arm around him.

He was a thinner version of his father; he wore the gaze his father had always had, the dark eyes that flashed when he got angry or felt happy. Recently his eyes had burned with fury, with frustration.

"You can keep them under your bed."

He shook his head. "I don't need those things anymore."

He leaned forward and held his hands in front of him. Looked down at the ground.

"I'm not a child anymore. Frank offered me a job. He thinks it's time I support myself."

"You're too young to work. You have to stay in school!"

She took hold of his arm. David twisted out of her grasp and looked at her seriously.

"And who's going to pay for me to go to school? You?"

Adriana leaned against his shoulder, and he put an arm around her.

"I'm sorry," she said. "I haven't been the mama you need."

David shook his head and clenched his jaw. He had nothing to say.

58

It was unusual that it wasn't windy in San Cristóbal, a place most people simply drove past en route to Las Palmas. As a rule the water crashed against the high wall that protected the beach promenade with such frenzy that you almost took it personally. But today the forces of nature had left the little town in peace.

Although the big city of Las Palmas loomed on the horizon, there were people in San Cristóbal who had never set foot there. They were born, lived, and died in the quiet neighborhood by the sea, which seemed completely unaffected by the metropolis only a few miles away. Here they had everything they needed: cafés, restaurants, fish from the sea, love, and community. The inhabitants lived like a family, and San Cristóbal was their home. It was as if the village didn't want life to change. Some people thought that was the very thing that made the little suburb of Las Palmas unique—the lack of desire for change.

It was calm and quiet where Kristian sat with yesterday's edition of the Norwegian newspaper *Aftenposten* and a beer in the sun outside Mar Cantábrico. The sun painted his dark shadow on the rough yellow wall behind him. The red plastic chairs and tables, faded after years in the sun, balanced on thin legs on the uneven ground. They took an involuntary dance step every time he set the bottle on the table or turned a page.

The Norwegian newspapers had given extensive coverage to the murders of Erika Bergman and Luísa Hagen, and pictures of the two victims had adorned the front pages the past few days. Kristian had read the Norwegian news on the Internet, but now he could read a print newspaper, which someone had left behind at the consulate.

The sun was still high in the sky, and he felt its heat from behind his sunglasses.

The first time he'd come to San Cristóbal he'd been fascinated by the different colors of the buildings, which were like a chain stretching out to the sea. The salt-drenched damp had given them a rustic character. He'd heard they were painted the same colors as the fishing boats, so even out at sea a fisherman could see his home, where his family was waiting.

Kristian didn't own a boat, but he'd thought about painting the Vespa the same light blue as the facade of his building. At the moment, though, he had other things to think about.

"You haven't been around lately."

Kristian raised his eyes from the newspaper.

"Hola, Jorge," he said, pointing at the chair beside him, to invite the old artist to sit down. "I've had my hands full."

Jorge raised his hands self-deprecatingly. "You're reading the newspaper, I won't disturb you."

"It's no problem. The paper's a day old anyway."

"Has the world really become so small that it's uninteresting after only one day?" said Jorge, sitting down. "Is that a Norwegian newspaper?"

Kristian nodded.

He'd met Jorge soon after his move to San Cristóbal. Kristian had been sitting at the same table as he was now, looking out over the sea, and Jorge had started talking with him. He made art out of plastic bottles, mobiles that moved and twirled on their own axis in the wind. Kristian bought one of them and hung it up on his balcony.

Jorge placed his hat on his knee and pulled his hand through his gray mop of hair. He had unusually thick hair, which in a peculiar way made him look younger. As if his hair had only changed color but hadn't followed suit with the rest of him as he grew older. He wore a gray jacket made of thick fabric. He'd sewn it himself. On the outside it looked rather ordinary, apart from the red silk cloth that stuck out of the breast pocket. But on the inside he had sewn various pockets: one for pens and brushes, a larger one for a sketch pad, another that had room for a watercolor pad, a box of watercolors, and a pocket camera. Jorge had shown him the jacket the first time they met, when he took out the sketch pad and drew Kristian's portrait in soft pencil.

"It's so I'll remember your face," he'd said and presented the portable studio inside his jacket. The sketch, on the other hand, he'd never shown him.

"You look worn out. May I get you a beer?" He didn't wait for Kristian to answer, simply waved to Maria, who ran the bar, and held two fingers in the air. "It's not good to think too much, believe me. I've often gotten headaches from less."

"Thanks," said Kristian, emptying his bottle as Maria set two fresh Tropicals on the table.

"No problem," said Jorge, raising the bottle in a toast. "I've just finished an installation that will be delivered next week, and I got a good advance. It's going to be mounted on the roof of a school. Young people need art."

"Do they?" Kristian asked absently, while his thoughts were somewhere else altogether.

"Of course, art reflects our society, our relationships, and thoughts. It tries to tell us something about life. And death. I would say that everything is art."

Kristian folded up the newspaper and looked at Jorge. What he'd said awakened something in him.

"What do you mean by that?"

"Art is culturally determined by the society we live in," Jorge answered enthusiastically when he noticed Kristian's interest. "Now, of course, you can maintain that art has no value outside itself."

"I don't maintain anything," Kristian replied. "My dad taught art and worked for many years at the National Museum in Oslo."

"It pleases me that you come from a civilized home." Jorge chuckled contentedly. "What I mean is that an artist creates a mirror image of reality that gives it a purpose. For that reason everything is art."

"Everything?" Kristian nodded at the portrait of the two victims on the front page of the newspaper. "Even murder?"

"I thought we were talking about art in general terms," Jorge replied. "Art in the general sense is about life. And death. I've heard that the perpetrator arranged his victims according to known artworks. I've read about murders that were arranged to make people think someone else did it. Perhaps this perpetrator is doing that, too."

"I have to admit that I don't quite follow you."

"The Norwegian painter Munch painted his sister on her deathbed. The stripes in the painting, which he made with a fork, show his tears. So when you look at the painting, *The Sick Child*, you see her through Munch's eyes. Perhaps the killer wants you to see the murders as he sees them. Maybe he wants you to understand why he did it and in that way say that it's really someone else who is guilty, someone who drove him to commit the murders."

Jorge took his bottle from the table and finished it.

"Another?" he asked.

Kristian observed the almost-empty bottle he was holding and nodded.

"Thanks, with pleasure. You won't live long on nothing but food and water."

"Very Hemingwayesque," said Jorge, waving to Maria.

Kristian smiled, impressed by the old artist.

The sea started to move restlessly, and soon the wind would pick up. Kristian thought about Erika Bergman and Luísa Hagen and what Jorge had said.

A feeling of worry came over him. A feeling of regret at not being able to be a father, about leaving his job in Oslo. But somehow this was good, too; he felt something that had been missing before in his life, small bits of value. It made him feel that he was alive, that he was breathing with his whole body. There had been so many times when he'd sat at home staring indifferently at the wall.

Kristian cast a glance at Jorge, who was taking a drink from his bottle of beer. The artist reminded him of the character he'd pictured when he'd read Ernest Hemingway's *The Old Man and the Sea*. He had a face formed by life, with deep furrows cut in his forehead and lines across the eyes and nose, like the roads and paths he'd taken. People he'd met, events that had made an impression. The sea and the wind, the sand and the memories he couldn't escape, but which had taken root and become part of him.

Behind the face that life had granted Jorge, Kristian could sense the young, attractive man he had once been.

Kristian reached for the bottle Maria had set on the table and let his gaze rest on the horizon. Would anyone be able to read his life in his face when he got older? Kristian sighed, but not because he felt sad or resigned. Something inside him was released—a thought. He was happy to be alive. Not necessarily because of how things were going for him right now or how they had gone in the past. He was simply grateful to exist.

And it was still calm out on the sea. The calm before the storm.

59

Sara came home late that evening. Both of the kids were sleeping over at friends', so she and Lasse were alone. He'd made dinner and opened a bottle of wine. When she saw the table set and the lanterns lit on the terrace and heard the subdued music, she felt deep gratitude for her husband. Just as she had so many times before.

"Sit down," he said tenderly, filling her glass.

"Thanks, darling. This is just what I needed."

She looked hungrily at the table where Lasse's homemade Skagen toast waited. Hand-peeled shrimp with black cod roe, dill, and lemon in a mustard mayonnaise on sautéed bread. Sara's mouth watered, and she suddenly realized just how hungry she was. It had been a long day, and all the responsibility on her shoulders was wearing her out. In two days Hugo would be back and she couldn't wait. The long, intense workdays were starting to take a toll. At the same time she felt recharged. She couldn't remember ever being so involved in a case. Every moment she was consumed in thought about the murders.

She was also pleased that the major tabloid in Stockholm was satisfied with her work and encouraging her to continue covering the story. But it wasn't just about the extra work, or the recognition. Sara loved the pulse, the intensity, the hunt for a story, finding out more. She probably should have worked for a pure news operation, but she didn't handle stress well. It was best for her as it was. Working on *Day & Night* she could use her creativity and direct the content without having to adapt to other people's rules or having a boss telling her what to do.

Although she was tired and would rather talk about something else, it wasn't long before their conversation turned to the sensational murders. Sara told Lasse the latest about Frank Hagen and his involvement in the massage place in Playa del Inglés.

"It's called Lotus Massage—have you heard of it?"

"No," said Lasse, getting up to clear the appetizer plates. "Keep talking. I'm listening. Just wanted to put the steaks on the grill."

"Women at the yoga center are referred there for massage treatments. Then they're offered something called massage erótico, something tantra-like, which is supposed to stimulate sexuality. Guess there's nothing wrong with that as long as they stick to massage. The problem is that they cross the line, and when the massage gets intense, the customers are offered sex for extra payment. Apparently it's encouraged by Frank Hagen, but it's completely off the books. He's not registered as a part-owner or employee anywhere. Some shady Canarians own the place. I was there myself yesterday and tried to ferret out a few things."

"So you got a massage from one of those guys?" He turned from the grill and gave her a teasing look.

"It was a way to get in and try to get information," she said, rolling her eyes. "The guy massaged my back and neck, nothing else—that I can guarantee. But I was actually offered massage erótico."

"As long as the masseur stuck to massage maybe that would've been a good idea. It would've been interesting to see the effect . . ."

He grinned as he set the salad bowl on the table.

"Ha-ha, very funny," Sara said sarcastically.

Their sex life wasn't great of late; she couldn't even remember when they'd last slept together. Recently her desire for Lasse had declined alarmingly. Maybe she was too stressed and had too much to think about. Maybe it was age or just the fact that they'd been together so long.

"So you think the massage place could have something to do with the murders?"

"It's not impossible. Both of the women who were murdered were close to Frank Hagen."

"Are the police sure it's the same perpetrator?"

"Yes, I think so. The murder weapon appears to be the same. Both victims were killed with a knife and both were arranged according to different paintings. Both were young and beautiful, and the perpetrator seems to have used an equally precise, studied method in both cases."

Lasse observed her with interest. "And how do you know all this?"

Sara cleaned the rest of her plate. "I have good contacts with the police."

"That's very impressive. Is it that Quintana?"

"You guessed right."

"I'm going to get dinner," he said. "But first, tell me what makes him tell you so much. I mean, I know he likes you. No one can help noticing that."

"Oh, knock it off," Sara said, feeling to her dismay that she was blushing. She reached for her wineglass.

"Good Lord, Sara, come on. Every time we see him he acts like a schoolboy around you."

"Now you're exaggerating."

"Not at all, and you know that as well as I do. But that can't be enough for him to reveal so much to you. What kind of hold do you have on him?"

"None at all. That's just silly. Maybe he does have a little crush on me, but I guess he's allowed to. It doesn't mean anything. He's never tried anything, if that's what you think. And if it benefits my work, I guess it's just fine."

"Sure, darling. If you say so."

Sara observed her husband as he skillfully set the steaks and baked potatoes on the plates. He was security, a good friend—but when had she last felt any kind of tingle?

They ate, and the conversation flowed as usual, without difficulty, practiced and familiar. She knew pretty much what he was going to say and think. With irritation she pushed her thoughts aside; she had far too much on her mind right now to reflect on her marriage. She stuffed yet another piece of steak into her mouth.

"And what's the next step in the murder cases?" Lasse asked after a while.

"We've started thinking that it could be a female perpetrator."

"Why not?" he said, taking a sip of wine. "It doesn't sound impossible. And Adam Fors was ruled out, thank God."

"Yes, it was a relief that it wasn't him. It wouldn't have been good to have a double murderer staying at the hotel. Not just because it would feel unpleasant, but there would have been a big risk of scaring away guests."

"Agreed," said Lasse. "I'm glad it wasn't him, but a woman? Are there women who were close to the victims?"

"I don't know," Sara said with a sigh. "Erika Bergman was on a yoga vacation, and Luísa Hagen seems to have lived a very isolated life near the yoga center. Both seem to have stayed in Tasarte for the most part."

"Have you talked to other residents in the area, looked at the women who live out there?" Lasse suggested. "Someone who's been lying low so far, but who is right in the vicinity?"

Sara gave him a long look.

60

Adriana stood looking out the window while the coffeemaker hissed. It was already getting dark outside. She was thinking that the darkness seemed to come earlier than before. The narrow road between the trees went down toward the yoga center. Not long before, she'd heard someone laughing loudly, but now she heard no voices. She picked up the coffeepot and poured a cup. She missed talk and laughter. There'd been so little of that in recent years, as if joy had died for her as she got older.

She'd seen the bus as it drove off with the guests, seen the outlines of the people. That's how they saw her, she thought: a quiet shadow along the wall, an outline of a person. No one really noticed her; she was just there. She missed the children, Adalia and Jonatan. But Samsara wouldn't say when they'd be coming home.

This wasn't how she'd thought it would be after Luísa's death. The children needed her. She was the source of security that could fill the vacuum now that their mother was gone. But no one seemed to understand that. The grandparents picked up the children without even asking if they wanted to go with them, as if their needs weren't important, as if they were forgotten. But she hadn't forgotten.

Every morning she'd stood and watched them go to school. Adalia always carried her backpack over her right shoulder, and Jonatan galloped across the road as if he were looking forward to a new day. She wiped a tear from the corner of her eye. Now only she and the silence were left.

Adriana had been there most of the time, taking care of the family's housekeeping. Every day, year in and year out. She'd cleared the table after breakfast, washed plates and tableware, put the fixings in the refrigerator, wiped the table. Then she would clean floors, put things away, make the beds. The double bed in the big bedroom, with the smells and sounds that still hung in the walls. Sometimes she sat on the mattress, felt the sheets against her palm. Closed her eyes and thought that it was warm, like when two bodies hold each other. Then she got up and went to make the beds in the children's room.

Every evening when she was done cleaning and making dinner she went home to her solitude. She'd accepted the situation. It was as if she no longer had a will of her own. No steam. It had gradually been taken from her over the years.

Sometimes he would come to her place, remind her that she was loved. Often he wanted her to console him, and she did that because he made her feel like a woman again. Those stolen moments made her raise her head and straighten up when she went past the mirror.

During the last few days he'd needed her even more. He didn't want to talk, just sat on the edge of the bed and watched as she undressed before he took her. But it was as if he didn't see her, not really. That was all he would give her. Still, she was grateful that he needed her. It wasn't much, but it was something. Something she could cling to when he left and she was alone again.

A movement outside the window down by the gravel road made her stop. She stood with her back against the wall and heard him coming up the road, heard the gravel crunching under his shoes, his steps on the stairs. There was pounding on the door. At first politely, like he usually did, and then harder.

Hesitantly she unlocked and opened the door. Terrified, she took a step back when she saw the two uniformed police officers outside.

"Are you Adriana Gonzalez?" one said.

She nodded.

"We want you to come with us."

61

Kristian stepped into the small offices of *Day & Night* in San Agustín. He was carrying two cups of espresso and handed one to Sara, who was sitting at her desk with her gaze fixed on the computer screen. By this point he'd learned how she liked her coffee. Sara took it gratefully.

"Was it easy finding my little back street?" she asked.

"To be honest, I had to ask someone. It wasn't that simple. It's nice in here," he said, looking around appreciatively.

"Thanks. It's nothing special, but it works. Sit yourself down," she said with a gesture toward the visitor's couch. "I'm just going to finish this article for *Aftonbladet.*"

"Maybe you'd like to hear what's happened first?" Kristian said, sinking down on the well-used couch. "Or with your police sources, maybe you already know?"

"No, I don't think so," said Sara, looking up. "What is it?"

"I just stopped by the Policía Nacional in Playa del Inglés. I had some papers to turn in. I talked with an inspector there I know slightly, Javier Herrera—do you know him?"

Sara shook her head.

"He told me that they brought in a woman last night. She'd just been arrested and was accompanied by several police officers from the Guardia Civil. They were actually on their way to Las Palmas, but she had some kind of breakdown so they stopped in Playa del Inglés so she could calm down. Herrera didn't know what it was about, but do you know where the woman came from?"

"No," Sara said eagerly.

"From Tasarte. She apparently lives right by the yoga center."

Sara stared at Kristian in amazement. The thought of what her husband had said at the dinner table the night before flickered past. Maybe Lasse was right.

"Who is she?" she asked. "Why haven't we heard anything about her?"

Kristian shrugged. "I don't know, and the police haven't said a word about anyone else living there or nearby. Unfortunately I didn't get her name. He didn't know it."

"Why hasn't Quintana said anything about her?"

"That probably means one thing: that she's considered a hot lead, and the police don't want to risk leaking it because it would harm the investigation."

"I have to call Quintana," Sara mumbled, reaching for the phone.

"Do you always do that? Jump on the phone and disturb people as soon as you think of something? Don't you think Quintana has other things to do? He's probably questioning her right now." Kristian shook his head. "If I were Quintana I'd have you arrested and held until the investigation was over, just to get some peace."

"You're right," Sara said with a small sigh, leaning back in her chair. "But who is she? Is she Canarian?"

"From what I understood she's not a tourist. But what connection she has to the yoga center—if she even has one—I don't know. Maybe she just lives nearby."

"Interesting. We were just saying that a woman could be behind the murders. The question is, what connection does she have to the victims?"

"Maybe she's just a mentally disturbed person who lives there and chose the victims at random."

"But if that were the case the victims wouldn't have been arranged like they were, and why take the trouble to murder Erika Bergman in the middle of Arguineguín. She could just as well have done it in Tasarte where the risk of being discovered wasn't as great."

"Okay, but maybe it was a false lead. Maybe she wanted to confuse the police."

Kristian finished his coffee and looked questioningly at Sara. "What is it with you and Quintana actually? Why does he reveal so much to you? He releases information to you, lets you into the forensic medicine department. Why is that?"

"Oh, he just likes me," Sara answered evasively, realizing she was blushing.

"Come on," Kristian persisted. "It can't be that simple. Tell me—what kind of hold do you have on him? If you tell me, I'll tell you a secret."

Sara observed him attentively. They hadn't known each other long, but she had already gained confidence in the somewhat slovenly ex-cop from Norway. He had a tousled, shabby charm that was hard for her to resist. She realized that she was starting to really like Kristian.

"Okay, but this stays between us—understood? Not even my husband knows about this."

"I'm listening," said Kristian, taking out his snuff box and pressing a pouch under his lip.

"Quintana has a daughter who's about twenty-five. Five years ago she got into serious trouble. She was partying a lot and involved with drugs. During that time there was a big problem with drugs being sold to Scandinavian young people here on vacation. I was doing a series of articles about that. While I was working on it I came in contact with a gang that was selling narcotics, mainly to adolescent tourists. One of the dealers was Quintana's daughter. I knew him from before, so I contacted him when her name came up."

"Did he know about it?"

"No. He'd noticed she'd started partying more, but he had no idea about the drug dealing."

"What happened?"

"He asked me not to contact the police, so I didn't. I wrote my series anyway, of course. Quintana sent his daughter to the mainland and as far as I know she got off drugs. I don't think she's used since."

"So you might say that you saved her? Both from drugs and the police?"

"If she'd been arrested it would have meant a multiyear prison sentence. Who knows how it would have ended."

"Didn't you have any ethical problems with it? She was selling drugs to teenagers, after all. Shouldn't she have been punished?"

"Maybe, but what good would that have done? The drugs were already sold, and who would it help for a young girl to end up in prison? In hindsight it was probably the best that could have happened. I don't have any qualms about it."

"So Quintana owes you?"

"I wouldn't put it that way. I've never asked anything in return. And I don't think for a moment that he would reveal details that would jeopardize an investigation or that wouldn't have leaked out anyway. It's just that I get to know things a little sooner than everyone else."

62

Frank noticed the suspicious looks at once when he entered the grocery store in Tasarte. People who usually greeted him, and who just days before had expressed their condolences for what had happened, now watched him slyly. He could see in their faces that they thought he'd done it, that he was the one who'd murdered Luísa.

He'd shopped here ever since he moved to Tasarte fifteen years earlier. At first he'd traded fruit for goods or shopped on credit when he didn't have money. In time he'd gotten to know the store owner, Julio, fairly well. Sometimes they even went out for beers together.

The fact that the police had repeatedly brought him in for questioning made his neighbors look at him askance. It didn't matter that he had an alibi, that one of the guests at the yoga center, Teresa, had told the police that he spent the early morning hours in her bed. That the police no longer considered him a suspect held no significance. In the eyes of the villagers, he was a murderer.

He had always been a respected man. With his yoga center he'd helped both the bakery and grocery store blossom. Customers streamed into the little village. Starting with two empty hands he'd built up the operation at the yoga center, made it work, contributed to the continued existence of the village, and eventually renovated his house to be the nicest villa in the whole valley.

There were always those who begrudged him what he had created, and he could live with that. But this was something else completely. The solid silence and the fact that the villagers—his neighbors and former friends—avoided him and talked behind his back hurt. They didn't even try to conceal their loathing. Even without saying a word they openly revealed what they felt and thought.

He picked up a few cans of corn and tuna in oil and set them in the basket with lettuce, tomatoes, and a red pepper. He would not let himself be broken, would not let the rumors swirling around the village force him to close himself up in the house. To hide as if he had something to conceal.

"Hola," he said as a woman passed him.

She turned her eyes away and continued walking, without a word. He noticed that she walked over to the checkout stand and talked quietly with the owner. Frank observed them out of the corner of his eye while he pretended to search for something on the shelf. The owner gestured indignantly, and the woman set down her basket of goods with a sharp thud. Julio shook his head and looked over at Frank, who was just putting a large jar of olives in his basket.

"Samsara!"

Julio waved him over. Frank paused.

"I thought everyone had stopped talking to me," he said sarcastically.

Julio needed to understand that he was master of the situation, that he didn't need to bend.

"I'm losing customers, Samsara." Julio threw out his hands. "I don't believe everything they're saying about you. I know you too well, but they won't shop here, and I have a family to support."

"What are you trying to say?" Frank noticed how his throat thickened; it was hard to swallow.

"For the sake of old friendship," Julio said, taking him by the arm. "Can't you shop somewhere else, at least until everything blows over? You know I don't want—"

"You mean I'm not welcome in your store anymore?" Frank felt himself getting agitated.

"Por favor," Julio said, gesturing for him to cool down while he nervously looked around, smiled at someone walking past with their bags. "For my family's sake."

Frank looked around, met the silent, accusing looks of other customers. It was a silence that hurt. It hit him like a pain in the gut. He looked down in his shopping basket. The cans of corn and tuna, the vegetables and the olives.

"I've shopped here since your children were little," he said quietly. "Our children play together. I've meant something to the community here . . ."

"Just until everything settles down," Julio said, placing a hand on his shoulder, trying to steer him to the exit. "You don't need to pay for what you have in the basket, it's okay."

Frank followed along. The basket weighed heavily in his hand, and his steps were laborious. He stopped when Julio opened the door.

"I didn't do it," he said. "I miss her. The kids and I—"

"I understand, Frank. I just need the basket. You can't keep that."

Frank stared at the basket in his hand and his fingers that clung fast to the handle. He saw how they let go and the basket fell down on the steps. It clattered against the concrete and down the stairs, where it stayed, the cans of corn rolling down the road and the jar of olives broken on the ground.

"That was unnecessary," said Julio, and Frank could hear that he was trying to maintain control.

Frank didn't bother to respond. He walked out to his car, which was parked by the side of the road. Didn't turn around, decided that he would never turn around again, never look back.

He stood with the key in his hand. A little beep was heard from the car as he opened it. He noticed that someone had made large scratches in the paint on the hood and across the doors. Fury shot up inside him, but he clenched his teeth, got in, and drove away. Away from what had once been familiar and safe.

Life had turned its back on him.

63

The window was cracked open, and it was cool in the room. Adriana lay on her bed, staring at the ceiling. She was back from the police station. It had been incredibly trying. Two detectives asked a lot of questions she didn't understand or know the answers to. They'd asked her whether she'd been in Arguineguín, but she hadn't. They asked whether she could confirm that, but she couldn't. They confused her. Showed her pictures she didn't want to see, black rocks by the sea, a beautiful woman with light hair sleeping with her eyes open. Luísa naked and bloody on a bed out in a field. They asked questions she didn't want to hear, much less answer. She only wanted to get out of there. And finally they let her go. By then she'd been gone for quite a few hours and it was night. She was shaken and had a hard time sleeping. She woke up late and stayed in bed all day. She still felt nauseated. And she was alone with her worried thoughts.

She clasped her hands in prayer, but she didn't pray, wanting only to close up inside herself, as if nothing existed outside. It hurt knowing that David was out there somewhere without her knowing where he was or how he was doing.

He'd begun to withdraw from her after he started working in Playa del Inglés. Samsara had arranged a job for him, and at first she'd been grateful. Heaven knows how hard it was for a young person to get a job these days. It started with him coming home late, eating the food she'd set out for him, and then going to bed. Then he stopped eating, only pushed the plate away and sat at the table without saying anything.

He'd started openly showing his loathing when Samsara would come to visit and ask him to leave for an hour. Adriana always went into the bedroom, undressed, and lay down on the bed.

She remembered the very last time.

After Samsara left her, David came back in, didn't bother finishing his food, and simply went to bed. He turned his back on her and refused to answer when spoken to. In the morning when she woke up, he was gone.

Adriana looked out the window. She remembered it as if it were yesterday, even though it had been some time ago. David took off and then she was alone in the little house.

The sun gleamed in the window. Adriana pushed off the covers and got up. She tried to avoid her reflection in the mirror as she went into the bathroom. She didn't understand why the police had taken her. The questions they asked made her confused, and she had a vague feeling that her answers were incoherent and meaningless. She thought of the light hair against the black rocks. *Like an angel of God,* she thought. After a few hours they let her go, insisting on driving her back to Tasarte even though she would rather have taken the bus. Adriana felt ashamed when the police followed her to the door. She wanted more than anything not to let them into the house, and as luck would have it they didn't ask to come in.

When she locked the door behind her she noticed that the police had been there anyway. They'd gone through drawers and cupboards, moved her things.

She turned on the faucet in the sink and let the hot water run between her fingers. She held her hands under the stream of water as long as she was able. The mirror fogged up. In the glass, a foreign gaze stared back at her. She bowed her head and put her hand on the mirror, drew her fingers over the smooth surface. The water formed small pearls and slowly ran down and gathered like a little pond on the sink.

Suddenly she was crying, sobbing. She felt how it started in her stomach and welled up into her chest. Waves of pain that wanted out. And she knew, when she bit herself on the hand so as not to scream out loud, that she had to hold back, could not let it break her. She had to pull herself together.

Adriana rinsed off her face, dried her tears, and went out into the kitchen.

On the kitchen counter there was a dead rabbit on a plate. It was bloody and not even skinned. Samsara must have brought it earlier in the day. He wanted her to make dinner for him.

At first when she and David moved out of the big house, Adriana hoped that Samsara would still have dinner with them, that they would try to be a family despite everything. Then perhaps in time he would want them to move back in. That he wouldn't bother with his other women and would care only about her. She still kept faith that one day he would see only her. That she hadn't waited for him in vain.

She took hold of the knife that was on the kitchen counter, drew her thumb over the edge to check how sharp it was. She opened the window above the counter before she let the knife slide in under the neck skin to loosen the rabbit's fur.

Then she set the edge of the knife against one front leg and pressed. A cracking sound as the knife hit the cutting board.

She remembered standing in the house where they lived together, looking at the sea. She loved that house, the view from the big windows, the garden where she grew herbs and vegetables. Samsara stood right behind her, with his hands on her hips. She'd been so happy. She worked the knife in under the loose skin by the throat and let it glide along the belly. The knife was sharp and cut through skin and fur in one slice.

Why had he treated her so badly? She'd loved him, higher and deeper than she'd dared at first. When they'd met, she'd wanted to wait, take it easy. Let the grief for her deceased husband settle down. For her sake and for David's. But Samsara had gone down on his knee before her, sworn that he'd never loved anyone so much.

She took hold of the skin and pulled the dark coat down over the meager meat. Heard it tearing loose from the body. She remembered the car ride from the hospital, the baby they'd lost, their little daughter who never got to go home with them. The nursery they'd set up, happy and expectant. Samsara had painted it white, the color of purity. Adriana would have had the child in her arms as they drove home, not sat with her hands in her lap. She'd left part of herself behind at the hospital. She stared at the mangled rabbit on the kitchen counter and thought about her dead child.

The knife loosened the tendons from the skin and she butchered the animal, cut off the head in one stroke before she threw it in the sink. She started cutting up the rabbit.

She'd been completely empty inside when they came home from the hospital. David disappeared up to his room, sat and cried behind a book. She lay down on the bed and stared at the ceiling. Nothing would ever be the same.

Adriana felt a strong pressure across her chest as she stood there in the kitchen, and she had a hard time breathing. A sudden pain made her stop, gasping for air. The rabbit was shredded into small pieces across the kitchen counter. It was completely destroyed. The meat was cut apart, and in the bloody mess her hand was trembling. She stood and looked at the remnants of the animal. She staggered backward, lost the feeling in her legs, collapsed on the floor, her back against the cupboard door, the knife between her quivering fingers before she let go of it.

"Por dios," she panted.

It had been a long time since she sought solace with God.

And it was a long time since God had seen her. She was only one of all the shadows that crept around alone on the earth.

64

Kristian poked a pinch of snuff under his lip and then got out of his car where it was parked in front of his home on the street in San Cristóbal and locked it. It had been a long workday.

The wind was blowing briskly in from the sea. He closed his eyes and drew in the salt air. Felt how it cleansed him inside. Blew away everything that had settled in there like dirty dust. The murders of the two women had pursued him home from work; the images branded in his memory didn't go away when he went to bed at night. Luísa's dead gaze as she lay there on the big iron bed, the blood that colored the thin mattress dark. Erika's hair playing in the wind down by the rocks, the slit throat. He knew the images would haunt him for years to come.

He stood with the key in his hand, about to unlock the front door, when he stopped. The door was slightly open. He looked up at the window that faced the street and thought he sensed movement. He turned cold inside. His first thought was that someone had broken in and that it had to do with the murders. He remembered what Sara had told him about the massage place. Maybe they'd been rooting around in something that was dangerous for both of them.

"Damn," he exclaimed out loud. He'd left all the notes about the murders in a folder on the living room table.

Some children were playing out on the street; otherwise it was calm. Unconsciously he held his breath, carefully pushed open the door, and went in. The Vespa was in the hall, but he immediately saw that someone had moved the engine parts. The can of oil was behind the front wheel, and the sheet the parts had been lying on was folded up next to it. He took a few cautious steps toward the stairs and looked up, but he couldn't see anyone. Under the stairs he found a big wrench, which he took with him.

With wrench in hand he slipped carefully up the stairs with his back against the wall, crouching down as he approached the landing. Kristian noticed that the door to the bedroom was open, and he heard someone moving in there. His grip around the wrench tightened as he came upstairs. He moved as quietly and smoothly as he could across the room and stopped beside the open bedroom door. He quickly looked around. The folder of documents about the murder cases wasn't on the living room table where he'd left it. But neither were the plates of leftovers or the beer bottles and glasses that had been on the table when he left. For a moment he wondered if he'd cleaned up himself. Then he noticed that the images of the paintings he'd taped up on the wall were also missing. He threw himself around the doorframe with the wrench raised over his head, ready to strike. At the last moment he stopped.

In front of him stood a short, plump, older Canarian woman with her hair in a bun and an apron around her waist. He stood paralyzed and stared stupidly as she set a laundry basket down on the floor and turned toward him. She looked at him skeptically.

"You mustn't frighten an old woman like me," she said reproachfully, taking a white sheet out of the basket. "Help me put this on the bed. You can take the other side."

She had an authoritative voice, and with her glasses sliding down on her nose, she reminded him of a teacher he'd had in middle school.

He lowered his arm but couldn't bring himself to say anything. He could not for the life of him understand what was going on in his home.

"You have made a bed before, or is this the first time?" She put her hands on her hips and shook her head. "Wouldn't surprise me. Didn't your parents teach you anything? Or your wife, if you even have one?"

"Who are you?" Kristian looked around, uncertain of what he was searching for. "What are you doing here?"

"It's pretty obvious what I'm doing here," the woman said. "I'm doing something you should have done a long time ago. I'm cleaning."

Kristian stared at her. He was still completely perplexed.

"How did you get in?"

"Your neighbor was kind enough to let me in. I couldn't stand and wait for you forever. The dirty laundry needed to be washed and dried and I can't stay here all day. Take hold of the other side now," she said, pulling on the sheet.

Kristian set down the wrench and reached for the sheet.

"Did you say who you are?"

He tucked the sheet in under the mattress on his side without protesting. There was something in her manner that gave no alternative but to obey.

"I'm Aurora Moreno, but you can call me Señora Moreno. I think it's appropriate to address people by their surnames; first names are only for close friends, and a person doesn't have many of those, right?"

Kristian sat down on the bed. "Aurora . . ."

She cleared her throat, a clear warning.

"Señora Moreno, I really don't know how to put this . . . It's very nice that you've cleaned, done the laundry, hung clothes out on the veranda, and made the bed. But what are you doing here, really? And how did you get here?"

"I took the bus," she answered simply, fixing her eyes on him. "I am what you need more than anything else right now. A human being can't live in chaos. I'll come here once a week and do laundry and straighten up your home, and I'm starting today."

"I can't afford cleaning help," he protested.

"Of course you can," she answered, packing up her cleaning supplies and going into the living room. "What you can't afford is to let it stay the way it is now. You'll need to arrange for an extra key next week so I don't have to ask the neighbor every time I come here."

"Who came up with this idiotic idea? I'm managing just fine myself. I don't need someone to clean and pick up after me."

Señora Moreno turned around and looked sternly at him.

"You don't seem capable of deciding what you need. There is nothing more to discuss—*basta!*" She glanced at her watch. "Now my workday is over. I'll come next week as agreed. I've already been paid so you don't need to do that this time. Don't forget the extra key now."

She took a bucket, detergent, and a brush with her and went down the steps.

Kristian stood there watching her, incapable of producing a single word. Señora Moreno turned around halfway down the stairs.

"I've put the folder that was on the living room table in the bookcase, along with the pictures you taped on the wall. Get some frames, or at least use tacks. The tape was terrible to get off. You have no idea how long it took."

Then she disappeared down to the entry hall, where Kristian heard her put the cleaning things away under the stairs. The front door opened, and Señora Moreno disappeared from his life and his apartment, at least until next week.

Kristian felt completely confused. As he went into the bedroom to get the wrench he'd nearly attacked Señora Moreno with, the phone rang.

"What do you think?" Sara's voice said on the other end.

"Sorry, Sara, but I've just experienced something incredibly strange. I can't really process it, and I have to admit I have no idea what you're asking me about."

"Isn't she just amazing? Señora Moreno?"

"You don't mean you were the one who sent her here?"

"I gathered you needed a little help at home so I talked with your neighbor about letting her in . . . Admit it, if there's something that needs to be put in order, it's your apartment."

"I don't know, Sara . . . She reminds me of my mother."

"Ha-ha, you'll have to take that."

"Sara!" Kristian said.

"Now I have to run. We'll be in touch. What do you say about lunch tomorrow, your treat? I'll call you!"

She hung up before he had time to protest. Kristian sank down on the couch and couldn't help smiling. Señora Moreno was right: a person doesn't have many close friends.

65

The narrow gravel road that led up to the house awakened many memories in him. The trees grew densely along the road, and the leaves rustled lightly in the faint breeze from the sea. He could glimpse the remnants of the police tape at the end of the little road that led to the papaya field where they'd found Luísa. To the left in front of him was the yoga center. There were no sounds or movements behind the high wall. Before, the yoga classes would gather in the garden and do a last evening session, and then some students would go down to the little bar by the shore. Sauntering along the road they would talk loudly and laugh, but now it was completely deserted, as if someone had put a lid over the community. Nothing but the wind.

Far off he could make out the sea as a deep-blue stripe against the horizon. A solitary boat with white sails drifted along.

David dreaded seeing her again. It had been so long since they'd talked. But he felt compelled; he would have no peace until he tried. He saw the house at a distance as he approached. He remembered the first time he came here. You couldn't see the entire house from the road; it was in a small valley, so you could only see the roof tiles. It wasn't fully visible until you came down into the valley—the modest little cottage with the even smaller veranda, the fruit trees around it, and the windows that reflected the sky.

Adriana was sitting out on the steps peeling potatoes when David walked up. He slowed down, observed her. She seemed to hear his steps in the gravel and raised her head. She stood up, letting the bucket of potatoes remain on the steps. For a moment she seemed confused and then she went inside and closed the door, turned the key. David went up the steps and set his ear to the door, listened to her heavy breathing on the other side. He knocked, carefully at first, and then a little harder.

"Why do you do this every time I come?" he asked loudly so that he was sure she would hear.

"Because you don't exist," she answered, and he noticed how her voice was shaking. "You always come when I'm alone, when I miss you the most."

David sat on the steps, picked up the knife she'd set down beside the bucket, took a potato from the water, shook it, peeled it, and set it down with the others. It took a while before he heard her unlock the door behind him and the door slowly open. He remained seated and took another potato from the bucket. Her steps approached. For a moment it felt as if it were his own feet against the steps. As if he were coming closer to himself.

Adriana put one hand on the back of his neck; it felt cold and damp. He looked up at her, but she was staring out over the little lot around the house where many years ago she planted an herb garden. He remembered how she would give him a basket and ask him to go out and pick basil, sage, lemon balm. He'd take the basket under his arm and walk down the few steps, across the gravel, and crouch and smell the herbs while he carefully cut off bunches of the ones that smelled the best. He could sit there a long time, simply enjoying the aroma until she called to him, and he ran in again.

"It's lovely here in the evening," she said.

"It's lovely here," he answered, thinking about the first time they came here, how much he loathed it. How he sat and looked out over the landscape, how miserable he'd been, how he'd disliked every stone, every tree, every puff of wind.

Adriana sat down beside him. David could feel the warmth from her, and he put an arm around her.

"The police have been here," she said quietly, as if she still felt the shame on her skin.

"Did you say anything?"

"What would I say?"

She looked at him; there was something in his eyes.

"No," he answered. "What would you say?"

"You always come when it's starting to be twilight, do you know that?"

"Yes," David answered. "Always."

"Why is that?"

"You know why," he answered.

"For a while he didn't come often," she said. "But lately . . ." She fell silent midsentence and got a tormented look on her face. "He says he's missed me."

David didn't say anything. His lips narrowed, and he felt a pounding in his temples. The knife slipped on the slippery potato and the blade scratched his palm; he dropped the potato in the bucket and blood dripped down on the step.

She took his hand in hers and kissed it, got blood on her lips but didn't notice. Pressed a kitchen towel she had in her apron against the wound on his hand so that it would stop bleeding.

"Do you miss him?" David asked.

"If I say yes, will you forgive me?"

David didn't answer. Adriana set her head against his shoulder and closed her eyes. Smelled his aroma: burnt wood, salt water, and something indefinable that reminded her of how he had smelled as a boy. Something innocent, harmless, like buds that fall to the ground without blossoming.

"Do you remember when you disappeared?"

"And you thought I was dead?"

"You will always live inside me," she answered. A sudden fear that he would simply disappear made her hug him hard. "Will you stay with me now?"

"You know I can't," he answered, and she could hear the sorrow in his voice.

Adriana started when she heard steps approaching. She sat alone on the stairs. *I must have dozed off,* she thought. Down by the road Samsara appeared; his face had a worried expression she hadn't noticed before. She thought he looked old. The years had suddenly caught up with him.

He crouched down before her and took her hands in his. She felt cold, wanted to go in and leave the chill that had come into her. But she would always carry it with her. It simply lay there waiting until she was alone before it came creeping and placed itself in her arms like an infant that never got enough to eat.

"Shall we go in?" he asked.

"Maybe David wants to eat with us," she answered.

Samsara sighed. "We've talked about that, Adriana. David no longer comes here. You have to try to forget him."

"Are you sure of that?" she said, her voice trembling.

"I'm sure," he answered soothingly. "You're bleeding—did you bite your lip?"

He used a corner of his tunic and dabbed at her mouth carefully.

He picked up the bucket, took her by the arm, and followed her up the steps. He opened the door, but she hesitated. Searched among the dark trees that surrounded the gravel road.

"David left without saying anything. He was here with me before you came. I'm sure he's out there somewhere. Let me go!"

Samsara put his hands on her shoulders and pulled her to him, led her into the house, and closed the door behind them. Closed out the darkness, but what he'd never understood was that she carried it inside her. Inside her was a darkness that she couldn't close out.

66

Thursday, July 3

The first thing Kristian noticed when he was back at Sara's office the next morning was that she was sitting at the computer, crying. She was sobbing loudly, her shoulders shaking, so completely absorbed in herself that she didn't notice him come in. This woman was really strange. She seemed to vacillate wildly between various emotions; sometimes she was completely closed off, other times hypersensitive.

And what in the name of God was up with her now? Had something happened? Then he noticed that she was playing music again. By that singer she insisted on listening to at all times of the day. "Sun, Wind, and Water," the title, was on the screen, along with a cavalcade of images of the singer and short captions about his life.

Kristian peeked over her shoulder. On the monitor he read that the singer's name was Ted Gärdestad and that he'd died twenty years earlier, at only forty-one years old.

"What's the matter?" he asked, consolingly placing a hand on hers.

"It's so sad," Sara said, her voice thick with tears. "He wrote his first song when he was only six years old. Mozart also wrote his first symphony at the age of six."

"He was eight, and you can't compare Ted Gärdestad with Mozart," Kristian said.

"Just think, as a fifteen-year-old he was discovered by Björn and Benny from ABBA." Sara sniffled, as if she hadn't heard or didn't care what Kristian said. "Then it ended the way it did."

She raised one hand in the air. "Listen. Hear what he's singing."

Kristian sighed and listened to the Swedish singer's clear voice maintain that life should have a happy ending.

Sara turned around in her chair and looked up at him.

"And you know how it ended. He committed suicide!"

"Yes, I know, you told me that. It's truly sad. Truly."

He had some difficulty understanding her strong passion for the fair-haired man with the beautiful voice who'd been dead since the nineties.

"Let's take a walk," he suggested, to get her out of her state of mind.

They walked along the water on the beach promenade, which wound along the sea from San Agustín all the way over to the sand dunes of Playa del Inglés. Sara seemed to have forgotten Ted Gärdestad, at least for now.

There was a brisk wind, and so far, other than some early-bird surfers already out in the water, the beach was deserted.

"Did you hear what happened yesterday?" Sara asked.

"No," said Kristian. "I haven't listened to the news."

He'd ended up at the bar with Jorge last evening. A group from Las Palmas that the owner, Maria del Mar, knew joined them, and they partied until late. He'd met a sweet young Canarian woman with beautiful long hair, and she'd gone home with him. Even if he and Diana did have a no-strings relationship, he still felt a little guilty.

Now he was hungover and dead tired, regretting that he didn't stay home the night before. It wasn't worth it anymore.

Sara on the other hand walked with quick, springy steps beside him, rosy cheeked, energetic, and fresh. Her hair smelled of apple blossom, and she had sturdy shoes on. She looked like the picture of health, and right now that irritated him incredibly. There was not a trace of the earlier crying jag.

In silence he observed the woman beside him while he struggled to maintain her pace. He couldn't figure her out. On the one hand her efficiency drove him crazy; on the other hand he admired it and felt a little envious. Everything seemed so much easier for her. She seemed to simply arrange everything, and there was a lightheartedness about her that was refreshing and attractive. Could he ever manage life so easily? Simply solve problems as they showed up and then leave them behind and move on? He wondered how much of it was about attitude and how much was simply circumstances.

"Two people disappeared in the waves," Sara said. "Tourists, of course. A Russian woman and a German man. People never learn. Even though there are red flags, and everyone knows the currents can be extremely strong, there are still people who are convinced they'll be okay. They found the German this morning, but the Russian woman is still missing. Thus the police helicopter."

She nodded toward the water where a helicopter was flying at low altitude along the surface. Several TV vans drove up and parked along the shore. Some reporters, microphones in hand and closely followed by cameramen, strode purposefully onto the beach in search of people to interview about their reactions.

"Won't *Day & Night* write about this?" asked Kristian.

"Of course, but fortunately my associate Hugo is back from vacation, and he's covering everything that's not about the murders."

"Okay."

"But before we talk more about that, I want to hear about that dream you have. About the boy eating ice cream. It was something you'd talked about with a psychologist."

Kristian looked at her, embarrassed. He had no great desire to discuss his private life. Especially something that had been buried in him since childhood.

"You truly have a talent for barging into people's personal lives."

"But that's the only way to find anything out. And I'm good at dreams," Sara said, smiling sweetly.

Telling the story that had pursued him in his dreams throughout his childhood was difficult. Kristian looked up at the sky before he put his hands in his pants pockets and pulled up his shoulders. On the other hand, maybe it would be good to talk with Sara about it. It felt right.

"It turns out my sister was two years old, and I was four. We were on vacation on Gran Canaria when someone stole the car we'd rented while I was standing outside a store eating ice cream and my parents were inside paying. My sister was still in the backseat. The car thief disappeared with her, and she was never found. I'd repressed it, and my parents never talked about it. I assume they have enormous feelings of guilt and thought it was their fault for leaving her alone in the car."

Sara took hold of Kristian's arm and stared at him in shock.

"What are you saying? That your sister disappeared on Gran Canaria when you were four years old?"

Kristian nodded.

"That's horrible. She was never found?"

"No. The police found the car the next day, but it was empty."

"But why didn't your family talk about it? I can understand it was hard when you were a child, but after you got older . . . It must be dreadful not knowing."

"We don't talk much about anything," said Kristian. "Maybe everything was destroyed when my sister disappeared. I don't know . . ."

"Maybe she's still alive?"

"I don't think so."

"What if she's here somewhere," said Sara eagerly. "Maybe I can help you investigate."

"Sara," Kristian said, a warning in his voice. "I appreciate your concern, but I don't think there's any point. Good Lord, it was thirty years ago."

"But you never know. When I get time I'm going to check on the case anyway. I'm sure a lot was written about it."

"I'm not sure I could bear investigating it. It's been a recurring nightmare since I was little. That's enough."

They walked on in silence. The sea spread out, wild, beautiful, and frightening. The helicopter continued its search. Kristian shivered; somewhere out there was a person whose life had ended in the waves. How much did she struggle before she drowned? What did she think and feel?

A thought took form in the back of his mind. The woman the police arrested the other evening, who lived in Tasarte. He took out his cell phone and called Chief Inspector Herrera at the Policía Nacional.

"I thought of something," he said to Sara. "Just have to check up on it."

The chief inspector answered immediately.

"Hola, buenos días," Kristian said. "Do you know anything more about the woman who was brought in on Tuesday evening? From Tasarte?"

"To be honest, I got curious so I checked around a little," Herrera answered. "Her name is Adriana Gonzalez. She's a widow and has a son in his twenties. It turns out that she lives in Tasarte right by the Samsara Soul yoga center and works as a housekeeper in the home of the man who runs it, Frank Hagen."

"You don't say."

Damn, thought Kristian. *All roads lead to that damned yoga guru.*

"Yes, and not only that. She had a relationship with him. They lived together for several years before Frank met his wife, Luísa."

"Who was just murdered."

"Exactly."

"Where is Adriana Gonzalez at the moment?"

"I heard she was released after only a few hours. I don't know why."

"Good Lord," said Kristian. "Thanks a lot. Bye."

He ended the call and turned toward Sara.

"We have to go to Tasarte. Now."

67

Earlier

The window banged in the wind, and the sun shone in the glass. Outside, the horizon was blue. There wasn't a cloud in the sky. Adriana wiped off the kitchen counter and put the last glasses in the cupboard before she went over to the window and closed it. She caught sight of a figure on the path that led to the house. Adriana watched the woman hurrying along the road. She felt a worried movement in her belly. She was both happy about the visit and dreading it. The woman looked like a little girl, slender and small boned in a dress with a ribbon around the waist. She skipped along the road, eager, as if there was something she wanted to tell and couldn't stop herself. Luísa was young, ten years younger than Adriana. Adriana saw Samsara's various romances as fleeting, dalliances that would slip away and disappear. She was always there waiting for him; *she* didn't slip away. Adriana had taken root. At the same time, she had a feeling that things with Luísa were different.

Adriana took two cups from the cupboard above the counter and put on coffee.

• • •

Luísa had recently moved in with Samsara in the big house. She had connected with Adriana at once and sought her out when she wanted to have coffee and talk. She'd already visited Adriana several times and told her that she came from Las Palmas, where she'd met Samsara at a yoga workshop he was teaching and where she was one of the students. Luísa described her and Samsara's love in sweeping terms, talked about how much Samsara meant to her. She acted as if she didn't know about Samsara and Adriana's love story. And maybe she didn't. Adriana didn't intend to say anything. The only thing to do was wait and see. In time he would come back to her.

Luísa held Adriana familiarly by the hand and told her about her love. Adriana nodded, told her she was happy for her. But in her thoughts she consoled Luísa, put her head in her arms and stroked her hair, held her, told her that she shouldn't be sad when Samsara got tired of her. Samsara's great love was her, Adriana. She was the one he would make happy, with whom he'd have children and start a family.

There was a knock at the door, light at first and then firmer. Adriana went to answer, but the visitor was already standing in the hall. Luísa smiled at her; she had a bouquet of flowers with her.

"I hope I'm not interrupting," she said, handing over the bouquet.

"Not at all," Adriana answered. "Come in. Coffee will be ready in a few minutes."

Adriana went over to the kitchen counter and put the flowers in a vase, which she filled with water. In the shiny faucet she saw a distorted image of herself. She picked up the carafe when the coffeemaker started to beep, signaling that the coffee was ready.

Luísa took the cup of strong, hot liquid but put it down at once, eager to tell what she had on her mind.

"You won't guess what's happened!"

Luísa put her hands together and held them up to her mouth. Her brown eyes glistened.

"No, I can't guess," Adriana answered, sitting down at the kitchen table.

As Luísa pulled her chair closer, the legs scraped against the floor. Adriana held her cup protectively in front of her. Her lips touched the porcelain, and she observed Luísa through the steam from the coffee.

"I don't know where to begin." Luísa could hardly sit still. "Frank proposed and I said yes. We're going to get married!" she said happily. "Isn't that just amazing?"

Adriana set the cup down on the table, her hands shaking lightly.

"Yes," she said quietly. "It's quite amazing."

"It won't be a big wedding. We're going to invite the immediate family and a few friends. Just a little ceremony down by the sea and a party out in the garden."

Adriana felt confused, as if she didn't really understand what Luísa had just told her.

"There's one more thing . . . I'm pregnant."

Adriana looked up at Luísa and felt something come loose inside her. A painful, hard clump that cracked and turned around in her. She didn't know what to do with herself. She just wanted Luísa to leave.

"I thought about you right away when Frank suggested we get household help. You'd be perfect. I bet you are wonderful with children. That would be just amazing. Will you?"

Adriana was forced to pull herself together so that Luísa wouldn't see how she felt deep inside. She felt ready to faint but forced herself to sit upright in the chair.

"I have to go now. I have an appointment with the doctor in a few hours. Frank promised to drive me there, and he's so particular about being on time so I don't dare be late. I just wanted to tell you. You're the first one besides him who knows I'm pregnant."

She smiled, and Adriana did her best to return it. But the smile plastered on her face felt like a grimace.

Luísa stood up and kissed Adriana on both cheeks.

"I have to go," she whispered. "I'm so happy that I could tell you everything."

Adriana stood with her hands resting heavily on the tabletop as she watched Luísa walk down the gravel road. The table was shaking; her whole body was shaking. She turned around toward the kitchen counter, took the knife that was there, and stabbed at the cupboard door. She raised the knife again and stabbed, stabbed, stabbed. Couldn't stop, drove the knife again and again into the wooden door, left deep gashes in the wood, chips flying around her. She leaned her head backward and screamed. She screamed as if someone had cut open her chest and torn out her soul.

At last she sank down onto the chair. The knife was sitting deep in the cupboard door. Everything was quiet. She hardly heard her own breathing. She closed her eyes and collapsed with her face hidden in her hands. There was nothing left of her, only an empty, dead shell.

68

The house felt deserted now that he was alone. Frank Hagen wandered through room after room and heard nothing other than the sound of his bare feet against the floor. The children's beds had been empty and untouched for several days, the blankets smooth. Their toys were put away in boxes and the wheeled plastic bins in cheerful colors that he and Luísa had bought at the IKEA right outside Las Palmas. Dolls and stuffed animals sat neatly lined up on the shelves he'd made and put up himself. It was as if the children's voices had settled in the walls and he could hear them as echoes if he listened carefully and set his ear next to the wallpaper with the flying elephants against a sky-blue background.

He remembered when he and Luísa helped each other put up the wallpaper. They'd laughed and joked and teased each other. And they made love wildly among rolls of wallpaper and cans of glue. When he thought about it, he'd never had so much fun with any woman as he'd had with Luísa. He'd fallen in love at once when he met her the first time, when she came into the yoga center in Las Palmas where he was teaching a workshop. She had black, shining hair that extended far down her back, and she was beautiful in a Canarian way, with olive-toned skin and dark eyes with a gaze he had difficulty resisting. She came from Las Palmas, a typical big-city girl who wasn't at all suited to living out in the country. But they'd quickly fallen tempestuously in love, desired each other hotly and passionately, and for the first time in his life he respected a woman deeply. When they got married, he felt truly happy.

Then time passed, and he didn't know what happened. He couldn't explain it. He fell back into his accustomed, decades-old patterns. The hunt for validation continued in the same way as it had before he met Luísa. Of course it affected the marriage. Gradually she pulled away from him. He noticed it but felt unable to do anything about it. Instead he betrayed her with their female guests, and he visited Adriana more and more often. His old lover was sliding increasingly into her own world, which he thought was nice. Adriana didn't bother him with questions, doubts, or demands. She simply did as he said.

Then suddenly evil had struck and his whole existence was turned upside down. He'd been a little in love with Erika, but they'd only had a week or so together before she was murdered so brutally. He'd been horrified and scared. She'd gone with him on his weekly shopping trip to Arguineguín, during which he also took the opportunity to visit his old friend Finn Nydal, who was the minister at the Norwegian Seamen's Church. They would play chess and drink Arehucas, Canarian rum. What had happened that afternoon while he visited his friend and Erika strolled around Arguineguín alone? Did she meet someone? He wasn't gone more than a couple of hours. When they'd met again to have dinner, she seemed like her usual self and didn't mention anything in particular. Frank didn't know how many times he'd wondered about this over the past few days; it had gone around and around in his head. He couldn't figure it out. They'd had the use of Finn's apartment. No one else knew about the arrangement. He and Erika had only intended to stay there for a few hours before they returned to Tasarte.

Apart from all the thoughts about who might have murdered her, he also worried that he might be a suspect himself. What if someone had noticed him and Erika when they were shopping in Arguineguín, or when they were having dinner at the restaurant? As always when he was with a lover in public, he'd worn a cap and sunglasses. He hadn't dared go to the police and tell them about their relationship or the outing to Arguineguín. He'd been afraid that suspicion would fall on him or that the yoga center would end up in a bad light. He simply didn't want to get involved. That had been a mistake, of course.

It had all come out, and he'd been questioned by the police several times. And then suddenly his wife, Luísa, was murdered.

Everything fell apart. He was worried and restless. His whole body itched.

He decided to take a bath to calm his nerves.

The bathroom was in a corner of the house at the far end of the corridor. There was a big window on each wall. The view of the mountains and the slopes with the orchards was usually enchanting, but right now he didn't see it. He opened a window and let the warm air flow in and listened to the chirping of birds in the bushes outside while he ran the water and undressed. He looked at himself in the mirror. He looked haggard. His face was sunken, and there were deep furrows under the suntan. His beard had grown out, and he didn't have the energy to shave or trim it. His eyes were tired and lackluster. He realized that he looked like a man on the skids.

Frank lowered himself into the hot water and heaved a deep sigh of pleasure. He reached for the bottle of herbal oil that was Luísa's favorite and poured a few drops into the water. When had they last bathed together? He couldn't even remember. The bottle was still there, but she was gone. He realized how much he'd neglected her and how he'd wasted the past years on a lot of shit that meant nothing. Why hadn't he realized her value? Why hadn't he appreciated what they had? He'd been an idiot, and now it was too late. He felt gloomy. He hadn't even had time to grieve for Luísa. He still didn't really grasp that she was dead. Suddenly he realized that he was crying there in the bathtub.

He was so deep in his thoughts that he didn't hear the front door opening. It was only when he became aware of a noise on the stairs to the top floor that he reacted. He straightened up and listened tensely. Dried his tears with the back of his hand.

All he heard was the chirping of the birds outside the open window. A rooster crowed far away. It sounded ominous. Was it his imagination?

He closed his eyes and let his head sink back against the edge of the tub and breathed out.

The air in the bathroom was damp with steam. His head got heavier, and he started to feel drowsy. Then suddenly a shiver ran through his body.

He heard a faint click and opened his eyes, sat up, and turned toward the door. He held tightly onto the edge of the tub and tried to peer through the vapors.

"Is anybody there?" he asked uncertainly.

The bathroom door started opening very slowly, inch by inch. Frank stiffened. He tried to get out of the bathtub but slipped on the smooth edge and fell back. The warm water splashed around him and stung his eyes. He turned around and reached out his hand for the bath towel that was on a stool alongside the tub. But before he could reach it he felt a hand on his shoulder press him down. He fumbled for the shadowy form of a person standing over him. Tried to take hold, but instead was pressed down under the water. A stream of air bubbles came out of his mouth and nose, rose up to the surface, and burst. Frank struggled to get loose from the hard grip, but the hand holding him was too strong. Everything was swimming before his eyes, and he saw small, blinking figures that sparkled and danced like beings, angels in the water. There was pressure in his chest, pressure on his lungs, and he started to feel dizzy, his heart hammering wildly. Warm water in his mouth, nose, eyes.

Then suddenly the grip was released. He screamed.

Before Frank could turn toward his attacker he felt a stab in his chest. For a moment all sound disappeared. It was silent. He looked down at himself, at the knife that was stuck in his chest. At the blood that quickly stained the bathwater red, how it was pumping out of him.

Frank felt no pain, only sorrow. As if not only the blood was running out of him but also his life force. He tried to take hold of the knife, but the strange hands held it firmly, did not let go. Then the voice against his ear, the warm breath against the face.

"I loved you, but you never saw me."

Frank opened his mouth, but the words ran out as bloody water down his chin and throat. No sound came out. Then the darkness approached. At first it rose like fog over the surface of the water, and then slowly it embraced him. His hands let go and slid down along his sides. His head got heavy, fell against the edge of the tub.

Then nothing.

69

Adriana pressed down the handle and carefully opened the door. She wasn't sure how it would feel to go inside. Now, with Luísa dead and the children gone. She hadn't been there since Luísa was murdered. Actually, she'd wanted to stay away until everything had been aired out, everything that had been—the sounds and the smells that reminded her she hadn't lived there for a long time. She wanted to wait until the walls and the floor again held the memories of her and her life. She who'd been there from the start. This was her home, not another woman's. Now that nothing obstructed her, she could come back. Everything could be like before. Order was restored. That was what she'd been waiting for. She was grateful she'd been patient. That she hadn't given up. That she'd waited all these years.

She stood quietly in the hall and took a deep breath. Ever since Samsara had opened the door and she took a step over the threshold, she'd felt that it was hers. Here she would live and walk across the floors and give birth to the child that was growing inside her. She would stand in the kitchen, prepare food, take bread out of the oven, and let the aroma of home baking spread through the rooms. All that had been taken from her. Now she would get it back.

Last night Samsara showed up at her house and asked her to help with the cleaning; he didn't have the energy to get the house in order. He'd cried, told her he wasn't doing well. Told her that he missed her. And she'd consoled him, sat and held him, rocked him in her arms. Whispered in his ear that everything would be fine. When everyone else had disappeared, she was still there. She would never leave him. Never again.

They made love and afterward he went home without saying a word, leaving his melancholy like darkness in her room. Once again she was sitting alone in bed, resting her head against her knees, feeling empty and exploited, but at the same time hopeful. Everything would be fine again. It had to be.

She called to him as she came through the door but got no answer. Maybe he didn't hear or he was out at the moment. The door was unlocked. She went over to the broom closet in the hall and found the cleaner, a bucket, and a brush. A sound made her stop. She set the things down. Called to him again, but no one answered.

Adriana went into the kitchen, where the food was still on the table. She opened the refrigerator and put away the milk, the tomatoes. Wiped off the kitchen table, pulled the curtains to the side, and looked out at the herb garden she had planted under the lemon trees. Turned toward the counter again, ran hot water into the sink, and started doing dishes, the same plates she had cleaned, rinsed, and put in the dish stand so many times before. There was the biggest kitchen knife. The detergent glided down over the blade. She felt the sharp edge with her fingers.

Again she heard a sound from the top floor. A scraping sound. Now she was certain; there was definitely someone there.

She went over to the stairs and placed her hand on the railing. She always had a hard time taking the first step. The pain from the time she fell and lost her child always came back to her. She felt pain in her abdomen. Slowly she went up, one step at a time.

The hall on the top floor was in darkness. She turned on the switch, but it didn't work. Farther away she saw that the bathroom door was ajar.

She went toward it hesitantly. Said his name—Samsara, Samsara—but got confused and upset by her own voice, which sounded foreign. Quietly she stood outside, felt the steam escaping from the bathroom. He was in the tub. That was why he hadn't heard her.

She pushed open the door and saw him sitting in the bathtub with his back to her. His head had fallen down against his chest and in the hand that hung over the edge of the tub he was holding a sheet of paper with something written on it, as if he'd fallen asleep as he read it. She took a few steps in and touched his shoulder. The room was wet and damp. His skin was wet against her hand. He slipped to the side, and his head fell backward, his eyes staring vacantly and frighteningly at her. His mouth was open, but he didn't say anything, as if a silent scream was inside him and wanted out. His chest was bloody, the water stained red.

She took a few steps backward and suddenly felt very dizzy; her throat was constricted. That was when she discovered that she still had the kitchen knife in her hand, the one she had just washed. The metal clattered against the tile floor as it slid out of her hand. She held her hand to her mouth. Then she screamed. Howled as if something bloody had been torn loose from inside her. She staggered backward, screaming out the pain as a shadow emerged from the wall, put its arms around her body, and pulled her with it down on the floor.

The figure put its hand over her mouth, whispered gently in her ear.

"It's over now. You don't need to be afraid anymore. He's never going to harm you again."

70

Kristian pressed the gas pedal to the floor, and the tires screeched as they drove away from San Agustín and onto the highway south. Kristian insisted on driving. Sara sat beside him and tried to call Quintana, without success. His phone seemed to be turned off. Again and again she listened to his formal voice-mail greeting and swore.

"Damn it all, he's not answering."

On the narrow serpentine roads up in the mountains it was harder to maintain high speed. They ended up behind a caravan of jeeps filled with tourists.

"Hell's bells," Kristian said quietly. "And it's not possible to pass either."

The minutes rushed by, and it took them an hour and a half before they could turn off toward Tasarte.

They turned onto the last little road toward Frank Hagen's villa, parked outside the wall, and went in through the gate. Once again Sara tried to call Quintana and finally he answered. It turned out that the police were already on their way to Tasarte.

"Wait for us in the car," he ordered. "Don't do anything until the Guardia Civil is at the scene."

"Of course, I promise," Sara said, clicking off the call and continuing forward. There was no way she was going to sit in the car twiddling her thumbs while Frank Hagen lost his life. The closer they got to the door, the more uneasy she felt. They couldn't get there too late. The front door was slightly open. She placed her hand on Kristian's arm to stop him before he opened it and stepped in.

"Listen, what if she's here? We're unarmed."

"Maybe you are," he said, sticking his hand inside his thin jacket. He took out a pistol and released the safety.

Sara stared at him in surprise. "Where'd you get that?"

"It's a leftover from my police days."

Whatever Sara thought about it in principle, she was grateful to Kristian. She was glad they weren't completely defenseless, considering what the perpetrator was capable of. Adriana Gonzalez. Sara hadn't even met her and suddenly realized she didn't even know what the woman looked like.

Cautiously, Kristian pushed open the front door. Because he had the gun, he went first, with Sara close behind him. In the hall they stopped and listened. Not a sound. Close together they slipped farther into the house. Sara's heart was pounding so hard she was afraid it would be heard.

In the big, airy kitchen everything looked tidy. No signs of struggle, no dishes left behind. Big windows faced out toward the valley.

They stepped carefully into the living room with its low couches, colorful floor pillows, Asian sculptures, and the big flat-screen TV that occupied one wall. The walls were decorated with colorful paintings and drawings, several signed by Frank Hagen.

They passed a workroom, a playroom with its own bouncy castle, and an octagonal-shaped room, which appeared to be a workout room with a black rubber mat on the floor and several floor-to-ceiling glass walls. One wall consisted of a single large mirror. *The house must have cost a small fortune,* Sara thought before they continued up the broad marble steps. On the top floor were the bedrooms in a row along an airy corridor, with high ceilings and wide white-plastered walls that were covered with abstract art mixed with Buddha figures and Hindu gods. It felt like walking around in a museum, thought Sara. The only thing that looked used was the master bedroom, where the bed was unmade and clothes were strewn around on the floor. Otherwise it was all very clean and tidy. They continued along the corridor.

"Wait," Kristian hissed suddenly and stopped. He raised his arm and pointed toward the bathroom.

Sara stared at the closed door. From the gap under the door came small clouds of steam. Slowly they stepped closer. Apart from Kristian's breathing, it was almost horribly silent. Outside the door they stopped. Kristian took a step to the side, while Sara carefully pushed the door open.

Both recoiled violently. In the middle of the bathroom was a deep bathtub on a tiled platform. Frank Hagen was sitting in the tub. His head was wrapped in a towel like a turban and had fallen to the side. One arm was hanging outside the tub. In front of him was a plastic tray placed across the tub, on which his other arm was resting. In his hand he held a sheet of paper.

There was an open wound in his chest, and the bathwater was stained dark red.

They'd arrived too late.

71

Suddenly, screeching brakes were heard outside the house. Car doors slammed, and voices called back and forth. Sara and Kristian stood dumbfounded, staring at the dead Frank Hagen in the tub. Quintana was the first policeman on the scene. In the doorway to the bathroom he stopped abruptly.

"Por dios, what's this all about? Move, damn it, get out of the room! You're in the way!"

He shoved them brusquely aside. Right behind him came several uniformed officers.

"Search the house!" Quintana ordered. "Cordon off the area and call for reinforcements! Get the K-9 patrol here. There's a good chance the perp is still in the area. And you two get out of here—now!"

Kristian and Sara did as he said without protest. In front of the house police tape had already been set up. They sat down on a bench in the shade under a tree on the other side of the barricade.

Kristian's face had lost all its color.

"Good Lord," he panted. "I know what artwork this refers to."

Sara looked searchingly at him.

"Tell me."

"The body in the bathtub, the towel wrapped around the head, and a wound in the chest. It looked like a stab from a knife. Did you notice the sheet of paper he was holding?"

Sara nodded. It had looked very strange. Frank Hagen was dead, yet he was holding a letter between his fingers. If he'd been reading it when he was murdered, he would have dropped it.

"It's *The Death of Marat*. An eighteenth-century painting from the French Revolution. Frank Hagen is arranged almost exactly like that painting."

Kristian nodded toward the top floor of the house and the open bathroom window.

Sara took out her iPhone and searched for the artwork. There it was: a handsome man in a bathtub with white cloth wrapped like a turban around his head. His eyes were closed; there was a bloody wound in his chest, and one arm hung outside the tub.

In front of him was a table covered with a green cloth, which disguised the fact that he was sitting in a bathtub. In one hand he was holding a letter and in the other, a quill pen.

"It's almost saint-like, like a painting of Jesus," said Sara.

"You're right," Kristian admitted. "The artist was a good friend of Marat and depicted him as a revolutionary hero who suffered a martyr's death. He was anything but, I can assure you."

She browsed quickly through the information on the screen.

"'Jean-Paul Marat was a newspaperman and revolutionary. One of the most important figures in the French Revolution and a mouthpiece for the radical forces in Paris. Marat saw enemies everywhere and thought that resistance could only be crushed by means of the guillotine. He asserted that several hundred thousand people had to be executed to restore calm to the country.' Not strange that someone wanted to kill him."

"He was murdered by a young noblewoman, Charlotte Corday," said Kristian.

"Why did she murder him in the bathtub?"

"Marat spent a lot of time in the tub. He had a skin disease that he is said to have picked up when he was hiding from his enemies in the sewers of Paris. In the bath he wrote letters and received people. Corday requested to meet him under false pretenses. She stabbed him to death with a kitchen knife."

"I happened to take a few pictures before the police arrived," said Sara.

Kristian shook his head. "You're out of your mind."

Sara brought up the pictures from the bathroom. She was well aware that she'd crossed a line. She gave Kristian a quick glance. Realized that more and more she'd started to consider him a colleague.

"Here—do you see?" she said eagerly, showing a close-up of Frank in the bathtub. She enlarged the picture of the letter. Sara zoomed in further, and suddenly they could both make out what was there. Just a single sentence. And a signature.

The deed is done—the monster has died.

—Dido

Kristian repeated the words out loud. Then he was silent for a moment.

"I recognize that line," he said at last. "I've heard it before, I'm sure of it."

"Dido. Who the heck is Dido?" mumbled Sara, who was off in her own thoughts.

Kristian pushed a pouch of snuff under his lip. His face brightened.

"Search on the name Charlotte Corday. She is supposed to have said those very words when the police came: The deed is done—the monster has died."

"The killer evidently calls himself Dido. Can that be Adriana's nickname?" Sara said thoughtfully.

"It strikes me that we're talking more about art than about the murders," said Kristian. "It seems like the perp wants us to see the motive rather than who killed them. As if we should see why they were murdered."

Kristian thought about what Jorge had said. Maybe the old artist had a point. That it's more about why than about who.

Sara dug in her purse for a cigarette. She looked over toward the entry to Frank Hagen's villa. More police cars pulled up into the yard in front of the house. Several K-9 units got out. Soon a helicopter was heard buzzing in the air. Sara took a couple of puffs and thought intensely. Where had she heard that name—Dido? She repeated it several times silently to herself.

Then suddenly it came to her. She turned cold inside. The massage center. The young, impudent guy behind the reception counter. She'd asked for the names of the masseurs, but only got the nicknames. Now she remembered clearly.

The young man who'd given her a massage was called Dido.

72

David parked on the street in the shadow of the palm trees that partly screened the setting sun. He opened the door, took out a pack of cigarettes, and shook one out. Took a drag while he looked out over the shabby houses and narrow stairs that led down to the sea.

He took the stairs to the stony beach. The incoming waves made his pant legs wet. David bent down, picked up a stone, and threw it into the water. He remembered clearly how he used to stand down here and throw stones while he waited for his papa to come home after being out fishing. He would peer out at the sea until his eyes hurt. Then he would catch sight of the boat, far out, at first only a dot against the horizon, and then growing bigger and bigger until he could see Papa standing and waving to him.

David stuck his hands into his pants pockets, drawing up his shoulders as if he was cold. He wished he was still standing there waiting for his papa, that the two of them could go up to the house where Mama was waiting with food, that he was pulling the stool over to the cupboard and getting out plates to set on the table while his parents hugged each other, that they were sitting around the table as a family. The sound of silverware scraping against plates, the aroma of food, the sea. The smell his father brought in with him and that never left the house they lived in. The laughter, the friendly voices, and the evenings when he was in his own bed listening to his parents' conversation and the clatter of china from the kitchen. Sometimes he felt so exhilarated and happy that he had a hard time falling asleep.

Happiness did not keep him awake any longer, nor did the sound of calm voices. It was hatred that kept him from sleep. He hated just as intensely as he had loved as a child. Hatred had made him into a person he could not fall asleep with. A person with a dark, incurable sickness that grew and boiled in his body. Like insects that crept and crawled inside him, eating his lungs, his liver, his mind.

He turned his back to the water and walked up toward the house, which was at the end of the narrow walkway along the water. The buildings were abandoned. It seemed as if everyone had moved up to the little village above, or even farther away where there were cafés, traffic lights, and jobs. He opened the door. It had been locked the last time he was here, but he'd left it unlocked. There was nothing of value, only memories that slowly faded with time.

Inside it was gloomy. The light that fell down through the cracks in the ceiling colored the walls a dull gold. He had to come here, even if it hurt. He passed through what had once been the living room; now only cockroaches and other insects occupied it. The rats scurried farther into the bedroom when they heard him crossing the floor. The marks were still there from the heavy iron bed—he had dismantled and taken it out—the impressions from the legs in the wooden floor.

A sound outside made him turn around. The wind had picked up and struck against the house; the door banged lightly against the wall. For a moment he could see his papa come in, see how he set his wet boots on the floor. The flames from the stove that danced and cast shadows in the room. He could sense the hours and days that Papa had been away like salt water against his skin. The unshaven face, the dark eyes that told him that Papa loved him without his needing to say a word.

He sat down with his back against the wall, pulled up his knees, and wrapped his arms around them. He held himself and felt consoled. Leaned his head back, felt the hard stone wall. He could see the sky through the cracks in the ceiling. His room had been on the top floor; now only the walls stood, like stage sets of his childhood.

He took the pack of cigarettes out of his breast pocket. It wouldn't take long before they started searching for him, but he no longer cared. He just wanted to get it over with. He wanted to enjoy the last moments of freedom before they came and arrested him. Nothing could be worse than the life he lived. He just wanted to see the ocean one last time as the sun burned at the horizon and colored the sky reddish orange, watch as the sea foamed and lived. One last time.

He closed his eyes and listened to the wind outside, how it took hold of the house, the sea, and the trees out there, how it lifted and tore at everything that wasn't firmly held down. As a child he thought nature was frightening, the forces around him dangerous and threatening.

He hadn't wanted Frank to die so fast. He'd read that it would take a long time, but it didn't. He thought he would be able to sit and tell Frank what a swine he'd been while the life ran out of him and into the warm water. Tell him why he'd killed the women Frank cared about: not because they'd done anything to him or deserved it, but because they meant something to Frank. That it was Frank who'd held the knife that had taken their lives from them. But Frank only said his name and then let out his last sigh.

Now he was sitting there like a beaker about to run over with everything he wanted to say but which Frank couldn't hear.

It was Frank who'd given him the nickname Dido, the same name he used when he worked as a masseur.

David struck the back of his head against the wall until it hurt so much he couldn't take any more. The pain made him nauseated and dizzy. *Your name is so beautiful you don't need a nickname,* his mama had said, stroking back the bangs that always fell down in his face when he was little. But Frank gave him one, and he felt sick when he thought about it. He could see the hazy eyes before him. The hands around his hips while the customers moaned his nickname during the act. David put his face between his knees and tried to contain the memories that were growing large and evil inside him.

He thought he heard the front door open and someone come in. Steps against the floor, the sound of glasses and plates on the table. Chair legs scraping. He dried his face with the back of his hand and smiled between the tears while he sat on the floor and listened to the sounds that the wind brought with it into the little house. He thought he heard his mama's gentle voice. *Can you run down to the shore and see if Papa is coming?*

Then he shut his eyes, and in his mind he ran to the shore and waited.

73

Kristian drove as fast as he dared up the curving road away from the Tasarte Valley while Sara sat with the phone pressed hard against her ear. The phone had rung a dozen times at the massage place without anyone answering.

Sara was about to give up when someone picked up.

"Lotus Massage, buenas tardes."

"Hi, it's Sara Moberg from the newspaper *Day & Night*. I was there the other day and got a massage. I didn't introduce myself properly. I talked with a guy in reception who gave me the names of all the masseurs—was that you?"

"Yes, that was me," the young man on the other end said, this time sounding considerably more accommodating.

"I need to get in contact with one of your masseurs. He calls himself Dido. I need a complete name and address. Right away."

"I don't know if I can give that out. I have to speak with the boss, and he's not here right now—"

His voice died away. Sara could picture how the otherwise self-confident guy was sweating behind the counter.

"I need the guy's name right now. Right this second. Otherwise I'm calling the police. Is that understood?"

"Yes, yes, wait a moment . . ."

There must have been something authoritative in her voice because she heard him start tapping on a keyboard. It took a few seconds.

"David Gonzalez."

A flutter in her stomach. She gave Kristian a quick glance. Adriana's last name was Gonzalez. Herrera at the Policía Nacional had told Kristian that Adriana had a son in his twenties.

"How old is he?"

"Twenty-two, I think. He's worked here a pretty long time."

"Where does he live?"

He gave Sara the address and cell phone number.

"When is he supposed to work next?"

"On Saturday. He starts at three o'clock. You don't need to tell anyone that I gave you this information, do you?"

Sara hung up and looked at Kristian.

"He lives in Aldea. Go left up at the main road."

"But why would he go to his apartment?" Kristian objected. "Isn't his home the first place the police are going to search?"

"That's true, but where else could he have gone?"

"He's Adriana's son, right? And she had a relationship with Frank and lived with him in the house. But what do we know about her and David's life before that? Where did they live before? Who was David's father?"

Sara looked at him, racking her brain. Who might know something about Adriana's earlier life?

"Wait," she exclaimed eagerly. "Do you remember the cook at the restaurant in Tasarte who met Adam Fors? She said she was friends with Frank Hagen's housekeeper. She must have meant Adriana!"

"Do you still have her number?"

"Sure, I always save my contacts."

She entered the number for Juanita Díaz and made a silent prayer she would answer. After a long series of rings a voice was heard on the other end. Sara introduced herself and explained her business.

"Adriana had a son with her husband, who was a fisherman," said Juanita. "Although she became a widow pretty young, when David was maybe ten or twelve years old."

"About ten years ago?"

"Yes, that sounds right. Her husband disappeared out at sea. Adriana took it very hard and moved from their house in Pozo Izquierdo. She opened a bakery in Aldea, but it wasn't long before she met Frank Hagen."

"And then she moved in with him?"

"That's right. She was probably happy at the start, but then she had a miscarriage and he met Luísa."

"Where in Pozo Izquierdo did they live?"

"At the end of the row of houses farthest down by the water, Avenida Gaviota. It's one of the last ones, a white house with a green door. I seem to recall that the window frames were painted blue."

Sara ended the call and looked eagerly at Kristian.

"Drive toward Pozo Izquierdo."

74

Sara could not tear her eyes from the dilapidated house in front of them. This is where Adriana had lived with her fisherman husband and son, and they'd been a happy family. Now it was only a mournful ruin, a tragic reminder of a previous life.

Kristian took the pistol out of his pocket and released the safety. "Shall we go in?"

"Is that necessary?" Sara asked, nodding toward the gun. "He's probably not even here." She looked up at the dilapidated facade, the boarded-up windows and green front door. "It doesn't look like anyone's been here for years."

"He's killed three people," said Kristian.

He tried the door. It was unlocked. They stepped into a small, dark hall where the sparse light filtered down through openings in the ceiling. The wood floor was broken in several places. It was unusual for these houses to have wood floors, Sara thought. Most were stone.

"Watch where you step," Kristian warned. "These old houses are swarming with cockroaches and rats."

"Fun," Sara said sarcastically. "Do you think I'm worried about that?"

She continued into the kitchen, or what had been the kitchen. There was a rusty sink and a walled-in stove that had cracked. The paint on the walls had fallen off in big sheets, and the floor swayed as she walked over it. Between the planks there were big gaps.

Kristian slipped into the adjacent room. He bent down and stroked the rotted floor with his hand.

"There was a bed here," Kristian said quietly, looking around.

There were deep marks in the floor, and a dark square was outlined next to the wall where it had been.

"Do you mean—"

"The bed with Luísa Hagen," Kristian said. "If it's that bed, then it was here."

Sara felt her mouth getting dry.

"Stay here," Kristian hissed, disappearing up the steps to the top floor.

Sara went over to the kitchen counter and saw a cracked cup in the sink. She carefully picked it up and wiped off the dust. Under the gray layer a light blue pattern was hidden. She put it back, opened the kitchen cupboard; a cockroach scampered out and fell down on the counter.

She started when she felt a hand on her shoulder.

"Take it easy," said Kristian when she abruptly turned around. "There's no one here, I've checked the top floor. The house is empty. He must be far away at this point."

"You scared me."

"I'm sorry. That's what happens when you're stuck in your own thoughts."

"Your nose is bleeding," said Sara.

Kristian brought his hand up to his face.

"Damn it," he said as he tasted blood on his lips. "Shall we go? I have tissues in the car."

"You go first. I want to stay a little while. It feels as if the walls are trying to tell me something."

"Of course," Kristian muttered, pulling a piece of paper out of his pocket and using it to try to stop the bleeding. "You're a journalist, of course the walls are trying to talk to you."

"Right now it looks as if you have a bigger problem," Sara said with a smile.

"I'll go ahead to the car. If you hear a shot you'll know I'm in trouble."

"Are you joking now?" said Sara as he walked toward the door.

Kristian opened the front door and grinned. "You've seen too many action movies."

He left, pressing the paper against his nose.

Sara felt sorry for him and his endless nosebleeds; at the same time there was something comic about it all.

She turned around and went over to what had once been the bedroom. On the wall she saw a Christ figure, a crucifix hanging on a nail high up on the wall. Sara let her fingers glide across Jesus's face and the open palms that were pierced by pain. For a moment she thought about all the suffering that was nailed to the cross, how it had spread over the room and covered the walls, the floor. *Like mildew,* she thought.

She went over to the wardrobe, which was slightly open. A movement among the old rags at the bottom of the wardrobe made her take a step backward. Faint, peeping sounds. She leaned forward and carefully pulled aside some of the cloth. Then she caught sight of four black kittens. She smiled to herself; the mother was probably out hunting or else she was watching Sara, waiting for her to go away. Sara left the room and went over to the stairs and looked up, tried to think about who had gone up these steps.

Suddenly she heard a sharp voice. "Who are you?"

She was so frightened that she stumbled on the stairs. Before she could scream someone placed a strong hand over her mouth. A young man stood over her, taking up all the space above and around her. She turned ice cold inside. It was the man who had massaged her in Playa del Inglés. The one with the long, wavy hair and the dark eyes. The one who called himself Dido.

Sara glanced quickly at the front door. David turned and looked in the same direction, as if he expected the door to be thrown open and someone to come in. During the moment he looked away, Sara tore herself loose and lunged toward the door. She didn't get far. A sudden pain in her leg and she lost her balance and hit the wall with her right shoulder, falling to the floor. He put a knee in her back and leaned over her. She held her breath when she felt the cold knife-edge pressed against her throat, right under the jawbone. The image of Erika Bergman lying on the rocks with her throat cut flickered before her.

"I recognize you," he said in a hiss. "You were at Lotus Massage recently."

"My name's Sara," she said, trying to keep her voice calm. "You're David."

"What are you doing here?"

"I want to get to know you better, understand what's happening," she answered.

"Are you alone?"

Sara swallowed; however she answered it might be wrong. She hesitated for a moment or two, closed her eyes, and felt the sweat running down her back. *I don't want to die this way,* she thought. *Not here and not now.* The planks under her were hard. The worn wood scraped painfully against her face. She was pressed against the floor, his knee in her back. She had to concentrate, felt the knife against her throat. The images passed through her mind. Erika Bergman against the black rocks, Luísa Hagen's gaze, the iron bed out in the papaya field where she lay bathed in blood, Frank Hagen in the bathtub.

"The bed was your parents', is that right?"

Sara didn't know why she said that—it just felt right. She wanted to get him to talk. He sighed heavily, and the pressure of the knife against her throat lightened.

"It's just me here. I'm a journalist," Sara continued. "I can write your story. Explain why you did . . . what you did."

"And why would you think I want that?"

"Why did you kill Erika and Luísa?"

"Frank destroyed . . . my whole life. He destroyed"—David swallowed hard—"everything that meant anything to me. Erika had nothing to do with it. She just . . . He liked her, but it could just as well have been someone else. I wanted to get revenge on Frank . . . It was Frank I wanted . . . I wanted to take everything from him."

Sara heard that David was out of breath, that he was trying to maintain his composure.

"He wrecked my whole life and left me and my mother in rags."

"I understand," said Sara, hoping he would believe her.

She had to get him to say more, get him to talk with her.

"You can't understand that!" His voice was hard and angry.

Sara curled up. The last thing she wanted was for him to lose self-control. Her jaw hurt from clenching her teeth. She was just waiting to feel the knife going in through the skin. To her surprise, he let go of her. He took his knee from her back, sank down beside her with his back against the wall. She peeked carefully, saw that he sat with his head bowed, eyes cast down at the floor.

"If you could understand that, you'd be as sick as me. I know I'm not completely healthy . . . I can't be."

"Don't say that. I'm sure that something has just gone wrong," Sara said, trying to change position without him noticing it.

"You're sure that something has gone wrong," he repeated sarcastically, letting out a bitter laugh. "That's a nice way to put it."

His voice died away. David stared vacantly ahead of him.

Sara moved slowly up into a sitting position. David didn't seem to care about that. She carefully put her knee under her. She wanted to be ready to get up quickly and get out of there as soon as she had the chance.

"Everything would have been fine if that bastard Frank Hagen hadn't shown up."

"And gotten involved with your mother?"

"At first he was the world's best stepfather. We moved to Tasarte, and it felt like he really cared about me. I was so stupid that I actually believed he loved us."

"Was he the one who got you interested in art?"

Sara continued asking questions. As long as he kept talking it was fine. Kristian was nearby, and it wouldn't be long before the police were on their trail. She had to play for time.

"Frank showed me a whole new world that I knew nothing about. He taught me to love art and music, the classics. He taught me to draw and paint. I could sit for hours and look in his art books while I listened to Mozart, Grieg, Puccini. He took me to museums and art exhibitions . . . and then he took everything from me and turned me into . . . turned me into a whore in Playa del Inglés. Turned Mama into his little . . . *puta*! Damn it . . ."

David took a deep breath, hit his head against the wall.

"And she still loves him. Can you understand that? She still loves him after all he's done to her, to her son, to us. I loved him like my own father, but what kind of father makes his son . . . prostitute himself?"

Sara stared at him. She saw the naked pain in his face. She reached out a hand toward him, and he laid his head in her arms. She stroked his hair slowly.

"I don't know what kind of father does that, David. I don't know."

75

Quintana heaved a sigh of relief when the car with the medical examiner pulled into the yard. They went into the bathroom where Frank Hagen was lying in the same position they'd found him in earlier. The medical examiner put on a pair of plastic gloves and bent over the body.

"How long has he been dead?" asked Quintana.

"I'd guess a couple of hours, no more."

"What do you know about the murder weapon?"

"Hard to say, but this only required a single stab. It looks like the weapon could be an ordinary kitchen knife, a larger one."

"Like that one?"

Quintana pointed at the knife that was on the bathroom floor.

"Absolutely."

"Other injuries?"

"From what I can see right off he doesn't appear to have fought back. Presumably it happened very fast." The medical examiner looked around. "Some water has splashed out on the floor, but nothing is over-turned and there are no signs of a struggle otherwise."

"Anything else?"

The medical examiner looked at Quintana. "The letter that's stuck between his fingers is extremely peculiar."

He bent over and carefully poked the sheet loose, held it in front of him, and read out loud: "'The deed is done—the monster has died/ Dido.' What the hell does that mean? And who is Dido?"

"No idea."

Quintana stared at the letter.

They were interrupted when an officer stuck his head in.

"We've arrested Adriana Gonzalez. She seems extremely confused and is babbling incoherently. She has bloodstains on her clothes and is raving about her son, David. It sounds like she just saw him."

Quintana turned to the medical examiner. "Continue here. We'll be in touch later."

Before he had time to answer, Quintana had left the bathroom.

Several police cars drove with blue lights and sirens on through the deserted mountain roads even farther west, in the direction of La Aldea de San Nicolás. David Gonzalez's apartment was in a picturesque building in the middle of the main street in the little town.

The cars circled the house and both neighbors and passersby watched wide-eyed as a dozen uniformed officers with weapons drawn rushed into the building. After a quick search they could see that no one was there.

"Cordon off the apartment and go through it," Quintana ordered when he was back out on the street. He sighed heavily. *Damn it. Where the hell is he?*

76

Kristian's nosebleed had stopped and after resting awhile in the car up on the street above Avenida Gaviota, he took the opportunity to look around. He had aimlessly wandered some distance away when he looked at the clock and realized that half an hour had passed since he left Sara. He jogged back to the car. Just then his phone rang. He recognized Quintana's voice immediately.

"Where are you two?" the chief inspector asked before Kristian could say anything.

"Pozo Izquierdo."

"What are you doing there?"

"We got a tip that this was where David and Adriana Gonzalez lived when David was a child."

"Damn it, you're not playing the hero as long as I have responsibility, is that understood? Do you realize you're exposing yourselves to danger? We have a witness who says he saw David in an old white Nissan pickup in Pozo Izquierdo an hour or two ago. Is Sara with you?"

"No, I think she's still in the old house—" Kristian felt a cold shiver down his spine.

"¡Mierda!" Quintana roared. "You stay where you are, do you hear? We're ten minutes from there."

"Okay," Kristian said weakly.

Kristian hung up and it got quiet all around. It was starting to get dark.

The streetlights were glowing with a warm yellow light that made the shadows move on the walls of the houses.

Kristian caught sight of a vehicle parked under a tree. It was a white Nissan pickup. He hadn't noticed it earlier. He felt a wave of worry in his stomach. He unlocked his car and leaned down, reached under the seat and retrieved the pistol, released the safety, and went over to the pickup with the pistol aimed at the ground. He looked for anyone sitting in the front seat but saw no one. Kristian opened the door. On the passenger seat was a CD case, on the floor a plastic mug and some papers. He leaned over the gearshift and reached for the papers while he continued to keep a watchful eye out. In the light from the street he could see that there were some bills, the last one a payment reminder issued to David Gonzalez. So he was there.

Kristian felt the pressure behind his forehead come back. *Not again,* he pleaded, *not right now.* And then his nosebleed started, the blood running down over his lips and chin. He dried himself with his arm, but that didn't help. The taste of blood and the feeling that something was about to go very wrong made his heart beat harder in his chest.

Kristian went down the steps toward the house where he and Sara had separated. He couldn't wait for Quintana. He should never have left Sara alone. He was such an idiot.

He remained standing by the door with his back against the wall, the pistol in front of him, and tried to slow down his breathing. Kristian thought he heard a voice but wasn't sure if it was the wind playing tricks on him or if someone was there on the other side of the wall.

"Sara!" he called. No answer.

Slowly he opened the door, prepared to throw himself to the side or to use the pistol. The hair on the back of his neck rose when a floorboard creaked. He stopped. Hardly dared breathe. It was as quiet as a Norwegian cemetery in January; only the wind blowing outside and the door made any sound. Kristian took a quick look around him. The adjacent room, the stairs up to the next story. He moved stealthily along the wall over to the bedroom. It was in semidarkness; the whole ground floor was dark. There was a wardrobe at one end of the room, but otherwise it was empty. The door to the wardrobe was closed. With the pistol aimed in front of him he tore open the wardrobe door. He almost fell backward when a cat ran out and slipped down under the floorboards.

"Damn," he whispered, lowering the pistol.

He'd almost fired off a shot when the animal came toward him. He stood quietly a moment to try to calm down. Where the hell had Sara gone?

Suddenly a thought struck him. Why hadn't he disabled the murderer's car in case he tried to run? Possibly taking Sara with him. He could have punctured the tires, opened the hood and ruined something, disconnected the battery, whatever.

Kristian looked at his watch. Quintana should be here any moment. He hurried over to the stairs, glanced up. No sign of life. His nose was bleeding, but he didn't even bother to try to stop it. Slowly he slipped up to the top floor. A narrow hall, three rooms in a row. Only one of them still had a door. He could see into the bathroom, where the sink lay on the floor; the tiles were cracked and revealed the gray concrete below. Only an old, rusty faucet and a drainpipe remained of the shower. The other room was empty. One wall had partly collapsed, and bricks lay in heaps on the floor. He looked up through the ceiling; the moon shone palely against the black sky. He stopped midmotion, thought he heard a sound but didn't know where it came from.

He braced himself and kicked open the door to the last room.

77

It smelled damp and musty in the cramped little space. Sara could hear the waves striking against the wall outside, so near that it almost felt as if the sea would force its way through the old stone walls. The ceiling was much too low to stand upright; she sat on her heels, and her legs already ached. The space they'd climbed down into must have been used as a pantry. She could make out a rusty old can on a shelf and a potato sack tossed in a corner. Her hands were tied behind her, and she felt the cold knife-edge against her cheek. David covered her mouth so she couldn't call for help.

He talked in a low, controlled voice, as if to calm her, but Sara was in a cold sweat and shaking with fear. She thought about her children, about Lasse, about her good life. Would it end here under the floorboards in a deserted house with a serial killer? She tried to breathe slowly, tried not to panic. Cockroaches were crawling around everywhere in the darkness. He held her, vise-like. She wasn't going anywhere, and there was nothing she could do about it. She started to feel dizzy, tried to breathe through her nose. And all these cockroaches. She felt the small insects moving over her body, crawling in under her clothes.

David froze when Kristian's shadow fell over them. Dust and dirt filtered down through the floorboards as he haltingly walked across the floor above their heads. It bowed lightly under his weight. His steps were like repeated strokes above them. He was so close that Sara could almost touch him. She tried to make a sound, but the pressure of the hand over her mouth increased, and the sharp edge of the knife scratched her cheek. He didn't say anything, but he was warning her.

Right above them Kristian stood quietly and seemed to be looking around. A drop of blood fell down on the plank and landed on the floor, then another. Sara could see the blood running through the crack. Kristian must have had another nosebleed. David's face was right next to hers; his glassy eyes stared up through the cracks in the floor. The sweat ran from his forehead, and his lips moved as if he were praying. She twisted a little, trying to change position as much as the limited space allowed. Her legs were about to go numb, and her back ached. David lightly shook his head. She felt the knife pressed against her cheek.

"Keep still," he hissed.

Sara closed her eyes, tried to think herself away, hope that everything would be fine, that soon she could go home and hug her children and her husband. But the smell of blood and death was far too strong.

She jerked and twisted her head to the side in pure terror when a cockroach darted across her face. The knife that David was holding against her cheek cut into the skin, and she moaned into the closed hand. Kristian had moved across the floor, but now he stopped over by the stairs. Sara's vision got blurry, and the pain was making her dizzy. She heard him go up the stairs to the top floor. The blood from the wound on her cheek ran between David's fingers. She tasted blood on her lips.

"Sorry, I didn't mean to," David whispered in her ear. "I don't want to hurt you. All I really wanted to do was hurt Frank. Do you think God is going to forgive me?"

Sara couldn't have answered even if she wanted to. He still held his hand just as hard over her mouth. Kristian had disappeared somewhere higher up in the house, and Sara wondered how long they would sit there in the same position. It was starting to become unbearable.

As if David had read her mind, the grip over her mouth loosened. He signaled to her to be quiet. Sara sat completely still in the same position, not daring to move. David's gaze was glassy, as if he'd entered another state of mind, inaccessible to the rest of the world. As if he were unreachable.

He raised up the wooden hatch that covered the access to the little food cellar and pulled it carefully to the side, trying to make as little noise as possible. When he pulled Sara up into the kitchen she kicked at a plank so that it banged on the floor. David's grip around her tightened and they stood quietly, waiting to see if Kristian had heard them. The seconds felt like minutes, but nothing happened.

"Don't do that again," David hissed. "I know it's over and I'm going to prison. I just want a little time to myself before the police get me. I'll let you go as soon as we get to the truck. Trust me. I just want to sit by myself and look out over the sea one last time. Por favor."

He pulled her with him, backing up toward the front door. He opened it carefully, but a movement in the dark made him turn around. A flashlight came on and blinded Sara for a few seconds before she could make out Quintana standing a short distance away on the narrow landing facing the sea, a pistol aimed at them. Behind him stood several policemen ready to draw their guns.

"Police," Quintana shouted. "Let her go!"

Sara felt how the young man collapsed, as if someone had taken from him the last thing that held him up.

"You don't understand," he said.

"Let her go," Quintana insisted, taking a step forward.

"I just want to see the ocean," he whispered.

Sara twisted. Her mouth felt dry, and her eyes stung. Quintana reached a hand out for her as a sign that she should come closer. For a moment she was uncertain. David seemed to be in another world, and the knife rested lightly against her cheek.

"David," she said calmly. "Let me go."

She took a cautious step toward Quintana. David stood there as if he didn't really understand what was happening.

"This wasn't how it was supposed to be," he said pleadingly. "I want to see the ocean . . ."

Sara turned around as she continued to move toward Quintana.

"I can't, David. We can do it another time."

"There won't be another time!"

Sara could see his desperation, as if he had just regained consciousness and realized what was happening, as if he'd just understood that the police were only waiting for her to get away before they threw him on the ground, carried him to the police car, and drove off. Sara could see the anxiety in his eyes.

Suddenly he lunged toward her, taking hold of her shoulder. An earsplitting detonation. The powerful sound exploded in Sara's ear. She squeezed her eyes together tight. It thundered as if someone had drilled a hole through her head. David tumbled over her, and they fell together over the broken railing and down onto the stone shore.

Sara looked in confusion at the patch of blood on his chest, which was gradually spreading over his dirty blue sweater.

"I just wanted to see the ocean," he whispered.

His gaze became vacant, and he looked right through her, far beyond the horizon.

Sara suddenly felt like crying.

78

Sara turned in the bed, the faintly pungent hospital smell in her nostrils. She'd dozed off, probably due to the strong pain relievers. She wasn't used to pain medication. She looked out the window, where she could see the ocean and the traffic that rushed in and out of Las Palmas.

Her mouth was dry, and she tried to sit up, but it was no use. The pain below her chest hit her with every movement. She reached for the water glass on the nightstand and took a few sips while semireclined.

There was a bouquet of colorful flowers from Lasse. Her eyes filled with tears when she saw them. He'd told her what the flowers were called, although she forgot the name at once. He was good at that kind of thing; she wasn't. She'd been close to losing everything: her family, her life. And she hadn't even turned forty-five. For a time she truly believed that she would die in that cramped, dark little space. That she would die like the others, Erika Bergman and Luísa and Frank Hagen. That she would be the fourth victim. That was how her life would end. Only now did she realize how afraid she'd been to die, and it made her want to cry. She longed for her kids and for Lasse.

Her husband had looked in on her before he went to work. A big group of tourists from Sweden was expected at the hotel that day, and he had to be there. The children were off at summer camp; she'd talked with them on the phone and managed to convince them that they didn't need to come home for her sake. Now that she was out of danger, everything was all right, after all.

Lasse promised to come back later that evening when he was done at the hotel. She wanted him to, even if it was late.

There was a knock, and the door opened.

"Are you awake?" the nurse asked, coming into the room. "How are you feeling?"

"I guess I've been better," said Sara.

"You have a visitor. Kristian Wede? Are you up for it?"

"Yes. Okay, I want to try to sit up."

"Of course. You've broken a couple ribs, and it will hurt a lot at first, but the pain will go away soon. We want to x-ray you and do some tests, so you won't get to go home until tomorrow."

The nurse took a firm hold on her arms and set her upright, fluffing up the pillows behind her back.

"Do you need anything? Juice, coffee, more water?"

"Yes, please, all of that," Sara said gratefully. "I think Kristian would also appreciate a cup of coffee."

"I'll do that. Do you want me to open a window?"

"Please," said Sara. She was so moved by the consideration and the nurse's gentle voice that a tear trickled down her cheek.

Good God, how sensitive I am, she thought.

"Is my bag here?"

"Of course."

The nurse retrieved it from a cupboard and handed it to her before she disappeared. Sara searched for a hand mirror and observed her face. It was pale, almost yellow. She shuddered when she saw herself. She had scrapes and was black and blue, one eye was swollen, and her throat was bandaged. It was worse than she thought. At that moment the door opened. Kristian came in.

"Are you putting on makeup for my sake? Were you thinking about seducing me?" He smiled broadly.

"Hardly in this condition," she said sarcastically.

She was happy to see him. She set the bag aside, and he gave her a light hug before handing her a bouquet wrapped in plastic, which he'd hidden behind his back. It was wet and looked a bit manhandled. She smiled inside when she saw what shape the flowers were in, but chose not to comment on it.

"These are for you."

"I never would have figured that out."

The banter between them was as usual, and Sara thought it was nice. At least something was the same.

With some difficulty Kristian managed to get the plastic off the bouquet. For a moment he looked confused while he searched for something to put them in.

"Thanks," said Sara, looking at the flowers.

A few of the stems were broken, others were drooping, and several flowers had lost their petals.

"I'm not so good with flowers," he said apologetically. "I don't think they liked the ride on the Vespa. I should have brought something else."

"Did you finally get it out on the road?" Sara said, smiling. "I never would've believed it."

"You'll get to ride it once you're recovered," Kristian said.

"And I think the flowers are nice," Sara said consolingly. "They remind me a little of you."

Kristian gave her a warning look before he sat down on the edge of the bed and took her hand.

"I'm so incredibly happy you're doing okay. For a moment . . . I was afraid I'd lost you."

Sara could not get out a word. Her throat got thick, and she was about to start crying again.

Kristian stroked her cheek. "You don't look great, Sara. But I'm proud of you, you know that? You're brave and strong. I'll be damned if you wouldn't have been an excellent police officer. I needed a partner like that."

Sara was a little embarrassed by his compliment.

"That would have been something," she said, smiling weakly.

The nurse came in with the drinks and rescued what was left of the bouquet from Kristian's hand.

"I'll put them in a vase," she said and went out again.

They sat quietly awhile. No words were needed. Sara liked that he was there and that he held her hand. He smelled good, like fresh air, a little motor grease, and aftershave. He smelled of life beyond the hospital walls. Life went on outside, and that felt like a consolation.

Finally he got up. The evening light was glowing outside the window.

"It's getting late," he said. "I should probably go."

Sara looked at the clock; it was almost eight. Lasse was probably on his way, if nothing had popped up at work.

Suddenly it struck her that the case was concluded, that their work together was over.

"Thanks for coming. It was nice working with you. I hope I'll see you soon. Maybe for a cup of coffee. That would be nice."

Kristian smiled.

"It would be," he said.

79

The sky was darkening over the little village with the tiny church. The shadows that ran through the streets and over the walls of the houses had crept under the trees looming over the many gravestones.

Adriana stood in front of the newly dug grave, staring down at the simple wooden casket at the bottom of the hole. Father Iniesta, an old friend of the family, stood behind her and placed his hand on her shoulder to console her. She thought it felt heavy and clammy against the fabric of the black dress she wore. It was the dress she'd inherited from her mother and which she should have worn in mourning for her dead husband when they were left alone, she and David. Now she was the only one left.

Few people came to the funeral. There were some young men, friends of David that Adriana didn't know, a couple of fishermen and their families from Pozo Izquierdo with whom they'd spent time long ago, and a few of her old girlfriends who still cared about her. All of them had thrown a fistful of dirt onto the casket, according to Catholic custom. She could not bear any gathering afterward, so the funeral attendees left one by one after they hugged her and quietly expressed their condolences. Condolences for a serial killer. She was surprised they even showed up.

Now only she and Father Iniesta were left.

"Now your son is resting with God," he said, still with his hand on her shoulder.

"I haven't been close to my God since the sea took the one I loved."

"That was long ago. Perhaps it's time now. With Him you can find solace."

She turned toward him and met his gaze, smiling faintly.

"Yes," she answered. "Maybe it's time. It's probably with Him I can find what I'm missing."

"That's good," the priest answered. "You can come to me any time, Adriana. You know that."

"I know," she answered. "I'm very grateful that you still care. There aren't many who want me around now."

"We are all God's children. God forgives us all, because we are all sinners. You have to be strong, Adriana."

She nodded and wiped away a tear from the corner of her eye.

"Come," he said, signaling to a man who was standing to one side, waiting to fill the hole in the ground. "I'll go with you up to the church."

"Thanks. I'll never forget everything you've done for me and David," she said.

A little later Adriana sat looking out the window of the bus. She had her bag on her lap in front of her. In it was a hymnal she'd received from the priest and a purse with the little money she had. She sat and held on to it tightly. Father Iniesta had offered to drive her home, but she wanted to be alone. He accompanied her to the bus that went down to the fishing village where she was born and grew up. Where she'd met the man with the sparkling dark eyes, the man who smelled of the sea.

Through the bus window she observed the lives that went on as usual. As if nothing had happened. Cars with families on their way home from the beach, open jeeps with tourists wearing sunglasses, goats climbing up the steep mounds of stones. At one point a dog ran after them, barking as it tried to chase the bus off the road. People walking back and forth, all on their way somewhere, all with goals and meaning in their lives. At last she was the only one left, but she didn't notice that. Just sat looking for the ocean, waiting to see the cliffs, the shore that met the water. The fishing boats, the foaming waves.

The windowpane was warm against her forehead. Her vision blurred from the tears that wouldn't stop. She recognized the streets, the houses where she'd been as a child, and then a grown woman and mother. The stores where she'd shopped for vegetables, cheese, flour, and meat. It had been a long time since she'd been here. The village hadn't changed that much, except that it was quieter. People had moved to get work and many of her old neighbors were no longer alive. They were in the same earth in which she had buried David. But the village was still as it had always been: the houses, the walls, the light—that hadn't changed. She was the one who was different. She was the one who had tried to grow away from the village.

"Last stop."

The bus braked and stopped. She started, the driver's voice awakening her from the thoughts grinding in her head. The doors opened. The bus driver turned toward her and watched as she got up, holding the bag next to her chest, and walked toward the exit.

"The last bus leaves here at five after eleven," he said.

She nodded. "Thanks," she answered. "But I'm not going back."

Adriana stood on the street and watched the bus as it drove away. Saw the dust that whirled up and settled like mist before the setting sun.

She went to the shore and the rocks where she'd walked so many times before, where she'd stood waiting for her beloved.

She leaned over and took off her shoes, set down the bag. Enjoyed the warm stones against her bare feet. The water that beaded against her legs, made her dress wet. She didn't notice whether the water was cold or warm, not even that it was wet, simply that it received her like an old friend welcoming her back. Adriana let her hands rest against the surface of the water. She moved her fingers through the small waves that lapped around her. Now the water reached her waist, and the black dress moved around her as if it were a living part of her.

She felt secure as she walked out, felt a kind of peace that she had long forgotten. She closed her eyes and continued. She thought she heard a shout behind her, far away, a little boy who was calling for someone. She wanted to turn around, see if he was the one who was calling to her, if he was the one who'd run down to the shore. But it was a long time since she'd heard him call to her, run after her when she left. She felt the absence of everything she had lost.

Adriana raised her head toward the sky. She was no longer touching the bottom, and she gasped for air before she disappeared under the water. The dress was heavy around her body, pulling her down. She felt a sudden panic. Her heart pounded hard in her chest, and her arms flailed in the water, but it didn't help. A little boy took hold of her, and she opened her eyes. She looked right up into a darker sky. A face against the sky, a pair of sparkling eyes. David held her by the hand, and he smiled at her.

"Come," he said. "Now let's go find Papa."

"Yes," she answered. "Let's do that."

80

The narrow road meandered up over the mountain, past steep precipices and a view that took the breath away from those who used the road to enjoy the natural beauty of Gran Canaria. Sara had put Ted Gärdestad on at high volume and sang lustily along with "I'll Catch an Angel." She shifted into higher gear as she accelerated out of a turn, and Kristian, who was sitting in the passenger seat, held tightly to the handle above the door. They passed several bicyclists struggling upward and an occasional car going in the opposite direction.

Sara glanced at Kristian, who appeared to be feeling poorly.

"Enjoy the view," she called over the deafening music, punching him playfully in the side with one hand.

"Keep both hands on the steering wheel," he said with a growl, scowling. He leaned over and turned down the volume so they could talk without having to scream themselves hoarse. "I'd be safer jumping out of an airplane with no parachute. Plus I was out yesterday, celebrating that we were finally done with this nightmare that's been hanging over us for the past few weeks. I have a hangover and to be honest I should be lying in bed right now. One more curve at this speed and I won't be responsible for the consequences."

"Try to be a little positive. You had fun last night, I assume?"

"Right now I'm asking myself whether it was worth it," Kristian said drily. "By the way, you really ought to be home taking it easy. You just got out of the hospital."

"I don't like taking it easy."

"Yeah, but you were almost manageable when you were in a hospital bed."

Sara braked hard when a bicyclist ahead of them pulled into the roadway to pass another, slower bicyclist.

"I've dreamed of this my whole life," Kristian said, moaning. "Getting killed in a car wreck to a Ted Gärdestad soundtrack."

"You see, you can be positive when you want to be."

"Keep your eyes on the road. I'm holding on."

After many miles Sara finally stopped, and Kristian heaved a sigh of relief when Ted fell silent. They were in the village of Soria, which was located among the high mountains, with a magnificent view of a beautiful, long valley. Kristian noticed a shop not far away and a sign for a brick-oven bakery. On the other side of the road was a simple restaurant where a group of people in hiking boots and matching clothes stood waiting for a guide to take them up the mountain.

"We're here," Sara said happily, reaching for the bag she'd set on the backseat.

"You still haven't told me what we're doing here," Kristian said, following her across the road and down to the restaurant.

They sat down at one of the outdoor tables, and Sara took out a pack of cigarettes and lit one. An older man who was sweeping in front of the entrance set down his broom and came up to the table. Close on his heels was a little puppy, who again and again bit on to the old man's trouser leg. Kristian leaned down and tried to coax the puppy over to him, but it was completely occupied and paid no attention.

"Would you like something to eat?" Sara asked.

Kristian shook his head. "No, thanks, I don't have much appetite after that crazy drive, but a cold beer would be good. I feel I ought to celebrate that there is life after death."

"Very nice," Sara answered. "I assume I've had a driver's license much longer than you and I've actually never been in an accident, so don't complain."

"Why do I have a hard time believing you right now?" said Kristian, giving her a teasing smile.

Sara shook her head and turned toward the waiter.

"A beer and a glass of red, por favor."

"Red wine?" asked Kristian. "I thought you didn't drink when you were driving. Are you trying to scare me even more?"

"I can handle one glass, and besides, I need it right now," Sara answered, looking serious. She pulled a folder from the bag she'd set on the table. "It's for you."

She pushed the folder over.

Kristian looked searchingly at Sara as she sipped her wine. He didn't really know what to think, but he had the feeling that she was uncomfortable and that it had to do with what was in the folder.

"Is there something you want to tell me?" he asked.

"I hope you don't take this wrong, but I haven't been able to let go of the story you told me."

"What story?"

"About the boy with the ice cream. And your sister. I called your parents."

"You did what?"

"I talked with your mother."

"I can't believe this . . ."

Kristian shook his head. He reached for the bundle of papers and started browsing. There were several black-and-white pictures of a car, along with handwritten reports. She saw his face turn pale.

Sara noticed that his hands were shaking. He stopped at one paper.

"My dad's signature, I see. Witness report?"

"I got it from the former police chief's private files. He's been retired a long time but could never let go of the case. For years he's been tormented by the fact that the case was never cleared."

Suddenly Kristian caught sight of something. He got up eagerly from the table and walked slowly across the road, leaving the open folder behind. Sara followed him until they were standing quietly in front of the shop.

He stared glassily at a spot farther ahead.

At the shop's entrance stood a plastic trash can. It was painted with red and blue stripes and the Kalise logo.

Kristian took a deep breath.

"So that's why you brought me here," he whispered. "This was where it happened."

ABOUT THE AUTHORS

Caroline Andersson 2015

Bestselling author Mari Jungstedt and award-winning author Ruben Eliassen are the duo behind the dark and dramatic Canary Islands Series.

Jungstedt is one of Sweden's most beloved authors. She has published twelve books in her popular Gotland series, which is available in more than twenty countries and has been filmed for German television.

Eliassen has published seven books in the award-winning Phenomena series, whose movie rights have been sold to an American film company.

ABOUT THE TRANSLATOR

Paul Norlen is a translator based in Seattle, Washington.